CHAINS OF
COMMAND

THE BOOKS OF WILLIAM J. CAUNITZ

Chains of Command
Pigtown
Cleopatra Gold
Exceptional Clearance
One Police Plaza
Black Sand
Suspects

William J. Caunitz

CHAINS OF COMMAND

A DUTTON BOOK

DUTTON
Published by the Penguin Group
Penguin Putnam Inc., 375 Hudson Street,
New York, New York 10014, U.S.A.
Penguin Books Ltd, 27 Wrights Lane,
London W8 5TZ, England
Penguin Books Australia Ltd, Ringwood,
Victoria, Australia
Penguin Books Canada Ltd, 10 Alcorn Avenue,
Toronto, Ontario, Canada M4V 3B2
Penguin Books (N.Z.) Ltd, 182–190 Wairau Road,
Auckland 10, New Zealand

Penguin Books Ltd, Registered Offices:
Harmondsworth, Middlesex, England

First published by Dutton, a member of Penguin Putnam Inc.

First Printing, September, 1999
10   9   8   7   6   5   4   3   2   1

Before he died, William Caunitz wrote approximately one half of this novel. It was completed later by his fellow writer and good friend, Christopher Newman.

 REGISTERED TRADEMARK—MARCA REGISTRADA

LIBRARY OF CONGRESS CATALOGING-IN-PUBLICATION DATA:
Caunitz, William J.
    Chains of command / William J. Caunitz.
        p.   cm.
    ISBN 0-525-94514-8 (alk. paper)
    I.   Title.
    PS3553.A945C45   1999
813'.54—dc21
                                                          99-28778
                                                                CIP

Printed in the United States of America
Set in Times New Roman

This book is printed on acid-free paper.

CHAINS OF COMMAND

One

Police Officer Johnny "Macho Man" Rodriguez walked out of El Cielo bodega carrying six bottles of Dos Equis beer concealed in a brown bag. As he crossed to the double-parked cruiser, his dark eyes raked the doorways and rooftops across 146th Street. He couldn't see the lookouts but knew they were there, crouching behind parapets, lurking in shadows, anxious for him to drive off so they could flash the "all clear" to the street dealers, or "pitchers," who peddled crack cocaine at designated locations throughout the precinct.

It was sixteen minutes before five o'clock, the second Wednesday in May. The sky was a cloudless blue dome, and the evening "white sale" thrived as the suburban trade stole into the Thirty-seventh Precinct to pay the day's market price for their drug of choice.

Reaching the blue and white, Rodriguez opened the passenger side door and placed the bag on his seat. Across the street a head sprang up along the roofline, then ducked back down. Macho Man smiled. He planted his elbow on the top of the car, cocked his thumb, took aim with his forefinger, and fired up at the roof. "Pow, pow, pow." He blew imaginary smoke from his fingertip.

Four stories up, behind the shallow roof parapet, an emaciated black man with sunken cheeks sat on the tar with his knees propped beneath his fuzzy chin. With a walkie-talkie in one hand and a Tec 9 machine pistol in the other, he thumbed the transmit button on his radio and lifted it to his lips. "They be leaving," he announced.

With a smile, his gold uppers gleaming, he reached overhead with the Tec 9 and fired a short burst.

"Giving us the slimebag *hasta la vista*," Officer Michael Francis Neary complained. He eased the cruiser into Amsterdam Avenue traffic.

Less than a minute later, the radio on the seat between the partners crackled: "In the Three-seven, a ten-ten report of shots fired from a rooftop at 1417 146th Street. Units going, K?"

Macho Man grabbed the portable and keyed it to reply. "Three-seven Adam to Central K. We're at that location. There are no shots being fired. Mark it ten-ninety-x."

"Ten-four, Adam."

Neary wore a stiff, displeased smile, prompting Macho Man to ask, "Whatsa matter?"

"Humps let go a burst to show disrespect, and you make the call unfounded?"

"You wanna charge up six flights to find an empty roof, amigo? You work the Three-seven, you gotta have a sense of humor. Whatsa matter? You losing yours?"

"No, I ain't losing mine. But you tell me. Why is it, every tour, we gotta show the colors on 146th Street? And to make matters worse, why you gotta always stop at Tío Paco's joint to get your beer? Dude is scum. Strictly a bad-news guy."

"That's why we do it, amigo. So Uncle Frank'll know there are cops in the Three-seven who can't be scared or bought off."

"Scumbag must hate the sight of you."

Rodriguez brushed a hand over his right trouser pocket to reassure himself that the parcel he'd just collected was securely tucked away. "You got that right, amigo. Every time he sees me coming, he gets one of those pissed-off, not-you-again expressions."

"Where to?" Neary asked.

"Let's hit the park."

Mike Neary drove the radio motor patrol car west onto 145th Street, passing beneath the Henry Hudson Parkway's stone underpass and emerging into the Riverside Park recreational area. With the transmission slipped into neutral, he let the car coast into deep shadow beneath a huge maple tree.

Ragged grass with rutted paths worn through it sloped down to a narrow cement walkway running along the top of the river wall. Beyond and to the right of them, the remnants of a chain-link fence protruded from a sandbox littered with liquor bottles and fast food takeout Styrofoam. Drug addicts had plundered much of the chain link and sold it to local shopkeepers, who bolted it across windows and skylights to prevent drug addicts from burglarizing their stores.

Across the gleaming river, the luxury apartments of Cliffside Park perched atop ancient cliffs, which towered out of the water. To the north, the gray, hulking mass of the George Washington Bridge dominated the horizon. Automobiles crawled along its double decks like trails of ants. Forty yards south of them, the fortress-like structure of the North River Water Pollution Control Plant sprawled across twenty-two acres of landfill like an alien invader from space, feeding on sewage from the entire West Side of Manhattan.

Rodriguez retrieved a church key from the glove box and liberated two bottles of Dos Equis from the confines of their bag. Caps removed, he handed one beer across to his partner.

Neary sucked deeply, relishing how the cold Mexican brew sluiced along his parched tongue and washed down his throat. They drank and stared out at the reflected sunbeams dazzling off the river, ears tuned to the low mutter of police calls.

Rodriguez was a broad-shouldered man in his late twenties with a swarthy complexion, flat nose, and long black hair. These features gave him the look of a peasant who had worked long, hard hours tilling the soil. In contrast, Neary was lean, in his early thirties, with chalk-white skin and blond hair. The Three-seven natives had, predictably, given him the street name "Paleface."

As Neary took another pull, beer spilled out over his lower lip, a trickle of golden amber sluicing down his chin. He wiped it away with the flat of his hand. "Did I tell you Barb's expecting again?" he asked.

"Geddafuckoutta here! Four in six years? Maybe it's time you tied a knot in that enchilada of yours, amigo."

"Bullshit. We love kids. Wanna have at least six."

Rodriguez pushed his hand out as if putting some foul-smelling thing at arm's distance. "Better you than me, amigo."

Neary looked unsure of what he would say next. When he spoke, his tone was tentative. "We'd like you to be the godfather, Johnny."

Rodriguez cocked his head and flashed him a grin. "It'd be an honor, partner."

An unidentified voice came over the radio. "What's a ten forty-five?"

Neary grabbed the portable. "Rapid Mobilization code signal. Four sergeants and twenty uniforms respond to the location."

"How soon after an arrest for DWI must the Breathalyzer test be given?" another voice asked over the police network.

"Within two hours of the arrest," Neary shot back.

"Let's cease with the unauthorized transmissions," Central admonished.

Catcalls flooded the network. The forthcoming sergeant's test guaranteed that the frequencies would be cluttered with such unauthorized transmissions: "students" eager to test each other's knowledge of police procedures.

Rodriguez tossed an annoyed look at his partner. "You *students* ever worry a cop might need help while you're tying up the network playing grab-ass?"

Neary shrugged. "We're getting antsy is all. The sergeant's test is only three weeks away."

Every time Rodriguez walked into the station house, he saw "students" walking around with flash cards, asking each other questions: What are the elements of Burglary First Degree? What's a code signal ten eighty-six? "Jesus," he grumbled. "Don't any of you guys ever think about pussy?"

"Not until after the test. Last one, I failed by two points. This time, I'm coming out top of the list. You raise a big family, it takes big bucks. I'm burnt out on moonlighting every swing, and being so tired my ass drags." Neary glanced at Macho Man. "Speakin' of pussy, you still seeing the Dominican chick?"

"Isabelle? Damn straight, amigo. Best blow job in Manhattan North. I'd be crazy to give something like that up."

"So why ain't you hitting the books? You don't wanna be a boss?"

Rodriguez let his gaze wander out over the river, and his voice go softer. "Me? I wouldn't make a good boss, Mikey." He took a swig of beer. "What I wanna do is make detective. Get my ass assigned to one of those silk-suit-headquarters squads, like Special Frauds."

"You gotta be hung like Secretariat to get into one of those shops . . . and have brass balls big enough to match," Neary complained. He tossed back another swallow of Dos Equis, lowered the bottle, and wiped his mouth with the back of his hand. "You speak Spanish, so why don't you put in for Narcotics? Eighteen months working undercover in the junk squad, you got a gold shield in the bag. Then all you gotta do is ask for reassignment."

Macho Man flashed him an annoyed glare. "Right, amigo. Like the Praetorian Guard would ever assign a Rican to a silk-suit-headquarters unit. They be using my ass to *habla español* in one'a their dirtbag undercover operations. When I'm burnt toast, they dump me into some shithouse detective squad."

Neary guessed it might be time to get off that subject. He was about to change it when the radio squawked again. "In the Three-seven, ten-ten shots fired at Edgecomb and 149th Street. Units going, K?"

"David going, Central."

"Frank'll back him up, Central."

"Ten-four, David, Frank."

Rodriguez listened to the rising crescendo of police sirens. "Shit's starting, amigo," he said.

The Thirty-seventh was one of twelve patrol precincts that made up the NYPD's Patrol Borough Manhattan North. Its southern boundary ran from the Hudson River and West 141st Street east to St. Nicholas Avenue, then north to West 165th Street at the Harlem River, and back across 165th to the west side of the New York Central Railroad tracks. The precinct was divided into eight radio motor patrol sectors with the alphabetical designations A through H.

The partners stared at the portable radio on the seat between them, waiting for the disposition of the gun run that sectors David-Frank had sped to. The radio barked, "Three-seven David to Central K."

"Go, David."

"Edgecomb and 149th Street, mark it ten ninety-two C, one to the house, under arrest."

"Ten-four, David."

Rodriguez raised his bottle in a mock toast. "To the end of the tour."

Neary held his eyes, reached to click the neck of his bottle with Johnny's, and nodded. "To the end of the tour, amen."

Francisco Xavier Santos strolled south along Broadway, acknowledging the furtive nods of respect from shopkeepers and passersby with a slight bow of his head. The thoroughfare was crowded with women pulling shopping carts, men polishing cars, and other men hovering over curbside checker and domino games. The jubilant sounds of salsa from a ghetto blaster filled the air from a rooftop halfway down the block. On foot, black pitchers wove through the congested traffic on 149th Street, hawking heroin and crack cocaine.

A woman wearing green Lycra tights, with a chartreuse scarf wrapped around a head full of jumbo pink rollers, rushed up to Santos pushing a baby carriage. "Tío Paco," she panted. "I've named my son after you!"

Beaming with pleasure, Uncle Frank reached into the carriage to pat his namesake's cheek. With a flourish, he pulled a hundred-dollar bill from one pocket and pressed it into the mother's hand. "Buy little Francisco a present from his uncle."

Gushing, she seized his hand and kissed it with the expected show of gratitude. *"Gracias, patrón."*

Aware of the approving murmurs directed his way by men loitering on the sidewalk outside of the Dominican Social Club, he smiled inwardly. That hundred dollars was the best kind of investment he could make. Response on the street renewed Paco's faith in his power in the community. He moved ahead. He had an appointment to keep with the Colombian.

With every step, pride filled him with satisfaction. This was his world, with its dazzling tropical colors, every building facade painted in glowing seafoam greens, deep blues, orchid purples, canary yellows, and varying shades of orange. Clutches of middle-aged men drank dark brown Brugal rum from small grooved glasses as they hung around their smoking charcoal grills. The zesty tang of Dominican cooking wafted toward Tío Paco as he veered from his course to approach one of those grills. There, *sancocho*, a thick stew made of five different meats, simmered in a large black pot. Another, filled with steaming chicken and rice, cooked alongside it. Rows of bananas were being basted with rum. As it hardened, it gave the fruit a glossy black skin. All of these things made the *patrón*'s mouth water, but it was the sight of *chicharrónes* that had drawn him here.

Seeing Paco's lust, the heavyset cook in a dirty undershirt grabbed a paper plate and used tongs to lift pork rinds from the splattering oil. Dumped onto the plate, they were handed across with his compliments.

"Mil gracias, amigo," Tío Paco thanked him. He plucked a handful of napkins from a stack on the sidewalk chef's table before continuing on his way.

The Irish who had settled Washington Heights at the turn of the century were long gone now. As were the Italians, the Jews, the Greeks, and the Armenians who came after them. Washington Heights belongs to us now, he gloated, and tossed a first pork rind into his mouth. I'm the *patrón* who decides who will do business here, who lives here, and who dies here.

Halfway down the block, Tío Paco tossed the plate into a garbage can and stood cleaning his fingers with a napkin. Out of habit, his gaze swept the street for danger. Sensing none, he crossed from the curb to the vestibule of a nearby tenement and shut the door. There, he drew a brown makeup compact from his shirt pocket and squinted into the round mirror in the lid. He was checking the crisscrossing scar etched above his right eyebrow, the result of a long-ago fight with a street dealer who had tried to cheat him on a shipment. Whenever he got angry or stressed, the welts turned white against his dusky complexion, like lightning bolts against a dark sky. He'd learned early on in the drug business that any betrayal of uncontrolled emotion could be hazardous to his health. To protect himself, he'd engaged the services of a Broadway makeup artist with a penchant for nose candy. They'd struck a deal. She would keep him supplied with a makeup that blended with his exact skin color, and he would be her candy man.

Paco noticed how the scar's lowest extreme peeked out from beneath the makeup he had applied earlier, and set to work feathering the vanishing cream down and outward toward his temple to cover it.

Under way again, he turned the corner onto 142nd Street minutes later, and cursed beneath his breath. The presence of a black BMW sedan and familiar Cali muscle outside La Rivista told him the Colombian had once again beaten him to the meet. He swore, yet again, that one day he would beat the sonofabitch to the mark.

At the door to the club, when a Columbian bodyguard attempted to frisk him, Paco slapped his hands away. He stood a moment locked with a pair of hooded, reptilian eyes, waging a battle of wills. Then, before it could escalate, he brushed past the man and proceeded inside.

A polished stone bar stretched along the right wall of the glitzy interior, with stools padded in coral leather to match the upholstery of semicircular banquettes. Red, yellow, and green floodlights bathed an empty central stage's tinsel backdrop, while a lone bartender restocked mirrored backbar shelves.

The Colombian had planted himself at a banquette table with an unobstructed view of the entire club. While approaching the Cali cartel's head man in New York City, Tío Paco made sure to keep his expression affable. They might both be *patróns*, but the man from Cali was the one with the bigger guns. As Paco watched Roberto Santiago lounge so confidently there, his gold cigarette case and Dunhill lighter on the surface before him, the Dominican *patrón* was all too aware of the contrasts between them. Tall, urbane, in his middle forties, Santiago wore an impeccably tailored light gray suit that flattered his athletic frame. Tío Paco was best described as squat, barely five feet four, with broad, heavy shoulders and big hands. At fifty-one years of age, he'd grown paunchy, his well-fed gut bulging beneath a loose-fitting purple *guyabara* shirt. His baggy gray trousers refused to stay up around his waist anymore, the cuffs bunching atop his shoes. But it was the color of their skin that revealed the main difference between the two men. Santiago's smooth olive-brown complexion reflected the mingling of substantially European blood with just the faintest bit of Indian. This tagged him as white, and placed him at the top of the race-conscious Caribbean pecking order, while Tío Paco's dark, rough Afro-Indian complexion branded him an *indio oscuro*. As someone who was not mostly black, his birth had placed him on the pecking order's next-to-last rung.

Santos kept his handshake with Santiago docile, and his demeanor submissive as he slid into the booth.

"Francisco, good to see you," Santiago greeted him. Reflected in colored lights from the stage, his teeth gleamed. "Something to drink?"

"What I would like, Roberto, is to know who is using cops to knock over my stash houses."

Santiago, with palms opened outward, raised his hands in a gesture of innocence. "It's certainly not us, *hermano*. We are in this together, no? Why have I heard nothing of this, and when did it start?"

Santiago had heard everything; of that much Santos was sure. Paco trusted the Colombian's word as much as he might a politician's. "Three weeks ago. They knocked over two of my places. Stole twenty keys and close to a quarter million of my dollars."

"They were Narco?"

"No. I think maybe local. They had too much of my intelligence."

"Then your problem is local, *hermano*. They had search warrants?"

"Not they. Only one man, that anyone saw. And he came to steal, not to make arrests."

"A description?"

Santos shook his head. "He wore a heavy jacket and ski mask. Came down from the roof. Armed with a fully automatic SPAS twelve-gauge."

Santiago knew how hard those weapons were to come by, and was clearly impressed. "So find out who he is, and kill him."

"Don't worry. But first I must find out who in my organization is feeding him information."

"How did he penetrate your security?" Santiago watched Paco closely as he asked the question, and added, "Have you made any recent changes that might make your places . . . vulnerable?"

Tío Paco felt like a lowly mestizo, being questioned this way by the white *patrón*. He laced his fingers beneath the table and squeezed hard. "No changes. We operate only in tenements we control. We only deal wholesale. The money and the product are not kept together. A customer must pass through our security before he is taken to an apartment to negotiate his purchase. We take his money there, then send him to a different apartment in the building to make the pickup. My men in the first apartment call ahead to make sure the order is ready."

The clatter of bottles being shuffled on the backbar drew Santiago's attention, and a glare of irritation. "You change the stash rooms every day?" he asked Paco.

"Of course." Frank slid his hands from beneath the table to fold them before him. "And only a small handful of trusted men know where they are."

"So get rid of the people who were working the day this cop took those tenements down. That way, you are certain to get the guilty one."

"Only after I learn who is giving him the balls to fuck with me; who this cop is working for."

"You got *policia* on your payroll. Why not ask them?"

"You think I didn't? None of them know."

"And you believe this?"

Paco snorted impatiently. "Of course I don't believe them. But not believing, and finding out who is doing this to me? These are separate things."

"You don't keep too much product around, correct?"

"Only what we are likely to need for any given time. Same with the money. We move it out, and restock product as supplies get low."

"How did this cop with the giant *cojones* get in?"

"One burst from that shotgun took out the door. No warning from our lookouts. My men inside were sitting ducks."

Santiago's manicured nails tapped out a rhythm atop his cigarette case. "A situation like this makes us, ah, uncomfortable, my friend. We worry that your problem could become our problem. Some might even ask if we are doing business with a man we should not. A *trafficante* who cannot control his own people."

Paco had to sit hard on the urge to gouge out this Cali *maricón*'s eyes. Instead, he forced a thin smile. "We have been doing *mucho* business for a lot of years, Roberto. You and your people know that I am a serious man. I don't see how my concerns could ever become yours. You and me, we make a deal, and then you are protected from all the rest of it. I make the pickup in Mexico. My men, not yours, are the only ones exposed."

Santiago contemplated him from beneath sculptured black eyebrows, his shiny brown eyes penetrating in their intensity. "Have any of your people been arrested lately, *hermano*?"

"Not that I know of. And all the people who work in my tenements have been with me a long time."

"We are in a business without a soul, Paco. You can trust no one." Santiago's eyes narrowed. "Why did you ask for this meet?"

"Because whoever ripped me off is peddling my drugs somewhere."

"Most likely in another part of the city," Santiago mused. "And you want me to find out who and where."

A nod. "If I wish to stand and fight, these are things I need to know."

Santiago's shrug said he was agreeable to such a notion. He was a businessman, after all. "I'll ask around, see if any of the heavyweight orders have fallen off over the past three weeks."

Paco nodded his appreciation. He reached across to pick up Santiago's Dunhill and toy with it. "Traitors and their families must be dealt with quickly. If not, others begin to suspect that they can cross you, too."

Santiago removed a cigarette from his case, tapped it against the lid, and beckoned for the return of his lighter. The mestizo handed it back to his *patrón*.

Roberto lit the cigarette, and for a long moment considered the hissing blue flame before he snapped the lid closed. "I watched this movie on the television last night. About a tribe in Africa that captures a safari and tortures all but one of them to death. *The Naked Prey*. You have seen it?"

Paco shook his head no.

"I was intrigued by this tribe's methods," Santiago continued. "They covered one of the bearers in mud, let it dry so he became entombed in a mold of clay, then slowly roasted him to death over a cooking pit. Can you imagine what it must be like to die that way, *hermano*? To be stewed alive in your own juices?"

Tío Paco nodded appreciatively. "I like it. Like it quite a lot. When I learn who is giving me up, I will make a fiesta. We will go someplace quiet, upstate, where all my people can watch this cop and his friends roast side by side, like suckling pigs."

"They will think long and hard before anyone looks to take you off again," Roberto said. He took another drag on his cigarette and sent several smoke rings floating toward the ceiling. "Meanwhile, I am having a problem in Queens. A reporter from *La Paz* is writing lies about my friends and me. Do you think you could take care of this problem for us?"

Paco shifted uncomfortably in his seat. "Killing a reporter can cause . . . problems."

"This spic must go. He knows no respect."

Determined to hide his feelings, Paco sighed, certain that Santiago had called him the same, or worse, behind his back. "We will make it look like an accident. *Sí?*"

"No accident. Messy, so that others will get our message. You don't fuck with us." Roberto drew an envelope from an inside pocket and placed it on the table. "Everything you need to know is here."

"It is taken care of," Paco assured him, and tucked the information into his waistband.

Santiago changed the subject. "I hear Darryl Johnson has begun to move some serious weight."

"Darryl is ambitious. He buys all his product from me."

"Ambition in a nigger can be a problem. I hear he is thinking of getting into your end of the business."

Paco masked his distrust of this Colombian behind a soft smile. Why was this Cali whore telling him this? And how did a big man like him even know who Darryl Johnson was? "Darryl is a pitcher. He will never be anything else. How could he? Nobody in our business trusts the black man."

"True enough, *hermano*." Santiago looked pointedly at his heavy gold Rolex Daytona, clearly ready to end the meeting.

"What happened to the one man they did not kill?" Paco asked.

"*¿Cómo?*"

"In the movie, about the safari."

"Oh. The usual thing. The brave white hunter outruns the niggers."

Two

Wedged conveniently between Harlem and the South Bronx—two of New York City's highest-crime-per-capita areas—Randalls Island was an ideal headquarters location for the Street Crime Monitoring Unit of NYPD's Special Operations Division. There, in an off-the-beaten-path setting beneath the Triborough Bridge, the crime statistics, data, and monitoring unit presided over by Deputy Inspector Gerald Mannion was responsible for gathering street crime incidence and trend information, and generating the computer statistics used by the commissioner and his so-called superchiefs during their monthly Compstat meetings with precinct commanders. Mannion was basically a bean counter at heart, happiest when crunching numbers and turning them into reasoned, well-ordered analysis. He liked that aspect of this duty he'd drawn almost as much as he *dis*liked running the liaison personnel responsible for gathering his raw data from the streets. While the brash confidence all of them exuded was part of what made them good at their jobs, he found most of the cops assigned to that task of a particularly thuggish bent.

A prime example of the type was Officer Clarence DaCosta, summoned to report to Mannion after regular office hours that Wednesday night. DaCosta was Street Crime's plainclothes liaison with Patrol Borough Manhattan North and was, in Gerald Mannion's mind, the epitome of everything he disliked about the eight patrol borough liaisons in his command. A lean, muscular man, half black and half Italian, DaCosta had piercing blue eyes, coppery, almost dirty-blond hair he wore in dreadlocks, and chiseled African features so striking they could easily be called beautiful. The first time they met, Mannion was instantly turned off by the young plainclothes cop's arrogance. Regardless of the fact that it could be an asset on the street, it was an impediment to a proper chain-of-command relationship. Tonight, DaCosta had arrived fifteen minutes late without excuse or apology. As Jerry Mannion shuffled together the flurry of faxes that had steadily accumulated on his desk that week, the Manhattan North liaison lounged in a chair before him, everything about his demeanor screaming disrespect.

"I'm hoping you can enlighten me, Officer DaCosta, as to just what the hell is going on at the Three-seven right now." Mannion made no attempt to suppress the irritation he felt. He held up the sheaf of faxes and shook them. "I've got everyone in the Big Building, from the PC on down, crawling up my ass about Washington Heights."

DaCosta eyed him steadily. "It's the hottest drug market in all the five boroughs, boss. It don't make for what you'd call your stable environment." He paused to point at the faxes in Jerry's hand. "I assume you're talking about them rumors been flying. Dominican stash pads being ripped off, and one shitheel getting his ass whacked in the process."

"They seem to be more than rumors."

"Nobody reported nothing, and nobody on our side ever saw no dead guy. That makes it a rumor. You ask me, I don't unnerstand the Big Buildin's beef. It's Dominicans *created* that fucking jungle up there, and mosta the predators living in it."

"One rumor has a police officer responsible," Mannion said coldly. "That he's the one who actually did the robberies."

If DaCosta cared, it wasn't evident. He looked almost bored. "Heavy dope traffic means lotsa loose cash. And loose cash creates temptations. Life's tough on a patrolman's salary. Ain't easy, keeping a wife an' kids in Pampers and sneakers, *and* tryin' to impress a girlfriend with what a swinging dick you are onna side."

A single man with none of the encumbrances he'd just mentioned, DaCosta was Street Crime's eyes and ears throughout the northern reaches of Manhattan. Mannion would admit it was a lot of ground to cover, but each borough command liaison had considerable resources. DaCosta drove an old blue Chevy gypsy cab to better blend into the territory he worked, and had in excess of a dozen snitches on his payroll. He also had access to the command logs and files at all eleven Manhattan North station houses to complement his complete freedom of movement on the streets. Right now, he seemed to be implying something that Mannion had not seen in any of his weekly reports. "You're saying it *is* a cop?"

The plainclothesman's attention drifted out the window toward the Fire Department's training academy across the way. There, a group of recruits was scaling an illuminated tower in a full-gear night exercise. Their yellow jackets, black helmets, and oxygen tanks gleamed in the floodlights. "Not that I've heard for certain, boss. But this rumor's been circulating for a while now." He nodded toward the scene outside. "You know what they say about smoke and fire."

One of DaCosta's reports, a couple weeks back, had alluded to such a rumor, but had supplied no details and hadn't seemed to lend it much credence. Now, he seemed to be admitting there might be something more to it. "Is this just you speculating?" Mannion asked. "Or do you have something specific to hang it on?"

Those chiseled features flashed an expression that was half irritation and half disgust. "I've got eleven precincts I'm monitoring. From rapists lurking in the bushes of Central Park to wiseguys dumping bodies inta Spuyten Duyvil, and a whole lotta badness in between. Specific? A corpse is specific. Little else about this duty is."

Mannion ignored the sharp edge of insubordination to press ahead. "The Three-seven is a potential major flash point, Clarence. The entire reason for the existence of this unit is to gather data from the streets, provide analysis, and pinpoint latent problems before they blow up in the city's face. I'm not suggesting you ignore the rest of the borough command, but right now I need you to focus hard on Washington Heights." He paused to consider what he'd just said, and where such a focus might very well lead. Cops committing armed robbery of stash houses made for very bad press. The powers at One Police Plaza knew it, and were painfully aware of what a scandal involving a rogue officer could do to them all. The current PC was a lame duck, rumored to be gone to Florida by summer's end, but everyone in line for his job was also directly in the line of fire. A major corruption scandal could well destroy all their ambitions. "Get me something more than rumors, for crissake," he demanded. "This is the Street Crime Monitoring Unit. We reports facts."

*   *   *

The slender concrete finger of Riverside Drive that skirted through the western edge of the Thirty-seventh Precinct fronted a mix of prewar apartment houses and nineteenth-century brownstones. The precinct station house, a limestone fortress with massive black lanterns dominating its ornate entrance, stood on a chunk of Riverside Drive between 146th and 147th Streets. The four-story building, with its rock towers and arches and terra-cotta quoins, had been built at the turn of the century. The city fathers at the time were pressured by the wealthy into building the new police station as protection from marauding gangs from the Bowery and East Side who traveled to the northernmost reaches of Manhattan Island to rob and plunder.

It was three minutes after midnight; Thursday, not Wednesday anymore. The first platoon set to hit the streets and greet the new day still had not begun to drift outside. The radio cars of the old day's third platoon were idling across the street in Riverside Park, hidden in the breeze-blown shadows.

"What's keeping them?" Mike Neary groused.

Macho Man opened his mouth to say something when the double doors swung outward and the fresh platoon began sauntering down the stoop. The park was suddenly filled with the clamor of slamming doors as crews abandoned their wheels. Macho Man and Neary crossed the park, heading for the station house. On the sidewalk, cops going home briefed the fresh troops on what was going down in their sectors.

Neary had just reached the curb when a female officer called out to him. "Hey, Paleface. Gimme the aggravating elements that raise a Burglary Two to Burglary One."

Macho Man continued on into the precinct's high-ceilinged muster room. He snapped the traditional salute at the desk sergeant and walked inside the glass-fronted clerical office past the elaborately carved teak front desk. The civilian clerical, a heavyset black woman with thick hair set in a sweeping beehive and a backside that spilled over the edges of her swivel perch, handed him a stack of reports to sign. Macho Man eased his arms around her to lean close and growl in her ear. "One day, Mary. Jus' you an' me. We gonna get it on, and I just know how finger-lickin' good you're gonna be."

Mary chuckled, deep and mellow, while shaking her head. "Child, you wouldn't survive the foreplay."

"But what a way to ex-pire."

Her phone rang and she snapped it up. "Three-seven clerical." Hearing the voice at the other end, Mary covered the mouthpiece to look up at Rodriguez. "You here, baby?"

"Who?" he mouthed.

"Sounds like Chiquita Blow-job."

Johnny took the receiver. "Hey, Isabelle," he cooed. "I was just gonna call you."

Mary rolled her eyes and went back to her paperwork. In the near silence of the office, the intensity from down the wire came through loud and clear.

"I been thinking about you a lot today, Johnny. You going to stop by tonight?"

"I gotta be getting home," he begged off. "Got court in the morning."

"Liar," Mary whispered, grinning, then shook her head in disgust at the gullibility of her sex.

"Just for a few minutes, Johnny. Please. I wanna feel you inside me."

"You sound like you need it bad," he murmured, his gaze locked with Mary's.

"I do, Johnny. Just thinking about it is making me crazy."

"I'll change and be right over. Sit tight." He handed the receiver back to the clerk, winking as she took it. "That woman be craving my body, mama. You taking notes?"

Mary swiveled back around to her keyboard, the glow of the monitor screen reflected off her scowling ebony features. "You don't know shit about women, Macho Man. A real one prob'ly kill your skinny ass."

Isabelle Melendez turned from the telephone to face the woman seated next to her. The gun the woman had pressed to Isabelle's ribs scared her, and she had to pee. Until ten minutes ago, she'd never seen the stranger who now held her life in one hand. She had just stepped out of the shower when a pounding shook the door of her second-floor tenement apartment. Pulling on a skimpy robe, she'd rushed to answer it. "Johnny?"

"I work with Officer Rodriguez," a desperate voice had answered. "He's been hurt and is asking for you."

Those words had sent a spasm of fear through Isabelle. She'd unchained the door with fumbling, frantic fingers, flung it open, and then went rigid. The woman on the threshold had jammed a gun into her stomach to propel her back down the hall toward her living room and onto the sofa.

The intruder looked nothing like any of the female cops Isabelle had gotten to know through Johnny. She wore running shoes, black tights, and a long embroidered vest. Her complexion was youthful and fresh-scrubbed. If it weren't for her hard body and the well-defined muscles of her bare arms, she might have passed for a teenager. Her coal-black hair was tied in a ponytail at the crown of her head, then teased and sprayed stiff, with softer tendrils left to trail loose at the nape of her neck.

Isabelle clutched her robe closed at the neck, eyes flashing panic. "I did what you told me. He's on his way. Please don't hurt me," she begged.

"I'm not going to hurt you, or Johnny," the woman replied. "I just want to scare the shit out of him."

Emboldened by this assurance, Isabelle flicked a cautious glance at the gun still aimed at her gut. "What did he do to you?" she asked.

"I'll tell you when he gets here."

"You got to keep pointing that thing at me?"

The 9 mm Heckler & Koch semiautomatic had a stubby tube screwed onto the barrel, and Isabelle sighed with some measure of relief as the muzzle eased aside.

"I guess not," the stranger replied, shoving the gun into her black vinyl tote. Somewhere in the distance, a car choked and backfired.

Isabelle examined the woman with new curiosity. "What's your name?"

"Gina." Bright, inquisitive eyes wandered toward an unframed oil painting across the room, to take in the sun-baked Indian depicted there. Stooped in front of a thatched-roof adobe hut, he wore his straw sombrero tilted at a rakish angle, gnarled hands gripping the neckline of his pure white serape. The woman's gaze then drifted on to take in the tight little living space with its green velvet furniture, the nap worn gray in places, and several pieces of cheap Chinese earthenware. "This building's a dump, but you keep a nice, neat place," she commented.

"Johnny likes a clean house," Isabelle replied. Her fear had started gnawing at her again. Besides the simple fact of the gun, there was plenty more to spook her about this woman's presence, beginning with how she'd entered, and including how detached she seemed now.

"I bet his wife keeps their house real clean too, huh?"

"I . . . I guess so."

"Rumor has it, you used to be one of Tío Paco's stashers. That true?"

A new kind of dread crept in around the edges of Isabelle's fear. "Not for a long time. Not since I started in with Johnny, and that been almost two years."

"Paco's got this thing about doing business with people who got close ties to cops, no?"

Isabelle shrugged. "You play the odds, maybe you wanna make sure the deck is stacked a little in your favor."

Gina yawned and stretched, one hand never straying far from the top opening of the tote. "Call me curious, but why's a pretty señorita like you waste your time on a married guy like Johnny Rodriguez? You gotta know it ain't going nowhere."

"I love him."

"Ah." The pitiful claim of every self-conning woman on the planet. "Men are lying dirtbags. You ain't figured that out yet?"

Isabelle shook her head, the smile she wore fanciful and dreamy. "Not my Johnny."

"I don't believe in love," Gina told her. "Except for how hot sex makes me feel."

Isabelle felt herself relax just a bit. Shared confidences about sex and the men in women's lives were a ritual as old as tribalism itself. "You single?" she asked.

Gina nodded. "Got a son, though. Name is Claude, and he's too gorgeous for words."

"Do you go around scaring people like this for money?" Isabelle asked. "Like a job, to help feed you and your baby?" The only thing she could imagine as a reason for a visit like this was that Johnny had gotten in deep to a bookie. He liked to gamble; that much she knew.

Gina shook her head, the expression she wore turning faraway again. "No, that's not at all why I do it."

A ragged metallic ringing interrupted their exchange, startling Isabelle but not seeming to perturb her visitor one bit.

"It's the downstairs buzzer." Isabelle felt her fear flood back.

"Let him in."

Isabelle stood and crossed to the tarnished intercom panel on the hallway wall. There, she pressed the downstairs door-release button.

"Open the front door and leave it like that," Gina ordered. "Then switch off the light on your way back here."

Once she complied, Isabelle lowered herself back onto the sofa in time to see Gina thrust her hand back into the shiny tote. When it emerged, the gun was once again in evidence, hefted with the spooky confidence of one long accustomed to its weight and feel. Without ceremony, Gina buried a single bullet in Isabelle's right temple, the impact jerking her body upright and snapping her head back. The dying body came to rest, slumped sideways, legs splayed and arms twitching atop the faded green cushions.

Gina reached quickly to switch off the table lamp, then heard the sound of feet hurriedly mounting the stairs outside the apartment. Seconds later, a man stood in silhouette on the threshold, backlit by a bare bulb on the landing.

"Isabelle, baby?" he addressed the darkened room. "Your Macho Man and his big throbbin' bone-on are here."

Rodriguez advanced eagerly as he spoke, and it wasn't until he'd almost reached the living room that he registered the puzzling scene now before him. There wasn't just one woman awaiting him there on the sofa, but two. One figure was slumped at an odd angle, while the other sat rigid, both hands in front of her. It was the sharp smell of cordite that prompted his reaction. His hand darted to his belt but never quite reached the off-duty Smith & Wesson 9 mm tucked there.

Gina fired, the slug taking him mid-chest and slamming his body backward into the living room wall. With the impact, he started to slide toward the floor, lax jaw fallen to his chest and eyes full of surprise. As a stain began to spread downward from the hole torn in his shirt, his entire body was racked with quick convulsions. Then he lay silent.

Singing softly to herself, Gina rose from her seat to approach the corpse, prepared to put an insurance round behind her target's left ear. "Macho, macho man. I wanna be yourrr ma-cho man." With the toe of one sneaker, she eased a lifeless hand out of her path, leaned with the weapon extended to probe with the barrel to find the sweet spot, and pulled the trigger a second time. The back of his skull exploded, sending blood, bone, and brain matter spattering across the wall. She dropped the weapon back into her tote, the stink of cordite now quite strong, and turned to survey her handiwork. She noticed that one of the dead woman's breasts was left exposed where her robe had fallen open, and crossed to tug the lapels together. "Sorry, Isabelle, honey," she murmured. "But you coulda given me up."

On the street outside the murdered woman's Hamilton Place tenement, headlights from the cars of upmarket druggies, desperate to score before a night on the town, illuminated pitchers scurrying in and out of traffic. The night air pulsed with an unstable mix of rhythms blasting from car radios and CD players. From behind the wheel of a double-parked blue gypsy cab, the driver watched Gina bound down the building stoop swinging her tote, and thought: This bitch pisses ice water.

Gina ran to the taxi to pile into the backseat.

"Any problems?" He studied her reflection in the rearview mirror.

"Nuh-uh. Let's jam."

He pulled into traffic while dialing 911 on his cellular phone. When the emergency police operator answered, he spoke with an exaggerated Spanish accent, reporting a shooting in a second-floor apartment at 2148 Hamilton Place. The call completed, he keyed off and flipped the phone shut. When he leaned over to set it on the seat beside him, a shiny silver object fell from inside his partially unbuttoned shirt. Dangling there on a heavy silver chain, it gleamed in the mercury-vapor streetlight. The numbers 4061 were embossed across its bottom, beneath the seal of the New York City Police Department.

Three

Thursday morning at six forty-five, Matthew Cosgrove Stuart burrowed deep into his oversize pillow to spend a few indulgent moments savoring the familiar sounds and smells of the two-story colonial his grandfather had built during the Great Depression. Fifteen minutes earlier he'd heard his grandmother's ornate William and Mary pendulum clock, downstairs in the entrance foyer, gong the half hour. The aroma of fresh coffee wafted up from the automatic coffeemaker in the kitchen. This bed was no longer the bed of his childhood, but this was the same house he had lived in all his life, on Harbor View Terrace, dominating a knoll overlooking all of Upper New York Bay. The section of Brooklyn was called Bay Ridge on maps, but to Matt Stuart and others who'd grown up there, it was simply "the Ridge."

A light wind off the bay swept through the open bedroom window to rustle the curtains, carrying with it the scent of magnolia, lilac, and tangy salt water. Stuart lay quietly, listening to the steady drone of traffic moving below him on Leif Ericson Drive. When he listened hard, he could even hear the lap of the bay against Brooklyn's shoreline. "Time to join the real world," he grumbled to himself, and tossed off the sheet.

After a shave and shower, Matt dressed in lightweight gray slacks, a white shirt, maroon tie, and navy blue wool blazer. He tucked a yellow silk pocket square into the blazer and gathered the tools of his trade from atop his dresser: Smith & Wesson 9 mm semiautomatic, handcuffs, and an ammo pouch containing two fifteen-round magazines. He clipped all of these onto his belt and slid his worn leather shield case into his trouser pocket.

On arrival downstairs, Stuart dragged open the tall teak pocket doors that separated the entry hall from the dining room and walked into a room flooded with dazzling spring sunlight. The cherrywood Hepple-white table and chairs gleamed with a high polish as he sauntered past, and again he felt the sort of contentment that comes with easy familiar-ity. Everything in this room, from leaded-glass china cabinet, to side-board, table, and huge crystal chandelier dated from a time long before his birth, when his proud first-generation grandfather had purchased and shipped them from the Stuart clan's native Scotland.

In the kitchen, he poured a mug of coffee and carried it into the living room to stand at the expanse of windows overlooking the harbor. A con-tainer ship piled high with rust-streaked cargo boxes lolled at anchor while gulls screeched and wheeled above her. Since he was a boy, Matt had liked to start his day watching the gulls, the wind playing with the surface of the water, the yellow ferries from Staten Island plying back and forth to the tip of Manhattan, and all manner of other nonstop ac-tivity that characterized this bustling scene now spread at his feet.

Stuart stood at just under six feet tall, with crow's-feet etched deep around his eyes. He could no longer lay claim to the boyish hank of brown hair that once fell forward toward his brow. Today, his wavy hair was salted through with gray and was worn combed more or less straight back from a high, weathered forehead. The impish glint that had ani-mated his dark green eyes in his youth was faded now, leaving him with a look of intensity that sometimes surprised him when he glimpsed him-self in a mirror. Next October he would be forty-six.

From the window, he carried his coffee to his grandmother's Steinway concert grand and sat down to run through a series of scales using just his left hand. He'd taken lessons as a kid, and started up again five years ago, but could never seem to find time enough to get his skills as sharp and crisp as he would have liked. Once he'd run through a few dozen rudimentary scales, he stopped, took a sip of coffee, and forced his re-luctant eyes to focus on *the* photograph, standing in the midst of other framed family pictures atop the piano. It was taken at David's third birth-day party. In it, Pat and he beamed with joy as they stood behind their son and watched him blowing out the candles on his cake. They had been a family that Saturday afternoon in June, seven years ago. Today, all Stuart had left was the Job, and this big empty house his grandfather had built.

Fifteen minutes later, Matt was in his car on the Brooklyn-Queens Expressway, en route to his assignment at the 72 Poplar Street headquarters of NYPD's Intelligence Division, when his cell phone chirped. He aimed his reply up toward the hands-free microphone implanted in the sun visor. "Lieutenant Stuart."

A woman's voice with an officious edge to it replied, "I have a notification for you, Lou." She used the diminutive of lieutenant, routinely used as a sign of respect within the Job.

"Go ahead."

"You're to report forthwith to the Big Building. Room 1406."

"Ten-four," he affirmed, his mind racing. He hadn't heard from the occupant of 1406 in five months, and now she was having one of her flunkies give him a forthwith. As he took the Brooklyn Bridge over the East River and left it at the Park Row exit, he wondered what she might want.

One Police Plaza is an orange brick cube resting on concrete stilts, known throughout the Job as "the Big Building." As it loomed in front of him, Matt let his gaze drift upward toward the fourteenth floor. The power floor. The police commissioner's office was located in Room 1400. Room 1406 housed his first deputy.

Suzanne Albrecht had been the CO of the Personnel Bureau when she and Stuart first met, three years ago. As far as anyone in the Job knew, she had no personal life—including a sex life—and did not socialize with anyone in the Job. She was known as a hardworking, career-minded boss with the toughness and verve necessary to claw her way onto the fourteenth floor. Her aloof brand of political correctness and severe, no-nonsense business attire had earned her the sobriquet "the Ice Maiden."

She and Stuart had carried on a "sneaking around" love affair, until five months ago. It was then that he made the mistake of telling her he'd fallen in love and wanted her to openly share his life.

Suzanne had tearfully explained that marriage to him was impossible. Her goals in life were different from his; she wanted to be the city's first woman police commissioner, and no matter how much she loved him, she loved her lifelong dream even more. It was something she would never willingly give up.

"You could be the first *married* female PC," he'd argued, but to no avail.

Avoiding his eyes, she'd told him she had shunned just the kind of consuming relationship he wanted simply because it might alter her single-minded focus and sap the energy crucial to any drive to the top.

Telling her where she could shove the PC's job, he'd driven off in a fury and left her on the sidewalk in front of her apartment building.

As first deputy police commissioner, Suzanne now worked as executive aide to their overall boss, and acted as PC in his stead in the event of absence or disability. While she also commanded all administrative units within the Job, her real power came from her proximity to the throne, and the fact that she controlled all of the department's "field associates"—rookies recruited while they were still in the academy, who, after graduation, were planted as Internal Affairs spies in precincts throughout the city. It was their job to root out corruption and report it to their overseers in the first deputy's office. Suzanne Albrecht had the power to squelch a career-destroying corruption case, or to whisper a word into a forever-grateful ear about a pending investigation.

When Stuart's former lover came out from behind her desk to greet him, her well-practiced smile was full of cool confidence. They stood at arm's length, each searching out the other's face. Matt felt his pulse quicken. He wanted to sweep her into his arms, feel the swell of her breasts against him, tell her how much he'd missed her, and how empty life had been without her. He saw nothing in her eyes to give him hope, no flicker of love, no longing for lost lust. After a brief, uncomfortable silence, all he could say was, "How have you been?"

Her smile lost some of the cool, and may have betrayed just the slightest relief. "I've been okay. Thanks for asking." She motioned him toward a grouping of blue leather sofas.

As Stuart followed her he took in the smartly tailored black business suit, hemmed at a conservative knee length. The oversize tortoiseshell glasses that partially concealed her beautiful face had always bugged him. Her disguise, she used to call them. Today, her auburn hair was pulled tight to her skull and gathered into an unflattering bun, giving her a look of sharp severity. Sturdy black shoes with low heels worked to lessen the impact of her otherwise shapely legs. In keeping with her Ice

Maiden persona, she wore translucent lip gloss and no other makeup or jewelry. He watched her lower herself next to him and felt pleasure in the secret knowledge that somewhere inside her lurked a voraciously sexual and assertive woman. Memories of their shared times made him feel uncomfortable. "Why am I here, Suzanne?"

"A cop and his girlfriend were killed in the Three-seven last night."

He frowned. "I heard about it on the radio this morning. Off-duty, no?"

She rose quickly and started to pace, hands hugging her shoulders. As he continued to sit, Stuart noticed an absence of police memorabilia and personal mementos on the tables, on the credenza behind her desk, and on the walls. The Ice Maiden's lair, he thought. Cold and surgical. A place where painful things could happen.

She stopped, fixed him with a stare, hesitated, and then plunged on. "Matt, the PC will be gone by Labor Day. He's joining Citibank as their vice president for worldwide security. I stand a good shot at getting his job. Better than good, actually."

"Congratulations. I hope it turns out to be everything you thought it would be."

"Are you being sarcastic, Lieutenant?"

"Me? Naw."

She gave him a mirthless smile and sat down next to him again. "I want you to know I haven't slept with anyone else, since."

"Neither have I," he replied, and leaned forward to kiss her.

When their lips met, she opened her mouth and slid a hand around his head to hold him close. Then suddenly she let go and pulled away, hastily patting the edges of her overly severe coif. "I wish you hadn't done that," she said, her tone scolding.

"Sorry." He wasn't. "You still get my testosterone boiling."

"That's something you're going to need to keep in check."

The smile he flashed was weighted at the edges with a heavy sadness. "Yeah, I suppose it is. So. Why *did* you bring me here?"

"Rodriguez, the cop in the Three-seven who was killed, was one of mine. A field associate. He had a wife, a little boy, car payments, and no money in the bank. But when the patrol sergeant searched his body at the scene, he found five thousand dollars in an envelope stuffed into his waistband."

Stuart grunted. "A lotta green for a cop to be carrying around. Any chance it was planted?"

"Pretty much soaked through with blood. The crime scene people doubt it was put on him after the fact." She shifted to face him more directly. "FAs in adjoining precincts have been monitoring rumbles. Word on the street is that someone in the Three-seven has been booming."

"Dealers?" Matt asked.

She nodded. "Several stash houses have been taken off. Cash and drugs."

He thought about it, focusing his line of inquiry. "I can guess what they do with the cash, but what about the drugs? Any idea where they're laying them off?"

She shook her head. "That, we don't know."

"You got any hard evidence it was cops?"

"Or just cop. No. Only the rumors."

"How long had Rodriguez been spying on his brother officers?"

The way she contemplated him turned blood-chilling. "We need field associates to keep our brother officers honest."

"How long, Suzanne?"

"Four years."

"And in that time, what did he give up? Just out of curiosity."

"Petty stuff, mostly: eating on the arm, cops getting it on with girl-friends during their tours, shopping at discount prices, accepting Christmas gifts."

"Anybody get popped as a result of his information?"

"No. This office is interested in the meat eaters, not the grazers."

"Somebody might mention to this office that minor corruption turns cud chewers into carnivores."

The shrug she returned was nearly as rueful as it was impatient. "I suppose. You forget what it's like, working on the street, sometimes, you work this close to the throne."

"What have they come up with so far? On the shooting."

"Nothing. No witnesses, no physical evidence. I spoke with the Three-seven whip this morning. They're not even sure Rodriguez was the mark. Apparently, his girlfriend used to stash for a major *trafficante* up there. She could have been the intended victim."

"Probably wishful thinking," Stuart mused. "In scumpits like the Three-seven, you can buy a hit for a quarter gram. And once the mutts take you down, they steal everything on your person, including your

Nikes. No way a local shooter would leave five large in this guy's pocket. A pro did your trusted FA."

An awkward silence settled between them. At length, Suzanne spoke first.

"There's smoke coming out of the Three-seven, Matt. Enough to make me fear I have a corruption problem brewing. Could be it's nothing. And could be it's so minor I can quash it without a ripple."

"And could be it's getting ready to blow any shot you've got at the throne right off the mayor's organizational chart."

The expression he saw on her face surprised him. Was she appealing to the bond they'd so recently shared, and *she* had cut? That's how the look she focused on him felt. "I'd make a good PC, Matt. You believe it, too. No matter how you feel about me."

He struggled to keep his own expression neutral. "I know how badly you want it," he replied. "And if you thought I might hurt your chances, just imagine what your little problem in the Three-seven could do, it turns out to be a big one."

She pushed quickly past any accusation she knew he'd implied. "I'm asking you for your help, Matt. Even begging for it, if you like. I need a pair of eyes up there; someone I can transfer in to have a look and report back." As she stared at him now, there was nothing of the boss-surbordinate dynamic remaining in her attitude. She was clearly beseeching him. "I want you to do it for me."

Stuart felt a tiny prickle of unease disturb the hair at the back of his neck. "Why me? Why not someone from IAD? Or your own office?"

"Because there's no one else I can trust. Not to use what they find to maybe knife me in the back."

"I'd say that's pretty sad. Wouldn't you?"

Her eyes fell to her hands. "Yes, it is."

"You've gotta know my transfer out of a silk-suit assignment like Intelligence Division, to an uptown shithouse like the Three-seven is no lateral move. I expect it'll raise some eyebrows. You thought about that?"

"It's why I'm getting you 'the money,' " she replied. "It will be the explanation for your transfer."

His current assignment didn't warrant a detective commander's compensation. The whip of the Three-seven squad did, and "the money" was the Detective Bureau's most sought-after contract. Seven thousand extra dollars a year, all fully pensionable. The city's Administrative Code set a quota of seventy-five such designations among the 380 sergeants and lieutenants assigned to the division. Only the politically connected, the "hung of the hung," got this prize.

Stuart refused to trust what she was attempting to establish between them again after five months of not hearing a word from her. To him, it presumed an awful lot. "Sounds like you're trying to bribe me," he said, keeping his tone good-natured.

"Not to worry, Matthew. You'll earn it, and then some."

"Nobody likes a bent cop. They betray the Job, their families, and themselves. But nobody likes a rat, either, and that's what you're asking me to become."

She pushed her glasses up on her forehead, a move that totally transformed her face. "I'm asking you to investigate and report. Nothing more."

"It's the 'investigate and report' that bothers me, Suzanne. I take the job, you know I'll do it. And you know me well enough to know that if I come up with any dirty cops, they're going down the tubes. That could dump an even bigger scandal onto your plate."

"When you raised your hand and took the oath making you a boss, you separated yourself from the pack, Matthew." At last, her tone was taking on the chiding edge of a superior officer admonishing a subordinate. "If that means being branded a rat in order to do a job for me, well . . . it's one of the things you get paid to do."

He nodded. "I do what I'm ordered to do, that's correct. But I want to know what I'm getting into. If you're gonna be square right on down the line with me, you know I'm not afraid to stick my neck out."

She returned his stare for a moment, and then reached out to lightly lay elegantly tapered fingers on his forearm. "I don't want you for this just because I know how passionate you are about corruption," she said softly. "I also want you because I know you'll do the right thing by me." The return gaze she met was intent enough to force her to avert her eyes. "You know I wouldn't ask you to do anything that might compromise your integrity, Matthew."

"Good. I'm happy to hear it."

"I wish everyone on the Job had your zeal."

"Most do, going in. It's the reality of the work, makes it so hard to sustain."

"Which makes you all that much more remarkable, considering what you've been through."

Seven years ago, at three o'clock on the afternoon after the framed photograph atop his piano was taken, the operations sergeant working the desk at Brooklyn North Detective Headquarters had telephoned Matt at home. Two detectives in the Seven-one squad had just been shot and killed. He was given a "forthwith" to the crime scene. After collecting his gun and gear, Stuart had rushed to his car, his son trailing him into the drive. Once he kissed David a hasty good-bye, he'd slipped the transmission into reverse while checking behind him for traffic. Only he hadn't moved the shift lever to where he thought he had, and when he hit the gas, the car had shot forward, crushing his son between its front bumper and the garage door. The sound of that one awful crunch was the thing of recurring nightmares. That, and his wife's anguished, hysterical shrieking.

He waved Suzanne's reference to his troubles away, suddenly impatient to get more details of the scheme she was proposing. "Tell me how you see this drama being played out," he prodded.

"Joe McMahon, the Three-seven's current whip, will be promoted to captain this Friday. You'll be promoted to detective commander and transferred in as the new whip, effective 0100 Friday."

Though he didn't say so, it sounded to Stuart as though she'd been planning this move since before the Rodriguez hit. She had too many ducks already in a row to have cooked it up on such short notice. Still wary, he turned to the actual specifics of the assignment. "Who's the Three-seven's second whip?"

" 'Martini Al' Goldstein. I believe you two have a history."

He conjured a mental picture of the squat, balding Goldstein with those tufts of black hair protruding from his ears and the ever-present cigar. "We go way back, Al and me," he agreed. "There's another small problem comes with moving me uptown, Suzanne. I'm working a couple undercovers on real short leashes. I'm the one put them under, and I'd like to keep running them. Anyone else tries to take them over, I foresee problems."

The look she gave him was calculating now. "I hope none of these people were inserted, ah . . . inappropriately."

"Of course not."

The first deputy uncrossed her legs and stood. She moved to the window and stared uptown across the city's jagged skyline, lost in thought. "You'll have enough on your plate, Matt. Get someone you trust to run them. You and Chief Ogilvy work it out."

Simon Ogilvy was CO of Intelligence Division and someone with whom Stuart had an excellent working relationship. Suzanne would know this. "Whatever you say, Your Worshipness," he replied.

She spun from the window to face him. "Don't fuck with me, *Lieutenant*. I'll have your balls for breakfast."

"Just like old times?"

They laughed.

"I guess I haven't totally lost my sense of humor," she said, a hint of relief in it. Returning to the sofa, she sat again. "I've already leaked word of your transfer to the grapevine. By tonight, the whole Job will know you're on your way uptown."

He planted his hands on his knees and heaved himself to his feet, thoughtful again as his mind wandered, mental pictures of Washington Heights streets and the citizens who peopled them vivid in his imagination now. "Sounds like you've thought of everything." When he turned back to her, he watched that beautiful face closely. "Anything about this caper you haven't told me, Suzanne? You know how I hate surprises."

She seemed to stiffen, ever so slightly. "You, of all people, should know I could never be anything but up-front with you, Matthew."

"I get in a jam up there, I don't want to be left swinging by my short hairs."

"You won't be. I promise you that."

He wanted to believe her. Hell, he *needed* to believe her. Still, that prickle of unease was still there; his cop guardian angel blowing on the back of his neck, warning him to keep a tight asshole. He studied her face for another long moment, and nodded before starting for the door. "Guess I'll be seeing you around."

Four

Later that morning, after wasting fifteen minutes searching for a parking place, Stuart spotted a green Ford Fairmont two blocks ahead, battering its way out of a tight spot in front of Cadman Plaza. He switched on the siren, slapped the dome light onto the roof, and wove quickly through traffic, timing his arrival just as the Ford surged clear. Matt jockeyed his department Buick into the vacated space, killed the engine, and tossed the vehicle identification plate onto the dash. When the hostile glare of a motorist he'd beaten to the punch greeted him as he emerged onto the sidewalk, he spread his hands in a what-can-you-do gesture.

A light spring breeze tugged at his tie, but Stuart was all but oblivious to the glorious May day, and the brilliant green of new leaves now starting to cloak long-barren trees. During the drive here from headquarters, he'd continued to turn his meeting with Suzanne Albrecht over in his mind, examining it from as many sides as he could see. He'd always known that their paths would sooner or later cross again. It was the nature of working as a boss in the Job. He'd wondered how he would handle that first "Hello, how've you been?" but had never suspected he might wind up working for her. Each time he heard himself ask why she'd picked him to investigate the Rodriguez hit, he also heard her answer. "Because there is no one else on the Job I can trust." His cop guardian angel was arguing the case for extreme caution, warning that

Matt had heard just part of the truth. As much as half? he wondered. How could he know? What she might have more truthfully said was that he was the only one on the Job she could trust to protect her political ass. He knew as well as she that if Rodriguez turned out to be part of some bigger dirty picture, she would be painted with the same broad brush. Johnny Rodriguez was one of hers, and other bosses up and down the chain of command, all equally ambitious, would use that fact to crucify her. She could kiss her precious PC's job good-bye.

There was another thing Stuart had to admit, at least to himself. Suzanne Albrecht was carrying a few of his markers around in her pocketbook. Their affair had come at a time in his life when he'd desperately needed TLC. She'd given him as much of that rare commodity as she was capable of giving anyone, and he knew it. For that alone, he owed her. And then there was that Friday night, three years ago. They'd just made love and were relaxing in the warm, cozy aftermath of it when she'd shifted onto one elbow and asked if he was happy being whip of the Seven-one detective squad. He admitted he was tired of all the paper, and the endless cover-your-ass statistics crunching. Most of all, he hated the monthly Compstat meetings at the Big Building, where resident desk warriors got off on playing God. "There are months I have to spend more time doing paper and going to those bullshit conferences than I do supervising investigations," he'd complained.

She'd run the slow, hot tip of her tongue lazily across his earlobe and asked, "If you had your druthers, where would you *like* to work?"

He hadn't had to think long and hard about it. "Someplace where it's the good guys against the bad guys." The following Monday, he was transferred into Intelligence Division. Today, he confronted the notion of payback. And just as he'd always feared, it was going to be a righteous pain in the ass.

While covering the four short blocks to his office, Stuart passed bustling streets named Pineapple and Orange; arteries crowded with upscale coffeehouses, chess parlors, and restaurants. He reflected on how a wave of disgruntled, rent-poor Manhattanites had poured into blighted Brooklyn Heights in the sixties and transformed it into a trendy, gentrified part of the city where rents were now equal to those its occupants had rushed to escape.

He strolled past a crowded outdoor café with a long orange sidewalk awning and saw a young woman reach across her table to caress her dining partner's face. Matt felt a sudden stab of jealousy.

Poplar Street was a one-block thoroughfare running east–west between Hicks and Henry Streets, lined on one side by nineteenth-century warehouses and a stretch of near-identical brownstones on the other. On the south side of the street, mid-block, Intelligence Division occupied one of those old warehouses as its headquarters. Stuart liked the way massive green lanterns bracketed the ornate entrance and its heavy double doors.

He stepped into the vestibule to glance up at the security camera, keeping his stare impassive. The door buzzed and he pushed through to be met by a uniformed cop with sagging bags beneath bloodshot eyes.

"Howzit, Lou," the cop greeted Matt as he advanced to sign the command log. Even if he was trying, the uniform couldn't prevent his face from clouding with the old "leper's stare"—a tight-eyed, deadpan expression reserved for other cops being shipped out to busy, less-than-desirable assignments. It said, "Better you than me, pal, and please, don't get too close, it might be contagious. You might somehow drag my ass out into the cold, along with yours."

"Just wonderful," Stuart replied. He signed himself present for duty at 1040 hours, thinking that when the Ice Maiden got it in her mind to shake the grapevine, she didn't waste any time grabbing hold of it.

"When you get a chance, Lou, the chief left word he'd like to see ya."

Stuart thanked him and took the stairs to his third-floor cubbyhole office two at a time. Three detectives stood talking in the narrow stretch of well-lit corridor, and Matt hurried past the glass-fronted offices on both sides. They tossed him the "leper's stare" and broke it up to wander off toward their own cubicles without further conversation.

"Assholes," he grumbled.

Two green file cabinets with black combination locks in their drawer faces stood to the right of his doorway. His desk was typical quartermaster issue—green, metal, battered, the surface inlaid with a stained gray plastic laminate.

Once he squeezed around his desk and sat, Stuart switched on his computer. He grabbed the phone as the machine's hard drive whirred and clicked through its routine warm-up and a warbling tone told him he had voice mail. He punched in the retrieve code. A familiar voice came on the line. "Raymond. It's a beautiful day." Translation: his undercover would meet him today at the agreed-upon time and place. He hung up and turned to the computer keyboard.

A coded identification number cleared Stuart to use the Intelligence Division data banks. His own code had a double-X prefix that granted him entry to all but three of Intel's data banks. Once he'd gained access, he pulled up Intel's profile of the Thirty-seventh Precinct and watched as the split screen displayed a boundary map of the patrol precincts that made up Patrol Borough Manhattan North. It also listed the name and pedigree of the Dominican drug lord who controlled sales within the Three-seven: Francisco Xavier Santos, alias "Tío Paco."

When the phone rang, he snapped it up. "Stuart." A smile blossomed when Matt heard "Martini Al" Goldstein's gruff reply.

"What's dis I hear, you're getting the money and taking over the shop, heah?"

Stuart eased back to prop his feet up on his desk. "You heard right, buddy."

"Tell 'em to keep their fucking money. It ain't worth it."

"A good marine goes where he's sent. You know that, Al. So tell me. How've you been?"

"Pretty good, considering this shithole I work in. Squad keeps me on my toes."

"How many cases you catch a year?"

"It's only five months in, and already we got twenty-eight hunnerd. Not much choice but to shitcan mosta them, and give the homicides and rapes our best shot."

"Homicides mostly drug-related?"

"Ninety-nine percent of 'em."

Stuart's voice lost its casual tone. "Looks like I'm inheriting the Rodriguez case."

"How about we meet for a taste later?"

Matt could hear urgency behind the casual invitation. "Sure. Where and when?"

"Seven? At the birdbath place on the West Side?"

"Sounds good. I'll see you there."

"Oh, and while I got you. We're throwing a promotion racket for Joe McMahon. Next Wednesday at the Amber Light. A yard a pop. Count you in?"

"You bet. See you later, Al."

Stuart returned to his monitor screen, where the boundary map of the Three-seven made it easy for him to see why the precinct's location had resulted in more cocaine and heroin moving through its streets than any other precinct in the city. It was flanked on the west by the Harlem River Drive, a main artery connecting the Bronx and upper Manhattan to New Jersey via the George Washington Bridge. To the east, the Henry Hudson Parkway ran north-south through the precinct, a funnel down from the moneyed suburban communities of Westchester County and Connecticut. Just across the Harlem River on the Bronx side, the Major Deegan Expressway ran north to connect with the Thruway and all of upstate. It was a drug wholesaler's dream: access from every point of the compass.

Stuart was still in his office digesting intelligence reports on Francisco Xavier Santos when a detective poked his head in. "You're summoned to the throne room, Lou."

Minutes later, Matt found Deputy Chief Simon Ogilvy, commanding officer of Intel, relaxing on the brown settee in his office, casually screening a series of surveillance videos displayed on an array of six monitors. He used the remote control in his hand to surf from one screen to the next, and gestured to Stuart to have a seat alongside him. As Matt lowered himself onto a cushion, he glanced over at the screens to see Suzanne pushing her way through a crowded restaurant. Simon depressed a button to shut the monitors down, one after the other, then twisted in his seat to regard his lieutenant. "A favorite trough of wiseguys and movie people was torched last night. You hear?"

"Caro's?" Matt kept his face straight, betraying no interest in what he'd just seen on that one screen.

"You got it. Hear anything on it?" Caro's was an Italian eatery on Pleasant Avenue, way up in East Harlem. It had a vaulted brick ceiling, blue-and-white-checkered tablecloths, no menus, and outrageous prices. Twelve of its fifteen tables were owned by wiseguys and Wall Street titans. To eat there on any given night, you had to "borrow" a table from an owner. Celebrities liked to go there, to ogle connected guys. Or *had*, by the sound of things.

"I hadn't heard a thing," Stuart replied. "But I'm meeting Raymond later. If it wasn't an accidental grease fire in the kitchen, he might know what went down."

As Ogilvy crossed his long legs, he took care not to sit on the hem of his Pierre Cardin suit jacket. "I'm sorry to be losing you, Matt."

"I'm sorry to be going, boss. But that's the Job. As soon as you think you're settled, they ship your ass somewhere else."

Ogilvy was reading Stuart's face, gauging. "I hear you're getting 'the money.' "

"Looks that way."

"Next month, I'll have forty years on the Job, and I'm still amazed at how many things that happen within the ranks depend on a roll of the dice."

Stuart knew better than to take that bait, but was still curious where Ogilvy might be headed. "How so, Chief?"

A smug smile stretched the CO's lips into a thin line. "A married cop is whacked, along with his girlfriend. The squad whip who caught the case is promoted to captain. You're given 'the money,' which, by the way, I didn't put you in for. Then you're shanghaied uptown to fill McMahon's slot. All in a day. It's almost like there's a puppetmaster somewhere in the Big Building, pullin' all our chains."

"C'mon, Chief. That's not the way the Job works."

"Yeah, you're prob'ly right. My wife is always complaining I'm too cynical."

To ask his next question, Stuart pitched his voice a bit lower. "What about Raymond, boss?"

The Intel chief's face muscles tightened. "We'll need to find him another control."

"He's not likely to sit still for that. Raymond knows he can trust me, and his ass is hanging way out in a very cold breeze." Stuart stared hard at his chief as he said this. "I could continue to run him."

"Might prove a little difficult, with you working all the way uptown."

"Not as difficult, or as dangerous, as letting someone else know of his existence. Not to mention the fact that the Intelligence Oversight Committee was never asked for the okay to insert him."

Ogilvy eased both liver-spotted hands along the sides of his head, patting his hair to make sure it was perfect. "It's too bad those ACLU pukes were able to ram that goddamn committee down our throats. Civilians telling cops how we can conduct our business." He spat that last part out, making a face like it had left a disgusting taste in his mouth.

Stuart refused to be diverted. He continued to press Ogilvy as hard as he dared. "Either way, we inserted an undercover into a noncriminal enterprise without IOC approval. That's a castrating offense."

"*We* inserted?"

"I inserted," Stuart quickly corrected.

"You know the PC is on his way out?"

"That's the rumor of the day," Matt replied.

"You also hear the Ice Maiden's gotten buddy-buddy with Hizzonner, and is the current front-runner to fill the vacancy?" Ogilvy flashed a cagey smile. "She was the hook got you into Intelligence, wasn't she?"

"You know I got here on merit."

This evoked a grunt. "Just like the rest of us. Glad to hear it." As he spoke, the chief brandished one spit-shined shoe, attempting to catch his reflection in the gleaming Italian leather. "She's a strange bird, that one. No private life to speak of. The Job seems to be the only thing she gets off on. Prob'ly be one of the great police commissioners, she actually lands the job."

Stuart feigned indifference. So far as he was concerned, Bill Bratton was a great commissioner, and look how long he'd lasted. "PCs come and go, boss. The Job itself remains the same."

"You know her on the outside, don't you?"

Stuart had to struggle to keep his attitude casual. "Nope. What gave you that idea?" Did Ogilvy really know something, or was he just taking potshots in the dark?

"Dunno," the chief said, shrugging. "Just had it in my head somehow that maybe you did. It'll be interesting to watch her make her moves. Especially since she collects almost as much intelligence as I do. You aware that the CO Intel used to run the field associates?"

"Yeah, I am."

"Did you also know that she's the one responsible for shifting that responsibility to the first deputy commissioner's office? Three weeks *before* she was appointed."

"How'd she manage that?"

"By doing her homework, and making sure every weapon she's got in her arsenal is loaded for bear. Suzanne Albrecht knows where a lot of the old memo books are buried, and that fact scares the shit outta some people in this Job."

Still extremely uncomfortable with the turn their conversation had taken, Stuart tried to steer it away from his former lover and onto safer ground. "So what about Raymond, boss?"

Ogilvy waved a dismissive hand at the question. "When you see him later, find out what he knows about events at Caro's last night. If there's something heating up we don't know about, we need to get on top of it, posthaste." He seemed to be acknowledging that Raymond was still Matt's man, without saying it in so many words. "So how you feel about working with 'Martini Al' again, Matthew? How long's it been?"

"August, nine years ago. And I feel fine. It's the one aspect of this assignment I'm actually looking forward to."

Ogilvy fumbled distractedly with his remote control, and one of the monitors came alive again, revealing the bustling interior of Caro's. "Canal Street, wasn't it? Where the shoot-out went down?"

"That's right. Good memory." Stuart flashed back to that stinking-hot summer day when he and Al Goldstein were both assigned to the Major Case Squad. The sidewalks near Canal's intersection with Mott Street, at the north end of Chinatown, were jammed with pushcart vendors hawking everything from fresh produce to fake Rolexes and Fendi, Chanel, and Hermès knockoffs. Ice-packed bins outside storefronts overflowed with fish, and everywhere tourists loitered to gawk at curiosities. The detectives had an arrest warrant for one Ching Li, a shooter for the Golden Dragon gang. They were tailing him through those teeming streets, waiting for an opening to develop. As the slightly built shooter hurried ahead through the crowd, Stuart momentarily lost sight of him. Frustrated, he'd pressed ahead, searching shop interiors as he went. Al Goldstein's "Watch Out!" caught him flat-footed just as Li stepped out from a stall, a 9 mm semiautomatic in one hand. Goldstein had leapt in front of his partner just as the gang shooter let loose with two. Both caught Al in the right shoulder as Stuart dropped into a combat crouch to return fire. His first shot caught Ching Li mid-face and exited the back of his skull. The explosion sent jet hair, skin, bone, and brain matter spewing all over crates of snow peas, bamboo shoots, beetroot, and ginger. Matt shivered now as he vividly recalled that chain of events. Al Goldstein was six weeks at home convalescing before his return to limited duty. He'd most certainly saved Matt's life.

"So. What about Raymond, boss? He took this assignment, I gave him my word. I'm behind him for the long haul. Someone else screws up and gets him compromised, he gets a bullet behind the ear, sure as I'm sitting here."

Ogilvy used the remote to change his view of the restaurant interior, focusing on a familiar Hollywood starlet. The neckline of her red dress plunged almost to her navel. "I'm sure you'll work it out. Just keep me posted."

Matt started to rise. "Fine. I'd better go clean out my desk."

Stuart stood on the corner of Forty-second Street and the Avenue of the Americas that Thursday afternoon, watching the lunch-hour pedestrian parade. Despite the beauty of the perfect spring day, few of the people crowding the sidewalks seemed to be paying much attention to an unusual freshness in the air and the warm, gentle sun. As always, they avoided eye contact and moved purposefully, each intent on his or her own business, insulating themselves with that essential personal space that enabled them to function as New Yorkers. One exception was a tall, lanky black bicycle messenger. He'd leaned his bike against the stone wall of Bryant Park and was lounging alongside it, muscular legs spread before him and head tilted back to bask in the sun. It struck Matt that he'd rarely seen one of these messengers, so vital to the functioning of business in the city despite the electronic age and information superhighway, actually stop and rest. Like the city itself, they seemed to be in constant motion. In New York, time was money, for Wall Street bond traders, corporate CEOs, and bike messengers alike. After ten minutes spent contemplating this slice of everyday Manhattan life, Stuart started east across the avenue to the opposite sidewalk and started up the steps into the peaceful oasis of green that was Bryant Park.

In a space dominated by the back end of New York's main Public Library, the lunchtime crowd was starting to bag up their garbage and think about heading back to the office. A Hindu woman with a bright red caste mark, dressed in a maroon sari, was lecturing to a walking-tour group beneath the shade of a London plane tree. She explained that the tract of land now shared by the park and the library was originally set aside by the city in 1823 as a potter's field. Later, in 1842, the Croton Reservoir, with levees fifty feet high and twenty-five feet thick, was constructed on a four-acre parcel on the Fifth Avenue side of the library.

Most of the park's lightweight green chairs and benches were still occupied by loitering lunchers and sunbathers as Stuart walked past, headed for the outdoor terrace bar at the east end of the park. A flock of cooing pigeons pecked at the stretch of lawn to his right, and Matt caught a blur from the corner of his eye. He turned, startled, to see a peregrine falcon swoop to snag a bird in its deadly talons. As the sleek bird of prey started skyward again on powerful wings, headed toward its nest atop a towering Forty-second Street office building, Matt was reminded again of how fleeting life could be. And that nothing was safe in this town.

The bar of the Bryant Park café was packed with customers drinking beer and cocktails from plastic cups. They were six deep out front of the main stretch of mahogany, forcing Stuart to sidestep his way around to reach a barmaid. When he caught her attention, he ordered a draft and watched her deftly fill the plastic schooner.

"Five dollars." She said it curtly, forcing herself to punctuate it with a smile.

Matt reached an arm over the shoulder of another customer to place six singles in her waiting palm, collected his drink, and sipped while stepping across to the stone balustrade with its vase-shaped spindles. So far, he'd seen no sign of Raymond. As he looked out over the park's central lawn, his thoughts drifted back to that morning eleven months ago when Simon Ogilvy had summoned him to his office. The chief had hefted a bulging folder at Matt and said, "This damned thing's been knocking around the shop for years. I want you to take a look at it, see whether or not you think this guy is dirty. If you think he's clean, close the damned thing out. If not, come up with some kind of sting we can use to put his ass behind the wall."

The file was on Angelo "Cheesecake" Albeneti, a man who was, according to the findings of an exhaustive NYPD investigation, as honest as a cold shower. At sixty years of age, he'd never been arrested, never been issued a traffic summons, associated only peripherally with known criminals the way every guy who'd grown up on the streets of New York did, and was the founder of Mom's Pie Company, with eight retail outlets spread around the five boroughs. The nettlesome thing about Cheesecake was that his name occasionally cropped up on wiretaps, and during informer-debriefing sessions. According to these sources, Angelo "Cheesecake" was a made guy, and one of New York organized crime's major players. Born in Sicily, he'd immigrated to the United States with his parents when he was eight years old. He left school at fifteen to take a job as an apprentice at Dominic's Bakery on Mulberry Street in Manhattan's Little Italy. When he was twenty he opened his own bakery on Pleasant Avenue in East Harlem. At twenty-two he married Rose Marie

Sabatino. They had one child who was killed by a drunk driver in 1981, and were divorced in 1986.

Stuart had spent the rest of that week absorbing every detail of the "Cheesecake File." Late Friday afternoon, he'd picked up the phone and asked to see his boss. Once seated in Ogilvy's office, he'd slipped the file onto his desk and made sure he had the chief's undivided attention.

"Too many sources, over too many years, all say this guy is a bad apple. I'm recommending we take a closer look at him. A *lot* closer."

Ogilvy grimaced. "We've already pissed away an awful lot of the taxpayers' money trying to do just that, Matthew. I'm gonna authorize more, your idea better be fresh, and better be good."

Stuart eased back in his chair, confident that he'd thoroughly thought this through. "We can't hang a wire on him because we don't have 'reasonable cause.' No judge would ever sign the order. We've tried surveillance teams and they haven't worked. They're man-hour costly, too. I think we need to attack this guy where he's vulnerable. Through his dogs."

The Intel CO stared at him like he'd developed a hole mid-forehead. "Come again?"

"He's got this pair of Shih Tzus he dotes on. Rocky and Magee. And I mean *dotes*."

Ogilvy closed his eyes. "I'm listening."

"He had this girlfriend for close to ten years after his divorce. A few years back, she gets fed up with his mutts and gives him an ultimatum. Either they go, or she does. He threw her out."

The chief's eyes were open again. "Still listening."

"She was so pissed, she threatened to have the dogs killed. Word on the street was that she even paid some junkie to do it. Someone tipped Cheesecake and the junkie disappeared. Later that same week, *she* disappeared. By all appearances he's a very busy man, but twice a day he takes time to walk them. Only person he'll trust them with is a woman who runs a grooming parlor down the street."

Matt leaned forward in his chair now, warmed to his narrative and getting more animated. "I say we send an undercover to his main shop on Pleasant Avenue looking for a job. A cop who knows dogs and can pass for something like a former vet's assistant or groomer. We have him read up on Shih Tzus so he can wow Angelo with all he knows and how crazy he is about the breed."

When Stuart was finished, Ogilvy sat a moment frowning at the ceiling. "It's kinda wacky, but it might just be wacky enough to work."

"Technically, we plant an undercover into a legit business, we need IOC approval," Matt cautioned.

Ogilvy had reached out to retrieve something from his blotter and started to read it. "I'm sure you can work out that minor detail," he said distractedly.

Still leaning on the balustrade of the terrace bar, Stuart finished his beer and pushed off to toss the empty cup into a trash can. When he looked over to survey the walkways of the park again, he spotted Raymond down by the chess tables, leading two Shih Tzus on blue leashes.

The undercover cop was tall and lean, his handsome face raw-boned, and his black hair slicked back off his forehead. As he strolled at a sedate, casual pace, his dark, intelligent eyes drifted around the park searching out other eyes that might refuse to meet his. He wore a black silk shirt open at the collar to expose a set of heavy gold chains.

Watching his cocky undercover man lead the two black and white, short-legged dogs with those mushed faces and bulging black eyes brought a smile to Stuart's face. A light went on in Raymond's eyes when he saw his control, but he kept his distance. Carefully, Stuart sidled down off the terrace to approach in a roundabout fashion. Neither spoke until they were shoulder to shoulder, both pretending to watch a sunbather.

"Magee, Rocky, say hello to your old Uncle Lou," Raymond told the dogs.

Stuart squatted to let them nuzzle his hand, tails wagging and bodies wriggling all over. "Watch that old shit," he said.

Raymond chuckled. "Bet I'm the only undercover in the Job works as a baby-sitter slash bodyguard for a couple of dogs. Gives whole new meaning to meaningful pursuits."

"You cool with the route you took to get here?" Matt asked, straightening.

"Not to worry, Lou. Three different cabs, East Side to West Side and back again, then here."

Stuart nodded. "What sort of luck you having?" he asked.

Raymond started to stroll, dogs out front and Stuart alongside him. "Our pal Cheesecake didn't skate all these years because he's careless. Much less stupid. He don't take chances, I'll tell you that much."

"He hired you."

A shrug. "Only because I managed to dazzle him. Did you know a Shih Tzu's hearing's so sharp that Chinese emperors used 'em to guard their concubines?"

Matt shook his head. "Afraid I didn't."

Raymond smiled. "Neither did Cheesecake. Ate all that Shih Tzu lore shit up."

"You managed to get any closer than the last time we talked?"

"Maybe. He's started to let me work the counter a little, just to relieve the boredom, y'know? Couple things I've seen there got me thinking. Like, if he's connected, how does he keep in touch with his crew? He's always in the store, hardly ever talks on the phone, and when he does, it's all bakery shit." When Magee took an interest in a greasy, crumpled piece of deli paper, Raymond jerked her leash to yank her away. "He don't gamble, he sure ain't no party animal, and he certainly ain't no clotheshorse. The dames from the neighborhood clothesline brigade who work in the shop say he's got a new girlfriend, but I ain't never seen her. One thing has occurred to me, though."

"Feed me," Stuart prodded him.

"I'm wondering if maybe he keeps in touch with his crew by putting messages in cake boxes."

"What would make you suspect that?"

"The cakes that regular customers pick up? They're stacked on aluminum trays just behind the front counter. The flaps are left open so they can look at 'em, you know? Make sure Happy Birthday and shit are spelled right. But boxes scheduled for delivery to the other stores are stacked in a different spot, near the loading dock at the back of the shop. All of them are taped shut."

"Ye-e-a-ah?" Stuart had a picture of the setup in his mind.

"Well last week, Cheesecake comes out of the back while I'm working up front. He hangs around; keeps checking the street like he's expecting someone. Next thing I know, Tony Nails shows, and you know what they do?"

"I know you'll tell me."

"They walk outside to stand right in the middle of Pleasant Avenue, plant hands to hide their lips, and start bullshitting, traffic detouring around them."

Tony "Nails" Fortunado was a name familiar to Stuart. A suspected soldier in the Albanese crime family, he'd been the target of an Organized Crime Control Bureau investigation a few years back, though he, like Angelo Albeneti, had never been arrested. "Sounds like a classic evasion technique. Wonder what it was about?" Matt mused. With the current technology available to surveillance teams, wiseguys often went to elaborate lengths to avoid having conversations picked up via laser or parabolic microphones. "Suspicious as hell, though, isn't it?"

"I'd say," Raymond agreed. "OCCB don't know for sure Tony Nails is an actual made guy, but evidence they've gathered suggests he's a pretty big earner. As an all-around gopher, y'know?"

"What happened after that?" Stuart asked.

"The thing that got me to thinking. Tony stays out on the sidewalk while Cheesecake comes back inside. Rather than pick up one of the cakes behind the counter, or even a fresh-baked one just then being put inta boxes, he goes over to the stack by the loading dock and pulls one buried three from the top. It's *that* one he takes outside and hands to Tony Nails."

This was interesting, indeed. "You ever try to sneak a peak inside one of those boxes?"

"Wouldn't be a smart move, Lou. Old Angelo's got eyes in the back of his fucking head. What I'm trying to work out now is how his people get back to him."

Stuart and his undercover paused simultaneously to admire the figure cut by a particularly attractive young redhead in a cream-colored business suit. She noticed their attention and surged ahead with a scowl of irritation. "Just continue to keep your eyes open," Matt told Raymond. "This is real progress."

"Why do they do that?" Raymond asked. "Turn themselves out looking like a million bucks and small change, then act pissed when a dude throws an appreciative look their way?"

Stuart smiled. "One of life's sweet mysteries. By the way, the chief wants to know if you've heard any scuttlebutt on what went down at Caro's last night."

"Just what's all up and down Pleasant Avenue: that a couple nights ago Frankie 'the Nose' shows up with his new girlfriend and Jimmy Caro is so blinded by Hollywood glitz, the dumb fuck tells Frankie there ain't no table for them. The Nose storms out, comes back last night with some guys from his crew, and they toss a couple Molotovs through the plate glass."

"That oughta teach Junior not to forget his roots, huh? The boss would also like you to keep an ear out for who might have been on the guest list last night."

Raymond hauled in the leashes to pull his charges toward him, and squatted to scratch them between the ears. "I'll see what I can do."

Stuart moved to a nearby bench and sat. "I've got something else we need to discuss," he began, and went on to tell Raymond about his transfer.

When he finished, his undercover's eyes were focused on some unseen distant object. "You know what the ACLU scumbags call an undercover who works a legitimate business without IOC approval?"

"An infiltrator."

"That's their word for a cop who's violating some innocent citizen's civil rights." Raymond leveled his stare at Stuart now. "I went through all that shit once before, Lou. They put me inside a labor union without the IOC okay. Couple months later, my control throws in his papers, and I draw a new one. Things start to get a little hairy, and all of a sudden this asshole don't know shit about me not having the oversight committee's blessing. Shit hits the fan, mosta it lands on me."

Stuart held the other man's gaze. "What are you saying?" he asked.

"I'm telling you I ain't gonna trust my ass to anyone but you, Lou. If you go, I'm outta the dog-walking business."

"I'm going to hang with you," Matt assured him. "Only now, you'll have to contact me at the Three-seven. I'll leave my new confidential number on your voice mail."

"Ogilvy give his blessing on this?"

"He said he was sure I'd be able to work out the problem."

"Which means, do what you gotta do, but don't get me involved." Raymond shook his head in disgust. "That ain't scrambled eggs on his hat brim, it's chickenshit." He rose from his squat to stretch a kink from one leg. "You know who Sal Sapienze is?"

Stuart frowned. "Yeah. You."

"That's right. And I'm tired of being Frankie, Joey, and Louie. I'm doing this shit too long, Lou. Look." He held out a hand and showed Stuart how it trembled ever so slightly. "My nerves is all but shot. I wanna be able to use my own name, work a squad, chase inta this crowd after that redhead with the fabulous ass, take a shot at convincing her I ain't the same as all these other horny fucks."

"You finish this job for me, Sal, you can pick your squad or put in for one hundred percent disability if you want. I'll call in every marker I've gotta call."

"What's so important about this one, Lou? You mow one down, three grow back in his place."

"This Job's taken more from me than you know, Sal. I need to keep believing it isn't all a waste."

Raymond looked at him in a way he'd never looked at him before, nodded, and stooped to lift the two Shih Tzus into his arms. "Magee. Rocky. Kiss your Uncle Lou bye-bye."

Five

Police Officer Clarence DaCosta, Special Operations Division's Street Crime Unit liaison to Manhattan North, lay on his back in the sleeping loft of his Hudson Street apartment in Greenwich Village. He'd been halfheartedly daydreaming about screwing Gina Galati, but was too preoccupied to find the focus necessary to fuel a decent masturbation fantasy. The apartment was located in a gentrified former tenement building a block north of the western reaches of SoHo on Hudson Street, just off the corner of Clarkson. Rented as a one-bedroom, with a tiny airless sleeping chamber little bigger than a walk-in closet, it featured an open, fairly large living room/kitchen combination with twelve-foot ceilings. The height gave the place an exaggerated feeling of spaciousness, and DaCosta had taken advantage of that fact, installing a sleeping loft at one end, above his big-screen TV and home entertainment center. He liked the feeling he got, sprawled naked on his mattress, Sinatra or Connie Francis playing loud on the stereo system just beneath him, the rest of his crib wide open, floor to ceiling, below. It made him feel free of the outside world, secure in his own secret thoughts.

The display on the clock radio alongside the bed read THURSDAY 1:18 PM. He was scheduled to work a four-to-midnight today, but had an appointment to keep first and would need to get moving soon. Eyes closed, he stared into the mirrors of his mind, wandering again through every memory he could recall of his long-dead mother. His mother's beautiful, golden-tanned face, tawny hair, and long, graceful neck were vivid enough to still seem alive. Any recollection of her radiant smile brought a smile to his lips. As a boy he was forever falling and scraping his knees. He'd run home crying and his mother would clean and bandage his wounds, singing soothing songs from her childhood in northern Italy.

Sophia DaCosta had worked in Bellevue Hospital's pediatric intensive care unit. She met Sergeant Clarence Poole the night he appeared in the emergency room with an abandoned infant girl. Tall and ruggedly built, with a con man's soft brown eyes, he was also black, with a wife, two kids, and a row house in the gentrified Sugar Hill section of Harlem. Years later, DaCosta's mother told him she'd named him after his father because she'd loved the man and wanted Clarence to have his name. She also wanted him to know his father had never lied to her about his other life. She'd known about that wife and kids from the very beginning, and had accepted it. She'd tried, and failed, to get her son to accept it, too.

His first memories of his father were of a huge black man who would visit them in their Chelsea apartment a few times a week, sweep him up into his powerful arms, and try to lay claim to him with jovial words and kisses. Clarence used to wriggle and kick, struggling to escape his father's embrace and all that it implied, resenting him for intruding between him and his mother. He was in kindergarten the first time a peer ever called him a nigger, and at the time he had no idea what it meant. Still, he could feel the strength of presumed superiority and the power of an eons-old anger that fueled it. But he wasn't black. He and his mother were Italians. Only the intruder was black; the one who had destroyed all links Sophia DaCosta once shared with her family and her people with the black baby he'd given her. From that day on, each time Clarence had assured his mother he understood and accepted their "situation," he'd told her a lie.

Clarence was ten years old the first time he saw the small gun on his father's hip. "I'm a policeman," his father had explained. In yet another attempt to build a bridge, he'd taken the gun out, unloaded it, and let his son hold the weapon. That experience, like the time he'd suffered his first racial insult, was seminal, but not in the way the hated Poole had hoped. Clarence felt the power his father drew from the badge and the gun, and how much he seemed to cherish it. He knew then he would one day be a policeman, too, but for entirely other reasons. He became obsessed with the NYPD and set out to learn everything he could about it. He would spend his school lunch hour in the library reading everything he could find on the police department, its organizational structure, the history of its politics, and its corruption scandals. After school he would read and clip articles about each of these subjects from newspapers and paste them onto the pages in his rapidly filling scrapbooks.

By the time he was twelve, Clarence could recite the Job's table of organization. The city's five boroughs were divided into seven borough commands, with Brooklyn and Manhattan—because of the volume of work—divided into Patrol Boroughs North and South. He knew the patrol divisions that made up each borough command, and could rattle off the precincts that formed each division. Throughout his teenage years he studied the Knapp Commission and how it had worked to root out the worst of the old police corruptions, all the while hunting for and identifying possible loopholes in new department procedures.

As the years drifted on, visits from Clarence's father became less and less frequent. Whenever he did appear, he seemed more aloof and in a hurry to get away. He and Sophia fought, and after one of those stormy visits, she locked herself in her bedroom for hours.

One July day in the summer of 1986, when Clarence was seventeen, he watched his mother trudge up the stairs to their third-floor walk-up and knew something was very wrong. She was pale and out of breath, all the robust energy that had made her seem so vibrant drained out of her. When he asked if she felt all right, she'd taken him into the front room, sat him down, and explained she'd been diagnosed with an inoperable brain tumor. The next day, she'd quit her job at the hospital.

While Clarence had no intention of contacting his father to tell him what was happening, Sophia feared he might and begged him not to.

"You're going to promise me right here and now that you will *never* contact your father," she insisted. "He has another life. We've always respected that."

"Fine," he'd replied.

And during his mother's terrible three-month fight for life, Clarence Poole never once paid her a visit. She died at 10:16 on the morning of Wednesday, October 12, 1986. Abandoned by her family for having a black man's bastard baby seventeen years earlier, Sophia DaCosta was buried in a simple grave by her half-black, half-Italian son.

Clarence had considered telephoning the roll-call person at the Two-oh, his father's then-current command, to leave a message that Sophia DaCosta had died, just to see what his reaction might be. After the funeral, he cut the obituary from the Bellevue employees' newsletter and mailed it to the precinct. He never heard from Poole, who had risen to the lofty rank of captain. Today, Clarence Poole was retired, divorced, and living with his second wife—a white woman—in Valley Stream, Long Island.

Stretching as he drifted up from his reverie, DaCosta glanced at the clock. It was time to get moving. He eased upright while avoiding banging his head against the ceiling, and headed for the steep wooden stairs.

After he showered and shaved, Clarence spent ten minutes tightening his dreadlocks and their decorative beads. Emerging from the bathroom, he stepped around a stack of yellowing scrapbooks to grab up a handful of darts. One by one, he pitched them at a super enlargement of the October 1982 cover of *SPRING 3100*, the Job's official magazine. The name was derived from the old telephone number citizens would call to report a police emergency before creation of the 911 network. This issue depicted a soot-smeared Lieutenant Clarence Poole, charging headlong like an NFL running back from a burning tenement, a bundled baby cradled tight to his massive chest. The surface of the glossy poster was shredded and defaced by thousands of strikes from wrathful, steel-tipped darts. The last one Clarence threw today embedded in the bridge of his father's nose, and he nodded with vengeful satisfaction.

"You uppity nigger fuck," he snarled, and hurried to finish dressing.

Gina Galati watched her baby boy Claude toddle after the blue beach ball. When he caught up with it, he slapped his hands over its sides and hefted it off the floor. Laughing, with drool running down his chin, he teetered toward his mother. His off-balance throw caused him to stumble backward and fall onto his diapered behind. There, he broke into gales of laughter as Gina scraped back in the kitchen chair and rushed to scoop him up in her arms. While he wriggled and giggled, she smothered his fat little belly with kisses.

Gina and Claude lived in a two-thousand-square-foot loft on the fifth floor of a Civil War-era factory building located on Brooklyn's John Street, a narrow block in a dreary warren of cobblestone streets and dark industrial buildings known as Dumbo, for Down Under the Manhattan

Bridge Overpass. The Brooklyn waterfront, once abandoned and left to ruin save for the Heights, had been colonized over the past fifteen years by artists forced to leave SoHo and Tribeca by high rents. Dumbo was now trendy, and landlords who once welcomed homesteading artists, grateful for their rent dollars, now had them under siege.

Gina's loft had fifteen-foot ceilings, faded brick walls, arched cast-iron-framed windows, and a virtual prairie of shiny wood flooring. The sleeping area, to the left of the open-grillwork freight elevator, had a king-size bed with a pink headboard. A tall chest of drawers with grooved wood knobs stood against the brick wall. Neighboring that space was a huge expanse of living room furnished with light-colored wood and burnt ocher leather couches and chairs.

As she deposited her son in his playpen, Gina saw it was almost two-thirty. "Time for Mommy to go to work," she said gently, and ran loving fingers through his sparse thatch of fine, corn-silk hair. Claude crawled quickly toward his fire engine and began blowing the Klaxon. Gina watched him as she undressed, tossed her clothes onto the floor, and started for the bath. The door left ajar, she started the water in the shower.

Ten minutes later, Gina emerged into the living room, toweling herself dry with an oversize bath sheet. At the cedar closet framed into one bedroom wall, she pondered what she should wear. Her best asset for the sort of work she did was her look of youthful innocence, and she settled on a loose, funky ensemble typical of what teenage kids were wearing right then. Oversize olive green fatigue pants with box sidepockets. Extra large black T-shirt bearing a logo of a dancing elephant, and over that a huge black and green plaid flannel shirt. Beneath it all she wore a black thong and no bra, just to remind herself she wasn't, in fact, a teenager out on yet another in an endless string of larks. Once her black hiking boots were tugged on and laced all the way up, she stepped back into the bath to dry her hair. As she studied herself in the bath cabinet mirror, she undertook a frank appraisal of her appearance. No way did she look twenty-four, she decided.

Once she changed Claude's diaper, Gina stuffed the squirming baby into blue bib overalls and a white cotton pullover. In the kitchen, she filled his diaper bag with the supplies he would need for the duration: diapers, juice, milk bottle, a change of clothes, snacks. On her way to the elevator, with the child hefted on one arm, she plucked her black vinyl tote off the back of a chair and inserted her control key to summon the freight car.

Naomi Ebbcomb was an attractive thirty-year-old painter with wealthy Lloyd Harbor parents and not much talent. She rented the second-floor loft in Gina's building, where her body of work—mostly large canvases splashed with bold geometric brushstrokes—stood propped against the walls. Naomi had the hots for Gina—unrequited though her passion was—and was more than happy to perform duties as her fantasy lover's unpaid baby-sitter. For Gina, the arrangement was perfect. Naomi was too shy to push her obsession, she never pried, didn't drink or do drugs, and genuinely loved little Claude. As soon as the mother and son arrived, the painter rushed over to smother the baby with cooed, unintelligible affections and kisses. As she collected him from Gina's arms, she purposely let the back of one hand drag across the nipple of Gina's left breast. For Gina, it seemed a small enough price. Paid baby-sitters in New York City cost an Arabian sheik's ransom.

To further stroke the hungry ego of her amorous friend, Gina nodded toward an easel set at one end of Naomi's well-ordered studio. "Show me what you're working on."

Too eager to please, the artist led the way. Along one wall of the studio ran a series of windows facing northwest and looking out on a breathtaking view of the Manhattan skyline. Unfortunately, the work in progress Gina encountered was nowhere near so inspired.

"The creation," Naomi offered proudly.

A gaseous orange fireball exploded in the center of the canvas, hurling out thunderbolts in bright, nonharmonious hues. Gina stared, trying to feign some measure of interest. "Ye—e-a-h. I can definitely see it. Very strong. Bold. And, I guess . . . disturbing, huh?" She turned to her neighbor. "You *do* mean it to be disturbing?"

Naomi nodded too eagerly. "That's right. So you *can* see it! I was so hoping you might!"

Gina glanced at her watch and made a face. "Damn. I'd like to hang a few minutes, but I'm already late." She brushed cheeks with her neighbor and gave Naomi's upper arm a gentle squeeze. "I fed him an hour ago, so don't let him lie to you. I should be back by dark. That okay?"

Naomi told her that of course it was as Gina kissed her son good-bye and hurried to the elevator. "Stay out longer if you need to. We'll be fine."

Gina hopped aboard the car, hauled the grillwork closed, and peered back through it. "I appreciate this, girlfriend. I really do." As the elevator motor kicked on and the car started its descent, Gina could swear she saw Naomi actually blush.

On John Street, Gina pressed west, her tote slung over one shoulder and tucked snugly beneath her elbow. She knew what a punctuality freak the cop was, and didn't want to be late. She turned left into Adams Street, a dank, urine-fouled stretch of uneven cobbles and potholes directly under the bridge's overpass. His beat-up blue Chevy Caprice gypsy cab stood idling at the curb.

Police Officer Clarence DaCosta sat behind the steering wheel and watched her through the rearview once she climbed into the cab. "Your stuff's on the floor," he announced.

From the floorboard, Gina retrieved a folded copy of yesterday's *New York Post* and removed the weapon concealed therein: a Star BKS 9 mm Luger with noise-suppressor screwed onto the barrel. She ejected the staggered-box magazine, examined the blue-tipped exploding rounds, and nodded with satisfaction. Once the magazine was slapped back into the receiver, she racked a round into the chamber, then dropped the gun into her tote. As she worked, she became aware, once again, of the familiar knot forming in the pit of her stomach. It was always present when she was with DaCosta, and she hadn't quite figured out the reason for it yet. No matter how physically attractive he was, it still bothered her, doing hits with anyone so clearly twisted. Was she frightened of him, or did she just want to fuck him? Probably a little bit of both, she decided, and pretended to look out the window while she studied his profile in her peripheral vision.

DaCosta had a smooth, cocoa-brown complexion, courtesy of his black, Harlem-born father and northern Italian mother. It made a dramatic backdrop for his pale blue eyes. Each cord of the interwoven, chestnut-colored hair that hung to his shoulders was adorned with a brightly colored bead. His tightly muscled arms and chest reminded her of those marble statues she'd seen of Greek javelin throwers, and she found herself wondering how strong and virile one other part of him might be.

DaCosta glanced back at his passenger. "That was a clean job last night."

"No problems on your end, then?"

"Zippo. No witnesses, no evidence, no nada."

"Tell me about today's."

He shrugged those strong, wide shoulders and she watched the muscles beneath his T-shirt dance. "A nothing job for someone like you. They'll be loose and happy, expecting I'm gonna spit up the people been giving up their stash houses." As he spoke, he headed them toward the bridge ramp that would take them across the East River and into Manhattan.

Gina felt nothing but scorn for every dope dealer in Upper Manhattan, and shook her head as she marveled at their gullibility. "Those morons ain't figured it out yet, have they?"

"Won't. Until it's too late," he said confidently. With the heel of his left hand planted atop the steering wheel, the renegade cop reached under the seat and pulled out a portable radio. Switched on, it filled the air with the drone of police calls.

"Why you always gotta listen to that shit?" she demanded.

"Hey. I'm a cop, right? Gotta know what's happening uptown on my beat. Us survivors are stone-cold allergic to surprises. Know what I mean?"

Late Thursday afternoon, Darryl Johnson lay sprawled atop the rumpled sheet of his bed with a glass of whisky balanced on his chest and an Uzi submachine gun at his side. "Some motherfucker out there be disrespecting me, man!" His rage thumped at his temples as he brushed an angry hand across tight cornrows of hair.

At twenty-three years of age, Johnson was boss of the Red Top crew, a gang of crack cocaine and heroin dealers who peddled their poison in glass vials with red plastic caps. They were responsible for twenty-seven drug-related homicides over the past thirteen months.

Three weeks ago, cops—from the Thirty-seventh Precinct, Darryl was convinced—had started raiding their stash houses, stealing their money and their dope. Johnson was also convinced that some about-to-be-dead motherfucker inside his own gang had unwittingly dealt crack to an undercover cop and was now selling out locations to keep his black ass out of jail. Right now, he was turning over a list of possible suspects' names when the electronic buzz of the cash counter broke his concentration. His main man, Fat Danny Washington, was running stacks of green through the box. When he was sixteen, Fat Danny's left cheek had been nearly sliced off by an angry girlfriend's straight razor, and surgeons at Columbia-Presbyterian had sewn the huge flap of skin back in place. The resultant handiwork looked like a shaggy patch of maroon skin glued to an acne-scarred moonscape, black as coal.

The stash house they currently occupied was located in a tenement owned by Tío Paco Santos on 155th Street, directly adjacent to Trinity Cemetery. It was a bare fourth-floor walk-up with a beat-up couch and an old bed with a chipped oak laminate headboard. Bags of cocaine and smack, stacks of money, and boxes of vials and stoppers littered the top of a long cafeteria table. Heavy drapes blanketed the windows, diffused sunlight leaking through at the seams. Darryl and Fat Danny were the same age; the only two "brothers" from their South Bronx childhood still surviving or not imprisoned. The majority had either been gunned down in the frenzied drug wars or had died of AIDS.

Fat Danny snapped a rubber band around a bundle of green and tossed it into a paper grocery bag. As his eyes fell on a blue porcelain bowl overflowing with cocaine, he grimaced and shrugged why not? Employing a carefully cultivated nail on the little finger of his left hand, he scooped a pile of the powder, lifted it to one nostril, and snorted hard. Then, wiping his nose with the back of his hand, he looked over at his friend. "Maybe it be those papaya-eatin' motherfuckers who be selling us out to the Five-O motherfuckers. Maybe they wanna move us off our territory."

"Ain't no Dominican wanna mess with Tío Paco, *or* with pitching shit onna street. They think that's nigger work, them being entrepreneur motherfuckers and all."

"So who else be knowing the locations, 'sides Nicky and Pigface?"

"That's just the problem," Darryl complained. "I gone over and over it in my head. Ain't nobody." He then turned his head slowly to regard his old friend as another possibility hit him. "You din't tell that bigmouth Airwick, did you?"

"C'mon, blood," Fat Danny protested. "Me? I wouldn't tell that limpdick motherfucker his own mama's name."

Darryl drained the whisky from the glass on his chest and rolled over to stand the empty on the floor. He swung his legs off the bed, stood, and crossed to the window to peek out past the curtain. On the street below, his pitchers were prancing along the curb out front of the cemetery wall, touting the joys of the Red Top product to any slowing motorist.

"You sure the half-breed motherfucker be knowing who's giving up our stash?" Fat Danny asked.

Darryl was partially preoccupied watching a patrol car cruise down the street. "Nigger's always been right in the past."

Fat Danny grunted. "Crazy motherfucker be thinking he's white, bro."

"He be a nigger just like us," Darryl assured him, then gestured to the bag his friend was stuffing with money. "Count it twice. Make *sure* there's twenty-five in there. Black or white, he ain't nobody we wanna get crossways with."

"I don't like making no fucking cop rich, bro."

"Price of doing business, m'man. Santos be out a quarter mil and the twenny keys them motherfuckers stole. We wanna stay on his good side, we ain't gonna gripe about no twenty-five large. It be cheap enough, we get the results DaCosta be promising."

"Some motherfucker gonna die in a lotta badass pain, bro," Fat Danny crooned as he recounted. He reached out to scoop another hit of nose candy and brushed his nose as the squeal of breaks coincided with his partner's sudden stiffening. "What that?"

Peering out past the curtains, Darryl watched his pitchers scatter in all directions as two more patrol cars arrived on the scene and uniforms emerged to give chase. "Sonofabitch!" he snarled. "Pig motherfuckers is rousting our people!"

Fat Danny tossed a last bundle of cash into the sack and hurried to join his buddy. "The Macho Man gets his honky ass ee-rased last night, and today his redneck pig pals are fucking with the whole street, bro." Several of their pitchers had managed to escape over the cemetery wall, but two more were now spread-eagled up against it, their captors reaching for handcuffs.

"It weren't us whacked his white ass," Darryl grumbled.

"The drums be saying it was other cops did him."

Johnson waved the notion away as crazy talk. "Cops don't kill other cops. Y'all know that."

"You sure, bro?"

There wasn't much Darryl could claim he *was* sure of right that minute. He shook his head. "No. Gotta say I ain't." He knew the realities of the drug business well enough at his relatively advanced age to know no one could be trusted. As he watched the police cars speed off with his shackled pitchers, he cursed again, then checked the time on his diamond-encrusted gold watch. With binoculars snatched from the windowsill and aimed into Trinity Cemetery, he followed a narrow gravel roadway as it wound through the green grass and tombstones. At the far end of it, near the cemetery's Broadway entrance, he spotted a blue gypsy cab idling in the shade of a huge old oak. Clarence DaCosta stood outside it, leaning against a front fender. "Looks like our friend be waiting on us, Danny."

"Ain't no friend of mine," Washington murmured. "He alone?"

"Course he be alone. That nigger don't like sharing his money."

The fat man grunted as he rose, lifted his Tech 9 machine pistol from the table, and stuffed it into his waistband and the roll of blubber beneath his sweatshirt. He grabbed the bag of money as Darryl plunged his arms into the sleeves of his Tuskeegee Airmen bomber jacket.

With towering columns of puffy white clouds gathering to enliven the sky over Washington Heights, the partners emerged into the late afternoon sunlight, cautiously checking the street for any sign of "the man." The absence of their pitchers stood as a powerful reminder that cops in the Three-seven were currently on the warpath, and the last thing they wanted to do right now was stand still for a frisk. They waited for a break in traffic, then bolted across 155th Street to the opposite sidewalk. There, they strolled east along the gray limestone cemetery wall toward the black wrought-iron entrance gates.

Trinity Cemetery stood atop a gentle, sloping bluff overlooking the Hudson River. The land had once been part of the farm of John James Audubon, the famous naturalist and artist. On Christmas Eve, carolers still visited the grave of Clement Clarke Moore, the author of "A Visit from St. Nicholas." And every day, as the sun sank toward the western horizon, the Gothic spire of the cemetery church cast a shadow that pointed like a finger across Broadway, to the east.

With eyes glued on the man they would meet, Darryl and Fat Danny feigned swaggering confidence as they moved along the winding footpath, headed toward him. There, among the more and less ostentatious stones set out to mark the final resting places of yesteryear's dead, a strange silence seemed to lock out the external world.

DaCosta watched those two clowns come ahead while the bitter exhaust fumes from his idling cab reminded him he was likely to exceed his monthly forty-gallon fuel allotment soon. He'd be forced to dig out one of his phony gas authorization cards, having no intention of paying for it out of his own pocket. On the other hand, he had no intention of switching the engine off and risking it not wanting to start again once this particular meet went down.

Gina Galati huddled just inside the entry alcove, outside the locked doors of the empty cemetery church. In her right hand, she clutched her only prop: a spray of tulips and daffodils. As she waited for the dopers to pass, a fantasy was blooming in her fertile imagination. She and Da-Costa were sitting in her living room smoking a joint and drinking red wine. They had the Stones playing on the sound system, singing "Get Down on It," while her stepfather sat on the floor watching them, his pants around his ankles, legs awkwardly spread, erect cock poking straight up. His wild eyes on her, her stepfather began jerking off as Da-Costa lifted her sweater and she pulled his face to her breasts. With Clarence hungrily kissing and sucking at her nipples, Gina glowered at Santino "Sonny" Galati. He worked himself furiously, unable to come.

Gina Galati had grown up in a brick row house in the middle-class Canarsie section of Brooklyn. Her father was a barber with a weakness for betting on long shots. Through her early childhood, the bookmakers always had their hooks into him. When Gina was ten, her father was dis-covered slumped in one of his own barber chairs, his face bruised and heart stopped by an apparent severe blow to his sternum. Shortly after the funeral, her mother began to date Sonny Galati, a bookmaker with Albanese family connections. Less than a year later, they were married. A week after their return from a Miami Beach honeymoon, Gina was in-flating a tire on her bicycle in the garage when Sonny cornered her. He dragged her kicking into the backseat of his big white Buick, and there forced her to take him into her mouth. Once he came, and as he wiped himself on the tail of his shirt, Gina bolted to hide in the bushes until her mother returned from shopping. Her mother's reaction to all her hysteria and tears had surprised her in a way that still outraged her to this very day. Constancia Galati beat her little girl with a saucepan, demanded she apologize to her stepfather, and called her a liar and a whore.

From that day, Gina never brought her mother a problem, nor con-fided to her a single inner thought. On occasion, throughout the night-mare that was her high school years, her stepfather made late night visits to her bedroom. She could do nothing short of killing him to stop him, and while he had his way with her, she would fantasize *how* she would kill him. Since then, her mother had died and he had moved far away, but she continued to have those fantasies to this day. When she first became a shooter, she told herself she was doing it for the money. The truth was, she'd begun to associate killing with sex, and found she could kill anyone her handlers pointed her toward with cold indifference.

Ears cocked, Gina listened for the crunch of the dopers' sneakers on the walkway gravel. Once they went past her place of concealment, she slipped into their wake to follow along behind. For a few seconds, she moved undetected, and then they heard her. In the next instant they'd leapt from the path, whirling to confront her. In response, Gina acted just as startled as they did, clutching her bouquet of flowers tight to her chest as she froze. As planned, the guileless innocence of her young face, along with the spray of flowers, was more than enough to disarm them. Sensing no danger from this virtual child—and a white one at that—their caution evaporated.

"Yo, bitch. Don't go sneakin' up on a man like that," the slender one complained.

"Sorry," she apologized. "I'm looking for my great-grandmother's grave."

He waved the explanation off, and he and his partner started on their way again. The instant their backs were turned, Gina plunged her hand into her tote, took three quick strides in their direction, and pointed her 9 mm at the back of the fat one's head. The weapon jumped twice as she dispatched them both, the discharges no louder than lids being pried from pop bottles. Their bodies jerked like marionettes suddenly yanked in wild directions by an invisible puppetmaster, then collapsed. Darryl Johnson's legs continued to twitch for another few seconds, while Fat Danny Washington's fingers drew listless circles in fragments of his own brain and face.

Gina tossed the spray of flowers across Darryl's back while DaCosta approached hurriedly to scoop up the brown paper bag fallen to the ground between the two corpses. "Let's hit it," he growled, surveying Gina's prey with disgust. "God, I hate dope dealers *and* niggers."

Six

Kamil Imbongi, a.k.a. Curtis Lee Brown, sat atop the brick parapet wall separating two rooftops on 151st Street. A loose-fitting ankle-length African mantua draped his beefy body, and a brown, yellow, and black box hat made of African kente cloth crowned his head. The ivory-handled fly whisk that stamped his self-image as a tribal chieftain rested across his knees. Kamil felt at home on these flat, hot tar roofs with their brick chimneys and earthenware-capped airshafts. This was familiar ground and he could cross it with relative freedom and escape peril.

As Curtis Brown he'd grown up not knowing his father and had watched his mother grow old and haggard cleaning the homes of white folks, washing and ironing their clothes, and serving food and drink at their parties. By the time he was ten, he had worked his way up to being a bundler for the Wild Bunch gang. His job was to gather vials of crack cocaine into bundles and deliver them to street corners. By fourteen he was promoted to pitcher and had renounced his white-slave-owner name in exchange for an African one. At that age, he'd dreamed of one day becoming a serious-weight, multikey dealer, and tonight it would seem he was on the verge of seeing that dream come true. He had prepared all his short adult life for this moment, quietly developing his leadership skills and learning the subtle ins and outs of politics on the street. Right now, in the calm of his rooftop oasis, he wanted to savor the moment at hand.

When the rooftop door flew open that particular Thursday evening, Kamil shook himself out of his reverie. The local Dominican *patrón*, Tío Paco Santos, emerged from the stairwell, followed by his ugly Cuban bodyguard and another henchman Kamil had never seen. Unlike the Cuban, who was huge, the second man was short and squat like Santos, with the same powerful forearms but less gut than the older man carried. Doing Kamil the courtesy of keeping his empty hands in plain sight, Santos approached to take a seat on the wall alongside him.

"Kamil, my friend. How are you this fine night? Perhaps a little spooked, no?"

"Who's this dude?" Kamil asked suspiciously, eyeing the second henchman.

"*Mi hermano.* Don't pay him any mind."

Kamil supposed the younger guy bore enough resemblance to the Dominican to possibly be his brother. "I din't expect y'all to come with no company."

"Relax," Santos advised. His tone was impatient. "I tell you he is cool, you take my word. But I do like the caution you show. It means you are smarter than your former boss, and that is what I am looking for right now. A man smart enough to know when to show caution, but still ambitious enough to show leadership as well."

Kamil continued to eye him suspiciously. "You gonna cut to it, or dance around it all night?"

Santos smiled. "I like that in you as well, Kamil. You have always been direct. So I will be direct, too. I have decided it is you I want to do business with, as the new boss of the Red Top crew."

As much as the murders of Darryl Johnson and Fat Danny Washington still disturbed him, Kamil was hearing precisely what he'd hoped Santos would come here to say. He felt his heart rate quicken with the excitement of this moment, and to keep control of it, he hauled his considerable bulk to his feet. Ivory-handled whisk in hand, he swatted at an imaginary fly and nodded. It was time to play crafty. He turned to face Santos squarely as he spoke. "Red Top crew chief is a shitloada responsibility, bro. And dangerous, it recently seem."

"With me backing you, I think you have no worries, Kamil. I have been watching you; how you run the pitchers on your block, compared to how others run theirs. You have a style they respect. In this business, respect is everything. You lose it, you have lost all control."

Kamil's expression remained noncommittal. "How do I know y'all can protect me, bro? Every nigger on the street got itchy feet right now, the way Darryl and Fat Danny gone down. They saying Tío Paco be losing his grip on the turf. Stash houses ripped off. Cops roustin' pitchers, then Darryl and Danny walking smack into a motherfucking ambush. Drums be saying that nigger Street Crimes cop is running the show up here now, not you."

Imbongi had never noticed the scar over Paco's right eye, and saw now that the *patrón* had attempted to hide it beneath some sort of pancake makeup. As Santos stiffened with anger, the scar became livid, like a lightning bolt streaking a dark, brooding sky. "This is my problem to fix, and not your worry," he snapped. "I supply your crew. You sell what I supply."

"It was Darryl's worry, and Fat Danny's too," Imbongi shot back. "Why shouldn't it be mine?"

"Darryl was greedy. It make him sloppy, Kamil." Santos had better control of his anger. He was lecturing now. "My people on the street, they tell me this DaCosta was parked near the cemetery today. They do not see what happens inside, but I think your crew chief and this cop have a lovers' quarrel. But you, Kamil? I think you are too smart to get into the bed with this cop. Which makes him my *problema*, not yours."

"And how do y'all figger we cut the cornpone?" Imbongi asked cautiously. "With me in charge."

Santos didn't flinch. "You get five percent of my profit."

"Ah." Kamil commenced to strut, fly whisk working the night air. "I see. I keep the street end cool. I keep all the greedy little motherfuckers honest. I sit on our stash houses and take mosta the risks. For this, I get five percent. Man, that be generous." His voice dripped sarcasm, and he slowly shook his head. "Ain't much of a taste now, is that, bro?"

"There are many fingers in this cornpone, as you call it," Tío Paco replied. Once again, there was a slightly disagreeable edge to his tone. "You must look at it another way. You are with me? And play by the rules that are agreed? *Es posible,* you live longer than any of your dead brothers did."

Mom's Pie Company occupied the street level of an otherwise dilapidated four-story brick building on the west side of Pleasant Avenue. A fire escape ran down the center of the facade, from just over the bakery door, to zigzag up toward the rooftop. Wired to the iron bars outside the first-level landing were an array of badly weathered stuffed animals that had once belonged to Angelo Albeneti's only son, Anthony. The five-year-old had been killed eighteen years ago by a drunk driver who careened onto the bakery sidewalk just as the boy emerged, eating a wedge of cake. Shortly after the incident, the driver had disappeared, his body never found. Angelo Cheesecake had wired the animals to those bars as a warning: You don't drive drunk on Pleasant Avenue.

When Gina Galati and Clarence DaCosta arrived outside the bakery, the eight o'clock closing hour was fast approaching. She directed the cop to double-park in front of the Manhattan Center for Science and Mathematics, diagonally across the street, and to wait for her.

"Why we gotta do this now?" he complained, clearly irritated by the detour through Harlem to this remote stretch of no-man's-land that he'd been forced to take.

"Because tomorrow's my little boy's birthday, and I wanna pick up his cake. When else am I gonna do it, this crazy schedule I keep?" Gina opened the door and got out.

Even at that late hour, customers still crowded the bakery. Two neighborhood women and a lanky, handsome Italian guy with a host of gold neck chains worked the counter. A half dozen trolleys with sliding aluminum trays lined the wall between the front of the store and the bakery, the stack of white cake boxes with customers' names scrawled on them having thinned somewhat toward the close of business. Out front, ricotta cheesecakes, tiramisù laced with dark Jamaican rum, cannoli shells, and sheets of Prato cookies filled the glass display case. Translucent slats of thick plastic curtained the doorway that led to the business end of the bakery.

Gina joined the line, her eyes wandering ahead over the shoulder of the woman before her. Between two of those plastic slats she spotted Angelo Cheesecake on his knees in the bakery beyond, cleaning a dough vat. Flour caked his shoes white. Beneath his stained undershirt, a dense mass of black hair matted his powerful chest, back, shoulders, and forearms. The overhead lights gave his bald head a dull sheen, and his heavy brow, downturned, obscured his pitiless eyes. When he glanced up at a wall clock, and then out past the curtain to scan the line of customers, his gaze fell on Gina. Gripping the rim of the vat, he heaved himself to his feet, wiped his hands on his apron, and wandered over to untie the leashes of his two Shih Tzus. Magee and Rocky, stretched out in their wicker dog bed, growled at the intrusion as he snapped leashes onto their collars. As he led them out into the store proper, Gina stepped out of line to crouch and pet them. "Gosh, they're cute," she gushed, fawning a moment over each in turn.

"Thanks, lady," Angelo replied gruffly. "C'mon, kiddos. Time to rendezvous with your fire hydrant."

The man in line in front of Gina was helped by one of the two neighborhood women, which left her face-to-face with the good-looking Italian guy.

"Help you?" he asked.

"Margolis," she replied, and handed him the order slip.

He turned to survey boxes on the trolleys, located hers, and pulled it. When he started to break the Cello tape sealing the lid to check the contents, she told him not to bother.

"I'm sorta in a hurry," she explained. "Got a meter running outside. Thirty-eight bucks, isn't it? She extracted two twenties from her tote, tossed them onto the counter, collected her box, and told him to keep the change.

Sal "Raymond" Sapienze waited until the young woman cleared the door before stepping around the end of the counter, ostensibly to retrieve a pair of napkins he'd let flutter from the counter to the floor beyond. Of all the cake boxes he'd handed to customers collecting orders over the past two weeks, hers was the first taped shut. When he'd started to open it, she hadn't exactly panicked, but took pains to make sure he didn't. Beyond the front window, the boss man stood shifting impatiently from foot to foot as Rocky and Magee relieved themselves, Rocky against the urine-corroded fire hydrant and Magee squatting in the gutter beyond the curb. There was no mistaking where Angelo Albeneti's gaze was focused, and Raymond followed it to a blue gypsy cab across the avenue. As the young woman with the mystery cake box opened the back door to climb in and the interior light came on, Raymond's eyes widened. He knew the man behind the wheel. A black man with dirty-blond dreadlocks and, if he remembered correctly, spooky blue eyes. The guy was a cop.

*   *   *

The squat, heavyset man with the thin jaw who slouched in the cordovan banquette in Aperitivo's elegant dining room had a dead cigar stubbed out in the ashtray and his stare anchored deep inside a ten-ounce martini glass. His short-cropped chestnut hair bristled with gray. His olive drab suit looked like something he'd grabbed off the rack at a fire sale.

"How's the shoulder?" Matt Stuart asked as he slid into the booth across from him.

Detective Sergeant Albert "Martini Al" Goldstein, the second whip of the Thirty-seventh detective squad, shifted his attention. "Whenever it rains, I get a little pain. No big deal."

Stuart lifted his chin at the economy-size martini glass. "Not many joints left around where you can still get a birdbath, huh?"

"Nope," Goldstein agreed, and lifted the glass to take a slow, loving sip. "So, how ya been, Matt?"

"Still kicking. Still collecting a paycheck."

"You dancing with anyone special these days?" Goldstein and Matt were still in close touch two years after that Chinatown shooting incident nine years ago. He'd been with Stuart through the ordeal of his son's death and subsequent divorce. After the accident that killed their son, Matt's wife was hospitalized for three months. Never quite recovering from her depression, she was eventually discharged; came home, packed her clothes, and left. Matt was away at work that day, and when he returned home, he found no note of explanation. Not that he needed one; he understood. In her mind, her husband and the Job had killed her son.

Stuart shrugged. "Not really. How's everything at your house?"

Goldstein flashed Stuart a sour smile. "Same shit. Martha and me are still doing it doggie style. I beg, she rolls over, plays dead."

"Sorry to hear that. I hoped things were better."

Al dipped a finger into his drink and licked the tip of it. "Women never forget, Matt. She catches me screwing around once, fifteen years ago, and I been paying for it ever since."

"Why do you stay?"

With a grimace of frustration, Goldstein raked fingers across his scalp. "Figured, sooner or later, I'd be able to make it right again. You know, the way it used to be. Hell, I've bought every self-help book on love and marriage ever published, looking for some way to turn it around. They're all bullshit."

Aperitivo's dapper owner, Louie, approached carrying a cocktail tray, brightly colored book spines patterning his Missoni tie. The birdbath he placed in front of Stuart was frosty cold. "Vodka up, cold and dry."

Stuart sipped appreciatively. "Thanks, Louie. It's got to be what? Six years? And you still get it exactly right."

The restaurateur beamed. "That's my job. You gentlemen going to eat? I've got an excellent Dover sole tonight."

Stuart ordered their famous veal chop, and Al took the sole. As Louie wandered off, Matt drew the blue plastic sword out of his drink and sucked the first of two olives off the blade. "Tell me about the Three-seven, Al."

The second whip held his glass up before him to study his reflection. "It's a down-and-dirty shithouse, Matt. Buried in homicides that ain't going nowhere, and knee-deep in natives that hate our fucking guts. Not a decent place to eat in the whole precinct. I been thinking seriously about throwing in my papers and going to live in Florida."

Stuart idly traced the outline of a fleur-de-lis crest woven into the white linen tablecloth. "Tough times go, but tough guys stay," he recited the axiom.

Goldstein gulped down the remainder of his drink and held up the empty glass to the waiter. "At the Three-seven? Like most shops that busy, there ain't much supervision from up the line. The suits in the Big Building don't wanna know what we gotta do to survive. Them war heroes in Internal Affairs are scared to cross a Hunnerd-tenth Street."

"How savvy are the patrol force supervisors?"

Martini Al laced his hands together and hunched forward over them. "Mosta them are pretty sharp, but they got their share of assholes. We got two affirmative action face-lifts from the Big Building spend most of their tours inna basement lifting weights and doing make-believe paperwork."

"What about the cops?"

"Lotta street moxie, I gotta give them that. Most on a razor edge. Downside is, they suffer from the old fuck-the-public, fuck-the-Job, us-against-them syndrome."

Stuart sighed and made a face that reflected his disgust. "You're off the street awhile, you somehow get it into your head that things might have changed. But they never do."

"Only the cast of characters changes, Matt."

"What about the precinct CO?"

Goldstein chuckled and shook his head. "Deputy Inspector Gordon Huntley was one'a the fair-haired boys. Praetorian Guard sent him to the Three-seven to make inspector. Instead, he got a taste of black pussy and went native."

"So who runs the shop?"

"He still attends the monthly Compstat meetings and pays lip service downtown, but the cops pretty much run themselves."

"Wonderful. Anyone downtown aware of this?"

"No doubt, but who they gonna send to replace him? He was the best they thought they had."

"And the squad?"

"McMahon ran a tight ship. I took care of the paper and watched his back while he supervised investigations."

"You happy with that?" Matt asked.

"Whatever."

"The detectives?"

"Two third grades, a second and a first. If there's any justice, the first, Jack Hogan, is gonna make sergeant this time around. I believe they're all solid people."

"You believe? Shouldn't you know?"

Goldstein eased back from the table and focused a level stare at his old partner. "I swear for myself, Matt. And myself alone. I can't sit here and tell you that none of our detectives is out there in the street doing things he or she shouldn't."

Stuart skated a finger around the rim of his glass as he gave it some thought. Al was right, of course. There was only so much any whip could know, eyes in the back of his head or not. "I hear a cop or cops in the Three-seven might be booming."

The waiter arrived pushing a serving trolley, handed Martini Al his fresh drink, and began to prepare their Caesar salads. Al took a first sip and smacked his lips.

"You coulda heard right. I can't get a handle on it, but I see too many cops whispering to each other at the end of their tours. That's a bad sign, generally. I don't care what kinda changes Bratton put in place, the detectives working any squad are never aware of all the intrigues going down with the patrol force. Still, I gotta tell ya, I been getting some bad vibes. The drums say there's bad stuff going on, too."

"The drums?"

"Street talk. In the Three-seven it's called 'the drums.' In my experience, they ain't often all that wrong."

"Who beats them?" Stuart asked.

"Most every block inna command's gotta stash house. All of 'em got lookouts, and nobody misses a fuckin' trick, Matt. It's uncanny. They see everything that goes down around them."

"These drums. They ever give up anything you could use before a grand jury?"

Goldstein grunted and used the tines of his fork to stab at the salad just set before him. "You kidding? Ain't no way any voodoo witch doctor junkie's gonna talk to us or any court. It all filters down. That's how we get drift of it. Offhand remarks made to cops or detectives."

Munching a crouton and savoring the piquant hint of anchovy, Stuart digested this information, bit by bit getting a better idea of what he was headed into. "What are the drums saying about the Rodriguez caper?"

The corners of Martini Al's mouth tightened. With exaggerated care, he placed his fork on the rim of his salad plate and stared straight back at Matt. "They're saying it was another cop took him out."

Stuart eased the napkin out of his lap to wipe his mouth. "Talk to me, Al."

"Rodriguez has a yard and a half in his checking account, not a dime in savings, and they find five large on him when they search his body. These drug dudes roll around the streets with trunks fulla cash. A cop stops them, they pop the trunk and say 'Merry Christmas.' "

"Or at least *Feliz Navidad*, huh?"

"You got it."

"So you're saying that Rodriguez, and maybe other Three-seven cops, are dirty?"

"I ain't saying nothing. But I can add two and two. I gotta acknowledge there's some serious temptation out on those streets, but that five thou wasn't kosher." Goldstein picked up his fork again to push a piece of romaine around in its dressing. "Seems pretty clear to me, Macho Man made some sorta score during his tour last night."

Stuart plucked that tiny sword out of his drink again to suck the last olive off the blade. He chewed thoughtfully. "We sure Rodriguez was the mark, and not the woman?"

"Absolutely? Nuh-uh. We think the girlfriend was used for the setup; that she saw the shooter, and hence, hadda get popped, too."

"What's with the Macho Man handle?"

"Dude was a real swingin' dick. Thought he was God's gift, you know?"

"Any ideas *why* he was whacked?"

Goldstein watched an attractive young woman in a very short skirt rise from a table across the room to make her way toward the ladies' room. "Not a clue, Matt. Not yet, anyway."

"What do we know about him? Other than how much money he had in his checking account?"

"A tough enough street rep. A cop needed backup, Macho Man and his partner could always be counted on to be two'a the first to respond."

The waiter glided quietly to the table to place another martini before the second whip. Meanwhile, the thick-necked date or husband of the woman who'd left for the rest room was busy trying to meet the eye of every other female diner in the restaurant. Al passed no judgment, seeing too much of himself at that age.

"Partner's name is Neary," Goldstein continued. "Seems less volatile to me than Rodriguez was. He swears nothing dirty went down during their tour, and I tend to believe him. Family guy. Ambitious to climb the Job's promotion ladder."

"They make any stops during their tour?"

"According to Neary, Macho Man went into Tío Paco's bodega to buy beer while he waited in the RMP."

Stuart recognized the nickname of Dominican *patrón* Francisco Xavier Santos from the intelligence file he'd read. "Tell me more about this Santos, Al."

"Inna nutshell? A lowlife who's developed management skills. He rolled onto the scene in the early eighties. Little tough guy, used to buy his product from Colombians in Queens. Didn't take him long to figure a way to up his piece of the profit. Negotiates directly with the Cali cartel, then makes his pickup south of the border himself."

"Cuts out a lot of greedy hands along the way," Stuart supposed.

"Uh-huh." Al watched the young woman emerge from the restroom alcove, admiring the sculpted turn of her long legs. Over at their table, her date was busy getting his eyes back under control. "A gram of coke sells for around fifty bucks these days anywhere else in the city. But in

Washington Heights, pitchers who move Tío Paco's product price it at thirty. A key he'll sell for sixteen to eighteen large, which is goddamn near wholesale. Anywhere else, it's twenty-two to twenty-five K."

"If he's his own importer, why the street pitchers? Why not work strictly wholesale?"

"It's one way to control his empire, Matt. Nobody peddles nothing in Washington Heights unless it comes through him. He also sells them the street corners where they do business."

"How does he get his product into the States? Anyone know?"

"Not precisely, no. Once he makes his deal with the Cali rep, he sends a couple of his minions down there, and they haul it back."

"Where'd the handle come from? Tío Paco."

"Uncle Frank? From his phony generosity. He gets off on playing the *patrón* role to the hilt. And guess what? It works. The measly few bucks he tosses around onna street buy him a whole lotta eyes and ears. Believe me."

Stuart tore a heel from the loaf in the napkin-covered basket and dipped it in olive oil. He nibbled thoughtfully. "You think Rodriguez was tangoing with him?"

"Possibility," Goldstein admitted. "Whether Neary knew or not."

"He was dirty, it could be he got what he deserved. We on the same wavelength there?"

Goldstein lifted his martini and gazed through the clear liquid at his former partner and new boss. "I'm reading you loud and clear, Matt. Ain't nothing I hate much worse than a dirty fucking cop."

A crack of thunder prompted Tony Fortunado to look skyward, where a throng of black-bottomed thunderhead clouds rolled eastward across the night sky. Any moment, a torrential spring downpour would be upon him. Don't got no umbrella, he thought, grabbing up the shopping bag and sliding out of his car. On the sidewalk, he depressed the remote button on his key, heard the BMW chirp, door locks engaged, then hastened across John Street before the rain came.

During the time of the Civil War, the buildings on the block where Gina Galati now lived were owned by the Schuman family. They manufactured barrels for the Union army. Gina's building had been the family's headquarters. Slate-gray marble sheathed the lobby walls. The floor mosaic depicted Union sailors rolling wooden barrels off a cargo steamer onto a quay at Vicksburg, while on the slopes above the harbor, the Stars and Stripes billowed over burning Confederate ramparts. Fortunado pushed Gina's button on the intercom panel and checked his reflection in the building-directory glass. The pompadour that crowned his head of dense black hair was a thing of beauty. He bared his perfectly capped teeth to search for any sign of the risotto he had eaten for dinner, spotted a bit of parsley wedged between his incisor and first molar, and worked at it with the tip of his tongue.

"Who?" he heard Gina's irritated query.

"Me. Open up."

Upstairs in her fifth-floor loft, Gina hung up the house phone and left the kitchen to head for the freight elevator. She slid the steel locking pin out of the hasp to unlock the grillwork gate as a chorus of clacks and groans from the cables told her he'd gotten under way, and then moved on toward her living room. There, she scooped up her tote, removed a .32 magnum Smith & Wesson Lady Smith, and sat on the sofa with the gun hidden beneath an open copy of *Elle* alongside her right thigh. She neither liked nor trusted her visitor. The slimeball was forever gaping at her breasts and making comments. If he ever did more than talk about her ass, she intended to ventilate his balls with a .32 hollowpoint magnum load.

When Fortunado dragged the rolling fire doors open, and then the ornate iron gate to step from the car, Gina nodded toward the cake box on a side table. "The one with Margolis on it," she told him, her tone heavy with sarcasm. "What genius came up with *that* handle, Tony? I look like a fucking Margolis, for crissake?"

"Could be your married name." He stalked to the table, deployed the blade of a butterfly knife with practiced expertise, and used it to slit the Cello tape sealing the lid.

"What, you think I'd mess with it?" she asked. "I'm fucking stupid, maybe?"

Undeterred, Fortunado glanced inside, then closed the lid and advanced to remove a small brown paper sack from inside his shiny leather jacket. Come July, guys like Tony would still be wearing that wiseguy clown apparel, Gina mused.

"This is for you," he said, and tossed the sack at her. "You don't need to count it. It's all dere."

Gina caught the sack deftly in her left hand and upended it to dump three letter-size envelopes into her lap. She opened one and fingered the cash inside.

"I said it's all dere."

She nodded, not breaking her concentration as she leaned to drag a triple-beam scale from beneath the coffee table. "Nothing personal, Tony. But my loving stepfather told me always to count it when it was his money I'm picking up. I'm gonna do less with my own?" It was six years since Gina had last made a pickup for Sonny Galati, but some lessons died hard. Indeed, maybe all the lessons Sonny had taught refused to die. With the scale set on the surface before her, she piled on the three envelopes and began pushing weights back and forth along the balance bars.

"Why you always gotta weigh it?" Tony demanded impatiently.

"Saves time. What I do for a living has taught me it ain't something I can afford to waste. *Capisce?*"

He shrugged indifference, sat in a chair opposite, and began cleaning his nails with his knife, occasionally glancing at her breasts.

When the arrow on the balance floated to the middle of its bracket, Gina frowned with displeasure. "It's short."

"Whaddaya mean, short? Dere's thirty thousand, just like dere should be."

"Forty, Tony."

He folded the knife and slipped it into his jacket pocket as he sat forward in his seat. "How you figure." He splayed a hand and counted fingers. "One cop, two niggers, ten apiece."

"You forgot the cop's girlfriend."

"C'mon. She wasn't on the fucking order form, and you know it."

"I get paid for every head that's gotta roll in order to fulfill the terms of the contract, Tony. That's our deal."

He opened his hand to argue, and she cut him off with an abrupt wave of her own. "I ain't gonna argue. You got a problem understanding plain English, let's go have a siddown with the main man."

Gina knew damned well that Tony had pocketed an extra ten large for himself, figuring if he pushed hard enough up against her, he might get away with it. For a long moment, they sat with eyes locked in a battle of wills. Just to be on the safe side, she eased her hand beneath that copy of *Elle* until fingers found the comfort of the Lady Smith's grips. She could hear the creaky mechanism of this scumbag's thought processes at work, weighing the typical mid-level wiseguy's options: "Do I pay this bitch or waste her? Just how important is she, and what kinda hell would I be likely to catch?" Eventually, common sense, even in limited quantity, appeared to win out. He looked away with an irritated jerk of the head. "I'll see what I can do about dat extra ten."

"Tomorrow," she replied. "After that, I start charging you vig."

He dug for cigarettes and had one halfway out of the pack when she stopped him. "Not in here you don't. I got a baby sleeping in the next room."

Fortunado glanced over his shoulder at the crib in the sleeping area, separated by a knee wall from Gina's big bed. He pushed the butt back down into the pack and tucked them into his pocket. "DaCosta got anything new for us?" he asked.

"He tells me a lieutenant named Stuart is taking McMahon's place at the Three-seven. A regular Boy Scout. Won't take so much as a bottle of Aqua Velva at Christmastime."

Tony grunted. "Fucking dinosaur."

"I think it's kinda heartwarming. To know there's at least one of them still around."

"Funny remark for a shooter to make, dontcha think?"

"I'm also a mother, hotshot. With a kid to raise in this cesspool of a world."

Fortunado heaved himself to his feet, feigning boredom. "Spare me the Madonna and child routine, uh? Tell DaCosta we want updates. The main man'd be interested to learn if the years have made Lieutenant Stuart any smarter."

Gina wanted this guy out of here, wanted to take a long hot shower and crawl between the sheets. "I'll pass it along," she told him. He slid another glance at her breasts, and she tugged the vest she wore closed, removed her hand from the Lady Smith, and folded her arms across her chest. "And while we're on the subject, why is it I'm running around with this renegade cop, I'm curious to know. All this exposure is starting to make me nervous."

"He's got the run of their whole fucking borough command, is why. Way I unnerstand it, he's the key to launching our whole deal."

"So why not have him do the hits?" she asked. "Dirty's dirty. Hell, he's an accomplice already."

Tony shook his head. "Don't fit with his image. Every crooked cop you deal with is gonna have this thing about how crooked he really is. In dere heads, it's okay to take drugs and cash off scumbags, even to set one up to get whacked. But actually pull the trigger? That's a whole other matter. Makes them bad guys. And besides, long as it ain't them that was the shooter, they can play let's-make-a-deal with the DA, things start to go sour on 'em." He wandered over to where he'd left the cake box, picked it up, and tucked it beneath one arm. Outside, lightning struck so close at hand, the resultant thunderclap made Tony Nails jump. "Got an umbrella I can borrow?" he asked.

"How about I sell you one for ten grand? You've got it in your pocket, anyway." Outside, the heavens opened, rain playing a sudden Buddy Rich solo on the window glass.

He reached into his jacket pocket with a sigh, withdrew a fourth envelope, and tossed it onto an end table. In response, Gina headed for a wardrobe alongside the elevator, opened the left-hand door, and removed a button-spring Totes umbrella to toss it across.

Tony accepted without gratitude. "I bet a lotta dudes have told you you got great tits, huh?"

"Only my stepfather."

"Huh?"

"Inside joke, Tony."

With a bewildered shake of his head, he stepped into the elevator and Gina used her key to release the car. Before sinking out of sight, he held up the cake box. "Ain't you curious to know what's in dese things?"

"Not in the slightest," she called back, and heaved the fire doors closed.

Seven

The rain stopped shortly before sunrise, but by the time Stuart drove his unmarked car onto Riverside Drive that Friday morning, heavy dark clouds were once again gathering. He cruised the roadway between 146th and 147th Streets searching for his reserved parking place out in front of the station house. Police cars and the private automobiles of on-duty cops jammed the street, without an empty slot in sight. Matt reached the end of the block, waited for the gray van on his tail to pass him, then threw it into reverse. In front of the Three-seven, he parked, blocking two cars nosed into the curb, and got out.

Designated parking places were always reserved in front of patrol precincts for key personnel: the CO, the XO, the desk officer, and the whip of the detective squad. This was done by stenciling those official titles onto the curb. When Stuart came upon the curb sign reading RE-SERVED CO DETECTIVES, he straightened to examine the parking permit placed on the dashboard of an interloping Plymouth. The legend on the plastic laminated document said the car belonged to a member of the precinct's community relations staff.

Matt did an about-face to take the wide flight of stone steps two at a time, reminding himself of the creed that the old-time Irish sergeants used to preach to rookies back when he first came on the job. "Eight t'ousand miles I come t' be ye boss, and be ye boss I'll be."

The doors of the formidable entranceway were painted a forest green, and the ornate brass doorknobs were the biggest he'd ever seen. He stepped into the marble-faced vestibule to find the precinct receptionist's desk—a long, narrow metal folding table—blocking his entry to the muster room. A uniform cop was perched on one edge of the table, leaning forward to coo sweet nothings at the woman seated behind it. She stared up at the guy with wide, admiring eyes and a toothy smile.

"Officer," Stuart addressed the uniform in a friendly voice.

The cop glared over icily, taking in the stranger framing the doorway. "Yeah, whaddaya want?"

"May I see you outside for a minute, please?"

"In a second," the cop said, turning back to the woman.

"Now!" Stuart snapped, his firm tone getting the cop's attention. Without waiting for a reply, he turned to step back out the front door. In the gathering gloom, he paused to survey a bronze commemorative plaque he'd noticed earlier, mounted to the right of the doors. Mayor William L. Strong opened the station house on July 1, 1895. Theodore Roosevelt was listed as head of the Police Board.

The cop who trailed after him had a name tag pinned over his left breast that read "Kelly." Matt dangled his shield case in the uniform's face. "I'm Lieutenant Stuart, the squad boss. You assigned to precinct security, Kelly?"

The cop nodded, expression wary. "Yeah, Lou."

"Last time I thumbed the Patrol Guide, I read that the officer assigned to station house security is responsible for the safety of all vehicles parked in and around the building. How do you figure you can do that, with your ass planted inside, hitting on that civilian?"

"Lou, she'd just asked me a question regarding traffic regulations."

At least he was quick and clever enough to have a ready answer. It was one of the first things they taught rookies at the Academy. Always have an answer for the boss. It can be a lie, a half-truth, or even a fairy tale, but the boss needs something to hang his hat on. "That spot is reserved for the CO detectives," he said, pointing to the trespassing Plymouth. "And that isn't my car, Kelly. I'd really appreciate it if you'd get it moved, like, forthwith. Unless you want to tag a summons on it."

"It's outta there, Lou," Kelly assured him, and turned to hurry back inside.

Stuart returned to his car and stood leaning against the front fender, waiting. Purple mourning bunting draped the stone above the precinct's arched entranceway, and the flag on the second-story pole was flown at half-mast. It was then that he realized the cop on security wore no mourning band around his shield, while tradition demanded that whenever a cop was killed, every cop in the Job stretch an elastic band around his or her shield. Two policemen emerged from the station house, and Matt noticed their shields were naked, too. Strange. What the hell was going on around here?

Drumming his fingers on the navy paint of his Buick, Stuart took a moment to orient himself to his surroundings and felt a first drop of rain. A ribbon of Riverside Park lay dead astern of him, its trees and undergrowth verdant with new spring leaves. In that block, only two other buildings stood on the same side of the street as the station house, each flanking it. The one to the north was an eight-story russet-colored brick apartment house embellished with ornate limestone trim. The other was a white Art Deco building with terra cotta accents. Bars and security gates covered the ground- and first-floor windows of both buildings. Colorful, spray-painted likenesses of murdered drug dealers were painted across the ideally suited white Art Deco facade. Ghetto folk heroes. Thick loops of razor wire crowned every roof parapet he could see.

The station house doors flew open and a fleshy-faced man in jeans, sneakers, and a tweed jacked hurried down the stoop. As he moved his car, he waved an apologetic hand in Stuart's direction. "Sorry, Lou. Won't happen again."

Matt didn't reply. He slid behind the wheel of his car and steered it into the vacated spot. On his return inside, he flashed his shield at the unsmiling receptionist and squeezed around her table.

The muster room, where the platoon coming on duty stood roll, and the sitting room, where cops coming on duty read the latest orders and received instructions from their sergeants, abutted each other, forming one cavernous space. Rococo moldings garnished the fifteen-foot ceilings of both rooms. Well-worn maple flooring stretched from wall to wall, causing footfalls to echo. At the far end of the muster room, a wooden staircase rose toward the second floor and beyond.

While advancing into the muster room, Stuart was drawn to the bronze memorial plaque, fringed in fancy scrollwork, mounted on one wall. Sixteen police officers assigned to the Three-seven had been killed in the line of duty since it had opened. The first was patrolman Brian

Bute, on January 1, 1898. The last to give his life was Police Officer Anthony Accera, on February 12, 1996. The official titles of the slain cops reminded him of how much the Job had changed. For the first hundred and fifty years of its existence, the cops in the NYPD were "patrolmen"; then around 1965, when the Job started to admit women into the patrol force, the title was neutered to "police officer." Matt's sad eyes moved down the columns, reading names and dates. He reverently placed the flat of his hand on the tablet in salute, then did an about-face. The sign hung over the broad, dark wooden staircase read DETECTIVES ONE FLIGHT UP.

On arrival upstairs, Stuart scanned the squad room, getting a feel for where he would spend God only knew how many weeks, months, or years. He'd always liked the high ceilings and wide-open spaces of the old detective squads, and instantly felt an affinity for this one. Nine green filing cabinets took up space along the west wall of the main room. The detention cage stood alongside, the lockup's steel bars painted in royal blue enamel. Cork bulletin boards overflowed with wanted posters, legal bulletins, line organization notices, and Detective Division flash warnings on the new high-tech weapons scattered across the urban landscape. Two rows of metal desks filled the central, open space.

Martini Al Goldstein and two detectives, one male and one female, were huddled around a desk covered with tagged evidence bags. Each bag had a Property Clerk invoice stapled across its Ziplock seal.

Stuart walked unnoticed into the squad, the police radio competing with an old honey-colored Grundig to mask any ambient noise. He stepped over and switched off what sounded like the Newark jazz station, WBGO.

Al and the two detectives turned to watch him walk to the command log set out atop a glass-fronted library cabinet, and sign himself present and in command at 0900. After lining off his entry, he straightened to approach them.

"Morning, Lou," Goldstein greeted him.

Stuart nodded. "Sarge." He glanced at the evidence on the desk. "What's this?"

Goldstein hurried to bring him up to speed. "We caught a double homicide inside Trinity Cemetery last night. Coupla big-time local pushers." He went on to describe the scene and probable circumstances of Darryl Johnson and Fat Danny Washington's sudden demise.

"We got anything on it?" Stuart asked. He picked up the plastic bag containing Johnson's Tec9 machine pistol, noting the time of occurrence listed on the property voucher.

"Nothing, Lou. Bodies weren't discovered until almost six," the female detective replied. "ME thinks they'd been laying there at least an hour."

Goldstein made introductions. "Detectives Rhoda Bolivar and Jack Hogan, Lou. Terry Gaskin and Josh Littel worked a surveillance last night."

As Matt shook hands with each of the squad detectives present, he catalogued those first impressions, attempting to read any initial negative vibes, and got none. Bolivar had an exotic look he didn't want to trust: undeniably attractive, with high cheekbones, a long, sculpted jaw and short-cropped black hair. He wondered how distracting the face, and her angular, lean physique, was to the other members of his command. Hogan, on the other hand, was cut from an old-school mold, from the thinning salt-and-pepper crew cut clear down to thick-soled wing-tip shoes. Maybe fifty, he was a big man with a round face starting to go pouchy. His gaze had that flat, distant look a detective gets when he's worked too long in a busy shop.

After the round of greetings, Stuart waved a hand at the station house at large. "I don't get it," he said. "One of the Three-seven's own goes down and I've yet to see a single mourning band."

"Married guy, off-duty, in his girlfriend's love nest," Martini Al reminded him. "Kinda touchy area in the new, politically correct Job. It ain't like it was line-of-duty."

Matt didn't much care what the circumstances were. Officer Rodriguez was a fellow cop. "How's the widow holding up? Or has anyone asked."

"Someone from downstairs probably has. Us? We're facing the real possibility we'll wanna search the apartment. Ain't likely to endear us, you know?"

Stuart focused on the investigation spread on the desk before them. He picked up a post-incident summary filed by Captain Glen Arnold, the watch commander, and quickly scanned it. "I'm surprised the canvass for witnesses came up so dry. A Hundred Fifty-fifth and Broadway is a busy place."

Bolivar grabbed that one. "When Jack and I went to interview the pitchers who work the cemetery wall through there, all of them were gone. Precinct anti-crime did a scoop right before the hit went down. Arrested two, and all the rest scattered. We drew a blank." Matt heard no trace of the expected Hispanic accent in her speech, and wondered where in the city she'd grown up.

"What time was that?" he asked. He'd noted the estimated time of occurrence listed on the Property Clerk voucher.

"Around four o'clock, Lou," Hogan replied. "We're guessing the hit went down four-fifteen, four-thirty. Citizen taking a stroll through the graveyard didn't spot and report 'till almost an hour and a half after that."

Stuart thought, Cops clear the street just before a double hit goes down. His voice took on a harder edge. "Precinct anti-crime units aren't allowed to make drug collars."

Hogan shot a quick glance at the other two detectives, his demeanor guarded. "This is the Three-seven, Lou."

"There are no dukedoms in the Job, Jack," Stuart replied. He picked up a stack of eight-by-ten photographs. Yellow crime scene tape, strung from tombstone to tombstone, cordoned off the blood-soaked bodies inside the frozen zone. Fat Danny Washington's right hand groped upward, clawed fingers stiff with rigor. On the walkway, two shell casings lay inside chalk rings. Sifting through the photographs, he came across a close-up of the entrance wound in the back of Johnson's head. A wide zone of powder soot surrounded the hole, indicating the murder weapon was so close when fired, the powder grains expelled from the muzzle had no chance to spread out and pepper the adjacent skin and hair. He shuffled through more shots until he came to one detailing Fat Danny's entrance wound. It told the same story.

"These guys were whacked point-blank."

"They were a couple of pretty savvy street thugs, Lou," Hogan said. "I don't see anyone sneaking up on them."

"More likely, they knew and trusted whoever popped them," Bolivar added.

Stuart examined a photograph depicting a broken spray of daffodils and tulips scattered over Darryl's back. Outside the squad, a clap of thunder ripped the relative calm. A sudden gust of wind rattled an open window, and then the rain came, its pelting making a dull noise on the tin windowsill.

"Weatherman said we could get as much as a couple inches today," Hogan reported.

Bolivar stepped sideways between two desks to close the window as Stuart picked up a plastic bag containing the chunk of aluminum which had bound the bouquet of flowers together.

"This being sent to the Latent Squad?" he asked.

"Within the hour," Bolivar replied. She'd returned from slamming the window to sit on the edge of a desk, one leg slung across the corner of it. "It and everything else where there's any chance they might find a print."

Stuart wondered what those long, slender legs might look like in a skirt. He gestured to the detention cage. "What's with the blue bars?"

"Our way of letting the mutts know it's us that run the shop, not them," Hogan told him.

Stuart found his office in the back corner of the squad, behind a frosted-glass wall and door. It had a window that overlooked the park, and a large portable blackboard positioned to the right of the doorway. Important phone numbers were taped to the wall to the left of a battered old oak desk. Overhead, a huge ceiling fan lazily chopped the air. He'd never seen department-issue office furniture as old as this stuff he'd inherited; probably original quartermaster issue. The wooden swivel chair had a slatted back wrapped two thirds of the way around the seat, its arms worn to a gray polished sheen with a century of use. In curious contrast, there was a computer perched atop a rolling metal stand off to one side.

Matt slipped out of his sports jacket and hung it on the corner coat-tree. He opened the window a few inches at the bottom and stood for a moment staring out through it, watching rain pelt the landscape beyond. He liked the incessant drumming of the rain; liked the fresh smell it gave the air.

Al Goldstein drifted in, leaning against the doorframe. He lifted his chin at the three separate stacks of folders set out on the desk. "Figgered you'd wanna look through the personnel files, and the case folders on a couple of the open homicides."

"What the hell is going on here, Al?" Stuart turned from the window to ask it. "Anti-crime cops clear the street just before a double homicide goes down. A cop is whacked and the other cops who worked with him are apathetic."

Goldstein sighed and shoved off from the doorjamb to pull over one of two straight-backed wooden chairs. As he sat, he regarded his old partner with a rueful expression and shook his head. "Honest wit'chew? I don't got a clue what's going on downstairs with the patrol force."

"How the fuck can you work here and not know what's happening downstairs, Al? You're the second whip, for crissake."

Goldstein sat back, an ankle thrown over a knee, and stared directly back at his new boss. "Maybe we need to get something straight between us, ol' buddy. Canal Street mighta been a long time ago, but I'm still the same cop I was then. One hundred fucking percent."

Uncomfortable with this turn, Stuart looked briefly past his second whip toward some unseen spot in the distance. When his eyes returned to his old friend, there was a measure of apology in them. "I know you are, Al."

A faint smile replaced the rigid lines frozen on Goldstein's face. "Word being flashed around the house is the new squad boss is one tight-ass sonofabitch."

"Shit. And I wanted them all to love me."

"Driscoll's storming around his office kicking the file cabinets."

"Who he?"

"Head community relations jerk-off. One was parked in your space."

"Him and the rest of the swivel-chair heroes are just gonna need to learn to cope." Stuart glanced at the plywood keyboard bolted to the wall alongside the window. "I see we've got three cars."

"Think of it as two. One of them is always in the shop for repairs."

"What's the shelf life of a set of wheels up here?"

"Nonexistent, really. Mutts know them all, department *and* personal. Attrition rate's pretty high."

"We got a Shylock?"

"You bet. Motor Transport runs a borough command motor pool outta the Penn Central rail yard. Other side of the Harlem River. We need a clean unmarked, we drive one of ours over there, do a lend-lease. Come back with a clean one. This way, cars don't get burned so often, and Motor Transport can keep shuffling the same cars within all Manhattan North."

"Toy Chest?" Stuart asked.

Goldstein pointed to a locker against the wall alongside the coat-tree. A combination lock was hung through the hasp. As Al fed him the combination, Stuart spun the dial and opened the door. Inside, the Toy Chest was jam-packed with disguises: wigs, mustaches, beards, sunglasses, rubber noses, chins, collapsible leg and arm casts, canes and crutches. A strongbox was welded to the bottom, and Stuart reached in the haul to open the lid. It contained four stun grenades, four smoke grenades, and two incendiary grenades, all military issue. He hefted a stun grenade, the size of a small orange with a pull pin and safety spoon. Equipped with a two-second fuse, it was designed to explode with a flash and bang guaranteed to get a bad guy's attention. An elfish grin spread across the whip's countenance. "Where the hell'd you get these?"

"You don't wanna know," Goldstein assured him, and reached in behind five hanging Kevlar vests to extract a manila envelope taped back there. He opened it and dipped in a hand to pull out a banded stack of greenbacks. "Play money for buys and other fun shit. Counterfeit, and you don't wanna know about it, either." He replaced it and returned the envelope to its hiding place.

"Looks like my stay at the Three-seven is gonna be, ah . . . interesting," Stuart murmured.

"Oh, I'd say so."

"I want to talk to Rodriguez's partner ASAP, Al. This guy Neary. Find him for me?"

"You got it. I'll run downstairs; check the roster."

Once his second whip left, Stuart started in on the personnel folders. Rhoda Bolivar's PD 406-143 Force Record card stated she was thirty-two years old and divorced, no dependents. Jack Hogan's showed he was fifty-one and married with three children.

After five minutes spent digesting the backgrounds of those and the two other detectives assigned to him, Stuart looked out at the partners currently present. Bolivar and Hogan reminded him of many good trans-cultural detective teams he had worked with in the past. Bolivar, shapely and statuesque, wore black pleated trousers, a man-tailored white shirt, and a black double-breasted blazer with a white pocket scarf. Big Jack Hogan was all rumpled beige.

Matt felt a stab of respect for McMahon, the previous lessee. One of a squad boss's toughest jobs was the pairing of detectives. If he made good marriages, the squad ran smoothly. Bad marriages, big problems. Those two looked like a good match.

When he finished with the personnel folders, he opened the Rodriguez-Melendez homicide case folder. A copy of the return roll call showed that Macho Man had signed off duty at 0010. Give him ten minutes to get out of the bag and into civilian clothes. Another ten to shoot the shit with a cop or two, and fifteen minutes tops to get to his girlfriend's crib on Hamilton Place. That put him there a bit short of one in the morning. The shooter is waiting in the girlfriend's living room. Macho Man walks in, gets whacked, the shooter walks out.

Matt pushed back from his desk and stood to walk into the squad. Jack Hogan was at a typewriter banging out a lab request for ballistics to run Darryl Johnson and Fat Danny's guns through their files. Rhoda Bolivar was staring at a photograph she had leaned up against a desk lamp. From the Rodriguez-Melendez crime scene, it showed Isabelle Melendez's body slumped on the sofa. Stuart stood over Bolivar to look at the photograph. She glanced up.

"Something about this picture's been bothering me, Lou."

"What's that?"

"It's her bathrobe. I couldn't put my finger on why at first, but now I think I know." She plucked a pencil from a coffee can and pointed to how the bathrobe's sash was snaked over the arm of the sofa. "Her robe was untied, and she had nothing on beneath it."

"So?"

"The victim was pretty well-endowed. Believe me. I saw her. And when that bullet struck, she had to be lifted up off the cushion. Head shot, which means she was dead weight on the way back down."

Matt frowned, watching the eraser of the pencil as she pointed it to different parts of the picture. "Not sure I get your drift."

"That robe should be open," she asserted. "Both her breasts, or at least part of them, exposed. But look. Both lapels of the robe are pulled together. I don't see how that can be, unless the shooter covered her up."

Stuart saw the sense of it. "So maybe he did."

"That's the problem I'm having, Lou. I just don't see a man doing that."

Stuart continued to study the photograph, fully understanding her point and its implications. "I want you and Jack to do another canvass of the crime scene. If this was a professional hit, it means the shooter didn't likely come from the neighborhood. And what that means is the slimebags working Hamilton Place would have tracked his coming and going."

"Or hers," she added.

Still thoughtful, Stuart nodded. "Be an interesting twist on it."

Hogan looked up from his typing. "You ain't dealt with this brand of mutt before, Lou. Ain't any of them gonna give up anything to us. That, I'll guarantee."

"We're talking about a dead cop here," Stuart fired back. "You lean on the bastards as hard as you need to. Just bring me back a name, a description, anything that points us in the right direction."

Eight

With his former partner now dead, Officer Mike "Paleface" Neary had been reassigned to the 8 A.M. to 4 P.M. tour and saddled with a young female rookie to break in. His wife was ecstatic about him working days again, but less enthused about Patrol Officer Connie Ferraro. Mike had described his new partner as a bleach blonde with an "ass as big as the back of a city bus," but Barb wasn't mollified. The way she and most cops' wives tended to view it, *any* female partner was trouble. Eight hours of daily fraternization created an atmosphere of intimacy. Sooner or later, someone was going to cry on a shoulder, get an itch, or start carrying a torch. As the mother of three kids with another on the way, Barbara Neary didn't like the odds of her husband remaining faithful to her, no matter how ardently he insisted he would. Men were fairly predictable animals.

To Mike, Connie Ferraro seemed like a good enough kid. The daughter of a Staten Island boatyard owner, she had a smart, tough mouth on her. Neary suspected she might be gay, but after working four years at the Sixth Precinct in Greenwich Village, he was easy with a whole range of alternative lifestyles. Before she entered the academy, Officer Ferraro had taken an A.A. degree in criminology from John Jay. Today, she was a bit heavy on theory and light on common sense, but Mike figured time would help strike a balance. If he passed the sergeant's exam, he would need certain leadership skills in order to be successful at that rank. The ability to pass along the wisdom of the street was perhaps the most important of those skills. And female partner or not, Connie Ferraro presented an excellent opportunity to get in some practice.

At eleven-fifteen that Friday morning, Neary and Ferraro received a call from the dispatcher ordering them back to the station house forthwith. It was thirty-six hours since Johnny Rodriguez took that bullet in Isabelle Melendez's apartment, and while Mike had already been questioned by squad detectives, the patrol force commander and a lieutenant from Internal Affairs, he suspected this summoning had something to do with his former partner's demise. Joe McMahon had retired and a new whip was aboard to take command of the Three-seven squad. As this new boss proceeded with the Rodriguez investigation, he would undoubtedly have his own questions to ask. An envelope containing five thousand dollars found on a dead off-duty cop tended to raise eyebrows.

At the station house, Neary was directed to report upstairs to the squad room while Officer Ferraro loitered around the front desk drinking coffee and shooting the breeze with the sergeant on duty. Sure enough, the new whip wanted to see him. Mike found him installed in the squad commander's office, Sergeant Al Goldstein also there, his butt parked in a chair.

"Officer Mike 'Paleface' Neary, meet Lieutenant Matt Stuart," Goldstein introduced the two men. "Our new whip."

Stuart had risen from behind his battered old oak desk with Mike's approach. At close to six feet, he looked solidly put together without having the paunch so many middle-aged bosses sported. His slightly thinning hair was liberally salted with gray. For some reason, the name was familiar to Neary, but he couldn't put a finger on why. "Lou," he greeted the squad commander as they shook hands.

"Have a seat," Stuart invited. He indicated the chair adjacent to Goldstein. "I'm guessing that most of what I want to go over is stuff you've already discussed with Sergeant Goldstein, but I wanted to hear it for myself."

"Unnerstand," Mike said as he sat. "I heard about the money they found on Johnny, it raised more'n a few questions in my mind, too. Like, where the fuck did *that* come from?"

Stuart studied him closely while nodding. "I read in the file that you're guessing it came from Frank Santos. Or at least you did at the time you first heard about it. That still your take?"

No matter how many angles he'd looked at it from, Mike kept coming to the same conclusion. He couldn't see any other answer. "Unless the broad was working as some sorta go-between, and she's the one paid him the bread, right before they were whacked."

"You know her?" the whip asked.

Mike shook his head. "Just by sight. I mean, I knew he was fucking her, just like everybody else in the station house, but we didn't, y'know, socialize."

Stuart looked down at the file spread before him on his blotter. "You were his partner for three years," he observed. "How would you characterize your relationship?"

"That same night, I told him my wife is pregnant, Lou. And that we wanted him to be the baby's godfather. Johnny Rodriguez saved my life at least twice that I can think of. We were buddies."

"Off duty, too?"

"We'd have a beer a couple times a week, after a tour." Mike paused to think back on those times, and slowly shook his head. "But I live up the Hudson in Rockland County. He lived in deepest, darkest Queens. Them's two different worlds."

Stuart made a note of something and leaned back in his chair. So far, Neary had no problem with how the new squad commander was conducting this interview. On his arrival, the scuttlebutt downstairs had him as a real hard-on. Mike could see an air of authority in the man, but knew all good commanders had to have one. He found no fault there. And the questions put to him were as direct as they were fair.

"Did you know that Isabelle Melendez worked for Francisco Santos?" Stuart asked.

"I'd heard the rumor. Yes, sir."

"And how did Officer Rodriguez justify consorting with an alleged felon?"

"Blew it off, sir. Said every Dominican in Washington Heights worked for Tío Paco one way or another. Only justification he seemed to need was the kinda head she gave."

"It weren't no secret he was putting the wood to her," Al Goldstein interjected. "Even up here. Most of the patrol force and civilian staff called her Chiquita Blow-job."

Stuart listened to this, then turned back to Neary. "Any guesses what he was selling for the money he got?"

For the past day and a half, Mike had thought about that question over and over. It still bugged the hell out of him. "Five grand or no five grand, I still ain't convinced it wasn't planted on him, Lou. Johnny was an arrogant little prick sometimes, but I never thought for a minute he might be dirty."

"The Crime Scene Unit's techs don't think it was planted," Stuart told him. "They think it was on his person when he was shot."

Neary had heard this through the grapevine, but remained unconvinced. "They *think*, Lou. I ain't quite ready to damn him, based on some science nerd's best guess. Like I said. I might be dead right now, it weren't for Macho Man Rodriguez covering my ass."

By noontime the dark clouds had vanished to the east and bright sunshine was refracted in a billion shimmering beads of rainwater scattered across the Washington Heights landscape. Seated on the passenger side of an unmarked car, Matt Stuart took stock of the neighborhood surrounding the heart of Tío Paco Santos's home turf. Rows of brick tenements lined both sides of 146th Street, their stoops covered with graffiti. El Cielo bodega was on the south side, halfway down the block. A short gray-haired woman in a canary yellow slicker hurried along the sidewalk carrying two plastic grocery bags. Her pace quickened as she passed a stoop. Matt spotted a lookout lurking atop it. In the middle of the street, three pitchers pranced through traffic, hawking crack at passing motorists. Their lookouts kept a suspicious watch on the two white men seated inside the unmarked parked at the east end of the block. Matt watched a hollow-eyed pitcher run alongside a cruising green Chevy Lumina, yelling the street name of the car's color.

"Yo, Emerald! Red Top make you feel good all over and bring you down real cool."

The white guy behind the wheel of the Lumina wore a white shirt and tie. When the brake lights of his car lit, the pitcher broke stride to trot toward the driver's side. The window came down and after a brief conversation the car's occupant slapped a wad of bills into the dealer's hand and drove off. The pitcher reached inside his voluminous Phat jacket and came out with a portable radio. Looking over his shoulder at the unmarked, he radioed a description of the Chevy, its driver, and the weight of the sale to his stasher. A thirteen-year-old standing in a doorway around the corner on Convent Avenue would take the weight out of a nearby garbage can and make the delivery as the car cruised past.

"Fucking mutts see us parked here and couldn't give a rat's ass," Stuart complained. "For them, it's still business as usual."

A mocking smile played at the corners of Al Goldstein's mouth. "The animals we got working this concrete menagerie are like the great grazing herds of the Kalahari, bwana. You wanna survive, you learn early on the difference between cops who hunt and them that don't. They know me, and know these wheels. They know precinct squad detectives don't generally make bantamweight drug collars."

"So they keep one wary eye out and continue to do business."

"You got it."

"I imagine Frank X. Santos knows we're here, too, then."

"I'd bet the old homestead on it." Goldstein looked Stuart's way. "Still got your heart set on paying him a visit?"

"Why not?" Matt asked. "Need to get a feel for how this bad boy thinks. You figure he's holding court in there, this time of day?"

Goldstein nodded. "Generally is. And I'm sure he'd like to meet you too."

Stuart checked the time. It was ten after one, and the lunch-hour deli counter traffic had started to fade. "Let's wait another five, then go on in and see if Uncle Frank might buy us a beer."

Seated with accustomed ease on his cane-backed chair, a dead cheroot clamped between his teeth, Francisco Santos was contemplating the checkerboard before him when the two detectives drifted into the bodega. He glanced up, made eye contact with the fresh face, smiled, and returned his attention to the board. The old man seated across from the *trafficante* combed fingers through a thick mass of wavy white hair and pushed a black disk forward into the next square.

A large, brutish-looking man who'd been watching the game over Tío Paco's left shoulder eased slowly around and into a protective position alongside his boss. As he folded his tattooed arms with their bulging biceps across his chest, the weight of his gaze fell on the two detectives.

Martini Al lounged by the door, hands loose at his sides, right foot braced against the wall behind. This was Stuart's show; one male top dog sniffing out another.

Matt took his time moving around the store and soaking up details: no alarm system in evidence, an accordion security grill rolled up over the plate glass window, two pit bull terriers inert on the floor, alert black eyes following his every step. Rotting black-skinned plantains, cheese, bloodred chorizo sausage, and barrels of coffee beans scented the air. The unpainted wooden shelves were stocked with dusty cans of soup, beans, artichoke hearts, anchovies, and black olives. Mouse droppings dotted the surfaces between the cans. A grimy display case was filled with bloody pans of chicken parts, steaks, pork chops, lamb shanks, and cold cuts.

Stuart looked up at the ceiling, where the stamped tin was painted blue with billowing gray and white clouds. El Cielo—The Sky. "Got any beer?" he asked no one in particular.

Santos slid a disk forward. "In the refrigerator."

Stuart moved around the counter to an avodaco-colored Kenmore, where bottles of Dos Equis crammed three shelves. He removed one and held it up to Goldstein, who shook his head, then nudged the door closed. There was a church key tied to the handle by a length of ratty twine, and he used it to pry off the cap.

Out from behind the counter, Matt took a sip and watched the players make their next few moves. The old man moved his disks with surefire thrusts, while Tío Paco's patient play became more tentative the longer Stuart said nothing. I'm getting to him, he thought, and smiled inwardly. To break the monotony of watching checkers, he scanned the yard art on the big goon's forearms and biceps. Below each tattoo was an inscription in Spanish, and a bearded saint on the right forearm caught his interest. A dagger thrust through the aurora and head of the saint dripped blood. He could make out only one word of the four-word legend, but it was enough: Folsom. There were few things about that small California town on the American River with which Stuart was familiar. There was a large water project dam somewhere nearby, and, more important, a famously notorious prison. He let his eyes roam again, and was brought up short by a trident adorning the web of skin between the right thumb and forefinger. It bore the words *Los Muchos*, and Matt was familiar enough with Cuban street lore to know criminals of that nationality advertised their specialties like this. The trident identified this hombre as a hit man with many scalps.

Tío Paco began a move, hesitated, and then abruptly pushed a checker into the next rank. The old man went wide-eyed and pounced on the mistake, double-jumping and turning his own disk into a king. Santos cursed softly.

Stuart eased back against the glass deli case and took another sip of his beer. "I'm the—" he started to introduce himself.

"New wheep," Paco cut him off.

"And you're hip to Job lingo. I'm impressed."

Santos threw him a taunting grin. "I know many things, Lou. Like how you kill your own son, and that your wife, she divorces you because of this."

Stuart felt a sudden loathing harden his expression.

"I know the shoot-out on Canal Street." Paco tossed a meaningful look in Goldstein's direction. "I know you come here from Intelligence, and that you don't take the money. What I do not understand? Why they transfer you here."

Stuart played it deadpan. "I'm a Marion cupcake."

"The what?"

"Part of a special squad of good guys looking to put humps like you in the dungeons of Marion Prison. You familiar with it? The hellhole John Gotti now calls home? He gets to spend twenty-three hours of every day locked in a six-by-eight cell."

The scar on Tío Paco's forehead brightened. "Marion is federal."

"We gather evidence and turn it over to the DEA, FBI, and IRS. They're the ones who'll prosecute you."

Across the store, Martini Al smiled.

Unwittingly massaging his scar, the Dominican *patrón* pretended to study the board while Stuart studied him. Brown makeup had been used to hide the scar, however ineffective it was at the moment, and it told Matt something about his adversary.

"You like this gig you got, Frank?" he asked.

"It's a living." Santos did not look up.

"I like mine, too. But I've gotta tell you, there are things about it that don't exactly thrill me anymore. Like to know what they are?"

Irritation colored the *trafficante*'s tone when he spoke. "I cannot wait."

"Mysteries, Frank. I don't like mysteries anymore. When I was younger, I used to get off on them. Now, the tough cases give me gas."

"Beans do the same thing to me."

Matt nodded, taking another swallow of Dos Equis. "Then we've got at least one thing in common, after all."

"What do you want here, Lieutenant?" Santos looked up to meet Stuart's eyes.

"I was kinda hoping you could help me with this mystery I inherited. You see, Frank, I've got this double homicide I just can't figure. A dead off-duty cop and his girlfriend. When they searched this cop's body, they found the five thousand bucks you slipped him when he visited here day before yesterday."

Santos pushed a checker ahead on the board.

". . . Then I've got the boss of the Red Top crew and his main man whacked in broad daylight, inside a cemetery of all places. Because all of this went down inside your *casa*, I've got to ask myself what exactly the five grand you paid Macho Man Rodriguez was supposed to buy you? Was it you who had him and his lady friend whacked? And Darryl and Fat Danny? And if so, why?"

The *patrón* looked up at him again and slowly shook his head. "You're talking *loco*, Lieutenant. I know nothing about these things."

Matt nodded. "Right. It's your own backyard, wired to the tits with wall-to-wall surveillance one block to the next, and you don't know shit. I'm willing to concede, even if you know something, you might not know everything; like who did kill them, if you didn't. Is there some other hump out looking to become the new *patrón* up here, Frank?"

The *trafficante* eased back in his caned throne to view Stuart with more confident disdain now. "I can imagine how it must feel, each time you look up and down Broadway to see all the beautiful tropical colors, and hear the *liquado* beat of our salsa everywhere in the air. They tell you it's the Dominican who is on top here now, not the gringo no more. *We* are the occupying army."

In one blinding move, Stuart slammed his beer bottle into the middle of the checker game, then whisked his nine out to ram it in the surprised Cuban bodyguard's face. "The Rough Riders just arrived, Generalissimo. And just in case Muscles here don't speekee no *inglés*, tell him he flinches, I blow his fucking brains all over your nice blue sky."

Paco held up a hand, instructing the Cuban to take it easy. He then turned to Stuart. "I *don't* know who killed the policeman. Or who killed the crew chief. If I did, Lieutenant, this mystery of yours would already be solved. I, also, am working on it."

Matt slowly backed away, the nine lowered to hang loose at his side. "Try not to work up too much of a sweat," he told the *patrón*. "And thanks for the beer. I'll stop by again sometime, have another of these chats. It's been educational."

As soon as the detectives left the bodega, Francisco Santos upended the crate with the checkerboard atop. Erupting from his chair in a rage, he stormed past the beaded curtain that led to the back of his store, and jerked the compact from his trouser pocket. He couldn't be sure if Stuart had noticed the scar or not, and examined it with the compact mirror to see how glaringly obvious it was. He'd met other cops like this one; assholes who could cause real problems. As he applied fresh makeup, he considered his options, and knew there was only one real solution. If Stuart became a problem, he would have to kill him.

Back inside the unmarked, Goldstein twisted the key in the ignition and the engine roared to life. "You've made a quick transition back to the streets," he commented.

"Survival of the meanest and the craziest, Al. It's the only law the other animals understand in this zoo."

The name on Benny Cool's rap sheet was Benjamin Collier. The eleven drug collars he'd taken since he was fifteen years old had resulted in his doing only eight months in the city penitentiary on Rikers Island. The "Cool Man" was nineteen years old. He was a member of the Red Top crew. His turf was the west side of Hamilton Place, the block where Isabelle Melendez and Johnny "Macho Man" Rodriguez were slain.

Less than twenty-four hours after the hits had gone down, Benny was still very much on edge over the murders of Darryl Johnson and Fat Danny Washington. It scared him any time he couldn't figure out what was going down on the street, and not knowing who'd iced his boss and his boss's main man made him wary. He had a nasty feeling that somehow, this was going to be one of those bad-luck motherfuckin' days, and as insurance against it, he'd stuck his big .44 magnum revolver into his waistband at the small of his back that morning.

"Bad shit be going down," he murmured to himself as he looked up and down the street, watching other pitchers work the Friday afternoon traffic. Overhead, lookouts peered down from the rooftops. A kid wearing

a black, orange, and green warm-up suit tugged the leash of a big German shepherd, trying to tie him to a parking sign. Everything on the
street looked cool, but the Cool Man's receptors were telling him something contrary. Bad shit be going down. He glanced up at the second-
floor windows of the apartment where Macho Man and his bitch were
hit, and felt a shiver run down his spine. It was bad shit, killing cops, he
told himself. Sooner or later, it touched everyone on the street, which
meant it was gonna touch him. He tried to shove the thought away, but
of one thing he was dead sure. That fat-ass Kamil Imbongi wasn't
mean enough, bad enough, or smart enough to run *any* major drug-
hustling crew.

A blue Jeep Cherokee with Connecticut plates turned into Hamilton
Place and a chorus of brand names flew back and forth, curb to curb. The
Cool Man's gaunt frame fairly swam inside his huge jacket, shirt, and
baggy pants as he jogged alongside the Cherokee, touting the joys of
Red Top-brand dope.

Before she left the squad that afternoon, Rhoda Bolivar had dipped
into the Toy Chest to pull out a chestnut brown wig, oversize nonpre-
scription eyeglasses, and a wedding band. On the street, lookouts were
forever searching for familiar cars and known faces, hunting for the
slightest signs of undercover cops. Still, with the volume of traffic, it
didn't take anything elaborate to throw them off the scent.

Rhoda braked the lend-lease Jeep and hit the window button.

"You lookin' to get cool, mama?" the skinny kid asked, his eyes probing the interior of the Jeep for any signs of cop: coffee containers care-
lessly discarded on the floorboards, blank forms, empty beer cans. "You
be a cop?" he asked.

"I'm from freaking Connecticut, for crissake," she shot back, feigning
a certain impatient nervousness.

"How do I know them license plates ain't bullshit, mama?"

She waved him off and started to straighten in her seat. "I've got the
money. Screw you if you don't have the time, buddy. I'll find someone
who does."

He reached in and grabbed her left wrist before she drove off. "Whoa.
How much y'all be needin'?"

"What's the price for two ounces?"

"Twenny-six hunnerd."

"Twenty-three," she countered.

"This ain't no motherfuckin' Kmart. Twenny-six be the price."

Bolivar eased her right hand into the crack between the driver and passenger seat as she nodded. "Okay," she told him. And in one deft move, she produced a pair of cuffs, slapped them on the wrist still grabbing hers, and ratcheted the other bracelet onto the steering wheel. Leaning left, she drew the .38 Smith & Wesson Chief concealed beneath her right buttock and aimed it at the Cool Man's surprised face. "You've got the right to remain silent, Mr. Benjamin Collier," she advised him.

"Motherfuckin' bitch pig!" he shouted, jerking at the handcuffs.

"Got him, Jack," she announced into the microphone in the sun visor. "Come on around."

From the corner of Amsterdam Avenue, Detective Jack Hogan appeared in another of the lend-lease program's unmarked cars. All up and down Hamilton Place, every eye was on the sudden flurry of commotion as his dirty white Ford Contour screeched to a stop alongside the blue Jeep. From the rooftops, lookouts radioed news of Benny Cool's arrest. In an instant, every pitcher on the block had vanished like so much windblown smoke. A description of both unmarked cars was radioed throughout Washington Heights.

Leaving the door open, Hogan heaved his bulk from the Ford and trotted over to his partner. "You okay?"

"Yeah. Let's get out of here," Rhoda replied, checking the street in her rearview. So far, all was calm, but she didn't want to stick around long enough for that to change. As Jack patted the kid down for weapons and took a big .44 magnum Ruger off him, she unlocked the bracelet from the steering wheel and waited while Hogan secured both hands behind the mutt's back.

Out on the street, Rhoda walked with her .38 at her thigh, helping escort Benny Collier to the passenger side of Hogan's Ford. Jack hauled open the door, grabbed the Cool Man's elbow, and placed the flat of one big paw atop his head.

"I'll get him to the house, you back up," he said, and pushed the kid down into the car. "You set?"

Rhoda nodded as Hogan slammed the door, then hurried back to the Cherokee.

*   *   *

"Bad-luck motherfucking day," Benny Cool complained repeatedly to himself as he watched the street scene outside the moving cop car. He'd never made it past his sophomore year of high school and could barely read or write, but he and the rest of the pitchers in Washington Heights were all expert on Article 220 of the Penal Code: Controlled Substances Offenses. They also knew the potential consequences of carrying an unlicensed concealed weapon in New York City. No longer warm and content inside the cocoon of heroin he'd snorted an hour earlier, his mind skittered like a pinball as he struggled to examine his current predicament.

Although no money had changed hands between him and the bitch cop, he knew it didn't have to in order for a drug sale to go down. All a pitcher need do was offer to sell, give or exchange, or *agree* to sell, and it's a sale. He thwacked his head against the headrest, angry with himself, angry with the cops, and angry at the world. "Loosen the fucking cuffs," he demanded. "They be fucking cutting inta me."

The big, crew-cut cop with the broken veins in his nose ignored him.

Benny tried to remember what penalties the "weights" could bring him. Two ounces was sale in the first degree: an A-1 felony. Add to that, possession of a loaded gun: a class C felony. His shit, most definitely, wasn't cool today.

Slowly, other things began to dawn on Collier, too. Like the fact that this big honky motherfucker was a precinct detective, not no beat or plainclothes anti-crime cop. Generally, they didn't bother messing with drug shit.

He be wanting something from me, Benny concluded to himself. Oh yeah, he and his bitch cop partner be wanting something from Benny Cool. Which might, just *might*, give him a little bit of an edge. Cops who wanted something were often willing to trade, especially a couple of detectives who wouldn't want to be bothered running a whole lot of drug-arrest paperwork through their pain-in-the-ass system. The thought made Benny relax a bit. The shit he was in might not be so deep after all.

Nine

Because of the high number of confessions extracted from recalcitrant slimeballs there, the interrogation room at the Three-seven detective squad was known throughout Manhattan North as the Intensive Care Unit. Tucked off to one side between the records room and the dormitory, the Thirty-seventh ICU was painted a nasty mint green and furnished with the original oak claw-foot table and five straight-backed chairs. In recent years, the one-way mirror had been removed, the hole drywalled and covered with acoustical tiles. A mini radio transmitter and a 16.5 mm pinhole camera were concealed in tile perforations. Their wireless signals were beamed to a twenty-five-inch video monitor in the record room, a drab, cramped space stinking of mold and lined with old metal shelves overflowing with NYPD storage cartons.

As he watched Rhoda Bolivar and Jack Hogan interrogate Benjamin "Benny Cool" Collier via the monitor, Matt Stuart was amused enough by the pitcher's theatrical arrogance to allow himself a slight smile. On-screen, Benny's bored eyes roamed the ICU as his pursed lips puffed in and out and his knees swayed back and forth. His entire attitude declared that Mr. Cool had nothing to fear. He was an old hand at this dance and was confident he wouldn't catch a beating from these detectives because they wanted something from him.

Stuart and the rest of NYPD had long since learned that the menacing good cop-bad cop routines popularized by television shows fell on deaf ears in the real world of drug dealers, street gang members, and other such sociopaths. When Matt had had his fill of as much arrogance as he could stomach, he decided it was time to turn up the heat.

"What's the combo to the Toy Chest?" he asked Al Goldstein.

The second whip looked away from the screen in disgust. "Eleven-nine-two-fifteen. It's on a Post-It, stuck to the back of the bottom desk drawer. What you got in mind?"

"Gonna mess with him a little," Stuart said as he stood. "I need fifteen feet of string and a hole punch. Think you could scare them up for me?"

Clearly puzzled, Martini Al shrugged. "Got a whole punch around here somewhere. What kinda string?"

"Something stronger than kite string. Butcher's twine. Anything like that." Stuart started out the door. "Meet me in my office when you find it."

Seven minutes later, when Goldstein returned from a trip downstairs to the basement, Stuart accepted a coil of cotton twine and a single-hole punch from him, and led the way toward the ICU. There, he threw the door open and waved Hogan and Bolivar outside. "Let's see what sort of tune he sings now," he said to Al under his breath. "Disappear a couple minutes and take Rhoda and Jack with you. Then wander back into the squad, looking aimless."

Collier slouched in his chair and regarded the new arrival with clear contempt as the whip entered the room. "Ah. The main poleese honky be comin' to see Mr. Cool," the pitcher crowed. "Kinda wondered what's been taking y'all."

"What makes you think I'm the boss?" Stuart asked.

"Them's uptown threads you be wearing, dude. Last asshole was strictly Sears. And the Spanish bitch is too good-looking to have any power."

"Interesting observation, Benny." Matt thought of Suzanne Albrecht.

Collier gestured with a limp hand toward the closed door leading to the squad. "Your troops be wanting me to give up who did the Macho Man and his bitch. Like right. Him that did them surely told Benny Cool all about it. Bragged on it up and down Hamilton Place."

"Your station was right across the street from her front door," Matt noted. "Could be he didn't *have* to say anything."

Benny had heard this already, of course, and got to work on a disdainful, glazed-over look. Eyes rolled up in his head, he sighed. "Why ain't y'all booked me, Mr. Boss Cop?"

"Not why we brought you in, Cool. Didn't go to all this trouble so you could entertain us with the same old shuck-and-jive dance, either. I'm more results-oriented, and a lot more impatient."

The Cool Man pried his gaze from the ceiling to throw Stuart a scowl. "Fuck's that s'pose to mean?"

Matt removed handcuffs from his belt and advanced to grab the pitcher's right wrist. He jerked it behind his back. "It means I want you to tell me a story, and I don't have all day to wait." One bracelet was clamped to the right wrist. He then looped the chain down and around a chair leg. Benny's left wrist went into the second bracelet, effectively immobilizing him with both hands behind his back. "You see," he continued. "I'm not here to work a trade. You're gonna go down for the gun, and for an A-felony sale of two ounces. *And* you're gonna give me what I want."

Betraying some confusion now, Collier tried to straighten out of his slouch and discovered he couldn't. The handcuffs rattled against the chair leg as the chain drew taut, stopping him cold. "You be dreaming, Mr. Boss Cop. You think this be the first time I ever sit in this chair?"

Stuart sat in the chair opposite and smiled patiently. "First time you've ever sat across from me, Cool." From a pocket of his jacket, he removed an incendiary grenade retrieved from the Toy Chest. He leaned to set it on the scarred surface of the old oak table, then produced the hole punch and fifteen feet of cotton twine. "Young stud buck like you really likes his pussy, huh?" he said distractedly. "Spend all that money you make impressing all the fine-looking poontang from the 'hood. I bet they just love that big meat whistle you got dangling." He made direct eye contact with the prisoner and winked. "Three, four years upstate, someplace like Attica or Greenhaven, you might get a little tired playing the one-handed sugar blues. But once you're back on the street, you're back in the saddle. Right?" Matt removed his wallet from an inside pocket, opened it to extract a twenty, and slowly creased one corner of the bill.

"Fuck you going on about?" Collier complained. He couldn't help flicking the occasional nervous glance at the grenade, and was clearly curious about the string, the hole punch, and the twenty-dollar bill.

Stuart shifted to get more comfortable in his chair, drawing an ankle up over one knee. With an attitude of affected casualness, he set to work punching a hole in the folded corner of the twenty. He then fed one end of the string through it, knotted it to hold it there securely, then held up his handiwork for Benny's inspection. "What am I going on about? See that closed door there? I plan to tuck this twenty beneath it. I figure a little more than half will stick out the other side, like someone might have accidentally dropped it. You get my drift?" He stood as he spoke and wandered over to squat before the door. "Tuck it underneath like so." He straightened after placing the bill beneath the door, and carefully uncoiled the length of twine as he started back to where Collier sat. "How long you figure it'll be before some sticky-fingered cop wanders by and sees that?" he asked. "And what do you imagine he'll do when he does? Leave it there?"

Collier continued to scowl, still confused.

"Not a chance, right? He'll pick it up." Matt sat again, grabbed the grenade off the table, and carefully looped the opposite end of the string through the pull pin. "You familiar with thermite, Cool?" He smiled at Collier and shook his head. "Probably not, huh? It's the stuff they fill an incendiary grenade with. A mixture that's part aluminum and part metal oxide. Burns at over fifteen hundred degrees. That's hot enough to melt right through steel." He paused to let it sink in, then nodded toward Benny's crotch. "Or sitting in a man's lap, for instance, hot enough to burn his dick clear off, burn through the seat of his chair, through the floor, and through the next floor, fifteen feet below, and on into the basement." That said, he reached over and dropped the grenade between the restrained man's legs.

"What you doing?!" the Cool Man hollered. "You motherfucking crazy?!"

"Don't know. Am I?" Stuart asked. He knew from his Marine Corps experience just how hard it was to actually pull the pin from a grenade. But Collier didn't know that. All his information was gleaned from movies and television he'd watched, and it suggested the pin of a grenade practically fell out on its own. Right now, Benny Cool Collier was having some serious second thoughts about where he stood. Or sat.

The whip eased back in his chair, folded his arms across his chest, and surveyed his handiwork with a nod of satisfaction. "A goddamn incendiary grenade of all things," he said, clucking his tongue. "I've got no idea how you managed to get your hands on it. Probably while I had my back turned in my office. You put that damned thing down your pants to hide it, and somehow, the pin came loose. Burned that big, beautiful Johnson you're so proud of clean off."

Collier was staring wide-eyed now, his panicked gaze flicking back and forth between the object in his lap and the bill tucked beneath the door.

Matt grunted. "They find out you don't have a cock anymore, those hard-ons at Corrections will have a dilemma on their hands. Do they send you to a women's lockup, like Bedford, or turn you out into the general population of a men's prison? Hell, you'd have every stud buck in the joint willing to fight to the death over you, Benny." He shrugged. "Hell, be a tough call."

Beads of sweat had formed at Collier's temples. His attention was riveted on the pebbled-glass partition separating the ICU from the squad room as he watched for the shadows of movement indicating the approach of anyone who might snatch up that twenty. "Y'all ain't fucking serious," he complained.

"You don't sound too convinced," Matt countered. "Somebody killed a cop, Cool. Me? I'm serious as a heart attack. Either you give me something I can hang an investigation on, or you've enjoyed your last blow job. You decide to stonewall me here, I hope to God it was a memorable one."

Stuart could see the pulse pounding in a vein now prominent across the pitcher's left temple. The kid's heartbeat had to be thundering in his ears right now, and he was probably feeling a little lightheaded. "Sad thing about sex, though, isn't it?" he continued to bore in. "Once it's over, it's over. No matter how good it was, the memory's never so sweet as the act itself."

Collier took another look at the deadly object in his lap, afraid to so much as twitch for fear of setting it off. His Adam's apple bobbed and tears began to fill his eyes. At the same moment, he heard hurried footfalls on the wooden stairs beyond the partition, and then saw the shadow of movement across the squad.

"Weren't nobody from the street did the Macho Man and his bitch!" the pitcher blurted. "It was that cop!"

Stuart extended his right foot to plant the toe of his shoe across the length of twine. "Which cop?"

With sweat pouring down his face, and eyes darting from Matt's shoe on the string to the shadows of movement in the squad, Collier rushed ahead. "Don't know his name. This scary blue-eyed nigger wears dreads. Motherfucker drives a beat-to-shit blue gypsy cab."

If it was indeed a cop, it sounded like someone working undercover. Matt had no idea whom. "Just this one cop, working alone?" he asked.

Collier shook his head, eager now to unload. "Nuh-uh. Had this bitch with him. Ain't never seen her a'fore. Young stuff. He wait in the car; she go inside. Macho Man, he show maybe fifteen minutes after that. Ain't there but a minute when she come wandering back out, cool as cream cheese."

"Could you describe her to a police artist?" Stuart asked.

"It was after fucking midnight," Collier complained. "Eye-talian-looking, maybe. Or Spanish."

So Rhoda was right. The shooter was a woman. Matt reached over to pluck the grenade from Collier's lap and started to reel the twenty in, winding the twine around the palm of one hand. "A few years upstate might not be so bad as it sounds," he said philosophically. "Life can be short on the street. Look at your old boss, Darryl, and his buddy. You stay in your line of work, how long before your number comes up, Cool?"

Collier glared sullenly, the sweat still glistening but no longer running in rivulets from his hairline. Anger had replaced the tears in his eyes. "Like you fucking care," he growled.

Stuart hefted the grenade in his open hand and smiled. "Enjoy your time upstate, Cool. Maybe read a few books."

Rhoda Bolivar and Jack Hogan waited to escort their prisoner across to the blue-barred detention cage as Stuart emerged from the ICU. Neither had asked what he planned to do with the grenade, string and hole punch, but to judge from their expressions, each was impressed with the results. As the whip watched them turn the key on Collier, Martini Al emerged from the records room carrying a videotape and wearing a thoughtful expression. To avoid being overheard by the prisoner, the four took their ensuing discussion into the whip's corner office. Matt sat at his desk, with Bolivar and Goldstein on the straight-backed chairs. Hogan propped himself on the windowsill, the late afternoon sun at his back.

"The woman shooter was a nice call," Stuart complimented Bolivar.

"We got any idea who this guy is, Collier described? He thinks it's a cop."

"Sounds a lot like Clarence DaCosta," Al Goldstein told him. "Special Ops Division's Street Crime Unit liaison to Manhattan North. Real strange duck. Works plainclothes. Shows his face in the Three-seven a lot. Drives a blue Chevy gypsy cab, just like the kid described."

Stuart digested this information and made a note to check Intel Division's database for anything out of the ordinary on the man. Street Crimes was one small part of a Special Operations fiefdom that included NYPD's Aviation, Mounted, Harbor, K-9, Emergency Services, and the Movie and TV units. Matt could imagine the latitude allowed, and freedom of movement afforded, anyone working as their Street Crime liaison in this stretch of the concrete jungle. He wanted to know whose ass this guy had kissed, or what special skills he possessed, to warrant his landing such a plum assignment. "Help me with the dreadlocks," he said. "Last name's Italian."

"Might be half," Martini Al replied. "But save for the light hair and blue eyes, he'd look as African as our friend Mr. Cool. You see his act, you'll suspect a serious ethnic identity crisis."

"Anyone ever hear of him working with a woman?" Matt scanned their faces and drew blank looks.

"Kinda surprises me," Hogan said. "Always struck me as a lone-wolf type, at least the way he relates to other cops."

Stuart leaned back in the old wooden swivel chair to stare at the stamped-tin ceiling. "So what gives here?" he asked. "The five grand found on Macho Man Rodriguez gives us reason to suspect he was taking money from someone. Now it seems possible another cop whacked him." He dragged his gaze down from overhead to make frank contact with each of the three detectives ranged around him. "Okay. Why?"

"Turf dispute?" Rhoda ventured. "Macho Man one day, the Red Top crew's big dogs the next. I'd say Tío Paco is either under attack, or he's suspicious of some kind of double cross. Maybe he's decided to install a whole new hierarchy."

"And uses a cop as his hired gun?" Matt was still having trouble with that. A lot of it. Robbing drug dealers was renegade enough. Murder for money was clear off the charts. "It's hard for me to imagine the guy I met in the dirty undershirt having that much muscle."

"Money talks. Big money talks big," Martini Al reminded him. "And appearances deceive. Santos may not look all that smooth, but he's the power up here. Ain't nobody dealing dope in all the five boroughs makes more mean green that our pal Paco."

From his perch on the windowsill, Jack Hogan craned around to scan the skyline above the New Jersey Palisades. He was hoping for any sign of an approaching storm, and though yesterday's clouds were long gone, he prayed more might arrive by morning. Otherwise, he would be forced to endure a first boat ride and backyard cookout of the season with his accountant brother-in-law in Bay Shore, Long Island. He dreaded those gatherings more than an inflamed case of piles. "We wanna have our ducks in a row before we start taking pot shots at DaCosta," he warned. "Right now, all we got is the word of one scared-shitless little street puke. Accusing a fellow cop of accessory to murder? That's as heavy as it gets."

From his in-basket, Stuart retrieved the Rodriguez-Melendez homicide file and opened it on the blotter before him. "Let me do some legwork on that count," he offered. "I've got some resources I can lean on; see if we can get a better picture of just who this guy is. Meanwhile, I see here Rodriguez's widow claims total ignorance . . . of the girlfriend and anything else. Why hasn't anyone done a search of the Macho Man's apartment? It's been three days now."

Goldstein made a face. "Your predecessor had this thing about dead cops, their widows, and a show of proper respect for their grief. Didn't want anyone charging over there and tearing her life apart while she was still white with shock. Y'know; from her loss."

"Even after they find five large on the corpse, and less than a hundred fifty bucks in his checking account?" The whip's tone was incredulous.

"McMahon's kinda old-school," Martini Al supposed. "To him, every murdered cop's a hero."

"We need to toss the apartment," Matt reiterated. "And what about a search of his neighborhood banks? For a possible safe-deposit box?"

Bolivar lifted her chin toward the cluster of desks mid-squad. "Jack and I have put together a list. Of banks with branches within two miles of his Elmhurst address. It's our next angle of attack."

Stuart considered the time frame. "I realize tomorrow is Saturday, but we need to turn the heat up here," he said. "You two free?"

Hogan looked like he might kiss him. "I don't know about Rhoda, but I can be."

His partner frowned at him. "Don't you . . . ?"

"Fuck that," he waved it off. "We got cops killing cops, my asshole brother-in-law can roast weenies by himself."

Ten

Friday night, a half hour after Mom's Pie Company closed its doors at eight o'clock, deep-cover police officer Salvatore Sapienze, a.k.a. Raymond, sat patiently behind the wheel of his five-year-old Nissan 240SX waiting for his control. He was parked half a block off West Street, beneath the westernmost tower of Manhattan's World Trade Center. For these evening meets, he and Matt Stuart had settled on this location as convenient to the Brooklyn Battery Tunnel, through which both of them would drive home. After rush-hour traffic died, Manhattan's Financial District became a virtual ghost town. Neither man harbored fear of being seen together here, which made these meets less stressful than the broad-daylight kind they'd undertaken Wednesday.

With his window run down, the balmy spring air and thrumming noises of a city at rough idle let in to keep him company, Sapienze wondered how much longer he could continue to live this double life. He not only liked Stuart but had a tremendous amount of respect for the lieutenant and his commitment to the Job. He knew about the death of his control's little boy, and the nasty divorce which had followed. It *had* to have affected Stuart, but one remarkable by-product was how he'd seemed to rededicate himself to the battle waged daily on the streets of New York. Given a choice between order and chaos, Stuart was still one of the good guys, no ifs or buts, and so was Sal. In their dog-eat-dog, it's-just-business world, the demands of being a good guy were wearying. It was a lonely bond they shared, and the loneliness of Sapienze's current assignment made the life he was forced to live even more difficult. At times like these, the ache of that loneliness manifested itself as a real physical pain in the pit of his stomach. None of the commitment on which he so prided himself could be allowed to shine through, and Sal wanted a normal life again. He wanted casual conversation and carefree sex with a woman who knew who he was. He wanted guys he could go deep-sea fishing with and not have to worry about every word from his mouth. Sal also knew that when he'd agreed to this particular assignment, he'd signed on for the duration. As long as it took to get the goods on Albert "Cheesecake" Albeneti was as long as he would go. A good guy was only as good as his word, and he'd given his to Lieutenant Matt Stuart.

The headlights of an approaching car filled the Nissan's rearview mirror as it swung in behind him. Once they were extinguished, the familiar shape of Stuart's Buick sedan gleamed in the glow of mercury-vapor streetlights. Sal eased an arm out the window to wave. His control stepped into the street to approach.

"Take a stroll, or sit?" Stuart asked by way of greeting.

"Sit. I been on my feet all day." Sapienze watched the lieutenant walk around the front of his car to open the opposite door and take the passenger seat. With more gray in his hair now than when they first met two years ago, Stuart still looked fit for a man pushing fifty with an ever-shorter stick. He also looked tired. Sal accepted the offered hand, and shook. "Nice night," he commented.

"Beautiful," Stuart agreed. "How you holding up, Sal?"

The taller, more angular man shrugged. "Could be we may see some light at the end of this fucking tunnel after all. It's an idea that kinda lifts my spirits."

Stuart's expression was curious but cautious. Sal had something, and Matt wasn't going to spoil his man's delivery. It was one of the things that made him an effective control: his patience.

"I'm working late last night, and right before we close, this good-looking broad comes in. To make a pickup. Young. Dressed like a tomboy. I ain't been working the front counter long enough to know if she's a regular or not, but the boss man definitely knows her. Gets up in the middle of cleaning one'a the vats the second he spots her. Decides it's time to walk the dogs. He's out onna sidewalk, right in her path, when she leaves."

Stuart didn't have enough information yet to understand where this was going, and waited through Sal's emphatic pause.

"First thing catches my attention is the fact she ain't wearing no bra—just this loose flannel shirt—and how firm and perky her titties are. Next is the name she gives me when her turn comes in line. Margolis. Even before I notice Cheesecake spot her, I think it's kinda strange, this good-looking guinea broad's got a name like that. Then, when I grab the box with her order in it, it's taped shut."

Stuart clearly remembered the gist of their earlier conversation in Bryant Park. "I thought only the boxes on the delivery dock . . ." He said it slowly, and let it hang, incomplete.

Sapienze nodded. "Uh-huh. And when I start to open it? Check the contents? She stops me. Says she's in a rush, she's sure it's fine. I get the distinct impression she don't *want* me looking inside."

"Which makes you think what? She's some sort of courier?"

Sal had thought long and hard about that one, and still wasn't sure what conclusion he'd come to. "Maybe," he allowed. "But that ain't the best of it, Lou. Once she races across Pleasant Ave and hops into her cab, I get a good look at the dude behind the wheel. And guess what?" He stopped to look directly into his control's eyes. "Man's a cop. Or at least was. Graduated same academy class as me, twelve years ago. Oddball with a badass attitude. Name's DaCosta. Clarence DaCosta. Half guinea, half black, all hard-on."

Jack Hogan and Rhoda Bolivar had worked through the dinner hour with a Queens assistant DA to hammer out details of the search warrants they meant to execute Saturday morning. It was 8 P.M. before they found a sympathetic judge in her chambers and were able to obtain her signatures authorizing them to conduct searches of slain cop Juan Rodriguez's apartment, as well as safe-deposit records at every bank within a two-mile radius. At nine-fifteen, they finally headed for Nassau County, Long Island, carpooling as they did most days. It was Hogan's Monday-Wednesday-Friday week, so he had the wheel of his aging Jeep Cherokee

Laredo. Rhoda slumped against the passenger door, one knee up against the dash as they headed out the Grand Central Parkway toward the Cross Island. Both were beat.

"I'm looking at the bright side," Jack was saying. "I wanna rebuild my back deck and add that spa we been talking about. I could use the overtime. *And* it gets me a pass on my brother-in-law's annual cluster-fuck and cruise."

When Rhoda laughed, it was in the light, melodic way she often did when it was just the two of them in conversation. Over the three years they'd worked together, she'd met Hogan's wife, Mary Kate, his three kids, and most of his extended family. Divorced for two years when they were first partnered, Rhoda had caused some consternation in Mary Kate. But once the two women got to know each other, Jack's wife came to see how silly any jealousy was. No question Rhoda was an attractive package, but she gave off none of the signals of availability that most gals on the prowl invariably broadcast. Hogan had never been as driven as some males to chase stray tail, and it made for a good fit, on the Job, and for a comfortable camaraderie off duty.

"He might be a jerk, but he does my taxes, too," she reminded him. "Careful how you sound to him on the phone."

The Baron of Baldwin—as Jack referred to his accountant brother-in-law—was the proud owner of a brand-new Trojan cabin cruiser. He was dying to see Hogan go green over it, and, weather permitting, had a midafternoon cruise planned from Baldwin Harbor across the East Bay to Jones Inlet and the open Atlantic. Mary Kate and the kids could still go, but Jack was happy to miss the Baron's pompous proclamations about how much his new beauty had set him back, how fast it would cruise at full throttle, and how many Harp lagers could be crammed into the galley refrigerator.

"I'll be the picture of abject fucking disappointment," he promised. "So gimme your impression of the new boss. He liked your thinking on the robe thing. I could tell."

Rhoda watched the taillights of cars ahead, frowned, and looked thoughtful. "You remember hearing his story, five or six years back? About him killing his little boy?"

"Who doesn't?" Jack murmured. He recalled it all too vividly and, as a father of three, could think of no worse nightmare.

"I know," she said, reading into his tone. "Big news not only on the Job but all over the city. I guess it ended up wrecking his marriage."

Hogan thought of the relationship he had with his own wife, and wondered if it might stand the test of such a catastrophe. Stuart was younger then; probably forty or thereabouts. Jack remembered seeing pictures of the wife in the tabloids: a pretty, slender blonde, nicely turned-out. He had no way of knowing, but guessed the ex-Mrs. Stuart might be a bit more fragile than his Mary Kate. Both he and his wife came from long lines of people tempered by adversity, from famine to occupying overlords, for eight hundred years. All the same, Jack never wanted to put his marriage to that kind of test.

"I don't care how cush his last assignment might've been, he wears the whip's mantle like it was tailor-made for him," he asserted.

Rhoda thought of Stuart placing the incendiary grenade in the suddenly frightened pitcher's lap and smiled inwardly. "Seems to, doesn't he? Some cops hate the street. They'll do anything in their power to stay off it. I think he realizes it's where most of the crime in this city goes down."

"Makes you wonder, though, don't it?"

"How's that?"

"Why a hotshot lieutenant from Intel Division gets his ass shipped to a shop like ours the day after a cop who looks dirty gets whacked."

Rhoda studied him intently now. "You implying he might be some sort of shoofly spy?" Shoofly was Job slang for an Internal Affairs cop, one of the police who policed the police. Most rank-and-file officers instinctively hated anyone from the IAD.

Hogan lifted a meaty paw from the wheel to pat the air between them. The gesture suggested she not jump to any conclusions. At least not yet. "IA don't work that way," he reasoned. "It ain't how they're chartered. But Intelligence? Them, I ain't so sure about."

"Intriguing," Rhoda mused. "With Benny Collier putting Clarence DaCosta at the scene when the hit went down, it could be this runs a whole lot deeper than just Washington Heights. I'll bet you dollars to dime bags, DaCosta knows something about the Darryl Johnson and Fat Danny Washington homicides, too."

"No bet I want any part of," Jack assured her. The implications of what she'd just said had been nagging at the edges of his consciousness, unspoken, for most of the afternoon and evening. In his estimation, they added up to just one thing. Someone was engineering a power play. And on a turf as rich as the streets of Washington Heights, nobody was going to roll over and let an outsider have the keys to his kingdom without a fight.

To a casual observer, the structure of a crack-cocaine-and-heroin-peddling operation like the Red Top crew in Washington Heights would undoubtedly appear lackadaisical and freewheeling. In fact, while most of the runners, pitchers, money handlers, and block captains, clear up through the hierarchy, were uneducated illiterates, the machine they serviced was a well-oiled apparatus built on the most basic of business principles. Throughout the centuries-long history of urban street crime, the basic philosophy of gang enterprise had evolved from trial-and-error experience, with each new undertaking spinning off from a basic set of principles to create its own turf-specific sub-rules. Twentieth-century dope dealing on the streets of New York was not unlike nineteenth-century pickpocketing in Dickensian London. In order to function, a crew needed a power structure where every individual employed in its business was answerable to another, one rung further up the ladder of command. Because the Red Top crew was huge, with bands of pitchers established on more than a dozen blocks off Broadway from 148th Street to Columbia-Presbyterian Hospital at 165th, the power structure was necessarily large and complex as well. During the tenure of Darryl Johnson as crew chief, thirteen Red Top block captains functioned beneath him as a sort of judiciary, executive council, and steering committee all rolled into one. As in feudal times, each had earned his seat at the table by being a little smarter, nastier, and stronger than his serfs . . . and simply by surviving longer than his peers in an extremely dangerous and inhospitable world.

Not everyone on the current Red Top executive committee was thrilled to see Kamil Imbongi anointed the new Red Top crew chief by Tío Paco Santos. Yes, Imbongi was as likely a successor to Johnson as currently existed in their ranks, but something about *how* he'd ascended to the throne rankled several of the more outspoken block captains. They'd called a meeting that Friday night to air their gripes and had gathered atop the same building where Imbongi had met with Santos the previous night. The weather had turned cooler and clouds were gathering low to threaten more rain. It did little to dampen the spirit of their debate.

"You niggers ain't listening to me," Little Richie Townsend complained. "It ain't that I got nothing against my brother Kamil." Tall, at six feet seven, and emaciated to the point of looking frail, Little Richie had taken three bullets from a Skorpion machine pistol in a street-corner confrontation two years ago and had remained standing long enough to mow down his three assailants. He fixed Imbongi with a steady stare as he spoke, his eyes bright with a spooky sort of strength his frail build belied. "He got a head for numbers ain't but one or two us others have. That ain't it. Before this, it was always us"—he drew a circle in the air with one finger to include them all—"decided who the next chief gonna be. Not some *no habla inglés* coconut-eating motherfucker."

"Remember. It be that coconut eater controls supply," O. J. Dixon reminded him. "And sets a price for it so low, we ain't in competition with anyone but our own motherfuckin' greed. Tío Paco ain't never been nothing but straight up with us, no matter that deep down in his heart he hates all our black asses." Dixon was the biggest of any of them in terms of sheer, hard-muscled mass. The same height as Imbongi, who stood six two and was a fat man, O.J. still outweighed him by ten pounds. He stayed in shape pushing weights made of manhole covers.

"He ain't the only motherfucker can supply us dope, he wants to start telling us how to run our sorry-ass lives," Corky Cochran piped up. He was the smallest of them, but mean as a snake. Local lore had it that last year he'd found his woman in bed with another man, had cut the interloper's genitals off, and made his lover eat them while he watched. The other man was no longer around to confirm the story, and the girlfriend wasn't talking, or seen going out much anymore. "Just last week, Darryl and me be discussing about them rip-offs Santos had. He didn't think ol' Tío Paco got the same strength here he once had. Not as much as the little spic prick want everyone to believe. Darryl be saying there was room he saw. To push up on these Dominican motherfuckers, cut out a bigger slice of the pie for us niggers."

Still clad in his African chieftain getup, Kamil Imbongi heaved himself to his feet and started pacing the outside perimeter of their circle. To his left, along the parapet wall overlooking 159th Street, two lookouts stood with walkie-talkies, armed with those new AK-47s that had recently shown up to flood the city's automatic-weapons market. Across the roof, three more armed brothers stood in a cluster sharing a joint. Kamil had grown impatient with what he saw as meaningless meandering. "Last week Darryl talks big talk like that, and where's the motherfucker this week, Brother Corky? Motherfucker's cold meat, onna slab somewhere downtown. I say we focus on the issue here. We got cops getting in our shit, big-time, from both sides of their law. Little Richie's man, Benny Cool, go down for bullshit today. Means to me the square cops don't know more'n we do. They bust Benny to squeeze his skinny ass."

"Drums be saying it was one of their own whacked the spic cop and the Melendez bitch," O. J. Dixon piped up. "They saying the blond nigger cop drives the piece-of-shit blue cab was on the streets around the time Fat Danny and Darryl go down. They saying the spic cop was Paco's, and Santos and the other bad-apple cops is drawing battle lines."

"Which ain't nothing we want no part of, ain't no motherfucking way," Corky Cochran said, addressing Imbongi.

Kamil squared around to face him, the anger he'd kept in check starting to burn at his gut. From an inside pocket of his robe, he extracted another Tums and popped it into his mouth before he spoke. "What motherfucking business we in?" he asked rhetorically. "We selling dope, correct? And because I or no other nigger in this circle happens to know no heavyweight Colombian, I don't see no way for us to cut Santos out. He the man. *Our* man. He say he want to deal with me. Y'all got a problem with that arrangement, I say you come up with a better one. Fast."

"It ain't you, bro," Richie Townsend started in all over again. "It's the *way* he gone about—"

"In or out?" Imbongi demanded, cutting him short. "I see our shit—both yours and mine—threatening to come unglued here, nigger. I'm the new chief, there's changes I need to make: tighten up security, anticipate where the heat be comin' from next. Y'all want the gig, just say so. We kick *you* around this motherfuckin' circle awhile." The way Kamil saw it, all they'd come here to do was bitch. Nobody really wanted the job. By continuing to sit right where he was, each of the block captains remained one step removed from the fate that had befallen Darryl Johnson. If the truth be known, Kamil was having more than his share of second thoughts about accepting this particular mantle of power himself. But five percent of the Dominican *patrón*'s net profit was strong incentive. Later last night, Kamil had run the approximate numbers. To the best of his reckoning, Santos cleared at least thirty million a year. His piece would be a million and a half.

It was 9:50 by the time Matt Stuart reached his Bay Ridge home and picked up a voice-mail message from Deputy Commissioner Suzanne Albrecht. After his meeting with "Raymond," and before starting for Brooklyn, he'd grabbed a quick nosh at his favorite Vietnamese haunt in Chinatown. It had been a long day and he was tired, but information developed in the course of his investigations demanded he sit quietly with it awhile, to consider the various implications. Before he returned Suzanne's call, he poured himself two fingers of Glenfiddich over ice and carried it into his study.

The message from Suzanne had been left at 4:40 that afternoon and simply asked that he call her when he got in, no matter the hour. He wondered if she'd intended it to mean as late as ten as he dialed her home number in Manhattan. Her answer, when she picked up, was brusque.

"Suzanne Albrecht."

"It's Stuart. Returning your call."

"You wait this late to check your messages, or just being obstinate, Lieutenant?" No doubting it, there was a slight edge of irritation there.

"Worked late, ate late, only just walked in the door," he replied. "Sorry."

"I asked you to keep me abreast of your progress uptown, and haven't heard from you in three days," she complained. "The paranoid side of my nature starts to wonder if you're holding out on me."

He took a sip of his scotch and let it glide back along his tongue, savoring the sweet glow it imparted going down. "To what end?" he asked. "Maybe I'm in cahoots with your FA's killer, or even ordered the hit on him myself?"

"Don't be an ass!" she snapped.

He grinned to himself, too tired to care if he'd managed to anger her. "You gave me a job. You trusted I'm competent enough to perform it. So maybe you haven't heard from me because I've got nothing to report." He wasn't about to tell her of the DaCosta development until he had more pieces of his puzzle assembled. What he offered, instead, was an explanation of his immediate strategy for trying to determine just how dirty Johnny Rodriguez was. "Tomorrow, if we find what we expect we might find, you'll be the first person I call with the news," he concluded. "Meanwhile, I'm beat, Suzanne. Been on my feet since sunup, and I'm back on them crack of dawn tomorrow."

"If I didn't know you better, I might suspect you're not telling me everything, Lieutenant."

"But you *do* know me better," he countered. "Which gives you every reason to just assume it. Good night, Suzanne. I'll be in touch." Without waiting for her reply, he hung up the phone, pushed back deeper into his favorite chair, and took another sip of his whiskey.

From outside the open window, the gentle whoosh of traffic on the Leif Ericson Drive floated up from below. For two years, Intel Division and the OCCB had been trying to conclusively link Angelo Albeneti to la Cosa Nostra. Tonight, Sal Sapienze had done even better. However obscure the connection, he'd linked Albeneti to a cop killer, and quite possibly to a conspiracy that, if real, could plunge the five boroughs of New York into an all-out drug war.

Alone in his bed an hour later, with the west-facing windows open and curtains being rustled by a breeze off Upper New York Bay, Stuart gave up trying to find sleep and thought again about Suzanne Albrecht. He considered how he'd actually felt on seeing her three days ago, after more than five months. If the truth be known, he had no idea if he was ever really in love with her. But just the same, he'd felt empty in her absence. A man of many complex emotions, he had spaces in his heart that ached to be filled by the kind of warmth only a woman could provide. Tonight, he saw no plausible means of accomplishing that end; not now, in this oddly transitional time of his life, which meant that after twenty-four years on the Job, the Job was all he had, other than this house and its memories. Once upon a time, Suzanne had represented hope; a means toward some semblance of emotional wholeness again. He wondered if he could ever expect to feel that kind of comfort again, or if he would spend the rest of his days alone, like he was tonight.

An image of detective Rhoda Bolivar surfaced, and as he thought about her—the handsome figure she cut in her dark-eyed, self-assured way—he also thought about fate, fog, and ships in the night. Most ships never saw each other as they passed. Some did, one admiring the other's sleek lines from a distance. Others, on rare occasion, collided. He and Suzanne had, and he reminded himself now that he was Rhoda Bolivar's boss. He needed to keep one eye on the murky waters ahead, and the fog of conflicting emotions now enshrouding him, and one glued to his internal radar.

Eleven

Before they left the Three-seven station house Friday evening, the members of the detective squad had agreed to meet at 9 A.M. Saturday in the parking lot of St. John's Hospital in Elmhurst, Queens. The two other detectives assigned to the command, Josh Littel and Terry Gaskin, had been working the past two weeks on an all-night stakeout of a warehouse beneath the George Washington Bridge interchange, waiting to nab a suspected automatic-weapons dealer. The new whip had met them only briefly, Thursday afternoon, and because they'd just come off their current detail, Stuart was reluctant to press them into service Saturday morning. Still, he needed all the warm bodies he could muster. When the two men arrived at the assembly site, both were red-eyed and visibly tired.

The day had dawned cold and overcast, which served to further dampen the mood. Stuart knew how hollow it would ring to play the cheerleader, and didn't bother. On his way up from Bay Ridge, he'd stopped to grab coffee and doughnuts, and handed a paper deli cup across as Littel climbed from his ten-year-old white Mustang.

"How'd it go last night?" he asked.

The tall, curly-haired detective peeled back the plastic lid from his cup and sipped appreciatively. "Thanks," he said. "Kid we busted's been locked down for fifteen days, so either the tip he fed us is bullshit, or what he gave us has leaked from somewhere. Twelve straight nights we're working that warehouse location, and not a fucking peep. Whole building's been as quiet as Grant's Tomb."

Stuart had read the case file and concurred with Littel and Gaskin that the expenditure of man-hours was warranted here, at least to a point. A group of Ukrainian immigrants were believed to have hooked up with a Jamaican posse, supplying them with bulk shipments of Czech-made AK-47 assault rifles and 7.62 mm ammunition. The guns were turning up all over the city, and had been used in several truck hijackings in the Bronx as well as a rash of drug shootings in East Brooklyn and upper Manhattan. "You think they've decamped?" he asked.

"It's the feeling we're starting to get," Littel admitted. "Meanwhile, my hopelessly insecure wife thinks I'm off chasing pussy. She treats me like a criminal every morning I drag ass home to bed."

It was hard not to crack a smile, but Stuart kept a straight face. He retrieved the box of doughnuts from the hood of his Buick and offered them across. "Maybe we need to put a scare into the kid you've got in custody. Say you're putting the word out on the street he's cooperating with us, and threaten to release him. See if he'll give up any more information."

Littel grabbed a glazed old-fashioned and took a nibble. "Couldn't hurt," he supposed. "God knows I'd like to wrap this thing, and how much I could use a decent night's sleep."

By nine, Stuart and all five of his detectives had assembled in the hospital parking lot. It was agreed he and Martini Al Goldstein, as the two ranking cops, were best suited to conduct a search of the Johnny Rodriguez apartment. Meanwhile, the two sets of partners would divide up a list of sixteen bank branches. Stuart and his second whip drove the three blocks to the dead cop's building on Seabury Avenue, Matt bringing Goldstein up to speed on what he'd learned from "Raymond" last night.

"The fucking plot does thicken, don't it?" Goldstein murmured as his old partner concluded. "First there's rumors it's a cop been booming the Dominicans. Then a slimeball like Macho Man Rodriguez gets whacked, followed fast by a local crew chief and his main man. Now we got a dirty special-squad cop holding hands with the Italian mob and playing chauffeur to a mystery woman shooter."

The whip tried to gauge what he saw in Goldstein's expression.

"You've been working Washington Heights for five years now, Al. Tell me what this means to you. What your gut feelings are saying right now."

Goldstein scooted further around in his seat to face Matt directly. "My gut feelings? Same thing yours are telling you, old buddy. That this whole thing's a lot bigger'n a one-precinct problem. We got us a major fucking territory dispute getting ready to go on the boil."

Stuart reminded himself this was a man who once took a bullet for him. If he was going to trust anyone on the Job, he figured Martini Al was as good a candidate as he was likely to find. "There are certain higher-ups who can't know about my guy inside Mom's Pie, Al. I didn't have IOC authorization to insert him. This blows up in my face, I take what measly pension my twenty-four years buys me, and a security chief's job at a Myrtle Beach go-cart track."

Goldstein peered hard at him. "You mind me asking *why* you did it?"

"It was as much Ogilvy's idea as mine. Couldn't lay it off on him, though, even if I wanted to. Man's Teflon-coated. We knew Albeneti was dirty, no matter what prior investigations had failed to turn up. There are things we couldn't accomplish with our hands tied, so we decided to take a risk. I agreed to take the hit, if one ever came."

Al turned to face forward again, and slowly shook his head. His disgust was clear. "Fucking Boy Scout is what you are, Matthew. I assume you believe you can trust this guy you got planted there? Trust him with your professional life?"

"He's one of the best I've seen," Stuart said. He reflected on how tired Sapienze had looked last night, and considered how he himself might feel, living that kind of life as long as Sal had. "But dangerously close to burning out. Sees this as his last hurrah, I think."

"He manages to walk away, ain't nobody can deny him disability, it's the route he wants to take," Al supposed.

Many cops who worked long deep-cover assignments had trouble returning to active duty. As such, they were eligible to apply for disability, on psychological grounds. It meant full pay until retirement and maximum benefits after that. Sapienze had worked assignments like his current one for over twelve years. Stuart believed it was some kind of Job record.

"I'm gonna talk to Ogilvy later today," he told Goldstein. "Request he set up surveillance on both Clarence DaCosta and Tony Fortunado. If they're part of the same pipeline, I need to know where it leads." He finished the coffee in his paper cup, crushed the empty, and flipped it over the seat back onto the floor behind. "Meanwhile, my deep guy will sit down with a police artist today. He gets us a decent likeness of the woman he saw, we'll show it to Benny Cool."

When they arrived at the apartment of slain PO Juan Rodriguez, neither detective expected to find his widow home alone. In times of grief, families tended to circle the wagons, and both cops knew this might pose a problem. Under current circumstances, their intrusion to execute a search warrant would not be received as either sensitive or timely. When the front door was opened to them, they found the apartment crowded with relatives, the dining alcove table laden with trays of cold cuts, covered casseroles, cakes, cookies, and other desserts. A red-eyed Elena Rodriguez approached when summoned, an infant cradled in her arms. Pending autopsy, her husband's body had not yet been released by the medical examiner, and a funeral wasn't scheduled until Monday. Stuart knew from personal experience just how agonizing that wait for closure could be.

Until presented with the search warrant, Elena Rodriguez assumed the two policemen in jackets and neckties, carrying gold detective's shields, had come to pay their respects. Realizing their actual intent, she became outraged. "What is this?!" she demanded, and threw the warrant to the orange shag carpet. "First they say this things about my Johnny and this . . . this *puta*! Now you come to my house an' treat me like a criminal?!" She spat the Spanish word for whore like it was a foul taste in her mouth.

As Matt held her angry glare, he tried to put himself in her shoes. The woman before him had smooth, coffee-colored skin, prominent cheekbones, and a full-lipped, pouting mouth. She carried a lot of extra weight, the kind so many young women fail to lose after childbirth. Comparing her to file photographs of Isabelle Melendez, Stuart considered the differences he saw. Even in death, the girlfriend had a more provocative and overtly desirable look about her: taller, and slender yet voluptuous. "Believe me, I'm sorry to do this, Mrs. Rodriguez," he said calmly. "But the woman in whose apartment your husband was killed was a known associate of the biggest crack cocaine trafficker in Manhattan. Your husband was found with five thousand dollars in cash on his person. Please don't make this any more difficult for you, or us, than it already is."

He could feel the heat of animosity building throughout the surrounding room. One of the men, old enough to be the widow's father or father-in-law, moved forward, followed by others who might be brothers or cousins. A fat, brassy blonde in stretch pants growled something in Spanish that triggered a murmuring among the women.

"What five thousand dollars?" Elena Rodriguez demanded. She turned, shifted the baby in her arms, and gestured at the apartment behind her. "Look at this, how we live. You think my Johnny steals money? You are *loco*."

Matt could feel Goldstein's impatience, and eased a hand onto the second whip's sleeve. "I need you to ask these people to leave us alone here for a while, Mrs. Rodriguez," he said. "The less trouble you give us, the quicker we can get this done."

The older man who had advanced to stand at the widow's side puffed out his chest, his nostrils flaring wide and eyes flashing fire. "This is what my son gets after he gives you people his life?" he snarled.

Matt wasn't going to mention that Johnny Rodriguez had died while off duty, in the apartment of a woman referred to around the Three-seven as Chiquita Blow-job. Instead, he again addressed the dead man's wife. "Please ask them to leave," he reiterated. "And accept my apologies. I don't want to be here any more than you want me here. Believe me."

Jack Hogan and Rhoda Bolivar visited five Queens bank branches, poring over five sets of safe-deposit records and striking out five times, before finally hitting pay dirt. At a Republic Bank on Thirty-seventh Avenue in Jackson Heights only a mile from his Elmhurst apartment, Johnny "Macho Man" Rodriguez had rented a box using his own name and Social Security number. Clearly, he was confident his secret would remain just that by virtue of the fact that he did his regular banking elsewhere.

To gain access to the box, the bank manager contacted a locksmith on Roosevelt Avenue. Because it was a Saturday, the shop was working shorthanded. The proprietor reported it would be at least an hour before he could free up someone to take the call. The partners decided to grab a bite to eat.

When Jack Hogan was a kid, that stretch of Queens was populated for the most part by middle-class Caucasians. Today, it was predominantly

Asian, with large pockets of Central and South American immigrants sprung up in Elmhurst, to the south. Former mayor David Dinkins had insisted New York was more a mosaic than a melting pot, and nowhere was this more true than in Queens, where one ghettoized immigrant community abutted but refused to commingle with the next. From Lebanese to Chinese to Guatemalan, those various populations remained as stubbornly insular as so many religious creeds. Along Roosevelt Avenue or Queens Boulevard, from one block to the next, shop signs would change from Farsi to Mandarin to Hebrew to Spanish. Where they overlapped, there was often tension, the attitudes and mores of two cultures clashing.

Before she left that bank branch for lunch, Rhoda Bolivar had reached Matt Stuart at the Rodriguez apartment via cell phone to tell him of their discovery. Now, as they slid into a booth at a Szechwan restaurant, she reported back to her partner. "I could hear the tension in his voice," she told Hogan. "Like he couldn't wait to get out of there."

"I can imagine," Jack replied. It wasn't a straw he would have wanted to draw. "They gonna meet us at the bank?" He checked his watch as he asked it: 12:35.

"He said they're hungry, too. Soon as he contacts Josh and Terry and tells them to go home and get some sleep, he and the sarge will meet us here. Asked me to order for them. Nothing too spicy. Goldstein's gut can't take it."

Jack deployed his napkin and watched a diminutive waitress pour two tiny cups full of steaming black tea. Rhoda glanced out the plate glass toward a sky partially blocked from view by the elevated tracks of the Flushing line. The day remained overcast and dreary.

"So. You wish you were out on Eamon's boat right now?" she asked.

Hogan was watching the face of the slender young Chinese girl, with its nervous, tentative smile. Her expression said she knew they were cops, and the way her eyes darted told him she probably wasn't legal. Not that he cared, so long as she didn't kill anyone. Half the populations of Queens and Brooklyn didn't own green cards. He investigated homicides and other violent crimes against humanity, not immigration violations. "Betcha twenny bucks, the asshole's too stubborn to call it off," he said. "Water gets rough, I hope one of my kids pukes on his galley carpet."

Her eyes sparkling, Rhoda laughed. "Nice, Hogan. Tell me how you *really* feel. Then tell me what you think we'll find in that bank box. And what you think Macho Man was up to."

"Squeezing Tío Paco would be my guess," he replied. "Could be he was selling protection it turned out he couldn't deliver."

"And how does Clarence DaCosta fit in?"

Hogan opened his menu and glanced down at it. "Dunno. Made Santos a better offer? Promised more comprehensive intelligence. And just to prove he can deliver, he removes a pesky leech like Rodriguez. Maybe throws in a couple uppity crew leaders as a bonus."

Rhoda raised her tea to her lips and sipped. It was weak, in need of more time in the pot. "The thought crossed my mind, too. That the hits are somehow connected."

"Coincidence is just too big," Jack insisted, looking up. "Think aboudit. Somebody's booming Paco's houses, which means he's got a major security leak. Then, inside two days, a major crew leader and his sidekick get replaced the old-fashioned way, and this swinging-dick cop who's dating one of Paco's former stash-house mamas buys a one-way ticket, too."

"You think Rodriguez might have played both ends against the middle?" she asked.

"You saw what a cocky fuck he was."

"But how stupid would that be, Jack? Offering to provide intelligence, then working to rip Santos off at the same time?"

"Give some guys a gun and a chunk of polished tin, they think they're invincible. Toss a little greed inta the mix, you never know what crazy shit they'll cook up. Believe me, ain't nothing would surprise me. I been watching cops step on their dicks for over thirty years."

Despite the pressure of the animosity they'd encountered, Stuart and Goldstein were careful to conduct a thorough search of the Rodriguez apartment. For Matt, it was particularly disquieting to search the dead cop's personal effects, to paw through the pockets of uniforms hung in his closet and the dozens of Italian-cut jackets, silk shirts, pairs of slacks, and shoes. Such a search inevitably revealed volumes about the personality, private preferences, and tastes of a subject. In the case of the slain officer nicknamed Macho Man, there was no fat envelope of cash hidden in a shoebox, or beneath a loose edge of the bedroom wall-to-wall carpet. There wasn't even a decent set of pots and pans in the kitchen, and the lingerie of the dead man's wife all showed signs of too much wear. In contrast, every thread of clothing Johnny Rodriguez had owned was first-cabin.

When the call came from Rhoda Bolivar advising them of the discovery of a safe-deposit box in Jackson Heights, Stuart and Goldstein were relieved to be called away from their own depressing task. Matt apologized once more for the intrusion as the widow stood, babe in arms, her mestizo features frozen in an expression of pure hatred. To escape the apartment, the detectives had to walk a gauntlet of equally outraged relatives assembled in the hall outside.

Once settled into the passenger seat of Stuart's Buick, Goldstein craned his neck to stare up at the third floor of the building they'd just vacated. He let out a long, weary sigh. "For a guy with a family living on a patrolman's pay, man spent an awful lotta money on his wardrobe. Get the feeling he was a little over budget?"

"Did like his designer labels," Matt agreed. "What do Gucci shoes run?"

"Too much."

"He owned eight pair."

"Cop I remember? Had that typical street kid's strut, Matthew. You know, like his balls are too big to hang comfortably between his legs."

Stuart pulled his seat belt across his chest and got them under way. "You heard his partner, Mike Neary, when I talked to him, Al. What was your impression of him?"

Martini Al shrugged. "As little attention as I pay to the patrol force, I still usually get a feeling someone's playing a particularly outrageous game. Rodriguez made me a little nervous. But Neary?" He shook his head. "A whole other animal. Dad was a cop. Grandfather, too."

"People inherit habits, good and bad."

"True," Al agreed. "But that ain't the sense I get. Not with this kid. Did he ever drink a brewski on the clock? Prob'ly. But either he's a fairly straight arrow, or the best fucking actor since Al Pacino."

Stuart steered them through moderately heavy Saturday traffic, his wipers set to clean away the persistent drizzle. A mile up Broadway, he turned north on Seventy-ninth Street, then right again onto Roosevelt Avenue. As they ran along beneath the elevated tracks, he scanned for Hogan and Bolivar's Szechwan eatery. "If we find nothing but Rodriguez family heirlooms in that bank box, I'm running out of ideas," he said. "Where we might look next."

"Then think positive," Goldstein advised. "And keep your fingers crossed."

The safe-deposit box rented by slain PO Johnny Rodriguez at the Thirty-seventh Avenue branch of the Republic National Bank in Jackson Heights proved to contain eighty-two thousand dollars, mostly in small bills. None of the Three-seven squad detectives present when the locksmith opened the box was surprised by this discovery, though all were curious to know what Macho Man had given up to Frank Santos in exchange. Matt Stuart put the cost of the clothes found in the dead cop's closet at upwards of twenty-five thousand dollars. There was no telling how much more money he might have squandered partying with the Melendez woman, but it didn't take a particularly active imagination to start the ante upward. In any information-peddling market, it represented a hefty chunk of graft.

Because she was the low person on the seniority totem pole, Rhoda Bolivar drew the duty of accompanying the whip across the East River to Washington Heights. No individual cop wanted sole responsibility for carrying that much cash to the evidence lockup, and if the truth be known, Stuart liked the idea of having her, in particular, along for company. He suggested she leave her car at the bank, and offered to give her a lift back to it once they finished up. They made the Saturday afternoon trip across the Triborough Bridge into northern Manhattan together in his Buick.

The drizzle had quit and the sky lifted somewhat by the time they reached the Randalls Island-Triborough Bridge Interchange. Their small talk ranged from where each was raised—Rhoda surprised Matt with her answer of midtown Manhattan's upscale Murray Hill—to where they lived now. Eventually, they wound their way around to the current investigation.

"What I'm still trying to puzzle is the connection between Macho Man and Clarence DaCosta, if there was one," Rhoda told Stuart. "I'm wondering where it might lead, and what made DaCosta decide to terminate the relationship."

From behind the wheel, in slow-moving weekend traffic, Matt considered what he now knew about DaCosta from Sal Sapienze, and tried to put it together with the fact that Rodriguez had been sleeping with a former Frank Santos insider. It seemed like as good a time as any to engage in a little more brainstorming. "Or, we could look at it from a whole other angle," he replied. "Think in terms of rival factions, rather than alliances."

Rhoda examined the new whip's profile as he drove. She remembered his tragedy, and looked for residual evidence of it. The gray in his hair was harder to read than the lines etched deep in his forehead and beneath his eyes. They hadn't been put there by laughter. She tried to guess his age and figured him to be just shy of fifty. "How so?" she asked.

Matt mentally reviewed what he'd told her, Jack Hogan, and Martini Al at lunch. He'd spoken cautiously then, fearful that sooner or later the nature of his relationship with "Raymond" would get back to either Suzanne or the IOC. He had to decide how forthcoming he wanted to be, and chose his words with care. "Tony Fortunado . . . the guy who Intelligence has tied to Angelo Albeneti and Mom's Pie . . . is Albanese family-connected. Even in the old French Connection days, the Albanese were less involved in heroin trafficking than some of the other families. But today, there's a new generation making the climb up through the ranks. Younger guys like Tony Nails see how much money they're missing out on, letting the Colombians, Chinese, and criminal elements from the former Soviet bloc control the flow of dope into New York."

Rhoda was assembling the bits and pieces of what lay *behind* Stuart's words. He was a guy who'd just returned to the street from five years working Intelligence, and had access to information to which few squad detectives were privy. She got the impression he'd made a study of the bigger organized crime picture, and possessed valuable expertise in that realm. "So you're thinking what?" she asked. "That maybe Rodriguez was the Dominican's dirty cop? And DaCosta belongs to the Italians? That the next Albanese generation is trying to engineer some kind of power play through DaCosta?"

"It's a theory I've been kicking around the past twenty-four hours," he allowed. "You think about it, it makes the executions of Darryl Johnson and Fat Danny Washington fit."

"Especially if it turns out the new Red Top leadership is less ambitious, and easier to manipulate," she agreed.

Matt nodded. "Johnson and Fat Danny were Santos guys, whether they'd be willing to admit it or not. He supplied them with product, set the prices, and thereby controlled cash flow. He let them strut their stuff on his streets and carry away enough cash to keep them happy, but he's the occupying army's general. He lets them do what they do because he doesn't want to do it himself."

"An enviable position," she mused.

"Exactly what the next generation of Albanese soldiers must be thinking, too."

"And thinking, you boom Red Top stash houses, it might be a good way to undermine confidence in Tío Paco's ability to control his turf." Rhoda had the ball and was advancing it quickly upfield. "Santos is the *patrón*, which means he should be able to buy the intelligence he needs to keep the cops at bay. If he can't, the pitchers might be willing to listen to someone who says he can."

"And who's more enshrouded in myth, and better positioned to seem credible, than the good old Italian Mafia?" Matt asked. "Most people still believe all that shit they saw in Scorcese and Coppola movies."

"And every time someone like John Gotti or Sammy the Bull grabs a headline, the wiseguy image is reinforced in all our minds. It doesn't matter the majority of them are soft and complacent now. What matters is that the old image still sells."

It was uncharacteristic for Gina Galati to hear from Clarence DaCosta unless Tony Fortunado called her first, to say something was in the works. When the phone rang at 3:48 that Saturday afternoon, she was trying to decide what she wanted for supper, and if she really wanted to make the trip to Staten Island tomorrow to visit her Aunt Rose Marie. It was several months since she last took Claude there, and she felt a certain degree of guilt. Rose Marie was her dead father's only sister. She was divorced and had lived alone for over ten years. Gina and little Claude were the only family she had left.

"Gina," DaCosta's familiar voice came to her from down the line. "You got dinner plans?"

While a vivid image of the rippling muscles across his shoulders and chest flashed before her mind's eye, she wondered what this was about. "Sounds like a leading question," she replied cautiously.

"I thought we could get a bite somewhere. You get the dyke to watch the kid?"

Gina hadn't accepted his invitation, and already he was lining up a baby-sitter. "Slow down a sec," she complained. "What's this about? I don't get it."

"You and me," he said matter-of-factly. "You know. Getting to know each other a little better. Seems to me, we've got a lot more in common than either of us wants to admit."

Like, how cold-blooded we both are, she thought, and it led her to wonder yet again about what actually drove him. She had clear motivations for why she'd chosen her own path, and supposed he had his, too. He was half black, yet seemed to hate anyone of African ancestry. She guessed it had something to do with who his father was, suspecting there was a whole involved story. While she doubted his and hers had very much in common, she still felt inclined to humor him. It was months since she'd gotten laid, and no man who came to mind embodied more physical appeal than DaCosta did. Not only was he gorgeous, but the element of danger surrounding him also fueled her fire.

"Where'd you have in mind?" she asked.

"Tommaso's? I ain't been there in years."

Gina could well imagine why. Tommaso's was a Bensonhurst, Brooklyn, landmark, catering to a boisterous Italian-American clientele that often wore its racism on its sleeve. A black man—tawny hair, blue eyes, and Italian surname or not—wasn't likely to get a warm reception. Nor was a woman who dined there as his date. "I'm more in a red-meat mood," she replied. "Peter Luger is almost walking distance from here. You game for that?" It was a Saturday, and the fact that Peter Luger was the gold standard by which all other steakhouses in America were measured didn't deter her from making the suggestion. If he wanted this date badly enough, he'd find a way to get a table.

"Not a snowball's chance in hell we could get a reservation," he complained.

"Use your considerable charm," she suggested. "I'll talk to Naomi, tell her you're picking me up at eight." And before he could discuss the matter further, she cradled the receiver.

Moments after he and Rhoda Bolivar arrived at the Three-seven, Matt Stuart received a call from the patrol force watch commander downstairs. Matt was at his desk when he took it, studying a police artist sketch that had arrived earlier, via fax. The subject of the drawing was a dark-haired woman in a Brooklyn Dodgers ball cap. She had almond-shaped, almost Oriental eyes, sharp cheekbones, and a wide, square jaw. To judge from the amount of detail the rendering embodied, Sal Sapienze had a good memory. One thing that struck both Matt and Rhoda was how young she looked.

"Yeah, Cap," he replied when the watch commander identified himself.

"You asked us to check into the sweep anti-crime made right before those hits went down Wednesday? I don't think you're gonna like what we turned up. Not any more'n I do, Lou."

"Hit me," Matt suggested.

"It wasn't the dispatcher put that call out over the radio. Someone tapped the borough command frequency. Had access to anti-crime's codes."

Which meant it had to be an inside job. Those unit codes were switched on a regular basis, to prevent just this sort of thing from happening. Stuart was led to the same conclusion the watch commander had undoubtedly reached. The interloper was a renegade cop. But unlike the watch commander, Matt now had a good idea just who the bad apple was.

Twelve

Deputy Chief Simon Ogilvy had spent much of that dreary Saturday in the basement of his Douglaston, Queens, house trying to assemble the new home entertainment wall unit his wife had purchased at one of those do-it-yourself furniture emporiums out on the Island. The piece was a monster, measuring five feet in height and eight feet long, designed to hold a big-screen TV, VCR, the components of a stereo system with Surround Sound capability, and a multitude of CDs and videotape cassettes. The individual parts, fabricated of flakeboard laminated with walnut veneer, each weighed a ton. The instructions were a muddled translation from the original Japanese or Swedish. Two hours into the project, Ogilvy's sixteen-year-old daughter, Corinne, had grown bored with the painstaking assembly process and abandoned the field. Left alone, he'd muttered curses each time a screwdriver slipped and he banged his knuckles, or Part A refused to match up with Part N. When Matt Stuart called at a few minutes after four to request an audience, Simon was still miles from the end of the tunnel, no light in sight, and nearly at wit's end.

Marjorie showed Stuart to the basement on his arrival, then remained behind a moment, arms folded, to survey the progress made since lunch. "I hope you're handy, Lieutenant," she told their guest. "It would be helpful if at least one of you was."

Ogilvy tossed the directions aside and struggled up from his knees to stand. "I'm blessed with a daughter who has the attention span of an Irish setter, and a wife who wishes she'd married a plumber." He shook Stuart's hand and led the way past the antique pool table toward an ornate corner bar. "But plumbers make too much money in this city, and as a small boy, I was assured by my sainted mother that all rich people go to hell."

Marjorie tossed her head and started back toward the stairs. "He's got a seven o'clock dinner engagement, Lieutenant. Means he should be headed for the shower no later than six."

Simon scowled as he stepped behind the bar to open a tiny refrigerator. "What would our lives be without them?" he asked. "Beer?"

"Sure," Stuart accepted. "After the day I've had, I could use one."

Clearly sympathetic, the chief gestured with a bottle of Beck's toward the partially assembled wall unit. "Tell me about it," he said. "Grab a stool."

"Didn't mean to interrupt your work," Matt apologized. He eased into the upholstered comfort of a bar chair and absorbed his surroundings. The walls of the bar area were done in raised-paneled oak, the wood stained dark like the interior of an old English pub. There was a good-quality dartboard hung on one wall, and the surface of the bar itself was mahogany, scarred by cigarette burns and decades of use. It had probably been salvaged from some venerable old watering hole destined for the wrecking ball.

"Not to worry," the chief told him. "Tomorrow's forecast is almost as shitty as today's. Relaxing as these projects are, I figure I'll stretch this out as long as I can."

Stuart accepted an opened bottle from his former boss and raised it in a toast. "Funny. You don't look that relaxed."

Ogilvy clicked his beer with Matt's and took a pull before leaning forward. "Fuck you, too," he said good-naturedly. "So what's so important, you traipse clear to the far reaches of Queens?"

The lieutenant reached to an inside jacket pocket, withdrew a folded sheet of paper, and opened it. "I told you what we found in the Rodriguez bank box. What I didn't say over the phone is we think we know who took him down." He flattened the shiny fax paper on the bar surface between them, turning the sketch of the young woman in Simon's direction. "Sal Sapienze saw her at Mom's Pie Thursday night. In the company of a Special Ops cop named DaCosta. He's their Manhattan North Street Crime Unit liaison."

Ogilvy knew who DaCosta was, and nodded. The nature of his assignment meant he had more freedom of movement than most cops, and more opportunities to stray. Chief Jerry Mannion was supposed to keep close tabs on all his liaisons, but in reality, how could he? In Ogilvy's estimation, Mannion was much more comfortable with statistics than with people, and by definition, his liaisons were a maverick, hard-to-control breed. They were spread out all over the city, working with extreme autonomy, moving from one precinct to another within their assigned sectors.

"He spends a lot of time in the Three-seven," Stuart continued. "An informant puts him in the beat-up old blue gypsy cab he drives on the street outside the building where Rodriguez and his lady friend were whacked."

Ogilvy studied the drawing, and then Stuart's face. He'd never seen the lieutenant look more serious. "How reliable is your informant?" he asked.

"Let's just say when he gave up that little tidbit, he was under extreme duress. I have every reason to believe its veracity."

"No idea who she is?" Simon was studying the face beneath the Dodgers ball cap: pretty, undeniably, but one that looked no older than his sixteen-year-old daughter's. The notion chilled him.

"No, but DaCosta does, and Sal thinks Angelo Cheesecake knows who she is, too." He went on to describe Sapienze's report on the series of events transpiring at Mom's Pie that night. "I want to pull Raymond out of there, Chief," he concluded. "If DaCosta knows him from the academy, he's in serious danger. The other night, he stayed in his gypsy cab. Next time, he might wander into the store."

Ogilvy tried to look at it from all sides as he took another slow sip of his beer. When he spoke, he was thinking aloud. "We could allege that your informant's tip, and a subsequent surveillance of DaCosta, is what led us to Albeneti. One dirty cop killing another is more'n enough justification for launching a full-scale Intel Division investigation."

A weary smile spread slowly from the corners of Stuart's mouth. "I was hoping you might say that. I don't have the manpower, and don't have the means of hiding certain information that might be crucial to the overall outcome."

Ogilvy wondered if he was just tired from a long day spent tearing his hair out. He'd just lost Stuart. "Come again? I don't get your drift."

"I've no idea which, or how many, cops, other than DaCosta, might be involved in this," the lieutenant explained. "Any corruption scandal, no matter the scope, could hurt people I have no interest in pissing off."

Ogilvy hadn't gotten where he was on the big-brass ladder by not being adept at reading between the lines. "Just how much of what you've uncovered *don't* you want Deputy Commissioner Albrecht to know, Matthew?"

Stuart shifted in his bar chair and contemplated his former boss for a long moment before responding. "Johnny Rodriguez was as dirty as the inside of a garbage can, Chief. He was also one of Suzanne Albrecht's FAs."

Simon registered surprise. "How do you know that?"

"She told me. The same day she called me into her office to say I was being reassigned to the Three-seven. She didn't like the looks of how her man took that bullet. If there was a brush fire, she wanted me to put it out before it got so big people noticed."

"She told you that, too?" Ogilvy asked, eyebrows raised.

Stuart shrugged. "In so many words? No . . . but yes. For all I know, she's suspected Rodriguez of being on the take for months. Could be it blew up in her face while she was busy hiding it under her hat. I doubt it, though. I think it caught her by surprise."

"One of her own goddamn FAs," Simon marveled, more to himself than to Stuart. "And how does DaCosta fit into this?"

Stuart described his rival-faction hypothesis to Ogilvy, admitting it was still in the formative stages. "We know Rodriguez was milking someone for a whole lot of money. We suspect it was Frank Santos, probably in exchange for intelligence. There's evidence connecting Da-Costa to Angelo Albeneti, and Sal Sapienze has connected Angelo to Tony 'Nails' Fortunado. That's a more or less direct link between Da-Costa and the Albanese crime family."

"And if DaCosta did in fact take out Rodriguez?"

"Along with those two high-level pitchers I mentioned."

"Right. It could be construed that the Albanese are positioning themselves for a major move into the Washington Heights heroin and crack cocaine trade, Matthew."

Ogilvy didn't need to say how much that notion scared him. Stuart, too, knew how fragile the peace between the city's major dope traffickers always was. The Colombians, Russians, Chinese, Jamaicans, Dominicans, and everyone else in the mix all hated each other. They only played nicely together because they had to. If what Matt had brought him this afternoon was even close to being accurate, the city was on the verge of a drug war the likes of which it had never seen.

"You brought this to me instead of your direct superior, Lieutenant," Ogilvy continued. "Allegedly because you need Intel's help to launch the appropriate investigation. Why do I think it's not the only reason?"

Stuart met it head-on, his gaze unwavering as he replied. "I know what Deputy Commissioner Albrecht's motives are, sir. By that I mean, how much she wants the big prize. And knowing that, I don't think the city of New York can risk it: her attempting to save her own political ass by trying to sweep this under the carpet."

Ogilvy doubted the lieutenant could have stated it more bluntly. He admired him for it: how little he cared about the political ramifications of the decisions he made. There were plenty of stand-up cops on the Job, but few who possessed a zealot's passion for the work as Matt Stuart did. Stuart only seemed to care how the judgment calls he made might affect the citizens he'd sworn to protect. "You're playing with fire and asking me to join you," he said matter-of-factly. "In the greater scheme of things, Suzanne Albrecht is my direct superior too, Matthew."

"I'm bringing you intelligence on a dirty cop. One who's likely had a hand in killing another dirty cop," Stuart countered. He pointed to the sketch still on the bar between them. "I'm bringing you a shooter with direct ties to Angelo 'Cheesecake' Albeneti, a man long suspected by your division of ties to organized crime. I've got a dead cop's dead girlfriend who used to stash for the biggest Dominican *patrón* in upper Manhattan. Before this ticking bomb blows the whole fucking city sky-high, I need your help trying to disarm it."

Ogilvy drained the remainder of his beer, slammed the empty onto the mahogany in frustration, and heaved himself away from the bar to pace. "You're gonna have to give the Ice Maiden something. A direction you're headed, if nothing else."

"I'll ask her what she knows about DaCosta. Say there are rumors. Nothing specific, nothing substantiated. That way, she won't be surprised to learn later that you're investigating him, too."

"So meanwhile, I authorize a surveillance of DaCosta on the QT. Him and who else?"

"Tony Nails, boss. Sapienze is convinced he's Albeneti's conduit to the Albanese organization."

"You realize if Deputy Commissioner Albrecht ever so much as *suspects* you've withheld crucial information from her, you and I never had this conversation," Ogilvy warned. "My people developed these leads through Intel Division's own investigative efforts."

Stuart placed his half-full bottle gently on the bar and stood, nodding. "I hear shopping mall security can be a nice gig. Air-conditioned summers; heated winters. And think of all the young mothers pushing baby strollers I could hit on."

"Not quite your cup of tea," Ogilvy growled. "Stay and finish your beer."

"Thanks," the lieutenant begged off. "I'm saving myself. For the women on the Brooklyn singles scene. It's Saturday, right?"

"There *ain't* no Brooklyn singles scene, smart-ass."

Stuart grimaced, pointed a finger at his old boss, and shot him with it before starting for the stairs. "Damn, Chief. Could be another lonely night."

Going west across Queens, hordes of Long Island theatergoers and other Saturday night revelers headed toward Manhattan with Stuart as he drove toward the Midtown Tunnel on the LIE. Forced to move at a crawl, Matt used the time to think about what he'd proposed to Simon Ogilvy, and how many ways it could backfire on him. Few people on the Job knew the power of the ambition driving Suzanne Albrecht better than he did. What he didn't know was how much his former lover might be hiding from him, what she already knew or might suspect. Within two days of being inserted to help save her ass, Matt had stumbled on Clarence DaCosta and what looked like a clear connection to the Albanese crime empire. It was too much, too soon. She *had* to know something she hadn't told him, and frankly, the notion bothered the hell out of him.

When Matt Stuart had called her home number late that afternoon to request a meeting, First Deputy Commissioner Suzanne Albrecht suggested he make it early. The CEO of a Wall Street brokerage had invited her to join him and the mayor for the Red Sox game that evening in his luxury box at Yankee Stadium. She didn't care much for baseball, but her host and his guest were crucial to her ambitions. Hizzoner was a shoo-in for reelection next fall, and he alone would choose NYPD's next commissioner. The money people responsible for financing his campaign needed to know their interests would be protected, and would want to feel they'd had a voice in his choice. Hence an invite like tonight's, where, in a relaxed, jovial atmosphere, they could test the waters, see what kind of team player this bright but reputedly hard-nosed career policewoman was. Suzanne had made a study of the mayor and knew precisely how she intended to work him. He, like she, was a political animal. Like many other dominant males of their species, his Achilles' heel was attractive women. She wouldn't dress to kill, but would lose the eyeglasses and soften the edges ever so subtly.

It worried her to wonder what Stuart needed to discuss so early in his tenure at the Three-seven. She was eager to keep the lid on any corruption that attached itself to Johnny Rodriguez, but couldn't imagine what Matt might have uncovered in only three days. Intelligence was notoriously difficult to gather on the mean streets of Washington Heights, where cops and the citizenry coexisted in a constant state of siege. In her experience, big breaks in homicides always came within the first forty-eight hours. Otherwise, an investigation of that sort could take weeks or even months to unfold. If the truth be known, she hoped it would take at least three months . . . and eight days: the amount of time left to expire before the current PC left his throne for a warmer climate.

It was five-thirty when the doorman buzzed from the lobby to announce Stuart's arrival. Not knowing how long this audience might last, Suzanne had already showered and dressed for her evening at the ballpark. When she answered the door to him, she fully expected the look of surprise that registered on his face. He knew how she felt about spectator sports in general, and baseball in particular, and yet there she stood in Yankees ball cap, a white silk turtleneck, and a blue satin warm-up jacket emblazoned with tragically dead catcher Thurmond Munson's name and number. The jacket was a gift from a well-meaning nephew more than a decade ago, and had hung in her closet ever since.

"If I didn't know better, I might think you were going to a ball game," he greeted her. "But naw."

"Off my case, Lieutenant. I'm being politically expedient."

"So I see. I thought only mayors and fathers of small children dressed in clown outfits like that." He moved past her into the apartment's foyer to gaze about. "Always saw you as more the pitcher type than the catcher."

"This a duty call or a social one?" she asked. "If it's duty, those last comments sound a whole lot like insubordination."

Stuart hadn't been in her apartment for nearly six months. He paused to take in the changes she'd made to the living room. "New carpet," he commented, ignoring her dig. "Persian?"

"Umm. Boteh Kermin. Circa 1910." She led the way onto and across its eleven-by-seventeen pattern of paisley and lotus blossoms gone mad. Choosing a blue leather armchair, she sat and nodded to the settee across from her.

He dropped onto a cushion, moving like a man who was tired after a long day. "I'll try to make this short and sweet," he said. "This afternoon, my squad discovered a safe-deposit box that your FA rented at a bank branch about a mile from his apartment."

Suzanne felt her heart rate quicken. "Bet you didn't come here to tell me about the car title and life insurance policy you found in it."

"Nope. Eighty-two thousand dollars, mostly small bills. And another twenty grand in designer threads hanging in his closet at home. His hand was in someone's cookie jar, Suzanne."

"It's definitely his signature on the signature card?" she asked.

"And definitely his clothes in his closet. Your guy was dirty. With a capital D."

"God*dammit*!" Unable to control her fury, she looked hard at Stuart, her mind reeling with all the implications of what he'd just reported. If the media got hold of this, it could spell disaster for her. "I've got to hand it to you, Lieutenant. You do work quickly."

He didn't seem ready to concede he'd accomplished all that much. "I have this nasty feeling we've barely touched the tip of this one, boss. We got lucky. I mean, what kind of idiot stashes almost a hundred large in payoff money in a bank box under his own name?"

"One who thinks he'll never get caught," she replied. It was hard for her to read Stuart's face. How much, she wondered, was he leaving unsaid? "Who's the money from?"

His gaze unwavering, he merely shrugged. "My best guess? The Dominicans. They're the ones running the show up there, and they're the

ones recently been ripped off. Word on the street says a cop was responsible for killing him. Could be Rodriguez was playing both ends against
the middle."

Suzanne's greatest fear was that her renegade FA had gone native, and
what Stuart was reporting seemed to suggest just that. During his brief
but dramatic tenure at the helm of the NYPD, former commissioner Bill
Bratton had tried to put safeguards in place to prevent just this sort of
thing from happening. Unfortunately, the throne's current occupant was
nowhere near the visionary or the zealot Bratton had been. The twice-
monthly Compstat meetings, aimed at keeping the channels of communication between patrol force, Detective Bureau, and the Big Building
open, had become monthly. The links of communication Bratton had
forged between local patrol forces and detective squads were also beginning to deteriorate citywide.

"If more than one cop was involved in those robberies, I need to know
how many and who, Lieutenant." She heard how cold her tone had gone,
and tried to find some measure of warmth. Stuart could be instrumental
in helping prevent disaster, or he could leave her in the breeze. "I'm
sorry if I sound upset," she apologized. "I'm sure you realize exactly
how much I've got at stake here."

"The whole city's got a lot at stake," he reminded her. "Not just you."

He wasn't making this easy. But then, why should he? He'd lost a
child and wife to the Job. He'd fallen in love with her and seen the Job
get in the way of it. All the while, his own dedication to the work never
wavered. Indeed, the adversity he'd faced had galvanized that devotion.
"Understood," she said.

"The name Clarence DaCosta ring any bells?" he asked her.

She frowned, scouring her memory banks, and shook her head.
"Should it?"

"Too early to know. He's a Special Ops cop. Street Crime Unit liaison with Manhattan North. Spends a lot of time in the Three-seven, I
understand."

"He would, wouldn't he? What of it?"

Matt wouldn't commit. "You've got access to a much bigger branch
of the grapevine than I do. You might shake it, see what the word on this
guy is. The rumblings I've heard are so faint, I wouldn't want to give
them any weight. Not without a whole lot more to go on."

"What sort of rumblings?" she asked.

"Not gonna go there, Suzanne," he said, standing his ground. "Too many good cops have been hurt by loose talk. Nose around. Let me know what you hear."

The only word Gina Galati could find to describe how she felt, seated across a table for two from Clarence DaCosta at the Peter Luger Steakhouse Saturday evening, was *strange*. Admittedly, the idea of what might happen between them later tonight excited her. Long ago, she'd learned how to separate the man from the act, and go far away to an isolated island of self-centered fantasy. DaCosta appeared to have all the requisite physical tools, and the sort of confidence it took to use them to effect. Still, he seemed nearly as crippled by some unspoken hatred as she was, and she'd never climbed into bed with anyone who embodied as much bitter anger and outrage as she carried locked inside herself. They would remain forever strangers, the two of them, doomed by an isolation that life itself had created in each, but she wondered, nonetheless, what made him tick. Where, for instance, did *his* fantasies take him when he found himself wrapped in a lover's arms?

To add to his air of mystery, DaCosta had appeared at her door in an elegant cream-colored suit with an open-collared black silk shirt. Now, he lounged slouching in the chair across from her, those spooky blue eyes flicking here and there around the crowded room, then landing back on her face to study it. "After the ball cap and baggy kid clothes, I gotta admit, you caught me by surprise," he said casually. "I'm watching the way men look at you. Clearly, I ain't the only one you've impressed."

Gina stared back just as directly as he stared at her, absorbing what was clearly meant as a compliment. She'd abandoned the loose-fitting garb she favored for her work and dressed for effect tonight. The simple Jil Sander knit dress she'd chosen left her back bare from shoulders to coccyx, and hugged every dip and curve from throat to mid-thigh. Apparently, it was working. Naomi had practically jumped her when she stopped to deliver Claude. On arrival here, a group of brash young suits with that aggressive, trading-floor look to them had fallen self-consciously silent as she passed.

"I'm full of surprises," she replied coolly.

Having since devoured a monster porterhouse, rare, with the steady, methodical concentration a leopard brings to eating prey, he grunted and pushed his empty plate away. Like every animal aspect Gina saw in the man, watching him eat had sent a delicious tingle the length of her spine. "It's funny, y'know?" he said. "I've been an outcast all my life. No matter how you treat me, I'll still resent you for being something I never can. And I ain't talking full of surprises."

"Being what? A woman?"

The blue eyes flashed fire. "Someone who knows who she is. I don't."

"And who am I?" she challenged, eyebrows arched.

"A beautiful Italian bitch, with ice water running in her veins. Some woman's daughter. Some daddy's little girl. All that apple pie shit, no matter what kinda twisted chick you think you turned out to be."

A sad smile creased the corners of her mouth as she met his stare. Slowly, she shook her head. "My daddy had a passion for the ponies. Couldn't control it, so his bookie sent a goon to see him. Got a little overenthusiastic. Beat him to death. But hey . . . every fairytale's got a happy ending, right? My apple-pie mama *married* that bookie, and lived out her days in the lap of luxury." She paused to brush aside an irritating wisp of hair fallen from the elegant twist she'd coiled atop her head. "Funny, ain't it? You wish you were full-blooded Sicilian, and I hate every Sicilian male in this city. With a burning passion."

He continued to stare at her, his expression now a mixture of surprise and confusion. "I don't get it. You hate them so much, why work for them?"

"Same reason you do," she replied. "Money's too good."

It was ten o'clock by the time Matt Stuart left the restaurant where he'd stopped to dine after his meeting with Suzanne Albrecht, and started up the street toward his car. He'd found himself at emotional loose ends, leaving her apartment, and with a hankering for Italian food. Lonely, he'd wanted an atmosphere filled with noise and life and people with no knowledge of his disappointments or his cares. He'd headed out Prospect Avenue in Brooklyn, his destination Tommaso's, on Eighty-sixth Street in Bensonhurst. The same maître d' who'd greeted him and Suzanne the dozens of times they'd dined there showed him to a quiet table along one wall. He tipped Matt to the existence of a 1990 Altesino Brunello di Montalcino, just arrived in their cellar, and left him alone to presumably dine in peace. Matt marveled first at his own stupidity for having come here, and then at the strength of the disappointment he still felt five months after Suzanne had thrown him over. His encounter with

her in her office two days ago didn't have the same effect on him as seeing her in her home. They'd never made passionate love on her desk, but
had, a hundred times, all over her apartment. At dinner, he came to realize he no longer had any real feel for who the woman was, but still
couldn't shake the ache of emptiness she'd created when she left. How
strange was that? he wondered. Apparently, he was still in love with the
idea of Suzanne, but no longer in love with the person by that name.

He'd lingered over the entire bottle of Brunello di Montalcino and was
slightly drunk by the time he reached his car. While fumbling the key
into the ignition, he realized it was way back in high school, the last time
he'd driven under the influence. Then, a vivid memory of the sound his
bumper had made when crushing his son to death against his garage
door forced him to switch the engine off again. A logjam of pent-up
emotion suddenly broke loose. Overwhelmed, he grabbed the wheel with
both hands, leaned forward to rest his forehead against it, and cried.

There was never any doubt in Clarence DaCosta's mind as to whether
Gina Galati would invite him upstairs after dinner. When he'd called that
afternoon to ask her out, he still wondered how mutual their attraction
might be. But one look at her little black dress told him everything he
needed to know. If he wanted to move, the light was green.

DaCosta's motivations for wanting Gina were complex. Regardless of
the fact that she had the kind of body that made the proposition pleasant
enough, she was connected to the Albanese crime organization. In order
to better access that venerable la Cosa Nostra family, and ultimately endear himself to it, Clarence needed the means to better understand it. His
only other Albanese contact, Tony "Nails" Fortunado, hadn't exactly
opened his arms to him, despite the invaluable favors he'd done. The way
all made guys were, Tony was arrogant and cocky in dealing with everyone who wasn't. He treated DaCosta the same way he treated women:
solicitous when he needed a favor, but always with the slightest edge of
contempt. That is, women with the exception of Gina. With her, he
seemed to fear the price he would pay if he ever gave her serious grief,
and that notion intrigued Clarence. He'd done extensive research on
Gina Galati and had turned up next to nothing. Her father was the victim
of a suspected example killing fourteen years ago. Her stepfather, a retired bookmaker named Sonny Galati, lived in Florida. Gina's mother

was dead. Gina lived alone with her little boy on the Brooklyn waterfront. When the necessity arose, the Albanese engaged her to do contract kills for them, which meant she was highly trusted. Her ancestry was pure Sicilian, so far as Clarence could determine. Because she was physically attracted to him, he hoped to use that fact to further cement the tenuous bond he'd established with the Albanese, the most ambitious of the old Mafia crime families in New York.

En route to Gina's floor, they stopped to collect her son, Claude, from his baby-sitter. At the elevator, Naomi Ebbcomb, clad in a clinging satin robe, greeted them. On seeing Clarence, she gave her neighbor a look that could have frozen alcohol.

"Heartbreaker," he murmured in Gina's ear as the elevator car got them under way toward the fifth floor.

Radiant with the flush of wine on her cheeks and her babe in arms, Gina flashed a wicked smile. "Wasn't too pleased to see *you* with me, eh, boyo?"

"I'd say she definitely had other plans. I ain't, uh, interrupting nothing, am I?"

She shifted the child on her hip, tossed her head, and sneered. "In her dreams. No matter how many times you say no, some people just don't get it."

When the car arrived at her floor, Gina handed Clarence the baby and heaved the slide-up doors open. Revealed through wrought-iron grillwork gates, the loft beyond was impressive in size.

"Welcome to my humble home," she said, and pulled the gate aside.

To the west, out a series of tall, cast-iron-framed windows, the whole of downtown Manhattan loomed huge, skyscrapers sparkling like gems in a jewelry case. The lights of the loft were left low, so that much of what illuminated the interior was the reflection of that skyline off an acre of polished maple flooring. There was a kitchen against the north wall, open on two sides with an island out front. Along the east wall, to Da-Costa's right, partial walls sectioned off what looked to be a sleeping area and a bathroom. In the center of the huge living room, pieces of burnt ocher leather furniture faced each other across a twenty-by-twenty square of white plush carpeting.

"Nice," he murmured, advancing. "I could fit eight of my place in here. Easy."

"And I'll bet your rent's still twice as high as mine." Gina carried

Claude to his crib, screened from her own king-size bed by a four-foot half wall, and laid him gently inside. She opened a closet and shrugged out of her light, spring-weight coat. All the while, she felt DaCosta again admire the tight, well-defined musculature of her shoulders and slender back. She turned after hanging the coat and caught him.

"Like what you see?" She advanced on him as she said it, her calves flexing with each step in her three-inch heels, her hips swaying seductively.

"What's not t' like?" he asked.

She stopped before him and reached to finger the lapel of his jacket. "Willing to observe two rules? You are, I think we can have a pretty good time."

"And they are?" he asked.

"One, you don't tell me *anything* about how you feel." As she spoke, she took a step back and peeled her dress from her shoulders, slowly drawing the knit fabric down toward her elbows. "Two, you don't tell me what you want, or ask me what I want. You don't say nothing at all." Her arms worked free of her dress, she tugged the garment toward her waist, the ripe fullness of bare, upswept breasts revealed. Then, without missing a beat, she hooked thumbs to wriggle the fabric down over her hips.

For the month he'd known her, it had been difficult for Clarence to get an accurate idea of just how spectacular her body might be. She'd always worn baggy teenage-kid clothes that did nothing to flatter the physique now revealed to him. She had a belly as taut as a drumhead and not a sag in evidence anywhere. It was hard to believe this was the mother of an eighteen-month-old child. Following the rules, he began to disrobe without a word.

Thirteen

The Spanish-language newspaper that employed investigative reporter Luis Esquivel bore the name *La Paz*. In his native tongue it meant "The Peace," and to him seemed particularly ironic. The streets of Queens and Brooklyn, New York, seemed only slightly more peaceful to him than those of his native Medellín, Colombia. There, when he was eight, his prosecutor father was cut down in the street outside his home by gunmen of the Medellín cocaine cartel. For the next ten years, until he matriculated to Rice University in Houston, Texas, he and every law-abiding citizen had endured the cartel's famed reign of terror. Today, in Queens, the car bombings of his childhood were fewer and farther between, but drug-related drive-by shootings were no less commonplace.

Twenty years ago, on the day of his martyred father's funeral, Luis had consecrated himself to avenging the death of Oscar Esquivel. For two years out of college after earning a degree in journalism, he'd worked for the Bogotá daily, *La Prensa,* reporting on the efforts made by an elite unit of the Colombian federal police—or DAS—to ferret out and destroy clandestine cocaine-processing factories. By 1995 Luis had become so incensed by an apparent lack of U.S. commitment to stemming the flow of cocaine and heroin beyond its borders, he took a staff job on the Queens, New York, paper. His ambition was to become a voice of indignation within the Hispanic community, to light a fire fueled by the horror of escalating drug-related violence, to fan it, and hope it might spread to other communities throughout New York City.

Within one month of his arrival, Luis was so thoroughly discouraged by the apathy he encountered everywhere—and a total lack of *simpatía* between the various Spanish-speaking communities—that he nearly lost faith. It was the murder of an eight-year-old Guatemalan girl one block from his Corona, Queens, apartment which turned his dismay into a fresher, more focused zeal than he'd yet to see in himself. The victim of a stray bullet fired during a turf dispute between a Guatemalan gang and Jamaican posse interlopers, Maria Elena Gutierrez lay sprawled in a pool of her own blood, half her face missing, when Luis arrived on the scene. The hysterical wailing of her grief-stricken mother had echoed deep down the halls of memory to a time when the wailing of his own mother had reached the same helplessly forlorn pitch. Eighteen years after the fact, he could vividly recall the murder of his father as if it had just happened, and what had then seemed so senseless to a ten-year-old boy now seemed even more senseless to him. His father had not worn jungle fatigues or carried a gun, but he was a soldier in the fight against social and moral corruption just the same. Maria Elena Gutierrez was no more than an innocent bystander, left shamelessly unprotected by the adult members of her society.

For the four years since, Esquivel had dedicated himself to an exhaustive investigation of the drug apparatus responsible for destabilizing the fragile fabric of New York's immigrant tapestry. Using contacts developed on the street, in the police department, DEA, and FBI, he had identified dozens of high-level players in the heroin and cocaine game. In weekly columns, he detailed who they were and the scope of their activities, one kingpin at a time, throughout the city's five boroughs. Week by week, as the picture of how tons of heroin and cocaine arrived in America, and as the channels through which they were distributed became ever more clear, three names stood out more than any others. In nearly every article, some mention was made of the Cali cartel overseer in New York, Roberto Santiago, and two former Russian KGB agents situated high up in the Brighton Beach branch of the so-called Odessa Mafiya. In an apparent alliance with tentacles that reached from the Amazon region of Colombia to the shores of the Caspian Sea, the Cali cartel, Russian organized crime, and immigrants from the Dominican Republic now dominated the supply side of the New York drug scene.

Over the past month, Esquivel had written four articles detailing how that unholy alliance worked, both domestically and abroad. He'd named dozens of names, tracing the organizational structure of the Odessa Mafiya from Brooklyn to Miami to Ukraine. On the Colombian side, he'd profiled Roberto Santiago and the billionaire puppeteers in his native country who controlled him. Word on the street was that those persons, so vividly drawn in his exposés, were none too happy about all the free press.

Unlike his father, Luis did carry a gun. He'd received his first death threat two years ago, and at the time, a DEA agent made him a gift of a 9 mm Beretta Model 92F. That Saturday night, once he finished putting the Sunday edition of *La Paz* to bed, Luis strapped the weapon and its lightweight nylon holster on the way he always did before taking to the streets. It no longer felt odd hanging there beneath his left arm, and tonight, his satin New York Cosmos warm-up jacket concealed it sufficiently should he choose to make a pit stop for an *aguardiente* nightcap at El Rhino, his favorite neighborhood watering hole.

Four winters spent in the American Northeast had still not seen Esquivel's equatorial blood acclimatized to cold weather. The dreary late May day that had greeted him that morning was not so cold as one typical of winter, but a spell of warm spring weather had made today's thirty-degree falloff objectionable enough. He'd donned a wool sweater and hadn't removed it all day. Tonight, as he left the newspaper offices and walked out into a bone-chilling damp, he was glad for it.

Always, since embarking on his crusade of exposure and constant harassment of New York's drug lords, Luis took care to be extra observant of his surroundings. Tonight was no exception. He scanned the sidewalks on both sides of Grand Avenue, and then the street itself, for anything that might seem unusual. His father's murder and the dozens of reprisal shootings and bombings he'd covered as a reporter were enough to persuade him to take threats against his own life seriously. On the other hand, as he started toward the newspaper's chain-link-fenced parking lot, he was aware of how little hope he actually had should anyone make a determined try at eliminating him.

The weather seemed to have dampened the city's spirits, with traffic at eleven o'clock lighter than usual for a Saturday night. Luis had finished up an hour earlier than he typically did, and entertained hopes of maybe meeting some attractive new woman at El Rhino. Now, he wondered what sort of luck he might have. In a city that literally never slept, it was rare when a main artery like Grand Avenue carried as little traffic as it did at that moment. He had just entered the parking lot, busy trying to come up with an alternative hunting ground should his first choice prove dead, when he spotted the shadow of movement beneath his car.

"Hey!" he yelled, and simultaneously reached to haul out his gun.

Startled, a black-clad figure reached up beneath the car to retrieve or adjust something. In the next instant, Esquivel's aging Honda Civic was engulfed in a huge ball of flame. The concussion from the explosion was so violent that Luis was stopped in his tracks, then hurled backward, a shard of metal grazing his left cheek only millimeters from his eye, and another impacting his right hip. He felt the wind knocked from his lungs as he landed hard on his back, but was too astonished at first to even fight for air. Flaming bits of debris rained down all around him prompting him to raise his arms to protect his face. Only then did he feel the panic of being unable to draw breath. All the while, he was cognizant enough to understand what had just happened. Someone had tried to kill him by wiring a bomb to his car. Luckily for him, that someone had screwed it up, and undoubtedly had just been killed in the process.

Frank Sinatra was singing "New York, New York" on the Yankee Stadium sound system when Suzanne Albrecht received a cellular call from the Operations Desk. On-field play had been slow that night, but the umpiring crew had not thought the drizzle significant enough to warrant cancellation of the game. It was nearly midnight by the time it was over, the home team losing to the hated Red Sox, 7 to 2, not that Suzanne had much noticed. For the most part, she'd been preoccupied with parrying her host's less-than-subtle sexual innuendo while, for the mayor's benefit, trying to appear the good sport. She wanted to believe Hizzoner himself was made uncomfortable by the Wall Street CEO's inappropriate behavior, but also recognized the awkward spot he was placed in. Politicians lived or died by how much money they could raise for their next campaign. Their host had influential friends with very big wallets and wasn't the sort of patron you wanted to anger with a lecture on politically correct behavior. By the third inning, Suzanne was chastising herself for failing so miserably to assess the potential problem. She hadn't called the right play when she'd softened her look to accomplish selfish ends, hoping the mayor might see her as more open and approachable.

Hizzoner was too busy ogling the tight-fannied twenty-something staffer who tended bar to notice how Suzanne had ditched the glasses and let her hair down. Meanwhile, she'd played right into his very married, philandering pal's hands.

The call relayed a message from Chief of Department Robert Dunleavy. Someone had tried to kill a popular investigative reporter at the Spanish-language daily *La Paz* by blowing up his car. Dunleavy was en route to the scene in Queens and thought the first deputy commissioner would want to join him there. The PC was in Washington that night, with a speaking engagement at the National Governors' Conference, and Suzanne was the highest-ranking cop within city limits.

Before she could explain the nature of the call to the mayor, he received one of his own from Gracie Mansion. Since launching a vitriolic print attack on reputed Cali cartel kingpin Roberto Santiago, together with his Russian organized crime and Dominican cronies, Luis Esquivel had stirred up new and significant outrage among the administration's Hispanic constituency. An attempt on Esquivel's life was big news and demanded a proper show of concern.

"I know you've got your own car, but if you would, I'd like you to ride with me," the mayor suggested. "Your driver can follow."

An event like a car bombing meant coverage by all five major TV news organizations, and God only knew how many wire services and newspapers. In light of that fact, Suzanne was now *really* kicking herself for leaving her glasses at home. The softened image she'd served up for her future boss was not at all what she wanted to project to the public, and the Job's rank and file. New York's first female police commissioner couldn't look fluffy. She couldn't look like she was even aware of her sexuality, but instead had to look tough, like Maggie Thatcher or Golda Meir.

The phalanx of uniformed cops and aides who constituted the mayor's entourage whisked them downstairs in a private elevator and across the sidewalk to his waiting Lincoln Town car. Once settled, they were under way, a patrol cruiser with flashing light bar in the lead, followed by a black Chevy Suburban with a red gumball going on its dash.

"I want you to know, you couldn't have handled Sterling any better than you did," Hizzoner murmured, one eye on the back of his driver's head. His tone was apologetic. "The one other time you two met, you had your game face on. I think tonight's look may have caught him by surprise."

So he *had* noticed. "A mistake on my part," she admitted.

In response, the mayor did something that caught her completely off guard. He moved his right hand from his lap to let it fall to the seat between them. There, it made slight but definite contact with her own. "I don't think so," he said. "I appreciate the idea of a good-looking woman knowing when and when not to use her tools. It's a dimension I hadn't seen before. One I think I like." Rather than let his hand linger, he withdrew it back toward his lap, his point clearly made.

Suzanne smiled slightly and felt the warmth of a pleasing glow crawl upward from between her breasts until it reached her cheeks. Her original strategy hadn't completely backfired. She'd meant to set a hook tonight, and had. "The Colombians have made threats against Luis Esquivel for nearly two years," she said, smoothly changing the subject. "So much time has passed, it kind of surprises me they were actually serious."

Hizzoner frowned. "How so?"

"They've got the same reputation the old Italian mobs used to have. You mess with us, we won't just kill you, we'll kill your family. It still happens a lot south of the border, but not here. They depend on their reputation, alone, to put the fear of God into people."

The mayor digested this thoughtfully. "This Esquivel doesn't scare so easily. Despite the threats, he's continued to be a pain in their asses."

The familiarity he used with Suzanne was a good sign. It meant he felt comfortable around her, which might indicate he thought they could work together. Still, she was careful to keep her own language more reserved. When those first threats were made against Esquivel, and he'd persisted in publishing his scathing pieces, she'd taken an interest. The FBI and DEA had files on him that made interesting reading. "His father was killed by them, eighteen years ago," she said. "Last year, he applied for a carry permit, which means he took those threats seriously enough. It was the DEA's New York agent-in-charge, of all people, who sponsored him through the bureaucratic maze, by the way."

"Would tend to indicate they took those threats pretty seriously, too," the mayor said. "Sounds like you've got your thumb on the pulse, Suzanne. I'm impressed."

"People make themselves targets of reprisal, I make it my business to familiarize myself with the details. It's my job." She paused, her expression turning rueful. "Not that it sounds like it did Mr. Esquivel any good."

At this, the mayor grunted and turned his head to stare out the window at the Manhattan skyline to the south of them. They were on the Major Deegan Expressway, headed for the Triborough Bridge and making slow progress through heavy postgame traffic. "Counting illegals, we've got no idea how many million people you and just thirty-eight thousand cops are expected to protect, Suzanne. Mr. Esquivel's alive. Considering the odds, I count him among the lucky."

Deputy Chief Simon Ogilvy was in midtown Manhattan, enduring the dancing portion of a rubber chicken and frozen snowball benefit dinner for one of his wife's charities. His deliverance came in the form of an attempt on a Queens reporter's life. As much as he hated to miss another earnest fox-trot with one of the board of directors, duty called. He made the appropriate excuses, then made haste.

Twenty minutes later, the scene Ogilvy encountered on Grand Avenue in Elmhurst was one of near pandemonium. This car bombing at *La Paz* had attracted as much media attention as the one at the World Trade Center ten years ago. Portable klieg lights burned everywhere, illuminating the earnest faces of talking heads, all gripping microphones. The flashing lights from scores of official vehicles reflected crazily off wet pavement, giving the scene a carnival-midway atmosphere. Directly adjacent to the chain link that fenced the *La Paz* employee parking lot, an Emergency Services Unit mobile command center was already up and running, the windows of the blue and white bus aglow, the shadows of occupants seen scurrying within.

It took Ogilvy a few minutes to locate Crime Scene Unit commander Captain Leon Grove, huddled up with Deputy Commissioner Ben Hunnicutt from the Organized Crime Control Bureau and his Narcotics Division commander, Chief Daniel Shoshany. Hunnicutt spotted Simon as the Intel Division chief shouldered his way past security.

"Nice night," he greeted Ogilvy, and offered a puffy paw. "You've got your own file on this Esquivel kid, I expect?"

"Sounds to me like it's his lucky day," the deputy chief growled. His gaze roamed the frozen zone inside a stretch of yellow crime scene tape. There, members of Captain Grove's team worked with practiced precision, carefully sifting scattered debris for evidence. What Simon presumed to be the reporter's automobile was a charred and twisted hulk sitting on four bare wheels. Even the tires were incinerated in the fire. Several surrounding cars were badly damaged by the explosion, the sides facing the blast staved in and charred black. "Looks like they meant business," he observed. "Any idea what material was used?"

"Bomb Squad is guessing plastic," Captain Grove replied. "Either Semtex or C-4." A slender black man who once held the New York City high school 800-meter record, he'd attended Columbia on a track scholarship and earned a B.S. in chemistry. From there, he'd tacked on an M.S. in forensic science from John Jay, and today was part of a new breed of NYPD cop who loved technology, knowing what it could do to aid an investigation. Once retired, he had a bright future as an expert witness. "Must have been at least a pound of the stuff, taped to the gas tank. Detonator was probably wired to the ignition system. I guess Esquivel surprised the bomber. He must have panicked. How he actually screwed it up, we may never know."

"Most Saturdays, Esquivel leaves the paper an hour or so later than he did tonight," Hunnicutt added. "Looks like the bad guy cut his timing too thin."

Ogilvy knew from the call he'd received that the bomber was killed and cremated in the explosion. "Any idea how he got here?" he wondered.

"We've got a car," Narco's Danny Shoshany replied. He pointed toward a late-model Nissan Altima sedan, bathed in floodlight. Its four doors were ajar, along with the hood and trunk lid, while Captain Grove's Crime Scene Unit techs worked it over. "Local squad detectives found it unlocked, keys still in it. Belongs to a rental outfit. Enterprise. We contacted them with the particulars. They're running a trace."

Ogilvy sorted through what he already knew about the target of tonight's attack. Over the past couple of months, Luis Esquivel had not only persisted in pissing the Colombians off, but had also managed to assemble some remarkably accurate details of how Russian organized crime now functioned in New York. Simon believed a renegade group of former KGB agents could be just as formidable as the Cali cartel, regardless of how new they were to this racket. They'd been ruthlessly schooled, understood discipline when it suited them, and were no strangers to bloodletting. "Virtually anyone with a phone bill and a checkbook can rent a car from Enterprise," he mentioned. "We may not have much luck there." And as he spoke, he spotted a disturbance out of the corner of one eye. He turned to look that way.

"Almost, but not quite enough security for the President of the United States," Narcotics Chief Shoshany growled. "I'm bettin' on the mayor."

Seated in the darkened depths of a black Mercedes 560SEL, with a beautiful fifteen-year-old Azerbaijani girl at his side, the Cali cartel's man in New York, Roberto Santiago, could barely control the violence of his fury. Two hundred yards up Grand Avenue, the night was streaked by blue, red, white, and yellow lights bouncing off building facades. The street was jammed with police cars, TV news vans, and hundreds of rubberneckers, but Santiago's focus was on the man facing rearward over the seat back before him. "What do you mean, the reporter is still alive?!" he demanded.

The bearer of bad tidings shifted nervously and glanced again at the ripe fullness of the teenage girl's half-exposed breasts. He swallowed hard as he nodded. "I see him with my own eyes, Don Roberto, before they put him in the ambulance. They are saying the bomb killed the man Santos sent."

The girl at Roberto's side was a gift made to him by one of his new Russian friends. One advantage of her, other than her voluptuous beauty, was the fact that she understood neither English nor Spanish. Roberto had always liked them young, but even to him, the idea of a fifteen-year-old seemed almost criminal. If it weren't for how ripe and womanly her body was, he might have felt ashamed of the strength of his attraction. Because of it, he felt no compunction of the sort.

"Take me away from here," he snarled to his driver. "To the *casa* in Manhattan."

Roberto would not dare admit it to a soul, but the fact of the Dominican's failure had him more than a little spooked. He had bragged to his new Russian allies that Esquivel was no more than a minor irritation, like a heat rash or mosquito bite. He would take care of him, *no problema.* Now, the powers in Cali who gave Santiago his stature and eminence in New York would hear of his failure. He had not made good on a boast, and they would not be pleased. There were many other good soldiers in the Cali cartel ranks, men hungry for the power Roberto wielded. He could be replaced in the span of time it took a bullet to stop a beating heart.

Roberto needed to move quickly, before the appearance of indecision did further damage. Just that afternoon, other disturbing news had reached him. In an area of Brooklyn still controlled by one of the old Italian Mafia families, purchase of Cali product had fallen off significantly the past two weeks. The Italians had missed the boat three decades ago by failing to create their own lines of cocaine supply. In the face of huge new demand, their once vaunted heroin-trafficking capabilities had also become insignificant. Still, like Francisco Santos in Washington Heights, they controlled important neighborhoods and streets. Roberto knew sales patterns throughout the city inside out. Street sales in the Italian-controlled sectors remained steady. It could only mean that lately, they'd found some other source for the product their pitchers were flogging. Either they'd stolen those drugs from the Dominicans, as Santos claimed someone had, or had forged a new alliance. Either way, Roberto's handlers in Cali would not be happy. He was sent to New York to guard their interests zealously by maintaining order and control.

Still glistening with the sweat of her exertions, Gina Galati watched Clarence DaCosta work to fluff his pillow. "What you doing?" she asked, her breath barely recovered.

"Getting comfortable," he replied. With a deep sigh of satisfaction, he flopped over onto his back and tugged the comforter up to his chin.

Gina rolled over onto one hip to peer at him through the gloom. He'd proven to be in as good a shape as he looked, almost effortlessly exerting himself during the more athletic segments of their lovemaking. Even now, as her heart hammered against her ribs, his chest rose and fell with the calm, steady rhythm of a man at total peace. "Don't bother," she advised him. "My report card says, plays and fucks well with others. It don't say nothing about sleeps."

His head came over, those unsettling blue eyes finding hers to lock on. "You throwing me out?"

Gina heaved aside the bedclothes to swing her legs over the side of the bed and sit. "You got it, champ. Not that I ain't grateful for all the good wood you just put to me. It's just that I sleep alone."

He grunted. "Always?"

"Only man ever spent a whole night with me was my stepfather," she replied. "I hate his fucking guts for it. So far, I still don't hate yours."

"Jesus Christ," he muttered. This was another of her surprises, he supposed; a little heavier than anything he was ready to take on right now, or maybe ever. Gina was a good-looking piece of tail, granted, but Clarence had just heard something he didn't want to know about her. Or any woman he'd just been intimate with, for that matter. He climbed out to search the floor for his trousers. "You're fucking serious."

"Oh yeah. Like cancer."

His pants recovered, Clarence moved on to locate his shirt. "Your stepfather fucked you." He dressed as quickly as he could manage it. "God*damn*, Gina. That's disgusting."

Once DaCosta beat a hasty retreat from the scene, Gina Galati was left alone with a rage that perpetually ate at her. As she listened to the elevator motor groan and then go quiet, the car having made its descent to the street, she stood before the full-length mirror in her bath, arms folded across her chest to hug her naked breasts. "You don't know the half of it, hotshot," she murmured. Her latest lover fancied himself a man of the world, streetwise and oh so jaded, but the chip he carried on his own shoulder obscured too much of his peripheral view. The only pain he was capable of seeing—centered on the fact of his half-black birth, she was certain—was his own. In his world, he was the only victim of injustice who mattered. "No idea of how disgusting it really was," she continued aloud. "You got no idea what it feels like . . . to have some motherfucker force you to suck him off. And no idea how much I hate my mother, may she burn in hell, for letting it be me instead of her."

Clarence DaCosta couldn't get away from John Street quickly enough, his anger mounting with every brisk step he took toward his car. Each time those last words Gina had spoken to him echoed in memory, the cold wind of something totally alien and unsettling tickled the nape of his neck. Her own stepfather. According to the file he'd read and picture he'd seen, the man was a fleshy-faced goombah; little-piggy pug nose with huge nostrils and a small, thin-lipped mouth. Clarence didn't know why the thought of sharing Gina with a man so physically repugnant made his stomach curdle the way it had, but right now he could barely restrain himself from vomiting.

Once behind the wheel of his beat-up gypsy cab, DaCosta made himself sit a moment, white-knuckled fists gripping the wheel. He needed to get a handle on his rage before he started the engine. How many times in his life had he worked to conjure an image of the act his own mother had performed to bring him, albeit accidentally, into this world? He did it again now, comparing his feelings of revulsion to those triggered by the thought of Gina Galati in her stepfather's arms. Clarence Poole hadn't forced himself, but had undeniably forced his blackness on the boy and now the man he'd left behind. His carefree comings and goings between his beautiful outcast mistress and his entirely separate life at home had eaten at his bastard son's heart. Eroded by the acid of such injustice, it had become a near-bottomless chasm of hatred, for him and everything he represented. Poole's were nothing at all like the comings and goings of Sonny Galati, but in each instance, a thing unspeakably ugly had defiled something beautiful.

As he twisted the key in the ignition and listened to the engine come to life, DaCosta saw Fat Danny Washington in a vivid flash of memory. Dying there on the cemetery's gravel access path, the Red Top crew chief's sidekick seemed to embody both Clarence's and Gina's separate but similar nemeses, all rolled into one. He was fat and physically repulsive, *and* he was a nigger.

Fourteen

When he considered the emotional shape he was in, hitting the hay Saturday night, Matt Stuart was surprised by how deeply he'd slept. He awoke at seven-thirty Sunday morning, happy to see that the weatherman's forecast for continued gloom had hit wide of the mark. His bedroom was flooded with sunshine. A fresh, rain-scrubbed breeze fluttered his curtains. This was likely to be his only day off this week, so he lounged in bed awhile before hauling it out to shave and shower. He weighed himself and discovered a four-pound loss, despite his having let his workout regimen lapse that past week. Beneath a soothing cascade of hot water, he took time to stretch the stress kinks from the muscles of his back.

The automatic coffeemaker was programmed to start brewing at seven forty-five, and the java in the carafe was still relatively fresh when he poured himself a cup at eight-fifteen. Seated next to an open window in the sun-washed breakfast nook, he sipped slowly and considered the idea of breakfast. His recent exercise lapse didn't prevent him from frying up six strips of bacon and whisking a little grated Swiss into his scrambled eggs. There was only so much a man could be expected to deny himself.

An hour later, Stuart was working his way through the Arts & Leisure section of the Sunday *Times* when the phone rang. It was Detective Josh

Littel, calling to report on last night's surveillance of the automatic weapons dealer's suspected warehouse location. He sounded whipped.

"Still not a fucking peep, Lou. You know how you get the vibe sometimes? Like they know you're watching? Two weeks ago, Gaskin and me had it bad. Now? Ain't got it at all. I think they've sniffed us out; shifted sites."

Over the years, Stuart had learned to trust his own and other veteran detectives' instincts in these areas. An animal being hunted in the wild can feel the weight of a hunter's eyes on him, and so, too, can many perps under surveillance. "Let's call it off," he said.

"Fine by us. Terry talked to Hogan last night. Sounds like the Rodriguez case is moving in strange directions."

"Is indeed," Matt admitted. "We're gonna need all the manpower we can get."

"Be good to get a decent night's sleep, I'll tell you that." Littel sounded like he meant it. "My wife'll think my girlfriend threw me out."

Matt chuckled and told him to get some rest. Then, no sooner did he hang up the phone than it rang again. This time it was Simon Ogilvy.

"You catch the late news . . . or anything this morning?" the Intel chief asked.

"Not if it isn't in the *Times*," Stuart replied. "Why?"

"Remember the rabble-rousing *La Paz* reporter we got the file on? The one been tormenting the Colombian drug kings and the Little Odessa underworld? Somebody tried to kill him last night. Bombed his car."

Stuart had done work on the Luis Esquivel file, and wasn't surprised to hear the people he'd targeted had finally struck back. The man was either fearless or just plain crazy. "Get him?" he asked.

"Nope. Lucky bastard wasn't in it at the time. Took some shrapnel is all." Ogilvy related how the reporter had apparently surprised the perp while the bomber was planting the explosive. "Bad guy was burned extra crispy. We found wheels at the scene we think are his. Unlocked, keys still in the ignition. A Nissan Altima, rented from Enterprise. They say it was reported stolen a little over two months ago."

"By whom?"

"Woman named Velasquez. Filed a complaint against her ex-boyfriend late March. Says he stole her car, credit cards and some jewelry."

Stuart knew that in the ghetto, it didn't so much matter where a player got a new car so long as he had one. With wheels from an outfit like Enterprise, it was a simple matter of peeling a little green *e* sticker off the bumper and, presto, a man could impress his pals and the chicks with a shiny new ride. "Any line on the boyfriend yet?" he asked.

"Nuh-uh. Nobody chased the complaint very hard," Ogilvy replied. "Squad at the Three-oh caught it, and you know how it goes in a busy shop like theirs. It ain't a rape, no one is bleeding or was hacked up into little pieces, it gathers dust. Mutt's name is Castillo. Eduardo 'Eddie.' Dominican citizen. Last known address, 582 160th Street."

Bells were going off, and Stuart understood why this call so bright and early on a Sunday. The perp in the botched car bombing was Dominican. One who'd resided in Washington Heights. Even if the perp wasn't this Castillo, it was someone he knew and trusted enough to lend him his car. "So," he said. "In the same week, we've got a murdered off-duty cop, together with his Dominican girlfriend. Then two top-dog pitchers, responsible for moving Dominican-controlled product. And now another Dominican's gone down, trying to kill an outspoken reporter."

"Beginning to look like a web, ain't it?" Ogilvy mused. "No matter how tangled."

There was an awful lot that still didn't make sense to Matt, and he was scrambling. "You know if Esquivel targeted Frank Santos in any of his print attacks?" he asked.

"Mentioned him once or twice. We never thought he hit him hard enough to make him a reprisal target. Not specifically. One interesting thing, though? Each time Santos's name came up, it was always in connection with Roberto Santiago."

After three years at Intelligence, Stuart not only knew who Santiago was but of his specific function within the Cali cartel's New York scheme. "How does this fit the bigger picture we're trying to draw, boss?" he asked. "We've got our eye on a play we think the Italians are ready to make. They pull it off, the Colombians and Odessa Mafiya will still be the suppliers, correct? I don't see it being the Chinese."

Over the past decade, the Chinese gangs had all but priced themselves out of the New York heroin market. In the face of fierce competition, they'd stubbornly stuck to high prices while the Russian-Colombian alliance worked to supplant them by giving away free samples of their South American and Caspian region heroin on the streets. Eventually, they'd undercut the Chinese kilo price for heroin by nearly half, giving them a virtual lock on supply.

"Not likely," the chief agreed. "I still don't know how it fits, Matthew. I only know it somehow does. You might wanna talk to the reporter."

"He took shrapnel, you say? How serious?"

"Cut a chunk of it outta his right hip at Elmhurst Hospital last night. Stitched up a nasty gash over one eye while they were at it. It's where he's laid up now."

Matt closed the Arts & Leisure section, refolded it, and set it with the rest of the paper. Ah well, he thought. So much for his one day off.

Gina Galati would have allowed herself the luxury of sleeping late that Sunday, but she had an eighteen-month-old child. Instead, she was up with the baby at daybreak, but once she fed him and got him settled with his toys in his playpen, she'd luxuriated for the next several hours in a mood of self-indulgent laziness. As a means of savoring the memory of last night's romp, she hadn't yet showered away the lingering musk of sex. It was noon, and she was still in her robe.

For every time that Gina had asked herself why, considering her history, she even cared about the attentions of men, there was a rare time like this morning when the answer seemed crystal-clear. She'd hated being brutalized at the hands of her stepfather, but had somehow managed to separate him and his deeds from the act of copulation. If she set the agenda and controlled the pace, the physical aspects of intercourse were things she liked with a fondness that bordered on fervor. In the throes, she wanted to hear nothing but the grunts of exertion, moans of pleasure, and the heavy breathlessness of honest exhaustion. Simply put, she liked the animal act much more than any object with whom she chose to perform it. She hoped her partners could find their own means of satisfaction somewhere far removed from her private emotional sphere. She'd heard it said that truly great sex was supposed to be all in the mind; that real lovers made love with each other's brains. So far as she was concerned, that was New Age crap. When she got laid and it was good, the man involved was little more than a vehicle, a mere conveyance. She was in the bed all by herself, hanging on for dear ecstasy, her limbs wrapped around an animal desire, and nothing more.

Clarence DaCosta was the rare lover who'd seemed to understand. Indeed, while he performed, he was every bit as capable of retreating inside himself as she was. All muscle from head to toe, and without being rough or rushed, he'd proven to be as athletic as he looked. A dirty cop and a cold-blooded shooter were an odd pair of bedmates, and the fact that he'd seemed so earnest in his efforts to give pleasure had somewhat surprised Gina. In her experience, most men didn't know how, even if they believed they did. DaCosta had worked his ass slippery with sweat beneath her hands, feeding on her the way a gourmand feasts, rather than a teenager at a fast food drive-up window.

The sound of the elevator interrupted Gina's reverie. It was headed upward, toward her floor, and the part of her that was forever on edge pushed her to take precautionary action. Five agile steps took her from where she lounged on her unmade bed to an armoire. Pressure from the ball of her left foot tripped the catch of a spring-release panel built into its base. It fell away to reveal a stash large enough to hold a small arsenal, and from it she grabbed the Franchi SPAS-12 assault shotgun—nine-shot, gas-operated semiautomatic—and a box of Remington "Express Magnum" buckshot shells. This hidey-hole was the largest of three such stashes located in strategic places throughout her loft. Another was in the bath, lest she find herself trapped there, and one in the island separating the kitchen from the living room.

The elevator arrived at her floor just as Gina took a stool behind the kitchen island, the shotgun propped against the knee wall, alongside her right thigh. She faced the ornamental gates, feigning an air of nonchalance. Theoretically, a visitor couldn't access her floor without a key, but in her game, Gina had learned not to trust presumption. The doors parted and she reached one hand beneath the countertop to grab the assault gun by the pistol grip.

The appearance of Naomi Ebbcomb, red-eyed and disheveled, wearing old gym shorts and a paint-stained T-shirt triggered in Gina conflicting emotions of relief and anger.

"How could you?" her neighbor demanded from beyond the filigreed ironwork of the gates. She sniffed and wiped at her nose with the back of one hand. "Ask me to watch your fucking kid so you can go out and troll for dick. Jesus, Gina. I saw what a cheeseball he was. I heard what time he left."

Her relief gone, but the anger still sharp, Gina contemplated her neighbor. There was pathetic defeat in the slump of Naomi's shoulders. In contrast to the pendulous, overlarge breasts hanging loose inside the

T-shirt, Naomi's slender, pretty legs seemed to belong to someone else. "How many times have I told you, Nay? I ain't gay. Give it up."

Still rooted where she stood, Naomi could no longer hold her tears in check. "I c-can't keep doing this!" she moaned. Her fists were clenched at her sides, knuckles turned white.

"Doing what?" Gina asked calmly. "Making passes at me that I ain't never gonna catch? I'm a cold-hearted hetero bitch. I get the urge to have the wood put to me now'n then. When I do, I go out and drag home a load of lumber."

Naomi winced with the word "wood." There was fresh vehemence in the way she shook her head. Behind her tears, her eyes flashed fire. "Watching Claude for you! I won't *do* this to myself anymore!"

An image of Clarence, all that beautiful, chiseled nakedness gleaming with a sheen of sweat, surfaced again in Gina's mind. She wondered what motivated a man like him to become what he had: a dirty cop, half black, who apparently hated other blacks with blind passion. Last night, he'd tried to prove something; of that she was sure.

Gina knew she had exploited Naomi and even she could tire of it, no matter how convenient all that free baby-sitting had been. She certainly found no sport in it, knowing too well the misery of being trapped in an emotional prison from which there was no escape. "If you can't, then don't," she said softly. "I'll find someone else, Nay."

Blinking the tears from her eyes, her neighbor stared blankly through the gates. "I love you," she moaned.

Gina shook her head. The anger that had burned bright just moments ago was replaced by something akin to pity, an emotion she had never felt for anyone but herself. A feeling of being set adrift attended it, and she found it deeply unsettling. "No you don't," she insisted. "You want me to want you, Nay. It ain't the same thing. Go home. We can talk about it later, once you get a grip."

She pushed back from the counter and stood, leaving the shotgun behind as she crossed the floor to disappear into her bathroom. It was at least half a minute before she heard the elevator motor kick in. Cables slapped as the car started its downward journey, and all the while, Gina studied her face in the medicine cabinet mirror. She tried to understand what she saw there. Was it anger? Of course. A part of her was always angry. Even as Clarence had labored to pleasure her, she'd been angry. It was anger that helped focus her on the goals she'd chosen, and gave her the determination she needed to strive doggedly toward them. But today, she also saw pity, and pity was something she'd never allowed herself to feel for another human being. The fact that she *could* feel it frightened her more than she cared to admit. A capacity for empathy, or whatever a shrink might want to call it, was nothing a cold-hearted bitch like herself could afford. Not one in her particular line of work.

The image Matt Stuart had conjured of Luis Esquivel, intrepid investigative reporter with more balls than common sense, was so wholly unlike the physical manifestation of the man encountered in a bed at Elmhurst Hospital, he felt himself blink when he first saw him. Esquivel looked impossibly young to have accomplished the kind of trouble-making he had. His was the round, brown face of a Latino cherub. His build—burly and still chubby with baby fat—was that of a teddy bear. Propped up at an incline to watch a soccer game on TV, he glared at Stuart on entry, then nodded.

"You look like a cop." He spoke with only the faintest trace of a Spanish accent. "The fact you made it past Cerberus out there? Probably confirms my intuition."

Matt produced his ID and gold lieutenant's shield. The reference to the three-headed guard dog of mythology was made regarding a capable-looking uniformed patrolman parked in a chair outside the door. "Lieutenant Matt Stuart," he introduced himself. "Commander of the detective squad at the Thirty-seventh Precinct. That's in Washington Heights."

Esquivel frowned, racking his memory for some elusive fact. "Stuart . . . Stuart . . ."

"Up until a week ago, I worked as a special-unit investigator for our Intelligence Division."

The reporter lifted an arm festooned with IV tube and wristband and snapped his fingers. "Gotcha. Italian mob stuff mostly, right?"

Matt might have been surprised if he wasn't already familiar with how thoroughly Esquivel ran down his various leads. Still, he was impressed. "Good memory, Luis."

"Comes in handy on occasion. So. Whose party did you piss on to get shipped from Intel to a hellhole like the Three-seven?"

Matt stared evenly back at him. It was hard for a cop to view any outsider as an ally, and Esquivel was an outsider. Then again, the guy knew more drug enforcement intelligence than most Narcotics Division cops, and had publicly declared war on all the same enemies. The bandage covering the left side of his face, and the fact of where he lay at the moment, were testimony to his commitment to the fight, and how much he was willing to risk to wage battle. "I'm not gonna jerk your dick, Luis," he said. "I'm here to do a trade, if you're amenable."

"Means what?" Esquivel asked, immediately on his guard.

"Means I'm prepared to tell you things you don't know. In exchange, I need some pieces to my puzzle that you might have." Stuart paused to let what he'd said sink in.

"The Three-seven," Esquivel said slowly. His eye contact with Matt never wavered. "There's this rumor, says a cop or cops have hit some stash houses up there. Stole money and drugs. A couple days ago, the top banana of a big street crew was whacked, along with his right-hand man." He stopped, tried to smile, and winced. "Let me guess. You didn't piss on anybody's party, Lieutenant. You're up there to stick your finger in the dike. Trying to stave off a major fucking disaster."

Matt turned, grabbed a green vinyl chair, dragged it closer to Esquivel's bed, and sat. "I'd like to know what you've heard about the Italians, and how they fit into all this, Luis. Like who might be getting ambitious, and where they've set their sights."

Sudden comprehension twinkled in Esquivel's eyes as he shook his head. "I thought we were trading, Lieutenant. You know: I show you mine, you show me yours. So far, I've done all the showing."

"It was a Dominican from Washington Heights who tried to kill you last night," Stuart replied. "I'm still trying to make sense of that fact."

This was new information to Esquivel; of that Stuart was certain. The reporter took a moment to mull it, and nodded. "Helps narrow it down some," he said. "Thought it might've been the Russians, but either way, Roberto Santiago was still behind it."

"Why Santiago?"

"Hates me, Lieutenant. With a holy, burning passion. I've dared to challenge his right to do business here. I've openly spit on that right, in a newspaper which prints in our common tongue."

Matt watched this man-child's face as he spoke. Esquivel wasn't bragging. He was merely stating a fact. "If it was a Dominican who tried to hit you, what makes you so positive it was Santiago pulling his strings?"

Rather than answer immediately, the reporter shifted, trying to get more comfortable. Stuart could see the pain the movement caused him. He motioned toward Luis's lap.

"How bad?" he asked.

"Missed my femoral artery by three inches, but I've still got the dick you promised not to pull. My hipbone stopped it, or it would have gone clean through me and out my ass. Rare for a reporter, huh?"

Stuart couldn't help chuckle. "No comment," he said.

Esquivel became serious again. "The Colombians and Dominicans do each other favors, Lieutenant. Not that they actually respect each other, but each has his needs. The Colombians might control the dope supply, but they don't have the ground troops the Dominicans do. Not in New York."

"So Santiago asks a guy like Frank Santos to do him a favor. Like killing you. And for it, what does Santos get in return?"

"Ah. You just asked the sixty-four-thousand-dollar question, Lieutenant. And I really don't have an answer. Francisco Santos has his own smuggling system in place. He negotiates his deals with Santiago, but takes delivery offshore. It means he gets his product for a lot less than other major-weight dealers, and makes a much larger profit."

"Enterprising."

"Very."

"Which means," Stuart mused, "that if Santiago wants a favor from him, he's gotta be in a position to supply him with something he needs, other than drugs."

As gingerly as he could manage, Luis shrugged. "There's also the matter of good will to consider, Lieutenant. Regardless of whether Santiago makes actual delivery, he's still Cali's man in New York. Still, in this case I doubt goodwill is all of it. Santos wants something else, I'm sure."

"Hazard any guesses?" Matt asked.

"If I was a betting man? I'd put my money on intelligence, Lieutenant. Most likely about who is stealing from him."

And to Stuart, suddenly, it all made perfect sense.

Clarence DaCosta was taking it easy that Sunday. He hadn't gotten home from Brooklyn until late, and had slept until almost ten. After some yoga and a leisurely shower, he'd wandered over to the East Village for breakfast in a greasy spoon on Second Avenue. The place was frequented by a brash young crowd of wannabe actors, artists, poets, and playwrights, all living on the cutting edge of hip. He'd loitered over his last cup of coffee, amused by the atmosphere of attitude and affectation, then wandered west again toward his Clarkson Street apartment. On Bleecker Street he stopped at Rocco's Italian bakery for a cannoli and sat on a bench outside to eat it. Yesterday's gloomy weather had given way, once again, to the warmth of late May sunshine. On a day as dazzling as this one, the people-watching was spectacular. Winter's interminable months of coats, boots, scarves, and earmuffs had finally given way. Pretty women now flocked the streets in sundresses, shorts, sleeveless blouses, and sandals.

For a few hours that Sunday, Clarence was able to lose himself and forget the inner turmoil that perpetually gouged at his soul. Last night, he may not have actually made love to a beautiful Italian woman, but he had fucked her brains out. It seemed to be exactly what she'd wanted, and there was a measure of satisfaction in that knowledge. Today, the world was full of beautiful women, many of whom seemed to sense the animal satisfaction he was feeling when he made eye contact in passing. Several flashed covert, knowing smiles, while others seemed to fear what they saw. Both were turn-ons.

DaCosta returned to his building at the corner of Hudson and Clarkson at two that afternoon, ready for something mindless like an old movie on TV and maybe a nap. He considered calling Gina to see if she wanted to get together later, but guessed it might be too soon. As a means of establishing certain territorial guidelines, she'd run him out of there last night, and that was fine. She was the prize and he the contestant, not the other way around. She'd liked the sex well enough to want him back, of that he was confident, but like a twelve-pound fish caught on four-pound test, he had to allow her to run until *she* chose to circle back.

He'd neglected his apartment last week. It was something of a sty, but he had no desire to do much cleaning on so laid-back a day. Instead, he spent a few minutes picking up soiled clothes and stuffing them into the laundry bag, then ran water in the sink to rinse dirty glasses and coffee mugs. He was placing them in the dishwasher when the doorbell rang. Not the intercom buzzer from the lobby downstairs, but the bell on his landing.

In the back of his mind, a dirty cop always wonders when those he's betrayed will get wise and move to drop the net on him. He prepares for this eventuality in a variety of ways. To date, Clarence was directly responsible for the armed robbery of five Washington Heights stash houses, and was an accomplice to three homicides. For him, prison was not an alternative he was willing to face. He'd always figured, when the time came, he might take his own life. His existence in his current incarnation wasn't one he could claim he really treasured, the occasional roll in the hay with a woman like Gina Galati notwithstanding. Before he approached his door to peer out the security peep, he grabbed a .357 magnum Colt Python from atop the television.

Fifteen

Detective Jack Hogan's wife hadn't reacted well to the levity in his tone Saturday night when he'd asked how her brother's party had gone. It was late by the time she and the kids returned from Baldwin, and Jack had spent the afternoon and evening tinkering contentedly in his basement shop. That's where Mary Kate had found him. A completely reassembled lawnmower—previously strewn about the floor in pieces—and an empty pizza carton prompted her to wonder aloud why he hadn't joined his family if he'd gotten home so early. With his lame excuse all prepared, Jack explained how he'd expected them to pack it in early, the weather being as lousy as it was. It failed to explain why he hadn't called, and Mary Kate was quick to point that out.

Early Sunday afternoon, the new whip had summoned Hogan to a meeting at his house in Bay Ridge, Brooklyn. As he and Rhoda Bolivar drove toward it, Jack was looking for a more sympathetic ear.

"So there I am, up to my elbows in grease, six beers to the breeze, and of course I gotta open my big yap."

"Let me guess," Rhoda offered. Stuart had reached each of them an hour earlier to suggest this brainstorming session. Pieces of the Rodriguez homicide puzzle were quickly falling into place. Apparently, what he wanted to discuss couldn't wait until morning. Rhoda had picked her partner up and had the wheel. "You told her you didn't call or join them because her brother's a jerk. Probably added something colorful, like you'd rather hit your thumb with a hammer than go for a ride with him in his new boat."

Jack had cut his thumb on the mower's engine cowling. He sported a gauze and adhesive tape dressing. "I didn't hit it with a hammer," he defended himself.

She waved a dismissive hand. "Whatever. Am I right or am I right?"

He grunted. "Eamon *is* a jerk. You can't deny that."

"I'm sure Mary Kate wouldn't deny it either. But that's not the point, Jack. Aside from you and the kids, he's the only family she has. The old blood-and-water cliché has roots, buddy boy."

"And I just can't help pissing on them, huh?"

Typically in a hurry whenever she drove, Rhoda cut hard around a dawdling Sunday driver and sped into the next gap. The Belt Parkway, as it skirted Jamaica Bay, was congested with travelers on day trips to Long Island beaches. Rhoda kept pace with the most impatient of the youth element as she stitched her way in and out of slower-moving traffic. As always, Jack was intrigued to see how calm and purposeful she remained at the helm.

"You said it, not me," she replied. "You've got eight brothers and sisters and can take or leave the whole brood. With only one egg in a much smaller basket, Mary Kate doesn't have that choice." She paused to glance quickly at her partner. "I understand these things. I've got the one sister and that's it."

Hogan wasn't getting what he'd hoped to get out of this exchange. He slouched in his seat and made a face of disgust. "I've met your sister," he growled. "How couldn't anyone like her? She's a doll."

"Immaterial to what I'm trying to say," she argued. "Siblings help us maintain focus on where we're from, and where we want to go. Eamon probably provides plenty of reminders for Mary Kate of where she *doesn't* want to go."

Admit it or not, Jack had come to treasure these little exchanges with his partner, as impossibly logical as she was. He was more the seat-of-the-pants, gut-reaction type, and all that cold logic helped to ground him. Mary Kate possessed it, too, and he wondered if it might be a woman thing. "Eamon don't remind me of any of that crap," he complained. "Just gives me gas. So what did the whip say to you when he called? Just told me he's gathering the squad. We need to talk."

"Nice smooth segue," she murmured. Her concentration was on the next gap in traffic through which she aimed to shoot. "Not much more than he said to you, really. Just that he'd called Littel and Gaskin, too, and he'd been to Elmhurst Hospital to talk to that reporter someone tried to blow up last night."

Hogan's eyes narrowed. Sulking, he'd skipped the newspapers that morning. "What reporter is that?"

The look it earned him carried a mixture of disgust and disbelief. "What? You don't watch the news? You're a detective, for crissake."

"You start nagging me too, I'm applying for reassignment, Bolivar. I'm either fixing broken shit to save my family a few hard-earned bucks, or got my wife crawling up my ass for shirking family obligations. When do I got time to watch the fucking news?"

Since Saturday afternoon's conversation with the new whip, Rhoda had caught herself thinking more about Lieutenant Matt Stuart than the pragmatic street cop side of her considered advisable. Regardless, the young, vibrant woman at her core was forced to admit an attraction to the man. He had to be least fifteen years her senior, but possessed a forthright, no-nonsense manner she found refreshing. In a world awash in hypocrisy and affectation, she had grown tired of the slick come-ons perpetrated by the kind of smooth operator she always seemed to attract. If Stuart was tempted to stray across that line, he'd at least had control enough to check himself. Thank God. Rather, they'd talked about their origins in a generally curious, nonobtrusive way: where each of them had grown up, gone to school, and where each had been assigned since coming on the Job. He was good-looking in a rugged, Anglo way that appealed to her, and what concerned her now was how strong the combination of his looks and his apparent sensitivity was. She wondered, as she and Hogan approached the man's house for this meeting, how she would respond to it today.

The neighborhood she entered in the eastern reaches of Bay Ridge was perched on a bluff overlooking all of New York Harbor, Staten Island, the Verrazano Narrows, and the Financial District of Manhattan to the north. Stuart's street, Harbor View Terrace, ran north and south, paralleling the water. It was lined with substantial, older houses dating back to the twenties and thirties.

"You don't buy an address like this on any lieutenant's pay I ever heard of," Hogan commented. He shifted around in his seat to get a better view of his surroundings as Rhoda drove up the block.

Following her partner's gaze, Rhoda thought she better understood now how a man who'd lost a child and a marriage to this place might still choose to stay, especially if he'd grown up here. She had always loved the sight of open water and the smell of salt air. The houses, too, had a primal kind of appeal, the way they projected solidity and substance. Yesterday, in their exchange about origins, his knowledge of Murray Hill in mid-Manhattan had been firsthand and relatively wide. Hers, of Bay Ridge, was based mostly on hearsay. None of these houses was really opulent, but she hadn't imagined his would be quite as impressive as this.

"Told me he grew up here," she said. "Yesterday, while we were talking in the car. His grandfather built it, right before the Great Depression."

"Probably means he ain't got a mortgage." Hogan's tone dripped envy. "Gotta be nice, huh?"

"Only the memory of running over his son in the driveway," Rhoda reminded him. "Makes his life a real bed of roses, I bet."

Hogan blanched and shelved the jealousy. Rhoda recognized Terry Gaskin's Pontiac Bonneville and pulled into the driveway behind it. The house, perched on a knoll up a steep incline of lawn, was white clapboard with black shutters. A sweeping veranda wrapped around one side above the garage. Flower beds below overflowed with mature azaleas, rhododendrons, and lilacs, all in full bloom. In the center of the lawn stood a pink dogwood a week past peak. Without intending to, Rhoda glanced at the garage door as she stepped from the car. With it came a vivid image of a small boy's crumpled body. A cold shiver ran the length of her spine.

Dressed casually in a white polo shirt and tan chinos, the Matt Stuart who opened the door to them looked surprisingly fresh and at ease for a man who'd been on the run all morning and hadn't had a day off in seven.

"C'mon in," he invited. "The sarge and Gaskin are here. We're still waiting on Littel. The living room is ahead of you, on the left. Get anyone coffee?"

"Only if it's already made," Jack replied. "Nice digs, Lou."

Behind Stuart's nod, given to acknowledge the compliment, Rhoda thought she saw the sort of wall many people erected to insulate themselves from pain. Or was she just reading her own projections into it? She started forward, taking in her surroundings. Dominating the entry was a huge grandfather clock, flanked by a beautiful mahogany side table. Both were either very old or excellent reproductions. In the living room, occupied by Terry Gaskin and Martini Al Goldstein, all of the furnishings were from that same—what? eighteenth century?—period. The parquet floor was covered with a huge oriental, while the built-in cases on each side of the fireplace were crammed with books. Rhoda sat in a wing chair diagonally across from where Gaskin lounged on a matching settee.

"How'd it go last night?" she asked the raw-boned, crew-cut detective.

Terry had been assigned to the Three-seven squad and partnered with Josh Littel less than three months ago. Rhoda thought him arrogant at first, but as time wore on, she'd recognized it as little more than a shell he'd created to protect himself. He'd gone through a nasty divorce a year ago, the story being he'd caught his wife doing the wild thing with a plumber making a house call.

"We ain't seen so much as a rat scurry across that loading dock the past eight nights," he replied. "Whip agrees it's probably time to give it up."

Stuart entered the room carrying a tray with five cups and a carafe, along with bowls of corn chips and salsa. "Thought someone might be hungry," he said, offering the first cup to Rhoda. "I'll leave the chips on the coffee table. Feel free to help yourselves."

When the doorbell rang a moment later, Stuart disappeared to return with Josh Littel. Once all of them were settled, he apologized for the inconvenience, thanked them for coming on such short notice, and got down to business.

"As you're no doubt aware, an attempt was made on the life of a reporter from a Spanish-language newspaper in Queens last night." He went on to outline how Luis Esquivel had led a virtual one-man campaign against the Cali cartel, Odessa Mafiya, Jamaican posses, Dominican street traffickers, and anyone else he could identify as part of the huge apparatus created to sell drugs in New York City. Rhoda was not a regular *La Paz* subscriber, but was fluent in the language and had read enough of Esquivel's work to know how ardent his outrage was. "From a rental car found abandoned at the scene, we've learned the dead bomber was probably a Dominican, residing in Washington Heights," Stuart continued. "Esquivel believes his attacker worked for Tío Paco Santos; that Santos sent him on this errand as a back-scratching favor done for Roberto Santiago." He stopped and let that tidbit hang in the air.

From where he sat in another chair alongside Rhoda, Al Goldstein chewed thoughtfully on an unlit cigar, then spoke around it. "Be my educated guess, Santos wants to know who's attacking him, and where they're laying off his dope. Esquivel's too?"

Stuart nodded. "And mine. I asked him if he's seen any evidence might lead him to believe the honeymoon is over between the Dominicans and Cali. He says he hasn't. Thinks that no matter how much they might dislike each other, it's too good an arrangement for both parties."

"Which would mean," Josh Littel interjected, "that the Colombians are under attack, too. And that doesn't make any sense to me. Where else is anyone gonna get cocaine?"

Listening to this exchange, Rhoda was aware of something lurking just below the surface of her consciousness, its dorsal fin visible for a moment, then disappearing again, like a shark circling. By blocking out the mutterings and speculations of the others, she was better able to concentrate and finally get a fix on it. "I don't think it's about cocaine," she said slowly.

Other conversation ceased. Stuart turned his attention her way. "Care to expand on that?"

The idea was still taking shape as she took the plunge. "We think it's the Albanese who whacked Johnny Rodriguez; that they're engineering some sort of move into Washington Heights. I know it sounds crazy, considering how deeply the Dominicans are entrenched. But . . ." She paused, still trying to organize the direction of her thoughts. ". . . Suppose they've taken a page from the Colombian-Dominican-Odessa Mafiya playbook . . . and undertaken to forge a competing alliance of their own."

She watched Stuart consider the idea, aware that Hogan was hunched forward and frowning at her. "A minute ago, you said maybe it ain't about coke," Jack said. "Which means you're thinking smack, correct?"

"It's the business they used to be in," she replied. "Some of the lessons learned aren't forgotten all that quickly."

"But most of those lessons are about how they fucked up on the supply side," Terry Gaskin argued. "Not about controlling the streets. They never knew fuckall about the streets. The blacks always handled that end for them."

Warming to her little brainchild, Rhoda nodded eagerly. "Exactly. And who says the blacks are all that loyal to the Dominicans? Or anyone else they do business with? Far as my experience goes, they seem to resent everyone, brown, yellow, and white, pretty much equally."

"Rhoda's got a point," Goldstein agreed. "The blacks know the Colombians and the Russians hate them every bit as much as the guineas ever did. Or the Chinese, for that matter, when *they* were the primary pipeline."

Rhoda watched Stuart process the input, clearly intrigued by her thesis. "So," he concluded, speaking slowly. "It's possible the Albanese have found a means of challenging the current order; that they're trying to drive a wedge between the pitchers on the street and the people who supply them."

"You look at the chain, I'd say the Dominicans are the weakest link," Littel offered. "How many of them you think envy Santos his position in their community? Little runt struts the streets up there like he owns the fucking place."

"Whoa there," Martini Al cautioned. "One big problem I got with all this. Your wonderful new organization you've got theorized? They got no dope to sell. The guineas been outta this game so long, their old lines of supply gotta be practically petrified by now. And even if they weren't, cocaine is something they ain't never trafficked in."

"You've got a point, Sarge," Littel agreed. "But they wrestle control of the game from the Cali alliance, you think nobody'll supply them with the dope they need to sell?" He shook his head, his mop of curly dark hair glistening in the sunlight that poured through the window at his back. "Bullshit. Santos ain't the only ambitious Dominican. No more than the Cali organization is the only bunch of ambitious Colombians. Escobar and his Medellín crowd ran the show before Cali. You get too high-and-mighty, seems there's always some backstabbing asshole waiting in the wings."

Stuart looked Rhoda's way again, a twinkle of something in his eyes she hadn't seen there before. It was subtle and aimed directly enough so that no one else in the room was likely to catch it. The message was clear and made her pulse quicken ever so slightly. It said he was pleased, and maybe a little intrigued, too.

*   *   *

Neither Fu Chiang nor Lyman Fat had ever been to the Canarsie section of Brooklyn before. But that sunny Sunday afternoon, both men found themselves aboard a luxury yacht moored in the Paerdegat Basin, on Jamaica Bay. They'd traveled there from Chinatown in downtown Manhattan at the request of Augustino "Gus" Barone, head of the Mafia's Albanese crime family. The occasion was meant to be a celebration of sorts, and on the surface, a strained gentility prevailed. Like diplomats, Chiang, Fat, and Barone had spent the past month doing the ritual dance of give-and-take, always civil no matter what disagreeable undercurrents existed, negotiating an agreement ultimately acceptable to both parties. They had ironed out money differences, crafted a comprehensive plan of attack, and were now ready to launch a mutual return to the marketing of heroin.

Both factions represented at the meeting today had once had a virtual lock on the smack trade, and that knowledge continued to nettle each man now seated in the boat's opulently appointed salon. Out of pure and simple greed, their predecessors had dropped a very lucrative ball. Today, neither of their factions was capable of picking up that ball and running with it alone. The forces standing in their way were formidable, having forged a coalition that many, on both sides of the law, considered unbeatable. If either the Italians or the Chinese had any hope of becoming competitive again, circumstances demanded they forge an alliance of their own.

Regardless of why he was here, Lyman Fat wished this meeting had been held almost anywhere else. Ever since 1975, when he and his parents were forced to flee South Vietnam in his father's small commercial shrimper, Fat hated boats, the smell of the sea, and most everything else he associated with them. Before reaching the teeming boat community in Hong Kong, he'd spent five months crammed into that shrimper's stinking confines. For twenty-five years he'd been unable to escape a nightmare that still visited him at least weekly. In it, the exterior air smelled precisely as it did right now, even if the air in the salon did not. Rather than of fear and cramped human contact, this air smelled of onions and garlic.

Fat, whose build belied his surname, had chosen a seat at one end of a built-in leather divan facing Gus Barone. He sat with his slender shoulders hunched slightly forward, trying hard to hide the mild panic that such a setting produced. He wasn't quite able to, and knew it, while in contrast, Fu Chiang was the picture of graceful ease. Lounging alongside him, Chiang calmly accepted a glass of the champagne just poured while Lyman took his own glass too quickly. Its contents sloshed across the back of one hand, Fat sat with elbows on knees, his white-knuckled fingers wrapped to hold the glass steady.

"A toast," Barone proposed. "We're back in the game, and this time we're playin' to win." He raised his glass, the black hair on the knuckles of his manicured gorilla hand glistening in the salon's soft incandescent light. They had pulled out of the basin and into the bay to avoid onshore listening devices. The portholes were covered with blackout curtains, which made Lyman Fat feel even more claustrophobic.

Both Fat and Chiang ignored the implications behind the toast as they raised their own glasses, then sipped. It was true that their forebears had not played to win in the past, and therefore had been supplanted by others who did. Lyman knew that many of the Mafia's older policymakers had no taste for the drug trade. It was alien to their culture and they had no real feel for how commerce in it should be conducted. The Chinese who had once run the heroin business in New York, on the other hand, were simply too greedy. One moment they were the dominant heroin marketers in the United States, and the next, their single largest American market had fallen into the competition's hands. In a move that smacked of genius, the Colombians and their Dominican henchmen had undertaken to *give* samples of their own product away on the street. To make matters worse, they had so seriously undercut Chinese wholesale prices, orders for Golden Triangle heroin had dried up entirely. Convinced the Colombians were bluffing, the older Chinese had stuck stubbornly to their outmoded pricing structure. That was five years ago, and in the time since, the Colombians had forged a new and powerful alliance with Russian organized crime. Their new partners controlled the flow of heroin from the vast poppy fields of former Soviet states on the Caspian Sea, and today, the Colombians had sources of supply from Asia *and* South America.

"A fine toast, my friend," Fu Chiang replied, still holding his glass in a ceremonial attitude before him. Heavyset and quite tall for an Asian, most of his body was covered with intricate and colorful tattoos. These, and the slight scowl that twisted his battered face, gave him a sinister, thuggish appearance that he found quite useful in his work. "And a profitable arrangement, we now all agree." He let his gaze drift from one face to another in the Albanese godfather's party.

The man on his feet to Barone's left was called Tony "Nails," a lieutenant in charge of a crew run by Albanese capo Angelo "Cheesecake" Albeneti. He had an appetite for violence that compared to Chiang's, and was a rising star in their organization. Albeneti himself was seated to the Mafia boss's right. A baker who ran a large, quasi-legitimate front business, he had an excellent head for finance. Fat did not know it for a fact, but guessed Albeneti would manage the money-laundering end of the Albanese operation through his string of baked goods outlets and other related businesses located in New York City, in New Jersey, and on Long Island.

"But while we think of the future," Chiang continued, "let us also hold close to our hearts the lessons of the past." He raised his glass a second time, knowing he need say no more.

Sixteen

Early Sunday evening, Matt Stuart visited the Douglaston, Queens, home of Deputy Chief Simon Ogilvy for the second time that weekend. There were recent developments his former boss wanted to discuss ASAP, and Sunday or not, Stuart's weekend respite was now thoroughly shot.

An old hand at hosting the impromptu brainstorming sessions called by her husband, Marjorie Ogilvy opened the front door to Matt wearing an easy, welcoming smile. Her dinner was undoubtedly rushed and her relaxed evening at home turned into something other, but she would betray none of this to their visitor. "Good to see you again, Lieutenant," she greeted him.

Matt took her offered hand, no longer surprised as he once had been by the firmness of her grip. "And you, ma'am. How's the project progressing?" He flicked a look in the direction of the basement.

"All finished, believe it or not. Matter of fact, Corinne is down there right now, watching some dreadful horror movie. Simon even managed to get the Surround Sound to work."

Stuart was impressed. His patience with new electronic innovations was limited, evidenced by his reluctance to accept CDs for years after they became the industry standard. He was still unable to program the recording function on his VCR and very begrudgingly tried to stay abreast of advances in computer technology. He'd given in there only because the computer had proved so useful to him in his work.

Shown to the chief's study off the living room, Matt found Ogilvy relaxing with a cocktail. An old Tony Bennett recording from the sixties played low on the sound system. The song was "Danny Boy," and in the background, Stuart recognized the distinctive saxophone style of jazz great Stan Getz.

"Have a seat, Matthew. Thanks for coming on such short notice. Something to drink?"

Stuart thought a scotch and soda sounded good, and waited as the chief rose to pour it. On delivery, he took a first sip, closed his eyes to savor it, and was reminded of just how hectic his day had been.

"Tired?" Ogilvy asked.

"Been running pretty hard," Stuart admitted. "You know what they say about rest and the weary."

The chief sat and picked up a folder set before him on his ottoman. "I suggest you brace yourself, Lou. Before this case cuts you any slack, you could find yourself running even harder. It's starting to take some interesting turns."

Tired or not, Stuart heard intrigue in Ogilvy's voice and felt his interest piqued. "Do tell," he urged him.

Simon settled back into the comfortable worn leather of his chair and opened the folder in his lap. "After our talk last night, I decided not to waste any time and got right onto the Angelo Albeneti aspect of your investigation. I assigned two of my guys to a Mom's Pie surveillance, hoping that sooner or later Tony Nails might happen by."

"What about DaCosta?" Matt asked. "Shouldn't we be set up on him, too?"

"You know how carefully I'm gonna have to tread here, him being another cop and all. I can't assign just anybody to a detail like that."

He had a point, and as eager as Stuart was to get a line on the scope of DaCosta's malfeasance, he knew he couldn't press Ogilvy in that regard. He nodded toward the material in Simon's lap. "I'm assuming your guys hit pay dirt?"

"Maybe the mother lode," the chief replied. "At three this afternoon, Cheesecake Albeneti takes the subway from 125th Street and Lex to Union Square. My guys took a chance and decided to follow, one on the train and one in a car. At Union Square, Cheesecake changes trains and rides the LL clear out to Canarsie."

"The heart of Albanese country," Stuart murmured. "To do what? Join the family for Sunday dinner?"

"It gets better. At the Rockaway Parkway LL stop, who's waiting there to collect him but our friend Tony Nails. Then, rather than drive him to Gus Barone's social club on Remsen and Avenue M, he takes him to the marina in Paerdegat Basin." He paused to toss a grainy eight-by-ten photo of Albeneti and Fortunado walking past cabin cruisers and sail-boats at Stuart. "They park, take a stroll along the boat docks, and go aboard this shiny new fifty-foot Trojan yacht. It comes complete with two goons in leather jackets, dockside." He removed a sheet of paper from the file in his lap and slipped on a pair of reading glasses. "We ran the registration. Surprise. Boat's owned by a corporation, home office Freeport, in the Bahamas."

"Who'd they meet there?" Matt asked. He'd been running Raymond undercover at Mom's Pie for six months. In all that time, they'd never caught Cheesecake Albeneti at anything more incriminating than meeting another wiseguy for a conversation in the middle of Pleasant Avenue. The man was *that* careful, which made today's developments unprece-dented. Something very big had to be in the wind. Nothing less would warrant Albeneti's taking such risk.

"This is where it gets really rich," Ogilvy said. "Yesterday, your theory was that the Albanese are setting up to make a move on Washing-ton Heights. Today, I think we may know how." He removed another grainy black and white from the file and handed it across. "Recognize ei-ther of these guys?"

Matt didn't, but the fact that they were Asian got his heart beating a little faster. The taller, more solidly built of them drew most of his atten-tion. His arms were exposed from wrist to elbow and solid with the kind of tattooing seen frequently on Asian gang members. This man and his slender, almost frail-looking companion stood on the companionway of a sleek, wedge-shaped luxury yacht. "This is who Albeneti and Tony Nails met with?" He looked directly at Ogilvy as he asked the question.

"Among others," Simon replied. He handed Stuart a third picture, of three other men, all approaching the same boat. "These guys I assume you *do* recognize."

The dapper, middle-aged man graying at the temples was Gus

Barone, the Godfather himself. He was flanked on one side by a hulking Albanese capo named Louie "the Crab" DiCaprio. On his other side stood Alfonse Palma, his consigliere and oldest friend.

"Jesus," Matt murmured. "Italian muscle and organizational know-how joined with Chinese lines of supply."

"Kinda looks that way, right? You ask me, it's damn near inspired. The guineas been out of this game practically forever, and all of a sudden this new generation gets a hard-on to be back in the mix again. So who do they hook up with but a faction that's been knocked out of the box so recently they can still taste the blood." Ogilvy's eyes shone as he spoke. "For crissake, Matthew. It's a marriage made in fucking heaven."

Stuart's mind raced as he worked to get all the various elements sorted into some semblance of order. "The Colombians and Russians control heroin supply from the Mideast and South America, but with the Chinese, the Sicilians have a time-tested source of supply again. Meanwhile, Tony Nails works with Clarence DaCosta to destabilize Washington Heights enough to make the Dominicans there vulnerable to attack. I still can't figure how they intend to pull it off, but I doubt it will be long before they show us."

"Won't be a full frontal assault," Ogilvy contended. "Not Gus Barone's style. He's less ham-fisted and more slippery than the old Mustache Petes. He wouldn't have called this meeting"—he paused to tap the photo Stuart had just handed back to him—"without having an entire strategy worked out."

That was Stuart's conclusion, too. "And it all points back to Washington Heights, boss. Frank Santos's turf is the figurative high ground. You take it, you've won a significant battle in the war." As he spoke, Matt was confronting how much he needed to learn. Fast. The evidence collected by Ogilvy's surveillance notwithstanding, the bad guys were still miles ahead of them. Indeed, that evidence, combined with other facts about the Rodriguez and Darryl Johnson-Danny Washington homicides suggested they'd already launched their first major offensive. The timetable would only accelerate from here. Of that he was sure. But where would the next assault take place? And how? "I won't be able to keep this from the Ice Maiden much longer, boss. No matter how much more groundwork we'd like to lay, too much is happening too quickly."

"You know she's gonna shit green, she realizes you've already kept her in the dark," Simon warned.

Matt was all too aware of that, but could see no alternative. "What can she prove if I tell her I only just now took what I've learned to you? That we compared notes and came up with what we have?" He pointed to the file Ogilvy held. "Until you showed me that, I had nothing but theory to go on, based on unfounded suspicions."

Self-styled performance artist Liquid Humanity had taken a break from rewrites of her latest one-person play, *Squeeze from Bottom Up,* to walk her dog. It was eight o'clock in the evening and Uzi, her brainless Irish setter, had been cooped up all day in their studio apartment while Liquid labored in the throes of creative frenzy. With Uzi trying to jerk her right arm from its shoulder socket, Liquid descended the stairs from her fourth-floor walk-up while reflecting on the progress she'd made that day. Three weeks ago, she'd paid an outrageous sum to rent performance space on SoHo's Wooster Street, and had put *Squeeze* on the boards for five disappointing nights. None of the press she'd contacted had bothered to come, despite her having spent close to a thousand dollars on an ultraslick mailing. The one agent she'd been courting sent an underling who looked like she'd just graduated from Bryn Mawr. Over drinks after the show, the fresh-faced little snot had the temerity to suggest the piece was in need of serious polishing. Liquid had gone away angry, and spent the next three days in a sulk. The handful of loyal friends who'd attended multiple performances and raved about the work's "raw energy" had been unable to jolly her out of that funk. It wasn't until she finally got furious enough to want to prove the world—and one ignorant little wannabe agent in particular—wrong that she found the motivation to tear her ninety-minute rant apart and painstakingly begin reconstruction. She was a week into the job and had to admit the product was significantly improved by the effort. Its edges, formerly fuzzy, were sharp as razor blades now. Points didn't simply impact, they *penetrated.*

While passing the second-floor landing—and the apartment door of her most mysterious and most attractive neighbor—Liquid nearly gagged on the strong odor of feces and urine that hung in the stairwell air. Uzi was in such a rush to get to the street, the artist had no time to ascertain from where the stench emanated, and could only conclude a vagrant had gotten into the building and used the second-floor hallway as a toilet. On her way back from Uzi's walk, she supposed she could ring the super's basement-apartment buzzer and advise him of the situation. She could only imagine how her gorgeous, blue-eyed black neighbor might react, coming home late at night to a stink like that.

As Stuart prepared to depart the Intelligence chief's house that night, he was still trying to figure how best to bring Suzanne Albrecht into the loop that he and Simon Ogilvy had created. He was tired. If the week ahead held true to last week's form, it was likely to be hectic. He needed to be fresh in the morning, and figured then would be soon enough to pay the first deputy commissioner a call. Suzanne was notorious for being at her desk earlier than any other superboss on the Job.

Chief Ogilvy escorted Stuart to his front door, where his wife interrupted them. She informed him he had an urgent call from Chief of Department Bob Dunleavy. He held up a finger, asking Matt to hang on, then took the portable from Marjorie's hand.

"Yeah, Bob," he answered brusquely. The Intel chief's expression clouded as he listened. He then made direct eye contact with Stuart. "Corner of Clarkson and Hudson in the Village? Got it. Jesus. I'm on my way." He depressed the cutoff button and handed the phone back to his mate, his expression now grave. "DaCosta's dead. Looks like a drug overdose on the surface, but detectives from the Sixth who caught it think something stinks."

Matt was caught so far off guard he was a moment just getting hold of the simple fact. He stared hard at Ogilvy as he groped to gather his thoughts. "What's at the corner of Clarkson and Hudson?"

"His apartment. A neighbor got a noseful going past his door, and got the super."

To Stuart, who'd never met DaCosta, the dead man remained a faceless renegade cop in dreadlocks who drove a beat-up gypsy cab and reportedly had a chip on his shoulder. He and a mystery woman hitter were Matt's only connection between Angelo Albeneti and Washington Heights, and now, just as suddenly as it was first established, that connection had ceased to exist. "You mind if I tag along?" he asked.

"Better yet, why don't you drive," Ogilvy suggested. "I'll rope a ride back."

The police commissioner wasn't due back from Washington until late that evening, which meant Suzanne Albrecht was still the ranking cop in the city when Officer Clarence DaCosta was found dead. Within fifteen minutes of receiving the call, she was under way from her East Eighty-first Street apartment to Greenwich Village. She had plenty on her mind throughout the ride downtown, trying to make various bits of information fit a bigger picture that was still uncomfortably unclear. That morning she'd learned that the perp killed in the Luis Esquivel bombing was not only Dominican but a likely resident of Washington Heights. It bothered her that Matt Stuart was privy to this information yet hadn't bothered to report it to her. Further, the FA she had planted inside Simon Ogilvy's Intelligence Division had contacted her that afternoon to report on a surveillance set up to watch Mom's Pie Company on Pleasant Avenue in East Harlem. The assignment was ostensibly to trace the movements of one Anthony "Tony Nails" Fortunado, a known soldier in the Albanese crime organization. What bothered Suzanne was the whisperings her FA had overheard. They implicated a mystery woman shooter whom the stakeout might also be looking to identify. Suzanne had since learned that a police artist had done a sketch of a young woman in a ball cap for Stuart, based on a description provided by a protected male witness. Stuart had passed that rendering along to his former boss, and scuttlebutt at Intelligence was that a renegade Special Operations cop might also be involved. Ogilvy was reluctant to set up surveillance on this cop because of the red flags it would raise up the command chain. Regarding crucial elements of a very sensitive investigation, it sounded to the first deputy commissioner like two of her subordinates were conspiring to keep her in the dark. She'd trusted her former lover with her professional future. The idea of his betraying her trust was making her see red.

While waiting for a detective from the Nineteenth Precinct to collect her for the ride downtown, Suzanne had asked Room 1000 at the Big Building to fax her Officer Clarence DaCosta's personnel file. En route to the scene of his death, she familiarized herself with his particulars. His PD 406-143 card listed him as single, with no children and no next of kin. He'd resided at the Clarkson Street address for six years, was a twelve-year member of the Job, and was formerly assigned to Narcotics Borough Brooklyn and Narcotics Borough Queens, both places in plainclothes. Assigned to Inspector Jerry Mannion's S.O.D. Street Crime Monitoring Unit two years ago, he was responsible for gathering statistics and other intelligence on street crime patterns throughout the eleven precincts that composed Patrol Borough Manhattan North. By the time she reached the dead man's address in the West Village, Suzanne had a fair picture, at least on paper, of the officer who had died.

Once Chief of Department Robert Dunleavy escorted her upstairs to DaCosta's second-floor landing, Chief of Detectives Roger Rose, together with the whip of the Sixth Precinct detective squad and the commander of the Manhattan South homicide squad converged on the first deputy commissioner. Several detectives had cigars going in an effort to dispel the stench of human elimination, and smoke hung heavy in the air.

"Short and sweet, Chief," Suzanne told Rose. "What, where, when, how." She and the C of D had never really gotten along, probably because they were fundamentally different personality types. He knew she was next in line for the throne and that he, therefore, would soon be looking for a comfortable retirement career. For a man of his intelligence and ambitions, that knowledge had to rankle.

"Massive overdose of something that hit him with the impact of a locomotive," he replied. "ME is guessing heroin, based on a field test of syringe residue. Victim hit the floor right inside the front door, which my guys think is odd. No tie-off to pop a vein. There's a spoon and lighter on the kitchen counter, but no vial or paper the stuff came in. Figure he's been dead about six hours. No other needle marks on him, or any other evidence says this guy was a junkie."

"Anything *else* strike them as odd?" Suzanne asked, the question dripping sarcasm. She scanned the interior of the apartment, visible to her through the open front door. The corpse of a tawny-skinned African-American male lay stretched in a grotesque attitude on the floor dead ahead. He had hair that could almost be called blond, worn in dreadlocks, and his lean, well-muscled torso was shirtless. His loose-fitting trousers were stained dark with the urine and excrement his dying body had expelled. She could not see his face, and was glad of that.

"Plenty," Rose replied. "Six scrapbooks full of articles on police corruption, cut mostly from newspapers, some dating back fifteen years. A poster-size blowup of an old *SPRING 3100* cover that'll give you goose bumps." He stopped to nod toward the Sixth Precinct whip, standing on his left. "Tommy's guys also think someone might've tossed the place. Real careful, like."

If Officer Clarence DaCosta had been murdered, not inadvertently killed himself with a hot shot of superpure smack, several pressing questions Suzanne had mulled on her way downtown came into sharper focus. Fairly soon, if Matt Stuart valued his pension, he was going to have to provide some answers.

A woman with multiple studs worn in one pierced eyebrow and a crown of thorns tattooed across her forehead scowled impatiently at Matt Stuart and Simon Ogilvy from the backseat of an unmarked Chrysler. They stood on the Clarkson Street sidewalk talking to the Sixth Precinct detectives who had just finished interrogating her. Stuart guessed her expression and overall attitude were part of the persona she'd created to go with the decorations.

"Come again?" Ogilvy asked the taller of the two detectives.

"Liquid Humanity, sir. Says she don't have no driver's license, but it checks out on her AmEx and Visa cards. Claims it's her legal fucking name. Says she's a performance artist, whatever the fuck that is. Lived upstairs from DaCosta the past two years. Never knew what he did for a living."

On arrival, Stuart had learned Suzanne Albrecht was already on the scene and upstairs. He knew he would have to speak to her sooner or later, but was in no rush. She was too smart not to know he'd been holding out on her, and no matter what he chose to say now, she was bound to challenge it in some way.

"Chief Dunleavy mentioned suspicious circumstances," Simon pressed them. "Making you guys think the hot shot he got might not have been self-administered."

The partners took Stuart and Ogilvy through what a medical examiner's pathologist, the Crime Scene Unit, and their own squad had developed after a search of the apartment. To Matt, the circumstances of DaCosta's death sounded more than just suspicious.

"How far inside the frozen zone have our friends from the papers and TV news been allowed?" he asked.

"By now, they probably know the dead guy was a cop. Otherwise, Chief Rose and Chief Dunleavy got a tight lid clamped on it."

"If it was a homicide," the second partner added, "they don't want the perp knowing he didn't pull off the overdose charade, y'know?"

Stuart was happy to hear it, considering what he knew of DaCosta's recent activities. If the killer was someone from Washington Heights retaliating for the murders of Darryl Johnson and Fat Danny Washington, he was likely to brag on it sooner or later. The same went for a friend or relative of Isabelle Melendez or Johnny Rodriguez getting even for their deaths. From experience, Stuart knew that killers who assume they've managed to fool the law are more inclined to be bold than those running with their heads down. "What about her?" he asked, nodding toward the performance artist. "She or any other resident of the building see anything suspicious? A stranger trying to get access, or loitering outside?"

"Nada, Lou. This one claims she was inside all afternoon, working. The stink of piss and shit was fucking overwhelming right outside his door, but nobody seen or smelled nothing all fucking day."

Several minutes later, Stuart and Ogilvy drifted away from the investigating detectives to a spot fifteen yards removed from the dead cop's front stoop. There, the Intelligence chief took a moment to survey the crowd gathered outside the cordoned-off corner section of sidewalk. Two remote news units were parked across Hudson Street, signaling that the vultures of the Fourth Estate had begun to circle in earnest. Both cops knew that once it was learned the deceased was a plainclothes, semiundercover cop assigned to work the drug-ridden streets of upper Manhattan, corruption speculation was inevitable.

"One of these bright-boy newshounds decides the homicides of Officer Rodriguez and this guy are too closely related to be coincidence, you're gonna see your ex-girlfriend throw an embolism, Matthew," Ogilvy warned.

Caught off guard, Stuart threw his old boss a sharp sideways glance. What he saw in the other man's face told him he had no room to maneuver here. "How long have you known?" he asked quietly.

Ogilvy continued to stare straight ahead, into the crowd. "Just about from Jump Street, I'd imagine. I'm the chief of Intelligence in this city, for crissake." He turned to look directly at Stuart. "I've never been too keen on spying on my own people, but the first deputy commissioner pulls strings to get some hard-charging detective lieutenant shoved up my ass, I feel like I've gotta defend myself. For a year, I couldn't believe you weren't one of her fucking FAs."

Stuart reeled from the implications. He'd worked for Ogilvy for over two years, which meant he'd been under suspicion for nearly half his tenure at Intelligence. "Jesus," he murmured. "What made you decide I wasn't?" He left the ultimate presumption of his fidelity implied.

"Gut instinct, mostly, but backed up by a lot of careful observation, too. I watched how things you worked on never surfaced anywhere else.

I watched how you dug into every assignment and seemed to give it your all. That's a hard thing to fake, friend."

Matt muttered "Jesus" a second time and again shook his head. "I presume you know, or have at least guessed, why I drew this current assignment?"

Before he could answer, something caught Simon's attention up the sidewalk. He directed Stuart's attention toward the door of DaCosta's building. There, Suzanne Albrecht, led by Chief of Department Bob Dunleavy and followed by Chief of Detectives Roger Rose, was emerging into the deepening gloom. The sun had set half an hour ago, and all color had drained from the evening sky. The amber glow of mercury-vapor streetlights, combined with the harsh glare of video kliegs, were the scene's only illumination.

"She wants that top-cop job so badly it makes her nipples hard," Ogilvy replied. "I doubt she knows that I know Rodriguez was one of her FAs, but I expect she told you. If it comes out that she was directly responsible for running him, and he went native on her, she can kiss her dream good-bye. Ergo, you're her knight in shining armor, Matthew. The champion sent to defend her tarnished honor."

Twice in two days, Stuart had been a guest in this man's home, traveling there to talk over things he'd uncovered in the course of an increasingly complex—and yes, explosive—investigation. On neither occasion had Ogilvy so much as batted an eye; not when informed of Johnny Rodriguez's evident corruption, and not when told that Clarence DaCosta was in bed with the Sicilian mob and had likely had a hand in killing a brother officer. It would be harder to play a hand any closer to the vest. "I guess the powers knew what they were doing," he said, a bemused smile crinkling the corners of his eyes, "the day they gave you the Intel chief's job."

Ogilvy made an effort to reassure him when he spoke again. "I've never once regretted her assigning you to me, Lieutenant. You're one of the best I've ever commanded, and I say that without reservation."

"Just one who isn't above accepting a favor, granted for personal reasons, no?"

Simon returned his smile. "We all live in glass houses, Matthew. I base my judgments on performance and try not to make a habit of throwing stones." He nodded toward the bottom step of the stoop, where the pair of superchiefs flanked the first deputy commissioner. A uniformed captain from the Job's Public Information Division was addressing a knot of reporters, while Suzanne awaited her turn. "I suggest we let her do her thing, then corner her afterwards. By the way, I've let slip a few bits and pieces of what we're up to, including the identity of the probable Esquivel bomber, to the FA she's got planted on my staff."

Familiar with most of the cops currently assigned to Intelligence, Matt peered curiously at him. "Who?" he asked.

"Pete Ogborn."

"Ah." Ogborn, a young, clean-cut go-getter, was someone with whom Matt had never worked an investigation. He didn't strike him as the sort to spy on his brother officers, but any FA who was good at his job wouldn't. He wondered what charms Suzanne might have used to lure him into her web.

"Came aboard just after you did," Ogilvy continued. "The back-stabbing little prick actually believes he's gotten away with their little charade."

Seventeen

While Suzanne Albrecht spoke to the media gathered on Clarkson Street, feeding them a few scant facts surrounding the death of Officer Clarence DaCosta, Stuart marveled at the agility and skill with which she handled their collective aggression. He also found himself examining her with new eyes.

"Let me ask this," a reporter from WCBS-TV News pressed her. "Why such a turnout of NYPD's top brass if this is merely a police officer who overdosed on drugs?"

Suzanne faced the tall, very blond, and fiercely serious reporter with imperious cool. "We don't talk in terms of *merely* when one of our own meets such a tragic end, Sharon," she replied. "The stresses of Officer DaCosta's assignment put him directly in a kind of harm's way that the New York Police Department needs to be sensitive to. Chief Dunleavy, Chief Rose, and I are here tonight in recognition of that fact."

"What, exactly, is a Street Crime Unit liaison?" a beat reporter from the *Post* demanded.

Suzanne worked without notes or support from the men on either side of her. While Matt listened to her description of DaCosta's assignment and what it entailed, he considered how much benefit of the doubt Simon Ogilvy must have given him. The man had known that Matt was screwing this skillfully manipulative woman, and also known that everything she did seemed to have an ulterior motive behind it. And still, he'd allowed Stuart the opportunity to prove himself, against strong odds. To him it meant Ogilvy was far cleverer and well suited to run Intelligence than anyone probably realized.

"Gotta admit she's smooth, Lou," Simon muttered in Matt's ear. "I couldn't imagine what you saw in her until I took a more critical look. Does a lot, trying to disguise what she's got."

The memory of the first time he'd seen Suzanne Albrecht unclothed flashed bright before Stuart's mind's eye. By then, he'd already decided she was a handsome specimen, and yet was unprepared for what greeted him as she emerged from the bath off her bedroom. All elegantly tapered limbs and breath-stealing curves, her naked body was downright stunning.

"Purge that faraway look from your eye, my friend," Ogilvy advised. "Fifteen minutes from now, chances are you'll never have so much as a friendly word with her again. I were you, I'd lock in my happy memories now."

Stuart was almost certain that Suzanne hadn't told him everything she knew about Johnny Rodriguez when she'd sent him north to investigate her dead FA's homicide. The circumstantial evidence he'd collected said she must have known Rodriguez would be killed. *Before* the fact. She'd had Matt's transfer all lined up the very morning after the Macho Man's murder. He'd seen something uncharacteristic in her demeanor and assumed it was just another part of the emotional barrier she'd erected: a studied, detached distance that even his passionate kiss had failed—but for a moment—to dislodge. Now he wondered if he'd seen the brittle edges of barely controlled panic. A major scandal would scuttle her shot at the throne, and he was her last desperate hope of quashing it.

Having fielded a dozen questions, Suzanne cut the impromptu press conference off and excused herself from the company of her superchief escort. She made a beeline for where Stuart and Ogilvy stood, her expression determined and her underlying grimness barely held in check.

"Join me in my car, gentlemen," she ordered. "We're going to talk." Without elaboration, she turned on her heels and strode up the sidewalk toward a black Mercury Marquis. The Nineteenth Precinct detective who had driven her there was leaning against its hood in conversation with a detective from the Sixth. On her approach, he broke off to open the left rear door for her. She signaled Ogilvy to join her in the backseat, while Matt moved to occupy the front passenger seat. Once settled, Suzanne waved the driver away at a distance and folded her arms across her breasts to fix Ogilvy with a scowl.

"Who, or what, prompted you to set up a surveillance at Mom's Pie Company without the Intelligence Oversight Committee's approval," she demanded. "Last report I read, an exhaustive investigation had determined it to be a legitimate business."

"Officer DaCosta was seen there two nights ago," the Intel chief replied.

Matt had to give it to him. He was meeting the first deputy commissioner head-on and apparently without fear.

"In the company of a woman who answers the description of Officer Juan Rodriguez's killer," Simon continued. "Officer DaCosta was identified as being in her company on that night as well."

If Suzanne blinked, Matt missed it. "By whom?"

Stuart answered for Ogilvy. "A street pitcher named Benny Collier. Member of the so-called Red Top crew. They work a twelve-block area between 143rd and 155th Streets." Suzanne's glare shifted to him as he spoke and he felt the intensity of her fury. "He was at work outside the Melendez woman's building the night the hit went down."

Suzanne continued to study him. There was accusation in those eyes. "We spoke just yesterday, Lieutenant. How is it you failed to mention these rather significant developments at that time?"

"I'd asked him not to," Ogilvy lied. It surprised the hell out of Stuart to hear him say it, and were he not already on his guard, he might have betrayed his astonishment. Simon, a master at covering his own ass, was voluntarily hanging it out in the breeze. "When he showed me the artist's sketch of the suspected shooter and told me of the DaCosta connection, she too closely resembled the woman seen in DaCosta's company at Mom's Pie Company. I learned a long time ago, the more widely information crucial to an investigation is spread, the more liable it is to be compromised."

Suzanne stared at him with a mixture of disbelief and outrage. "I'm your direct fucking superior, Simon. A police officer is suspected in the homicide of another officer, and you choose to withhold that information from me?"

"Perhaps it was a mistake," he admitted, not sounding like he meant it. "But yes, Suzanne. That's exactly what I did. The murdered officer was one of your FAs, and as dirty as the bottom of a Dumpster. I had, and still have, no idea how deep his corruption goes, or who else might be involved. You wanna run my decision past *your* boss, you be my guest."

Stuart knew Suzanne well enough to know how badly she wanted to lash out right now. While Ogilvy couldn't be seen as one of her rivals for further advancement up the big-brass ladder, he was still a rival for power. Intelligence Division was arguably as loose a cannon as existed within the tight structure of the Job, and Suzanne hated anything she couldn't screw down. Or anyone. By necessity, Intel often functioned outside parameters that the office of first deputy commissioner could control, and so did Chief Simon Ogilvy. Rather than confront his challenge head-on, she chose to change tack.

"Just how, might I ask, did someone see Officer DaCosta and this mystery woman at Mom's Pie Company, Simon? Prior to you ordering this morning's surveillance?"

He smiled a tight, don't-fuck-with-me smile. "I'm commander of the Job's Intelligence Division, Suzanne. My people and their sources see things. I'm not at liberty to reveal who; at least not at this time."

It had turned into a battle of wills and Matt saw that Suzanne knew she wasn't likely to win this one. Again, she changed tack, and turned back to him.

"Unlike Chief Ogilvy, I presume you *do* understand you are under my direct command, Lieutenant. Do you have any shared knowledge of who saw Officer DaCosta and your alleged female shooter at Mom's Pie on Pleasant Avenue?"

He didn't ask if the subject she referred to was an alleged female or an alleged shooter, but simply shook his head to indicate no. If the fact of Raymond's deep-cover existence inside Mom's Pie ever came to light, Simon Ogilvy faced professional castration. Suzanne Albrecht was angry enough at that moment to do anything within her power to get even. "I don't, ma'am," he replied. "I thought I might get lucky when I showed Chief Ogilvy the artist's sketch. That's all. My mention of Officer DaCosta being in her company was what set all the fireworks off."

Again, she turned to confront Ogilvy. "And the purpose of your surveillance on Pleasant Avenue is what, specifically?"

Simon was warming to this. He'd won the first round and his attitude was more relaxed. He even went so far as to ease deeper into the leather upholstery and draw an ankle up over one knee. "Lieutenant Stuart worked the Angelo Albeneti file for close to a year. Even though he never found anything he could pin on the man, he was not so convinced as you seem to be that Mom's Pie is a legitimate business."

"And why is that?" she snapped.

"An Albanese family soldier, Anthony 'Tony Nails' Fortunado, was seen making visits there. On one occasion he stood in the middle of Pleasant Avenue to have a conversation with Cheesecake Albeneti. It's hard to believe he's no more than another pastry customer."

"Seen by whom?" Suzanne demanded.

Ogilvy waved a dismissive hand. "Not material to what I'm telling you right now. What's material is the fact that this made Mafia guy has a conference with Albeneti that demands they stand with cars whizzing past in both directions. And right after DaCosta and this mystery tomboy shooter show their faces there, Matthew visits me with a story this dope peddler told him about the night Johnny Rodriguez was taken down. You're in my shoes, how do you react to all that?"

Without replying, Suzanne continued to glare at him. And try as he might to imagine what was going through her head at that moment, Stuart failed. He couldn't fathom why she was digging in like this, attacking the surveillance of a long-suspected Mafia front business. Her interest, and that of Simon Ogilvy, was supposed to be the same here. Root out bad guys. Throw them behind bars. Get them so dead to rights, the judge who passes sentence has no choice but to virtually throw away the key.

"Matter of fact," Simon continued, "I'm glad my people were where they were this afternoon. They saw no sign of DaCosta, but at three o'clock, Cheesecake Albeneti—who happens to own a brand-new Cadillac and a fleet of delivery trucks—takes a ride clear out to Canarsie on the subway. Tony Nails picks him up at the end of the line and they drive to meet with Gus Barone. For the occasion, he's gathered together several other known Albanese family members, and two high-ups in the Chinese heroin business."

Simon went on to describe the setting and the photographs his people had obtained. He detailed the roles currently being played in the Chinese underworld by Lyman Fat and Fu Chiang, and finished with Stuart's latest working hypothesis: the Albanese crime family and a Chinese faction with strong Golden Triangle ties were preparing to go head-to-head with the Colombian-Dominican-Russian drug distribution consortium. "It looks to me like we've got two dirty cops one way or another involved in a power play between the two most powerful factions in the history of organized drug dealing," he concluded. "Both those cops are dead, and one was under your direct command."

When Suzanne turned her glare back toward Stuart, the strength of her indignation had diminished somewhat. It was replaced, instead, by accusation. In the face of it, all he could do was shrug defensively. "I didn't ask for this gig, Suzanne," he said. "But I took it, and first and foremost, I've done the best job I knew how to do."

She started to interrupt, but he held up a hand to stop her.

"Simon didn't understate the problem just now. I think we're on the verge of an offensive launched by the Albanese and Chinese that could blow the roof off this town."

Ever since he'd heard the word late Saturday night that Eddie Castillo had failed in his attempt to kill Roberto Santiago's problematic reporter, Tío Paco Santos had kept a low profile. The car bombing at *La Paz* was all over the late news yesterday, and splashed across the Sunday afternoon edition front pages of the *Post*, *Daily News*, and *Newsday*. Media speculation over who was responsible ran rampant. Most glaring in each account was the fact that the bombing had failed and Luis Esquivel was still very much alive. To compound Castillo's failure, the mayor had proclaimed Esquivel a hero, and various Hispanic community groups were finally starting to make angry noises.

As valuable as his Washington Heights distribution network was to the Cali cartel, the Dominican *patrón* knew Santiago had to be furious. Losing face might not be quite as big an issue with the Colombians as it was with the Japanese, but a twisted sense of personal honor was paramount in Colombian culture. Luis Esquivel had been identified as a problem. Santiago had entrusted the specifics of taking care of it to Francisco Santos. Santos's failure would therefore be seen as Roberto's failure, all the way up through the cartel command structure to the seat of power in Cali. Depending on how displeased Santiago's handlers might be, they could make a move to replace him. Santiago knew that, and retribution against Santos was not out of the question.

A man who prided himself on his nerve, Tío Paco was a mess by ten o'clock that Sunday night. Ever since his own personal policeman, Johnny Rodriguez, had been whacked by the renegade mulatto cop, he'd had no access to police intelligence. He was flying blind. Just an hour ago, he'd learned the mulatto was also dead, apparently of a drug overdose, but knew better than to believe that aspect of the story. Suddenly, everything was very out of kilter in his world, and he was at a loss trying to find a way to set it right again. Like desert sands in a windstorm, the very topography on which he stood was changing before his eyes.

"I need air," he announced, and heaved himself to his feet in the back room of his bodega. He'd spent the entire day there, not daring to even look out to see who might have entered his store. Hector, his massive *marielito* bodyguard, had spent it with him, along with his sister's two sons. They had alternately played checkers and dominoes until all of them had grown bored and restless.

"Do you think it is wise, Don Francisco?" the older of his nephews asked. Pepe Fernandez was built along the same squat, powerful lines as his uncle, was twenty-six years old and the smarter of the two boys. "Until you have at least spoken to Don Roberto? Been given the opportunity to explain?"

"Explain what?" Santo grumbled. "There is no explanation for failure." He fingered the compact in the pocket of his trousers, wondering if he should step into the *baño* and check his scar before walking out in public. "But a *patrón* cannot fear to walk his own streets. The news of it will spread. When it does, I am finished here."

"Let us go see Santiago, Pepe and me," his younger nephew, Fredo, suggested. "He does not frighten us, Tío Paco."

Bigger than his older brother and more headstrong, Fredo was too impressed with his muscles and disrespectful of the wisdom that came with age. Without Pepe to hold him in check, his uncle believed the mean streets of Washington Heights would have long since swallowed him up. "Then you are a bigger fool than I thought," Santos scolded. "Today, Santiago also fights for his life here. We are cornered animals, him and me. The difference is that he can lash out, while I am without teeth or claws."

For nearly fourteen hours, Taras Pidvalna had been cooped up in the stuffy, darkened interior of a rented panel van parked across Broadway from bodega El Cielo, patiently waiting for any sign of the man called Tío Paco Santos. To Pidvalna, a recent arrival in New York from Kiev in Ukraine, the corner of 146th Street and Broadway on a sunny Sunday afternoon had been a source of constant fascination. Never in his life had he seen young people like these, so full of apparently aimless frenzy. Their elders were content to sit at sidewalk tables playing dominoes, gossiping, and eating food cooked on open-air grills, but the children, especially teenagers, could not sit still. The girls, many wearing tight, skimpy shorts and cropped, sleeveless tops in brilliant tropical colors were so brazenly provocative in their movements and attitudes that Taras, a seasoned former KGB agent forty-six years of age, had found it difficult to maintain his focus. In response to the girls and their musky sensuality, the boys behaved only as boys so severely stimulated must. They postured, pranced, revved their car engines, and tried to feign indifference. Doomed by biology, they so hopelessly failed at these attempts, they appeared quite comical.

In the middle of this circus stood a narrow, orange-yellow-and-aqua-painted storefront said to be the headquarters of local drug kingpin Francisco "Tío Paco" Santos. Pidvalna had a photograph of the man taped to one wall of the van, but could no longer see it in the darkness. No matter; he had the wide Indian-African face committed to memory, with its broad, wedge-shaped nose and strong cheekbones, the thinning jet hair combed straight back from a pronounced widow's peak. Through a hole drilled in the large *O* of an OLIVERA BROTHERS CARNES Y CHORIZO magnetic sign affixed to the van exterior, he'd waited and watched for any sign of the local *patrón*. The noise-suppressed Maunz 308 caliber Assault Sniper rifle leaning against the wall of the truck close at hand was a weapon with which Taras had only recently become acquainted. Still, he had no doubts as to its effectiveness in practiced hands. For fifteen years, Pidvalna had served within KGB ranks as one of the Soviet state's most proficient long-range target elimination specialists. The methods at which he was practiced were many and diverse—a sniper's bullet, for instance, would be an inappropriate end for the troublesome mistress of a party boss—but none suited this former biathlon champion better than an accurate, well-crafted rifle.

With his wary nephews out in front of him to lead the way, and the dispassionate "Havana Hector" Jaquez bringing up the rear, Tío Paco Santos stepped nervously from bodega El Cielo onto the Broadway sidewalk. Up and down the short city block between 146th and 147th Streets, the air was filled with strains of "Nadie Como Ella," sung by the Puerto Rican heartthrob Mark Anthony. It emanated from a boom box propped on a fire escape mid-block, and below it, a group of teenage kids loitered, many dancing. In the doorway of the laundry next door, four elderly Dominican men sat at a card table playing dominoes, the staccato clacking of pieces moving in quick succession punctuating their play. Here and there women sat in cheap plastic patio chairs, conversing in loud, excited voices with others leaning out of windows overhead. One of the men at the domino table spotted the *patrón*'s emergence from his place of business and raised a hand in casual greeting. The familiar voice of a woman hailed Santos loudly from the street.

"*¡Tío Paco! ¿Cómo está—bien?*"

Santos turned toward a small cluster of women leaning against the fender of a gypsy cab and forced a smile. But instead of returning it, they gaped openmouthed at two female figures kneeling inside the trunk of a battered Toyota, faces hidden behind ski masks. Each brandished a machine pistol and simultaneously opened fire.

Santos saw the head of Pepe explode like a ripe melon hit with a rock. A split second later, a hail of metal-jacketed 9 mm bullets ripped into his own torso, knocking him backward violently. When he slammed into the considerable bulk of Hector Jaquez, Havana Hector stumbled, tripped, and went down hard, the dying Frank Santos sprawled atop him. In the Dominican *patrón*'s final seconds of consciousness, before perception left him, all he knew was puzzlement. The voice of the woman who had hailed him was one he knew, but he failed to put a finger on whose voice it was.

Taras Pidvalna had seen the door of the bodega open. As the first of the Dominican *patrón*'s party stepped into view, he'd quickly brought the sniper rifle to bear. Sighting through the hole cut in the OLIVERA BROTHERS sign, he was waiting to get a clear shot at the shorter, older man behind two muscular young escorts when his target turned suddenly and all hell broke loose. Pidvalna watched in stunned amazement as two female figures in ski masks opened fire on Santos. Inside the confined interior of the van, the noise of those automatic weapons was deafening. He dove to the floor and lay flat on his belly, trying to present a low profile to any stray bullets, and only raised his head once the gunfire ceased. The van's darkened interior was enveloped in an eerie silence for just seconds before a woman started to scream hysterically.

Slowly, Pidvalna rose to his knees to peer out through his peephole.

The Sunday night revelers seen enjoying the balmy spring night just seconds earlier had scattered to the winds. A lone woman knelt wailing over the crumpled body of a child ten yards from where the bodies of the man called Tío Paco and his party littered the pavement. The two women shooters and their battered Toyota were nowhere to be seen.

Pidvalna's only interest now was in vanishing. With traffic still flowing normally past the scene, he forced himself to move confidently into the driver's seat, turn the key, and wait for a break to develop in the flow of traffic. Across the way, cars had started to slow as rubberneckers craned their necks to gawk. To avoid delays, Taras turned west on 147th Street, then south again on Riverside Drive. All the while, he tried to make sense of the events he'd just witnessed. He suspected that his employers in Brighton Beach, Brooklyn, might be confused by them as well.

Eighteen

For a man who had started out that Sunday savoring the idea of a much needed day off, Matt Stuart had seen fate play mischief with his best-laid plans. It was one of the aspects of the whip's life he'd conveniently managed to forget, especially a whip working out of a busy shop. At his last assignment before Intel Division, as whip of the Seven-one detective squad in the Flatbush section of Brooklyn, he'd slogged through many a seven-day workweek. Rarely, though, was any so fraught with intrigue as this past one had been.

He returned home at quarter past ten that Sunday night. By ten-thirty, he'd finished flossing his teeth and was prepared to tumble wearily into the sack. En route between the bathroom and his bed, the phone rang, the caller a sergeant working the Manhattan North Operations Desk. A multiple homicide involving Francisco Santos had just been reported in the Three-seven, on Broadway and 146th Street. The Dominican *patrón*, two of his bodyguards, and a nine-year-old boy had been killed by automatic gunfire. A third Santos henchman had sustained minor wounds. Two assailants, reportedly seen fleeing in an older-model Toyota Tercel, remained at large.

While reaching for a fresh shirt and underwear, Stuart asked the sergeant to roust the rest of his squad and have them meet him there. On his way through the kitchen to the garage stairs, he dumped the cold dregs of that morning's coffee into a cup and drained it. The stale taste was foul in his mouth. All the way north up the Gowanus and Brooklyn-Queens Expressways to the Triborough Bridge, he considered the implications of what had transpired and wondered if this was the first major offensive launched in the war he'd seen coming. He also knew that in the violent world of drug commerce, there were literally hundreds of people who might have had a beef with Frank Santos bitter enough to motivate taking him down. But experience told him the same sort of "gut feeling" things that the so-called drums of Washington Heights told Martini Al Goldstein. There were only two scenarios he was apt to take seriously at that moment. Either the Italian-Chinese coalition had declared open war, or a disenchanted Roberto Santiago was opting to replace Santos to save face.

The atmosphere in Washington Heights seemed surprisingly tranquil, considering what had happened that night, when Stuart eventually drove northbound into the Three-Seven via Broadway. Fewer people were seen loitering outside the all-night bodegas or lounging in lawn chairs enjoying the balmy spring night than he had expected. But then, as he approached the intersection with 145th Street, his perception of tranquillity changed dramatically. A block further on, the night was streaked by the bar lights of a half dozen RMPs and several EMS ambulances. Traffic was being routed east over 146th Street, with the left lane of Broadway kept clear for emergency vehicle access. The resultant jam-up reminded Stuart of midtown at rush hour. The sidewalk on the far side of Broadway was crowded with a throng of agitated pedestrians, some out to enjoy the spectacle and others visibly angered by what had taken place. With his flashing red gumball shoved onto the roof of his car, Matt could feel the hatred that radiated his way from many of the young Dominicans he rolled past and prayed that nothing would happen within the next several hours to further agitate them. A popular local *patrón* had just been murdered gangland style; one known for handing out hundred-dollar bills to the working poor and buying soccer balls and baseball gloves for local kids. It was a pittance compared to what he'd sucked from their lives, but theirs was a world where everyone sought to exploit them to some degree, and gave damned little in return.

At a blockade erected across Broadway at the corner of 146th Street, Stuart waited for a uniformed officer to haul a blue-painted barricade back and afford him access to the scene. He parked alongside several other unmarked units, surprised to recognize Martini Al's Chrysler among them. Goldstein, driving from his Spring Valley home in Rockland County twenty-five miles upstate, had beat him there.

The Three-seven squad's second-in-command was located inside the frozen zone at the northeast corner of Broadway and 146th, an unlit cigar clenched in his teeth and hands in his pockets, standing in conversation with uniformed patrol watch commander Captain Glen Arnold.

"Evening, Lou," Goldstein greeted him. "Real mess we got here." He nodded toward a forensic pathologist Stuart recognized. The man knelt over a corpse twenty feet removed from three others, all sprawled within five feet of each other. "That one's the nine-year-old boy. Caught a stray round in the face."

While staring at the dead kid, Matt got a vivid memory flash of his own son lying dead in his driveway. His heart went out to the boy's parents. "How long you been here?" he asked Goldstein.

"Ten minutes, tops. Glen was just catching me up. Says witnesses are claiming it was two broads did the shooting. They waited in ambush in the trunk of this beat-to-shit Toyota. Jumped out, did the deed, drove off."

"We found the car fifteen minutes ago," Arnold told Stuart. "Over by City College on 125th Street. Abandoned. Stolen tags. We're still running the vehicle ID numbers."

Goldstein showed Stuart where the shooters had parked. "The cap tells me he's got witnesses say a woman hailed Santos just as he stepped from his store. There's debate whether it was one of the shooters or another gal, maybe might've functioned as their lookout."

"Anyone recognize the voice?" Matt asked.

Glen Arnold shook his head, his expression turned rueful. "You know how closemouthed these locals can be. My guys are digging, though."

"One interesting twist," Goldstein added. He had the cigar out of his mouth and used it to point. "You remember that big fucking *marielito* with the Folsom tattoo?"

Stuart recalled the Cuban vividly. "The muscle Santos had with him in the store the other day."

"Havana Hector Jaquez. Badass fucking mutt if ever there was one. Lucky fuck's standing behind Santos when all the shit goes down, so Paco's dying carcass shields him from all the flying lead. Boss man slams into him and they both go down in a heap, the Cuban on the bottom of the pile."

"What's meant by minor injuries?" Stuart asked.

Goldstein jammed his stogie back between his lips and grinned around it. "Banged his head on the pavement going down. Nasty knot and a concussion. Otherwise, not a fucking scratch."

Gina Galati did not like surprises and had sought to control as many aspects of her work and daily life as she could with careful planning. She also kept tabs on the mood of her city, country, and world at large by staying abreast of current events, and each morning took time to scan the *Times* and at least one of the city's three major tabloids, front to back. Twice a day she watched CNN and local news.

Sunday night at 11:04, Gina was stretched atop the comforter on her king-size bed, propped against a pair of pillows as she watched the WNBC late news report. With her son sleeping noiselessly in his crib, she kept the volume of the television barely audible to avoid disturbing him. The lead news item was a late-breaking story from Washington Heights, where a powerful local drug figure named Santos had been killed an hour earlier in a sidewalk shooting. According to eyewitnesses, two women wearing ski masks had ambushed Santos and three bodyguards as they emerged from the El Cielo bodega on Broadway, killing them and a nine-year-old bystander.

When Gina accepted contracts from the Albanese organization via Tony Fortunado, she had one inviolable rule she always followed. She wanted to know nothing of her victims: whether they were married, had children, or what they had done to provoke Albanese ire. Such information about a victim tended to humanize them, and Gina wanted nothing of their humanity. The way she viewed these matters, an individual was already dead, whether they continued to draw breath or not, the instant Gus Barone decided he wanted them dead. Why should some other shooter get the ten thousand dollars she could earn performing a task that was really no more than a mere formality?

Tonight, as she watched the news, Gina felt herself start to breathe a bit quicker and sat up to pay closer attention. Twice that week she'd traveled to Washington Heights at Gus Barone's behest to kill three specifically targeted individuals and one woman who happened to be in the way. Presumably, all of them were involved in the drug trade. Her second victim was a cop. The last two were part of a large-scale street-dealing enterprise. To her, it sounded like Gus Barone and the Albanese were taking a hands-on interest in how the drug business was run in Washington Heights. Beyond that assumption, she knew nothing, and *wanted* to know nothing more.

It was the second news item broadcast into her bedroom that night that saw Gina's breath actually catch in her throat. Clarence DaCosta, described by the New York Police Department as a plainclothes Special Operations Division cop working the northern reaches of Manhattan, had been discovered dead of an apparent drug overdose in his Greenwich Village apartment.

As Gina gaped, unable to believe what she saw, a video clip of a woman holding a press conference replaced the face of the news anchor. A graphic identified her as Suzanne Albrecht, first deputy commissioner of the New York Police Department, but Gina was certain she'd seen her somewhere. Admittedly, this was an older version of the face that she remembered, but the woman had the same severely tied-back auburn hair, same strong facial bones, and same dreadful eyeglasses.

"The specific assignment Officer DaCosta had, and the function he performed, put him in grave danger on this city's worst streets for over two years," the woman told a cluster of reporters clutching microphones. "It appears that he succumbed to the kind of temptation he faced on a daily basis, and lost his own personal war on drugs in the saddest and most ironic of ways. But however you choose to view his death, we at NYPD want to remind you that Officer DaCosta was a hero," she declared. "We asked him to make what is literally a living hell his daily home. We cannot judge him for what happened here today, and can only view his passing as a terrible tragedy."

"Jesus Christ," Gina murmured. With eyes squeezed shut, she threw her head back, reliving the vivid memory of him there, in that very bed, just last night. It was hard to believe he was dead, but there was one thing of which she was fairly certain. Clarence DaCosta might have been twisted, and totally and irredeemably corrupt, but he wasn't any junkie. DaCosta loved his body the way an Italian grandmother loves the Virgin Mary. He hated drugs the way that same grandmother hates any woman who marries her son. There was no way he would willingly choose to defile his sacred temple with the poison of weak-willed pissants. To Gina, it meant one thing. Someone had murdered him.

One moment she was lying there, stunned, and the next she was all action. Clarence had called her at least six times in the past week, mostly from his cell phone. Those calls were traceable, either by the cops *or* by the people who had killed him. And either way, she was a sitting duck there on John Street. She had to get away, fast.

The Franchi automatic shotgun, an Intratec machine pistol, two handguns, and plenty of ammunition for each weapon went into a baseball bat bag with shoulder sling. She kept a packed bag of clothes, diapers, bottles, and food for Claude, along with a travel bag of her own in her bedroom closet for just such an eventuality. As she hauled these to the elevator, she considered the precautions she'd taken to cover her tracks, searching for anything she might have overlooked. Her phone was registered to a name other than her own, as were her Con Edison and cable TV accounts. The lease was in the name of a dummy corporation she'd formed. None of those safeguards would keep a determined pursuit at bay forever. They were only designed to buy her time. Right now, she needed as much time as luck would agree to give her.

Half a block up John Street, Gina had rented a derelict tire repair shop and parked a brand-new Land Rover Discovery behind its roll-up garage door. She'd only driven the car once, the day she picked it up from the dealer in Upper Saddle River, New Jersey. Since then, she had visited the garage once a week to make sure the battery was up and the vehicle would start on demand. When the elevator arrived, she grabbed all she could carry in one trip and started with it toward the street. Her plan was simple: load the car, grab the kid, and get the hell gone.

After two years spent assigned to the Three-seven detective squad, Rhoda Bolivar was accustomed to being called out of bed at all hours. Tonight, Jack Hogan had offered to collect her, and the partners had ridden to the scene of the Santos homicide together. Shortly after their arrival, it became apparent that the local population was every bit as frightened about what might happen next on their streets as the cops were. From what Rhoda knew of the Santos organization, his oldest nephew would have been the most likely candidate to take the reins in his uncle's absence. Now, he too had been killed in this housecleaning.

Interrogations were conducted with the several cooperative eyewitnesses the uniformed patrol had managed to locate. Then Rhoda and the other squad members joined the whip, Intelligence chief Simon Ogilvy, and Duty Captain Glen Arnold inside the El Cielo bodega. By that time, the corpses had been removed to the morgue, but the Crime Scene Unit was still searching for evidence that might help determine who had perpetrated the attack. Rhoda didn't hold out much hope there. She had no idea who the actual agents were, but felt strongly that this was the initial gambit in the power play she and Stuart had first theorized about just yesterday.

When Stuart addressed the collected company, he echoed Rhoda's thoughts. "Someone will step into the void here, and soon," he said. "And no matter who supplies them, the new front people will have to be Dominican. It's their neighborhood."

"And don't forget," Josh Littel added. "For all the *patrón* bullshit he spread around, the list of people who hated Santos has gotta be a mile long." He sat straddling a folding chair backward, looking disheveled in a necktie knotted haphazardly and a sport coat that seemed to have lost its will to live. "You consider how much money the man was making, you got *two* powerful motives for someone moving on him."

"A possible spotter and two shooters, all female," Stuart said. "Makes me wonder if we're not seeing some sort of divide-and-conquer strategy at work here."

"How so?" Jack Logan asked.

Stuart shrugged. "Only a hunch. But if I'm the Albanese and I want to move into an area, I think I'd want to destabilize the old power structures. How better to do that than start a gender war?"

"Matter of fact, there are strong matriarchal influences in Dominican culture," Rhoda offered. "Could be you're onto something, Lou. Women hereabouts have done a lot of Santos's bidding but hate the kind of macho posturing he engaged in. What they hated in particular is how its affected their lives."

Leaning with his backside propped against the angled glass of a deli case, Al Goldstein pointed the end of his cigar at her. "Like that broad you been squeezing the past couple months. Whatsername? The one who won't talk to nobody but you. That the attitude you're talking about?"

"Woman, Sarge," Rhoda corrected him. "And yeah. Candy Ignacio might be too strung out to be the kind of threat the Lou is talking about, but that's exactly the attitude." She turned to Stuart to explain. "One night back in February, the uniformed patrol found her freezing on the front stoop of her tenement. Her boyfriend was a Santos mule. Uncle

Frank sent him down to the islands to haul back a load of Cali cartel dope, and no one knows if he got killed, was arrested, or went AWOL. Two months after he disappeared, everything he'd left Candy to live on was gone up in smoke. One night she comes home to find her locks changed."

"And guess who her landlord was," Hogan added.

Stuart was intrigued. "Santos."

Hogan nodded. "Which makes you wonder if Candy's old man did something down in the islands that really pissed old Tío Paco off."

"Where's she now?" Stuart asked.

Rhoda glanced at her watch. "Somewhere between Twenty-third and Forty-ninth Streets, on Eleventh Avenue. Turning tricks. With her boyfriend and money gone, she had to find another way to feed her habit."

"Got a pimp then, I presume?"

"Black guy, pals around with one of the Red Top crew block captains. That's the connection, by the way, that got her started down this road in the first place. Her stepmother runs a stash house for the Dominicans."

Stuart considered this new information. "Right before the two shooters jumped from the trunk, most of the eyewitnesses say Santos reacted to a woman's voice that seemed to be familiar to him. Nobody is willing to say who they think that woman was. I think we should talk to your snitch."

"Her, and the Cuban," Martini Al interjected. "Man was like Santos's fucking shadow. If Paco knew the broad, Jaquez'll know who she is, too."

"Woman, Sarge," Rhoda corrected him again.

"Bite me, Detective."

"No thanks. Just brushed my teeth."

"People, " Stuart stopped them. "The sooner we wrap this, the sooner we can all go home to bed." He turned again to Rhoda. "When could you make contact with this woman?"

Rhoda recalled the last time she'd seen Candy Ignacio, and how frail and tired she'd looked. Her desire for rock had won out over the desire to survive, and Rhoda wondered how much longer she could live that life. "Rarely gets home before dawn," she replied. "Sleeps most days until two or three."

"Okay." Stuart swung around to address everyone in the room. "I don't know how fresh any of us will be on five hours' sleep, but let's all go home and get some rest." He nodded toward Terry Gaskin and Josh Littel, who stood together behind burlap bags full of greasy, dark-roasted coffee beans. "First thing tomorrow, I need you to hit the squad at the Sixth. See what they've managed to turn up from the DaCosta scene and where their investigation stands." He focused next on Goldstein. "I want you and Hogan to hook up with the surveillance Chief Ogilvy is running at Mom's Pie. If our tomboy shooter had anything to do with what went down here tonight, I'm hoping that sooner or later she'll show her face again at Albeneti's."

"What about Hector Jaquez?" Al asked.

In answer, Matt turned to Rhoda. "You speak fluent Spanish, correct?"

She nodded.

"Think Candy Ignacio will talk in front of me?" he asked.

Every time she and her new boss made direct eye contact now, Rhoda couldn't ignore the tiny tingle of intrigue she felt. On short notice, she'd turned herself out in very little makeup, khakis, a green polo shirt, and with her hair tied back. Still, she looked good and knew it, and knew that Stuart was seeing it, too. She reminded herself of how messy the fraternization she was contemplating could get, and guessed that he was trying to convince himself of much the same thing. "She likes having attention paid to her," she replied. "And likes the fact I'm interested enough in what she has to say to keep coming back. The fact that you're my boss might impress her."

"Lives where?"

"In a building on St. Nicholas Place. Where it dumps into Maher Circle. We hit her anytime before noon, we'll catch her dead to the world."

"Fine. And after her, we'll track down the Cuban."

She made arrangements to meet him at the squad at eight o'clock, and Stuart called it a wrap a short while later. It was nearly one by the time she and Hogan finally got on the road, still a half an hour from home. The five hours' shut-eye their boss had proposed was optimistic. She knew they'd be lucky to get four.

Nineteen

Having witnessed the killing of Francisco Santos and his bodyguards by a faction other than the one he represented, Taras Pidvalna had a nightmare of a time trying to find his way back to Brighton Beach, Brooklyn. Hampered by limited knowledge of New York geography, he'd gotten his directions confused at the Triborough Bridge and gone north through the Bronx and into Westchester County before realizing his mistake. By the time he turned himself around, he was angrier than was practical. In the parking lot of a Waldbaum's supermarket off McLean Avenue in Yonkers, he parked a moment to take several fortifying swallows of vodka. His nerves somewhat soothed, he carefully retraced his route back to the bridge, continued south into Brooklyn, and eventually found the Ocean Parkway exit off the Belt Parkway. It was almost midnight before he reported back to his former KGB section commander, Major Mikhail Neyizhsalo, in the office of his *dihskoteque* headquarters on Brighton Beach Avenue.

In the hour it took Neyizhsalo to debrief him, Pidvalna saw his boss become more agitated than he'd ever before seen him. During their session, the major had placed a number of electronically scrambled telephone calls. Once Taras was finished telling all he knew and answering questions asked by unknown parties at the other end of the line, he was ordered to occupy himself at the *dihsko* bar, but to not drink too much. There was someone Neyizhsalo wanted him to meet.

The bar area of Dihsko Volya was decorated with a vast expanse of bronze-tinted mirror, red velvet wallpaper, and brass-trimmed fixtures. At either end, the black laminate and leatherette-upholstered bar was bracketed by big-screen TVs on which patrons could watch a live video feed of the dancers imprisoned in gilt birdcages across the dance floor. Taras was more impressed with an Asian woman in a string bikini on the left screen than he was with the skinny blonde on the right, but neither held his fascination the way a sloe-eyed barmaid with long raven tresses, short-shorts, and slender dancer's legs did. He sipped his ice-cold Stolichnaya, trying hard to nurse the buzz generated earlier without letting it get out of hand, and watched how the woman moved, fascinated. It was three months since Taras had seen his wife of fourteen years. He couldn't honestly contend he actually *missed* her, but he did miss the free and easy access he'd once had to regular sex. In America, he'd yet to connect with a woman who didn't want money to sleep with him. He was sitting on seriously pent-up sexual frustration and needed to find another outlet for it. Soon.

"You watch that one any closer, you will be standing on the other side of the bar," Neyizhsalo growled in his ear.

Taras might have started with surprise if not for his years of conditioning. He was that absorbed in the vision of the lovely young woman before him, imagining what she would look like naked. Instead, he turned his head slightly, one eye still on the tight, perfectly rounded little fanny, and smiled. "Do not tempt me, Mikhail. I am a man of simple needs, and she is beautiful beyond words."

"The man I wish you to meet is here, Taras. Your time with women comes soon, but not now. Now is business." Major Mike caught the beautiful barmaid's eye, winked, and shot her with a chubby index finger. She flashed him a smile, tossed her head, and gave Taras a last glimpse of her backside as she hurried off to deliver a drink.

Pidvalna was envious of Major Mike and the success Neyizhsalo had found in America. In the former Soviet Union, the major was cunning, ruthless, and ambitious, but none of this was enough to succeed in breaking down the racial prejudices of their Russian masters. Because he, like Taras, was Ukrainian, he was excluded from rising any higher within the ranks of the KGB, no matter how useful his talents or loyal his service. Here, there was no such glass ceiling. The sky itself was the limit to how high a man could go when driven by cunning and luck. Following the broad, squat figure of his former and present boss, Taras again took note of the creamy silk of Neyizhsalo's tailored shirt, the perfect cut of his black worsted trousers, and the buttery soft leather of his Italian loafers. The clothes and the manner in which he wore them said Major Mikhail Neyizhsalo was a man who had arrived.

In the *dihsko*'s plushly appointed office, Taras found three men awaiting them. Two were clearly muscle, and of these he was most wary. Shorter, more thickly built, and less elegantly attired than the man they flanked, they had features suggesting a mixture of Mediterranean and Mayan blood, and furtive, watchful black eyes. They stood on either side of a black leather club chair occupied by a slender man of olive complexion with fine, aristocratic features. His jet hair was combed straight back and gathered in a tiny ponytail at the nape of his neck.

"Taras Pidvalna, meet Don Roberto Santiago," Neyizhsalo introduced them. "Don Roberto represents our Colombian friends in the alliance we have formed."

The Colombian met Pidvalna's eyes without blinking. Taras was surprised to hear the major identify him by name, and believed it signified just how strong the bond forged between their two organizations actually was. In such a relationship, a display of trust was crucial.

"Tell me everything you saw," Santiago said in lieu of greeting.

Taras described where he had parked, how long he had waited, and how the target had finally emerged from the little grocery long after sundown. "I then hear a woman call out to him, but do not see who. He looks south, but I am sighting my rifle, trying to get a clean shot. I am ready to pull the trigger when the big man behind him sees something. He tries to grab him, and that is when the firing starts. I see two women. They are wearing masks." He mimed with both hands as if pulling a ski mask over his head and face. "Both with machine pistols. Intratec, I think. Nine millimeter. I know the sound."

As he listened, Santiago toyed with the hair gathered at the nape of his neck, his expression intent. "Women. You are sure."

"It is not their bodies only," Pidvalna replied. "But how they move. Different from a man. These jab weapons at target like they have hatred. This is not how someone with training does this thing."

The Colombian closed his eyes, appearing to digest the information just imparted, then turned to regard Neyizhsalo. "Someone from inside his own ranks, I think. But still it makes no sense. No one has contacted me and sought my blessing. How do they expect to continue to do business?"

Major Mike had clearly been thinking along those same lines. "A different source of supply perhaps. If so, this power play as you call it reaches out beyond Washington Heights."

"It is not a market we can afford to lose," Santiago said slowly. "Last week, Santos brings me news of trouble. Someone has robbed his stash houses. He believes the police are involved. I have people of my own—Dominicans, just like him—who tell me it is not the police, but only one policeman. Tonight, I learn this one policeman is also dead."

Neyizhsalo and Pidvalna looked sharply at each other. "Why have I not heard of this trouble before now?" Major Mike demanded.

Santiago attempted to smooth any ruffled feathers with a casual wave of the hand. "We believed it was only a Dominican problem: between them and one greedy cop. But now I am more concerned. It is why I mention this to you now. The drugs stolen from this Dominican stash house in Manhattan were sold to Jamaicans who control the streets of East New York."

Neyizhsalo scowled, clearly not understanding. "But East New York is here in Brooklyn, far from Washington Heights."

Santiago nodded. "A place once supplied with drugs by the *siciliano* Mafia, just as Harlem once was. It is not with the Dominicans but with them that I think our problem may lie."

"And how is that?" Major Mike asked. "They buy the stolen drugs of a crooked policeman, and now you tell me this policeman is dead. Beyond him, we are the only source of supply."

"So we have assumed," Santiago replied. "Yet someone is bold enough to kill Francisco Santos without first seeking our blessing. Perhaps there is a new threat we fail to see."

"I say we contact these Sicilians who sell our stolen drugs," the major asserted. "They who once controlled the black man's streets in East New York. We must demand a sit-down, as they say. To reach an understanding."

"And if they do not wish to talk?" Don Roberto asked.

The look the major directed toward Taras Pidvalna was grave. "With us, I do not think they will want to fight the war."

* * *

Twice in the early hours of their 8 P.M. to 6 A.M. tour, Officers Joe Lozano and Pete Ogborn of Intelligence Division's Organized Crime Monitoring Unit were given reason to sit up straighter in the confines of their mobile listening station van. Each time, they made sure they had plenty of tape left on their cassettes. The conversation they monitored, at 11:54 P.M., was between Major Mikhail Neyizhsalo and a man called Taras. The latter was debriefed after witnessing the execution of Francisco "Tío Paco" Santos in Washington Heights. The second instance was an hour and a half later, when Roberto Santiago himself arrived at the Dihsko Volya to question this same Taras, now also identified by the surname Pidvalna.

"Jesus H," Lozano murmured. He eased his headphones askew to give one ear a break. "You believe this shit?"

It was only twenty-eight hours earlier that Intelligence had finally received permission from a judge to hang a wire in the Dihsko Volya's office, a move prompted by the attempt on *La Paz* reporter Luis Esquivel's life. It took the division's "spooks" another day to engineer a plan for planting the requisite device, and at nine-thirty that evening, that plan was finally executed. Two undercover cops worked as backup while an apparently drunk, seductively dressed policewoman of Ukrainian descent stumbled into Mikhail Neyizhsalo's office. Ostensibly, she was in search of the ladies' room, and before she was shown the way out, she'd managed to fall sprawling on the floor. From there, she'd planted a powerful microtransmitter on the underside of a club chair. Switched on and monitored from Lozano and Ogborn's remote listening location, the voice-activated device was designed to run for a total of sixteen hours on a lithium battery. By the time its juice ran out, the spooks were meant to figure a means of planting a more permanent solution. Meanwhile, this temporary device was yielding crisp, clear, and incredibly fortuitous intelligence.

"Sounded like the sonofabitch was practically wearing the fucker," Ogborn marveled. "This is a fucking gold mine, Joey."

Lozano reached for the phone at his elbow as his partner spoke. He punched in the Monitoring Unit commander's home number and waited just two rings before Captain Rick Holcomb came on the line.

"Yeah?" his sleep-heavy voice answered.

"Joey Lozano, Cap. We just hit the motherfucking load. Pete's cuing the tape now. You gotta hear this shit."

*   *   *

Sponsored into the United States by a fictitious brother with an electronics emporium in Sheepshead Bay, Taras Pidvalna had fallen into an Immigration and Naturalization Service black hole the moment he cleared customs at Newark International Airport late that past February. Rather than take up employment at the emporium—his stated intention on his visa application—he'd gone directly to work for his mentor and former commander, Major Mikhail Neyizhsalo.

The Odessa Mafiya controlled a wide variety of business and residential properties in the Coney Island, Brighton Beach, and Sheepshead Bay sections of Brooklyn, and it was in one of their residential buildings that Pidvalna was installed. Though cheaply furnished, the two-bedroom third-floor walk-up on Brighton Fifth Street that he now called home was more lavish than any place he and his family had ever lived in the former Soviet Union. Neyizhsalo provided for his maintenance, paying his rent and a weekly stipend of three hundred dollars, and sent another two thousand dollars a month back home to Pidvalna's wife and two children in Kiev. Other moneys were being held in a sort of informal trust for him, until such a time as he wished to invest it. The major had promised that, in time, he would be given an opportunity to take on a "piece of the action" himself, but for now he was expected to watch, listen, and learn while executing certain assignments that fell within his area of expertise.

While walking home in the wee hours of that Monday morning, Pidvalna contemplated what had transpired that night, and realized his earlier perception of it had changed. Before his meeting with Roberto Santiago, he hadn't been able to shake the feeling he'd somehow failed the major in a serious and perhaps unforgivable way. Now, he saw it differently. There was a power struggle in the offing. An adversary lurked in the wings of whom the major was previously unaware. Taras believed that Neyizhsalo was correct, contending that he should have been given the task of eliminating that nettlesome reporter. Yet if he had, he would never have witnessed those events that transpired in Washington Heights that night. Santiago and Neyizhsalo would be even deeper in the dark, and therefore ill prepared for the upcoming fight. Now, they could see the enemy coming, and would be prepared to meet him toe-to-toe.

Inside his building, while approaching his third-floor landing, Pidvalna stopped suddenly in his tracks, dropped to a crouch, and cleared the lightweight Glock automatic he carried tucked beneath his shirt. He'd heard soft music coming from his apartment . . . Ukrainian *troy-eestah moozihkah*, played on bass viola, dulcimer, and clarinet.

Staying low and hugging one wall, he hurried upstairs one flight to the roof access, raced soundlessly across the cold tar surface, and scaled the short parapet wall to descend toward his apartment windows via the fire escape. If an adversary lay in ambush inside his apartment, he wondered why the music, but knew he had to take these precautions. After living three months in Brooklyn, he had made no friends and had only a handful of acquaintances. No one but the major knew where he lived.

On the catwalk outside his apartment, he saw the bedroom and living room windows remained ajar, just as he'd left them to get fresh air circulating. What he hadn't done was leave the kitchen window ajar. It was open now, and from it emanated the distinctive odor of frying *kovbasa*, a traditional Ukrainian sausage made of pork and garlic. While confusing him, it also reminded him it had been hours since he'd eaten an unsatisfying dinner of dark bread and goat's-milk cheese. He'd had too much to drink on a relatively empty stomach, and was famished.

In a move as bold as it was incautious, Pidvalna took only a moment to scan his bedroom and living room for lurking intruders, then dove headlong through the screen covering his kitchen window. One shoulder tucked, he rolled and eventually came upright on one knee, his weapon extended to sweep the room. The barmaid from the *dihsko* stood just feet from him, clad in nothing but a black apron. With a spatula in one hand, she stared terrified into the muzzle of the Glock.

"W-what this is?" he stammered, his astonishment tying his tongue. Slowly, he lowered the weapon.

When she realized she wasn't in mortal danger, the barmaid turned to nonchalantly prod her frying sausage. Then, flashing a slow, sly smile, she shrugged. "I am told you have a long day, that perhaps you are hungry. I know I am, so I cook us something to eat."

Taras was unable to tear his eyes from the nakedness beneath her apron as he heaved himself to his feet. In contrast to her dark hair and eyes, her complexion was an almost translucent white. When she cocked a hip and turned slightly, he could see one of her small, pert breasts. Her legs, long, muscular, and shapely, were the stuff of lonely, late night fantasy. "A good idea, I think," he said slowly.

"Go wash," she said, and pointed with her spatula toward the door.

"Change clothes. Get comfortable. Then come, I feed you. *Holubtsi* and *kovbasa*, made by the chef at Dihsko Volya."

"The major sends you to do this?" Taras asked. There was more than just misgiving in his voice. Such fantasies never actually came true, at least not in his considerable experience.

She laughed. "Do not worry, Taras Pidvalna. Before Mikhail Neyizhsalo asks me this favor, I see how you eat me with your looking. I like this thing I see, do not worry. I go only where I want to go, not where others order me."

Doubt continued to cloud his expression. "You are saying you *wish* to be here?"

It brought forth yet another sly smile. "To a naked woman who cooks you food at two o'clock in the morning, you ask too many questions, Taras Pidvalna. Go wash. And change. Your appetite is showing."

Pidvalna glanced down to the throbbing bulge that had appeared at the front of his trousers. He gave up questioning his good fortune and hurried off, tugging at his belt.

Shortly after Joey Lozano reported in to the Monitoring Unit commander, Detective Pete Ogborn heaved himself out of his chair to stretch. He tried and failed to stifle a huge yawn.

"You cover it awhile, I'll see if I can find us some coffee," he said. "I'm dying to stretch my legs and get some air."

"No problem," Lozano told him. "Sounded to me like they're calling it a night in there. Can't be more'n a dozen people on the dance floor, and we ain't heard a peep since Santiago left."

The thumping bass of rock-and-roll music from the sound system occasionally penetrated the office with enough strength to trigger the sound-activated switch, but nothing of significance had been transmitted in close to half an hour.

"I get lucky, maybe I'll find a bakery open early," Pete said. He'd started toward the door separating the cargo box of the phony Con Edison truck from the cab. "Get us a fresh bialy or something."

"I'll take one of them *pampushky* things, they got them," Joey called over his shoulder. One variety of the Ukrainian pastry was much like a jelly-filled doughnut. Earlier that evening, Lozano had eaten three at one sitting.

Ogborn pulled his lightweight blue Con Ed jacket closed and zipped it against the chill night air as he climbed from the step-van. He drew the tangy salt air off the Atlantic deep into his lungs and moved with the easy amble of a union man working late-shift overtime. He stepped around the orange cones and barriers erected around an open manhole and started up Brighton Beach Avenue in search of a pay phone. Overhead, the elevated tracks running the length of the boulevard rumbled with the approach of a D train. Brakes squealed as the motorman slowed on his approach to the Ocean Parkway stop.

Two blocks along, at the corner of Brighton Second Street, Ogborn fed coins and a 212 area code number into a pay phone out of sight of his partner's position. From her apartment on Manhattan's Upper East Side, First Deputy Suzanne Albrecht answered on the second ring. Her "hello" sounded sleep-heavy, but any visions of sugarplums cleared the instant she heard her Intel Division FA's reply.

"Pete Ogborn, ma'am. It weren't the Colombians and the Rooskies whacked Santos tonight. They did have a guy in position to do the job, but someone beat him to the punch."

"Who?" she replied, her response clipped and terse.

"They ain't sure, ma'am. Two gals with machine pistols is all they know for a fact. They've put together the same bits and pieces my chief and your guy, Stuart, have and are convinced the Albanese are behind it one way or another."

It was met with a stretch of silence from the other end of the line. "And what do they propose to do about it?" she asked at length.

"Santiago and the Rooskie are going to ask Gus Barone for a sit-down. It comes to a war, they sound pretty confident they could win it, but I got the feeling they don't think they'll ever have to fight one."

The first deputy commissioner thanked her field associate for his report, advised him as always to be careful, and said good night. As Ogborn cradled the receiver and rounded the corner to head for an all-night deli he'd spotted earlier, he reflected on how long he'd been spying for Suzanne Albrecht, and how he felt about it now, four years down this road.

Though he'd been recognized as one of the best and brightest of his Police Academy class, Ogborn was still flattered the day the first deputy commissioner had singled him out in a clandestine, after-hours interview in her office at One Police Plaza. For that interview, the first dep had removed those outdated glasses she wore, let her hair loose, and left enough buttons of her silk blouse undone to give him a glimpse of the soft, pale curve of one breast. Despite her being at least fifteen years his senior, Pete had found her quite beautiful. The manner in which she'd engaged him, with such flattery, with such passion for the law enforcement path they'd both chosen, and with an ever-so-subtle suggestion of intimacy, had turned him to putty in her hands. Because he *was* one of the best and the brightest, she would have no trouble moving him into fast-track positions within the most sought-after special units. Any intelligence she asked him to gather would be reported directly to her, and *only* to her. There was so much ardor and intrigue infused into her proposition, he'd left that first meeting with an erection. For the four ensuing years, he'd nursed a crush on the woman which still persisted to torture him.

About a year after accepting her first assignment, Ogborn realized he'd been conned. He'd known he was thinking with his dick the day he took her bait, but still held out hope that a surreptitiously administered blow job or quick hump against the door of her inner office might someday come to pass. Nonetheless, since the day he'd said yes, he never again saw her without those glasses, without all the buttons of her blouse done clear to her throat, or her hair in anything but a tight, no-frills bun. Yes, she'd kept her promises of fast advancement and silk-suit-unit assignments, but for the privilege, the price seemed too high. For four years, Pete had lived with the guilty knowledge that he was a rat. He'd sold out the trust and confidence of his brother officers for thirty pieces of silver, and believed he knew exactly how Judas Iscariot must have felt. He wondered if the same sleepless nights had plagued Judas before the twelfth apostle finally decided to hang himself.

Events that transpired late Sunday evening had created quite a stir within the Washington Heights dope-dealing community. New Red Top crew chief Kamil Imbongi had called all his troops off the street the moment news reached him of Francisco Santos's assassination. It came too close on the heels of Darryl Johnson and Fat Danny being whacked. Dreading the worst for himself as well, Kamil was doing everything he could think of to ensure his own survival. In his heart, Imbongi knew that something was very wrong with the picture he'd been presented the moment Santos first appeared to anoint him. By then, Tío Paco had already lost control of Washington Heights, as evidenced by the raids on his stash houses, and by the fact that Macho Man Rodriguez, Isabelle Melendez, and the top nigger in the Red Top command structure all got themselves capped.

Earlier that night, around the same time Tío Paco was fed his lethal dose of lead soup, the local TV news reported the death of that renegade blond nigger cop who'd been plaguing the streets of Imbongi's turf since before last Christmas. Kamil didn't see the broadcast but heard word of it from a dozen different sources as he scrambled to get his pitchers to ground. He'd seen enough of Clarence DaCosta's act to have a fairly good grasp of who the uppity cop thought he was, and what his appetites were. There was no way he'd voluntarily OD'd on any drug; of that much Imbongi was certain. Someone had loaded up a hot shot and finished his sorry ass, probably because they no longer needed his services. Where DaCosta was concerned, the only questions bothering Kamil now were *who* the sorry fuck had been working for, and what this unknown component ultimately had in mind. Right now, it looked like they aimed to start World War III.

"Yo! Kamil!" a lookout called from across the darkened rooftop. Kamil had gone there to find calm, and to think. He bristled at this intrusion.

"I said no interruptions," he snapped in reply.

"Sidewalk says Little Richie be wantin' a word," the man persisted, ignoring the warning tone in his leader's voice. "Motherfucker's got two Dominican bitches with him, along with some greaseball gangster."

Imbongi's irritation turned to dread, the cold finger of it poking at his bowels. Word on the street had it that two women had killed Tío Paco and his nephews. Clearly, there was a power shift taking place within the Dominican organization, and Kamil was on the losing team. Santos had installed him as chief of the Red Top crew, not the new regime.

With his flywhisk nervously stirring the night air, Kamil shifted his grip on the Skorpion machine pistol in his other hand, cradling the weapon in the lap of his robe. "Let them come," he told the lookout. "And tell them niggers on the stairs to keep a sharp eye out." He told himself philosophically that tonight was as good a night to die as any.

An eternity of cold sweat and jangled nerves later, the door to the rooftop finally opened and the six-foot seven-inch Little Richie Townsend emerged from the stairwell, moving with the kind of confidence that comes from having survived multiple gunshot wounds. Imbongi remained seated in the shadow of a chimney, watching as Townsend ducked his head and passed through the doorway, followed by a woman a foot and a half shorter. Her fleshy hips were encased in impossibly tight Capri pants, her abdomen left bare below the knotted hem of a bright yellow T-shirt. Behind her, a taller, more statuesque woman appeared in an aqua blue tube top, white shorts, sandals, and straight black hair cut close to her head like a fashion model's. From the way she hung close to the goombah who appeared last, with his gold chains entangled in his chest hair and a walk like his balls were too big to fit between his legs, Kamil guessed she was with him. The older, stockier woman moved with an independent, confident air.

Little Richie searched for Imbongi in the gloom. "Yo. Kamil, m'man," he called out.

Imbongi intended to play Townsend, his most dangerous rival, cautiously. "Over here," he answered. "Who be your friends?"

Townsend advanced, the three others following. "Our new line of supply, way they explain it to me," he replied. "Meet Dona Raquel Gozon. She tell me she be the new *huéspeda* in these parts."

"I can talk for myself," the stocky woman snapped impatiently. She had advanced so Imbongi could now get a good look at her face. He was surprised by how striking it was, in a hard, fierce way. She had cheekbones that bespoke Indian blood, a slender, aquiline nose, and pouting lips. Her dark, flashing eyes were brazen in their directness. "Francisco Santos no longer controls the streets of Washington Heights, or commands the loyalty of the Dominican community here," she continued. "I, my sister, and our new supply partners do."

Imbongi glanced at the other woman with renewed interest. The bodies were hardly the same, but in the faces he noted a distinct family resemblance. On the younger, taller woman the features were softer and more classically beautiful, but the basic mouth, nose, and bone structure were much the same. "Your new supply partners," he said slowly. It was one thing to make a move on the local organizational structure within the Dominican community. Hell, women had been running stash houses and doing other high-level Santos bidding for years. He had no doubt they were capable, but to risk angering the Colombians? This sounded like craziness to him.

Raquel Gozon met the question without hesitation. "For five years we have dealt only with the Cali cartel, where once we had dealings with them, the Chinese, and others. Without competition, they control prices. The only way we can increase our profit is to take higher risks. My cousin Francisco did this by sending our people into harm's way." She glanced sideways at her sister. "Our brother, Jose, rots today in a Mexican prison. Why? Because Tío Paco was greedy, but unwilling to take those risks himself."

Her motivations might be clearer to Imbongi now, but how she intended to change the supply-side balance of power was not. The Colombians had a virtual lock on supply. They could set any price they chose. They'd driven the Chinese from the field by simply underselling them to death, and now that they'd formed an alliance with the Russians who controlled the poppy fields of the Middle East, they could do the same with anyone else who chose to enter the arena. "Our people," he said, moving the flywhisk in the air between himself and Little Richie, "pitch product, plain and simple. You control our price, same as the Colombian motherfuckers control yours. You still ain't told me where this new dope be coming from, and ain't told me who this motherfucker is." He glared hard at the goombah and saw the muscles of the guy's neck and shoulders bunch. "Listening to all our business."

"Easy, Marco," the self-appointed *huéspeda* said softly. "He don't know who you are, or who you represent. He knows this thing, he don't disrespect you in this way."

How this bitch went out of her way to smooth the goombah's feathers made Kamil uneasy. All he saw was another guinea with attitude; one who undoubtedly hated the fact he was standing on a rooftop in deepest, darkest Dominican land, meeting with a couple of uppity niggers.

"Meet Marco Fortunado," Raquel Gozon introduced him. "His brother, Tony, is a soldier in the Albanese family. Marco works in his crew. My sister, Beatrice, is his fiancée."

Ah. Everything Imbongi knew about the Mafia he'd learned mostly from movies like *Donnie Brasco* and *The Godfather*, but the Albanese name was as synonymous with la Cosa Nostra in New York as Gallo, Colombo, and Luchese were. None had been significant players in the dope trade for decades now, but it looked like they wanted back in. Imbongi wondered how cold and calculated this romance between the guinea gangster and the spic bitch was, and which side of the aisle thought they had the upper hand. Both, he guessed. "So you bringing what to the table?" he asked the mobster. "Better dope than Roberto Santiago got, at better prices? Why do I doubt y'all can do that?"

"Darryl Johnson didn't think we could, either," the mobster said evenly. It didn't take a semantics expert to get his implication.

Imbongi raised the machine pistol in his lap so Fortunado could get a good look at it. "We got guns, too," he replied. "And now we know who you are, it be easier to find out where you live. Don't threaten my ass, motherfucker. I'll shoot you dead where you stand."

"Gentlemen, please," Raquel Gozon complained. "Just like Tío Paco did, we know we need you to make our business work, Kamil. And Little Richie, and Corky Cochran, and all them, too. You are not our enemy, and we are not yours. The Colombians are the enemy, and the monopoly they use to strangle us."

"My crews peddle dope," Kamil reiterated matter-of-factly. "I don't give a shit where it come from. Long as it cheaper than any other dope in the city. It ain't? Motherfucker with the jones go on up the road to score. It be that plain and simple."

The younger woman, Beatrice, spoke for the first time. Her voice was softer than her sister's and more melodic, but no less sure of itself. "Marco, he represent a new alliance," she said. "Between the strongest of the old Sicilian families and the strongest Chinese tong. My sister and me? We represent the new power that today takes control of Washington Heights. On our side are the mothers who need the food to feed babies. After today, a Dominican man wants *dominicana* pussy, he jump through the hoops we tell him to jump through."

Imbongi realized he was gaping, and forced himself to shut his mouth. He wasn't well versed in either the language or the tenets of militant feminism, but realized he'd just been shown a glimpse of both. How long they'd been forming their ranks, and how strong these two women and their sisters-in-arms might prove to be, was a question only time could answer. But the evidence suggested they believed they were strong enough, and had already taken steps to claim the victor's spoils.

"We ain't gonna get in the middle of your politics," he said flatly. "Way I see it, y'all still got one big problem. The Colombian still controls the product that packs the pipe, and crackheads be a big slice of our market."

"The Cali cartel is not the only source for cocaine," Raquel Gozon answered. "And Roberto Santiago, he is not the whole Cali cartel. We control the marketplace, not them. They want to lose our market, we go shopping somewhere else." She paused to fix Imbongi with a glare even harsher than the one she'd previously had at work on him. Then, with slow purpose, she turned to give Townsend a taste of it, too. "That is our deal, amigos. You wanna sell dope on our streets, you do it this way or no way. We don't got time to fuck around, and Marco's people, they don't either. We both got people waiting to hear what you got to say."

Imbongi wondered what choice he and his Red Top crew had. What were their options? Call a general strike? Lay down in the streets to stop traffic like Mahatma Gandhi? He knew the guineas and the Chinese hated his nigger ass every bit as much as Roberto Santiago did, and that these bitches probably hated all men in general, be they black, white, yellow, or green. He was in business to sell dope, and wasn't inclined to haggle about where it came from. He glanced quickly toward Townsend as he spoke, trying to gauge the reaction of his most vocal critic at Friday's block captain meeting. Damn, it seemed like an eternity had passed since then.

"We want to sell dope," he replied. "Way I see it, we losing time *and* money right now, running our motherfucking gums."

Twenty

Four and a half hours' sleep would have to be enough whether Matt Stuart needed twice that much or not. When the alarm jarred him from deep slumber at six-thirty that Monday morning, he knew he had no time to dwell on how fuzzy with fatigue his brain still felt. Instead, he hauled himself out of bed and hit the shower.

Weekend events seemed to have added a dozen crucial pieces to his investigative puzzle, as scattered as they might be across Gotham's vast cityscape. He had the gut feeling that matters pertaining to the murder of Officer Juan Rodriguez, dead almost a week now, were about to come to a head. Run ragged or not, he needed to force his focus onto the task at hand. He was scheduled to meet with Detective Rhoda Bolivar at the station house in an hour and a half. From there they would proceed to roust a pipehead prostitute named Candy Ignacio.

At seven o'clock, as Stuart stood in his kitchen alternately hanging the tools of his trade from his belt and trying to gulp a cup of scalding coffee, the phone rang. The caller was Simon Ogilvy.

"Figured I'd wait awhile to call you," the Intel chief said by way of greeting. "Knowing how much you needed your sleep. We hit pay dirt with the wire we hung in the Russian mob's Brighton Beach disco last night." He ran through a quick recap of the meeting overheard between former KGB major Mikhail Neyizhsalo and Roberto Santiago. "I've got a surveillance team still set up there, another up the street from Gus Barone's social club on Remsen Avenue, and a third on Angelo Albeneti's bakery in East Harlem. Unfortunately, we didn't have enough manpower on the scene last night to get a line on Santiago when he left."

"They do the rush autopsy on DaCosta yet?" Matt asked.

"Not another needle mark on him," Simon replied. "There are bruises on his wrists, suggesting a struggle took place. The ME has pretty much ruled out suicide."

"Surprise," Stuart murmured. He took another sip of coffee, grabbed a banana from the fruit bowl, and told Ogilvy what he had on his plate that morning. "Any of the worms you're watching start to turn, I've got my cell phone," he concluded. "This Ignacio woman gives us anything, I'll make sure you're the first to know."

From the time she'd received the call from her field associate inside Intelligence Division, Suzanne Albrecht had suffered through the most agonizing six hours of her adult life. For twelve years, she'd lived with the specter of these events finally coming to pass, and had always wondered how she might deal with them when they did. Because she'd been driven by a consuming ambition to someday run the police department she so loved, she had always been able to rationalize a variety of scenarios in which she could dodge a bullet virtually aimed at her heart. In actuality, she'd known all along that when the time came, it was unlikely she would have any such luck. A decade ago as she started down this path toward self-destruction, she'd done it with the same kind of arrogance she'd brought to every task undertaken since childhood. But this time she'd bitten off more than she could chew.

At seven o'clock that Monday morning, Suzanne sat in her robe staring at the phone on her bedside table. Faced with what she was about to do, she couldn't control an angry trembling in her hands as she picked up the receiver and punched in the number of a phone located in an apartment above Mom's Pie Company on Pleasant Avenue in East Harlem. She listened to the ringing at the other end of the line and squeezed her eyes shut as tears started to roll down her cheeks. When a machine picked up, she nearly broke the connection, not eager to leave a recording of her voice. Instead, she persevered through the greeting, waited for the beep, then spoke with slow, measured purpose.

"Angelo. You know who this is and how to reach me. We need to—"

There was a high-pitched squeal and then she heard Albeneti's voice. "If this line ain't secure, I'll find some way, someday, to cut your fucking heart out."

Her teeth were gritted so hard her jaw ached. "It's secure. Yours?"

"You're fucking kidding, right? Far as the phone company knows, you're talking to someone in Rochester or some fucking place. Why you calling me here, Suzanne?"

"Your latest scheming, wherever the hell it's headed, is about to come crashing down around your ears. Murdering scum or not, the man you killed yesterday with that faked drug overdose was a cop."

"I don't know what you're talk—"

"Save it," she cut him off. "For someone else, not already fed up to her eyeballs with it. You want what else I know, and it's plenty, meet me at nine. You know the place. You're stupid enough to blow me off, we both go down in flames. We meet and talk, maybe we can think of something before you ruin both our lives."

"Nine's impossible," he complained. "I got a million things cook—"

"Just be there!" she snarled, and slammed the receiver back into its cradle.

Gina Galati hadn't slept at all well after arriving at her Aunt Rose Marie Sabatino's house in the New Dorp section of Staten Island in the wee hours of Monday morning. She'd tossed and turned in her guest room bed before finally giving it up at six-thirty. She'd checked on Claude, who slumbered without a care in the world, hit the shower, and then wandered into the kitchen clad in gym shorts and an oversize sweatshirt. The familiar figure of her aunt, frosted hair worn in a pageboy and her trim figure dressed in a fitted, pale yellow business suit, stood with her back to the room, pouring herself a cup of coffee.

To further distance herself from her cheesecake-king ex-husband, Rose Marie had dumped the surname Albeneti after her 1986 divorce and gone back to Sabatino. She'd moved from Brooklyn, across the Verrazano Narrows Bridge to Staten Island, gotten her commercial real estate broker's license, and made a new life for herself. Since childhood, Gina had been drawn to her father's only sister by the independent quality she'd always seen in her. She was too young at the time of her aunt's divorce to fathom the terrifying nature of a Mafia wife's decision to leave her husband, but knew it had taken uncommon strength for Rose

Marie to actually go through with it. This, Gina had learned about much
later in life. It only helped strengthen her burning hatred of all Sicilian men.

"Morning," she mumbled, stifling a yawn with one fist. "I didn't sleep
for shit."

Wearing a frown of disapproval, Rose Marie turned. "You want to go
anywhere in this world, you might want to lose the potty mouth, honey.
Coffee?"

"Yeah, sure." Gina pulled up a chair at the breakfast table, ignoring her
aunt's rebuke. She liked this house her aunt had bought, with its garden
full of rose bushes lovingly babied through winter cold and summer hu-
midity, and the big windows and French doors opening onto it. The house
itself wasn't lavish by any means, but was tasteful in the bright, crisp way
the interior was decorated. Each of the three bedrooms had its own bath;
there was a formal dining room and a less formal TV room or den. Absent
were the red-velvet-flocked wallpaper, heavily carved Italianate furniture,
and gold leaf of Gina's childhood. Her Aunt Rose Marie's tastes were
more contemporary and less influenced by the Old World mind-set of
ghettoized Italian enclaves like Bensonhurst, Bath Beach, and Canarsie in
Brooklyn, and Little Italy in downtown Manhattan.

"I appreciate you not telling me to fuck o—uh, take a hike last
night," Gina thanked her aunt. "And for not asking me to, you know, like
explain."

Rose Marie poured a second cup of coffee and carried it, together
with her own, to the table. She pulled out a chair to sit and contemplated
her niece a moment before speaking. "I'll only ask this, honey. Is the
trouble you're in serious, or just a man problem?"

Gina took a grateful sip of her coffee and shook her head. "Ain't a
dude thing, for sure. And I don't know yet, what kinda trouble I might be
in. Could be serious, though, yeah."

Rose Marie frowned at her. "Is Angelo involved?"

Gina reached to cover one of her aunt's hands with both of hers. "You
made the break from it all thirteen years ago, Rose. Why don't we leave
it alone?"

Her aunt bit her lower lip and stared past Gina's shoulder into her rose
garden. "If I'd known Sonny Galati so much as laid a finger on you, I
would have killed the bastard with my own hands," she whispered. "As
God is my witness."

"Sonny's my problem," Gina said softly. "And believe me, your little niece is pretty good at cleaning up her own messes. But enougha that. I got a question I need to ask. It's been bugging me all night."

Rose Marie focused back on her niece's face. "What's that, honey?"

"This police bitch I seen on TV last night. I don't know why, but she looked real familiar . . . only older than I remember. I think she's way up in the department, like a commissioner or something. I don't know why, but I got this feeling she's someone you used to know."

Eyes averted, Rose Marie hurriedly checked her watch, took another quick sip of coffee, and stood abruptly to carry her cup to the sink. "I didn't realize it was so late," she said. "I've really got to run, honey." Then, pausing, she feigned a phony quizzical expression and shook her head. "A police commissioner? I can't imagine who you're talking about."

"Why you giving me the bum's rush, Rose?" Gina complained. "You didn't even ask me to describe her."

Refusing to make eye contact, her aunt moved toward the end of the counter to collect her handbag. "If it's still bothering you later, we can try to figure out who you're talking about," she said, and slung the strap of the bag over her shoulder. "Right now, I'm late for a meeting. Probably be home for lunch. You gonna be all right, here by yourself?"

"Yeah, just fine," Gina grumbled. She had no intention of going anywhere that day, other than to a newsstand to purchase as many local papers as she could get her hands on. She didn't know how much they could tell her about what had transpired between the Albanese and the dope dealers of Washington Heights over the past twenty-four hours, but hoped there would be a picture of that honcho lady cop in one of them, and a caption to identify her.

Moments later, as Gina listened to the sound of her aunt's Oldsmobile being started in the driveway, she stared out across the sun-drenched rose garden. It looked like it would be another nice spring day. Claude could play in the sunshine, just like a normal kid, and she could stretch out on a lounge, nap a little, and try to get a handle on where she might turn next. She'd been frugal with the cash she'd earned the past two years, so money wasn't an object, at least for the time being. Maybe it was time to move to a place where her kid could have a relatively normal upbringing. Normal, considering he was the child of a single parent, and his mother was about to become a retired hitter for the mob.

*   *   *

Taras Pidvalna awoke at the decadent hour of seven-thirty that Monday morning, the barmaid whose name he'd either forgotten or failed to ask still slumbering soundly at his side. He had no idea who Mikhail Neyizhsalo had told her he was, or why she had treated him the way she had, but for two hours last night he'd enjoyed the most physically exhausting, voracious sex he'd ever had in his life. She'd brought him to the very edge of climax a half a dozen times, on each occasion backing away the instant before he would have exploded in her mouth. To distract him while his urge was left to subside, she'd ridden his stomach and ground her own fire against him, those beautiful breasts dangling in his face. Then, ever so slowly, she would go back at him again, first with just her tongue, then with her lips, and finally with her entire mouth. She'd teased him until he'd moaned aloud with the excruciating pleasure of it, and finally, when he'd been able to stand it no longer, he'd flipped her onto her belly and mounted her from behind. To his amazement, twenty minutes after he emptied what felt like his entire being into her, she'd eased her head into his lap, taken his spent organ into her mouth, and performed what could only be termed a miracle.

While Pidvalna lay watching the beautifully tapered back of the sleeping barmaid, her tangled black hair spread so close at hand that he could smell her perfume in it, he thought about his thick-waisted wife and the two children he barely knew. On his departure for America, he had promised Nina he would send for his family in a few months' time. She had cried, some of her tears shed for fear of losing the security he had always provided, and more shed over the idea of losing the only home she'd ever known. Nina and her mother and sisters had always been closer than he and she ever were, with him gone on assignments for long stretches of time almost from the day they were married.

Taras gazed again at this nameless barmaid, and thought of America and the opportunity it could offer to a man of his special talents, unencumbered by family. He decided he would put off contacting his wife for a while. As long as Mikhail could ensure that money was getting through, Nina would be happier living in Kiev with her mother than living here with him. More so, in fact. And it looked like he might be happier with that arrangement, too.

*   *   *

When Stuart collected her from the steps of the Three-seven station house at 7:35 that morning, Detective Rhoda Bolivar looked impossibly refreshed after only five hours' sleep. The minimal makeup she customarily wore to work was perfect. The creases in her black slacks were crisp, the open-collared white silk blouse neatly pressed. After pulling into the whip's designated slot, he watched the bounce in her step as she descended the stoop and advanced on his car, her camel-hair jacket slung casually over one shoulder.

"Morning, Lou," she greeted him with too much good cheer, and slid into the passenger seat.

Matt paused a moment to regard her before easing the shift lever into reverse. "Tell me the truth," he replied. "You've got a picture of a haggard, baggy-eyed woman hanging in your attic, right?"

She frowned quizzically, then let out a peal of light, musical laughter. "That's funny. You want the truth, I feel like somebody poured my head full of molasses."

Stuart started into Riverside Drive traffic. "Don't know about you, Detective, but I need another cup of coffee. I figured the one I gulped at home and the half-hour drive into town might've helped some. Face I shaved this morning belonged to some other, much older man. One Fifty-fifth and St. Nicholas Place, right?"

"Correct. And call me Rhoda, Lou. I promise not to bring you up on sexual harassment charges." Before she turned her head to stare out the side window, he saw bemusement play at the corners of that wonderfully sensuous mouth. "There's a bodega corner of Amsterdam and 155th makes the best *café con leche* in Washington Heights. You buy, I'll fly."

"Deal." He reached for his wallet and handed it across. "Leave me a little something for gas money, huh?"

Two blocks east, at a street corner across Amsterdam Avenue from Trinity Cemetery, Stuart watched the tight, compact roll of Detective Bolivar's backside as she hurried across the sidewalk into a little mom-and-pop bodega, and cautioned himself. It made him horny as hell to be around a woman as attractive as this one, but he was her squad commander. A little friendly banter with an edge of flirtation to it was fine, but both of them were here to do a job, not to find bedmates. He forced his mind onto the task at hand, knowing that any distraction while walking into a potentially volatile situation could mean a misstep that would cost one or both of them their lives.

Once they were under way again, Matt pressed Rhoda for more information about Candy Ignacio. "Tell me more about your snitch. You said yesterday she's on the pipe, and bitter as hell about her old man disappearing. How unstable is she?"

"You mean, is she dangerous? Not Candy, no. But her pimp, from what she's told me, can be when the mood takes him. I gather it's mainly when he's strung out and hasn't had much sleep."

"Makes two of us," Matt murmured. "What's his drug of choice?"

"Speedballs."

"Ah." A mixture of heroin and cocaine, a speedball could be unpredictable in the best of circumstances, and lethal in the worst. Some variant on that theme was what had killed the actor John Belushi. Stuart imagined rousting a speedballer pimp and his string of whores, not having any idea of how far up or down the guy might be. The idea failed to generate much enthusiasm. "I'm betting you've never had one of your sit-downs with Ms. Ignacio while this guy was anywhere close. Correct?"

"You win a cigar," she said dryly.

"No thanks. Things'll kill you."

"So might he. You watch my ass, I'll watch yours."

"Be my pleasure."

The same bemusement he'd seen earlier tweaked the corners of her mouth again. "I bet it will."

Despite the unusually mild spring weather, Candy Ignacio had endured a particularly rough night along her Eleventh Avenue and West Twenty-ninth Street stroll. Sunday nights were usually pretty slow in her trade, with most of the blue-collar population who trolled Manhattan's Hell's Kitchen for blow jobs either broke or partied out by then. That Sunday, she was so high by the time Rodney "the Weasel" Burns had turned her and Lola Marquez out to wiggle fannies and flash tit, she'd hardly known or cared where she was. If she'd known a national Promise Keepers rally was scheduled to start Tuesday, six blocks north at the Javits Convention Center, she probably wouldn't have let him turn her out at all. Some of the more fervent attendees had begun to arrive Sunday afternoon. By midnight, many who had failed to score in the cocktail lounges of their hotels had headed west and south in rental cars and cabs to exercise their freedoms as cash-carrying citizens of a free-market economy. Most were drunk, many were hatefully repressed, and all were searching for something that Candy Ignacio and her ilk could give them.

By dawn Monday morning, the Weasel had finally relented and let Candy and Lola haul their weary carcasses home to crash. Candy figured she'd administered more fellatio to angry drunks with flaccid penises in one night than she had in the entire past month. She had the battered lips, aching jaw, and hair missing from her scalp to prove it. The less aroused they were, the more frustrated and prone to act out they'd proven to be. Rodney was forced to pistol-whip one, and had threatened to cut the testicles off two or three more with his five-inch butterfly knife.

In bed at last, with Rodney stretched dead to the world beside her, Candy's mouth still tasted like latex. Her mind's eye was so alive with images of pasty, irate white faces, fists knotted in her hair, and limp organs being thrust at her, there was no way she could find sleep. Ever since Jaime had taken that trip to the islands for Tío Paco Santos and not returned, her life had become a living nightmare. It took a lucid moment like this one, as rare as it was, for Candy to see how far down she'd allowed the pipe and her beloved little rocks of crack cocaine to drag her. A basic instinct begged with fervent urgency that she find some means of escaping Rodney before he, the rock, or some other facet of this hellish existence finally killed her. The only problem was how little will she had in her current condition. As a teenager, before Jaime put the macho moves on her and wooed her away from her family, she'd been strong and directed. With better grades in school than most of her classmates, she had plans to attend City College and become a nurse. But today, at the ripe age of twenty, that ambition seemed like just another pipe dream.

Knocking at the front door, fifteen feet down the hall, failed to stir Rodney from his heroin-heavy slumber. At that hour, Candy had no idea who the caller might be, but rather than risk the ire of the Weasel, aroused anytime before noon, she figured she'd better go see.

With her slender, emaciated body wrapped in the tawdry Frederick's of Hollywood gown Rodney had ordered from a catalogue for her, Candy padded barefoot down the hall to peer out the security peep. Her pulse quickened and she broke out in a cold sweat on discovering the good-looking lady detective with an older, gray-haired dude on the other side of the door. As noiselessly as possible, she threw the three security deadbolts, shifted the bar of the Fox police lock from the floor plate, and eased the door open enough so she could slip outside.

"What is this?" she hissed at Detective Bolivar in Spanish. "You cannot come to this place. Rodney, he see me with you, he kills me."

"Someone killed Francisco Santos and his nephews outside his bodega last night," Rhoda replied in English, probably for the benefit of the gringo. Before now, the lady detective had never spoken to Candy in anything but her native tongue. "I figured you might not have heard."

Candy hadn't, and gaped at the cop in surprise. Hardly capable of strong emotion anymore, she still felt a flush of deep satisfaction and might even have flashed a gloating smile. "*Bueno.* I spit on his soul." She let fly with a glob of phlegm that hit the grimy ceramic tile floor at her feet.

"They are saying it was two women who did it," Rhoda told her. And as she spoke, Candy felt those cop eyes probing her own, ready to pounce on any involuntary reaction she might see.

Wary, Candy lifted her chin toward the gringo. "Who is he?"

"My boss. When I told him about your Jaime, he said it's possible we can help you find out what happened to him."

Candy stared at the gringo boss cop with deep suspicion, then threw a nervous look over her shoulder to scan the hallway behind. So far as she could tell, none of her neighbors was watching. "You can help me find Jaime?"

The gringo spoke for the first time, and Candy was surprised by how calm, gentle, and frank his voice was. "There's no guarantee he's still alive, Candy. Or that he didn't run off with the money he was paid. But if he was busted and thrown in jail, or killed and there's a record of his death, I have friends who can help me find out."

The idea that Jaime might no longer be among the living was one that Candy had long since accepted. For the past eight months she'd believed that if he was dead, she wished to be dead, too. It was why she'd let Rodney Burns turn her out in exchange for all the rock she could smoke. "You will do this?" she asked, and watched his face for any sign of deception.

"He doesn't play games," Rhoda said, this time in Spanish. "I would not bring anyone with me who does."

Candy continued to watch the gringo's face, looking for any sign that he understood what the lady cop had just said to her. When she saw none, she smiled inwardly. She liked this *latina* cop, as unlikely as that was. The woman listened to her without patronizing. Now, she'd just brought Candy a first glimmer of hope after nearly a year of darkness. When Candy spoke next, she surprised even herself by what she said.

"I cannot go back inside there." She hugged herself, arms wrapped across her breasts, and jerked a shoulder toward the Weasel's front door. "I do not know where to go, but I need to dry out. This, or I never stop until I am dead."

Rhoda quickly translated what she'd said for the gringo. He absorbed it, nodded, and gestured toward the stairwell. "For starters, let's get her to Bellevue. She wants to talk, we can do it in the car."

Candy was confused by this turn. He wasn't offering an escape from this hell as a trade for anything, and she didn't understand why. Men always wanted something for everything they did for her. This was a fact of life.

Rhoda seemed to sense her hesitation and placed a firm but gentle hand on one of her emaciated arms. "Helping people is his job, baby. Mine, too. It's not a new life he's offering, just a chance for you to find one on your own. Chances are, the dope's got too tight a hold on you, and you won't have the strength."

Candy wasn't so far gone she couldn't recognize a challenge when she heard one. She was too well aware of what kind of hold the rock had on her, and could feel the flush of bravery she'd felt a moment ago already dissipating. She craved just one quick pull on the pipe to bolster herself, and knew she couldn't do that. If she was going to accept Rhoda's challenge, that avenue of escape no longer existed for her.

"Lots of Dominicans in Washington Heights hated Francisco Santos's guts," she told the cops as they started with her toward the stairs. "When Jaime disappears, I start to hear more stories like his. Men who go back to the DR for Tío Paco, he cheats them. If they become too angry and complain too much, they are not seen again."

They started downstairs with Rhoda in the lead, the boss cop bringing up the rear. He spoke, addressing Candy's back.

"Which leaves their women here at home to fend for themselves."

She nodded. "All are not on the pipe like me. Many have babies to feed. Some have sworn an oath to get even with him someday. I believe they will at least try."

"Anyone in particular you think is more likely to succeed than the others?" the gringo asked.

Candy was of a mind that all women should try to help one another, not stab each other in the back. She also knew that when it came to winning the affections of men, and keeping them, too many women let their possessiveness and a consuming need for approval supercede any feelings of sisterhood. Before she and Jaime moved in together, he'd had an affair with an older woman whose husband ran one of Santos's stash houses. He'd sworn he had dumped her the moment Candy turned his head, but she'd always suspected otherwise. Then, one month after Jaime disappeared, his lover's husband also went south to the islands on Santos business. Until her own mate failed to return from that trip, the other woman had always snubbed Candy on the street. Afterward, she'd turned strangely friendly. And every time Candy saw her, she could also see a barely controlled rage boiling within her.

"Raquel Gozon," she replied as they reached the rubbish-strewn lobby. "Her husband also disappeared. And last month, the stash house he once ran for Tío Paco was robbed. Everyone says it was the police, but how do the police know where unless someone tells them?"

"If she wasn't on the inside anymore, how would she know where?" Rhoda asked. "They're moved all the time."

Candy shook her head. "Raquel fucks a block captain in the Red Top crew now. Little Richie Townsend. He is the friend of Rodney, my pimp. They say he has the manhood of a bull." As she passed beyond the front door and onto the stoop, Candy made a fist, crooked her arm, and shook it by way of demonstration. "Rodney tells Lola and me, Raquel cannot get enough of what Richie has."

All the way downtown to the Bellevue Hospital complex on First Avenue at East Twenty-eighth Street, Matt Stuart listened to the fiery opinions and crucial information imparted by the Dominican prostitute occupying his backseat. He also marveled at the relationship that Rhoda Bolivar had been able to cultivate with her. When they reached the hospital, it was another hour before they made the connection with the psychiatric social worker who would help process the new patient into the system. Before they left, Rhoda promised Candy she would get her the toiletries and basic items of clothing on the list they'd put together. It was nearly nine before she and Stuart stepped aboard an elevator outside the lockdown area of the detox unit. While headed for the ground floor, Matt's cell phone rang.

"Lieutenant Stuart," he answered.

"Your nephew Raymond, Uncle Lou. Four delivery trucks just left here. That cake you ordered left with them. Total comes to twenty-six seventy-two."

Stuart thanked him, saying he'd collect the cake later that afternoon from the Mom's Pie outlet in his neighborhood, and broke the connection.

"What's up?" Rhoda asked.

"Albeneti's on the move. Four trucks all left the bakery at the same time, with him in one of them. Sounds like he's trying to cover his tracks."

He quickly dialed Al Goldstein, working the Pleasant Avenue stakeout with Jack Hogan and whomever Simon Ogilvy had assigned.

"Sergeant Goldstein," Martini Al came back at him over the airwaves.

"It's Stuart, Al. You guys have four trucks on the move, correct?"

"That's a ten-four."

"Your quarry's in the one with the numbers two-six-seven-two on the plate."

"Gotcha."

"Don't crowd him, buddy. Give him plenty of line. It looks like his antennae are up."

"Appreciate the tip," Al grumbled. "Me being so new to this kinda work."

Matt smiled. He was so mentally tired right now, he was getting punchy. "Keep me posted, pal. Where he goes, how long he stays, who he talks to." He hit the END button and dialed again, this time reaching Simon Ogilvy in his Intel Division office. By the time the chief picked up, Matt and Rhoda had reached the hospital lobby and were halfway up a long, covered walkway toward First Avenue.

"Yeah, Matthew. I just heard Albeneti's on the move. You want your guys to stay with him?"

"Until I need them elsewhere," Stuart said. "We just got the name of a suspect from Rhoda Bolivar's snitch. It's a Dominican woman who's been shacking up on the QT with a Red Top crew block captain, name of

Townsend. It could explain why Darryl Johnson was removed from his leadership role last week."

"This loverboy the new guy running the street show up there?" Ogilvy asked.

"Don't know that," Stuart admitted. "At least not yet. If he isn't, whoever is had better watch his back."

Twenty-one

Relieved to be back working a regular shift again after three weeks of paralyzing boredom, Josh Littel had collected Terry Gaskin from his Staten Island home bright and early that Monday morning. Together, they'd appeared at the Sixth Precinct station house on Tenth Street in Greenwich Village at a few minutes past eight and found the detective squad whip in his second-floor office. Because a fellow officer had met an untimely and suspicious end, he was eager to help, providing them with an unoccupied desk in the squad and fresh-brewed coffee. The Clarence DaCosta file in hand, Josh and Terry pulled up chairs and dug in, poring over building occupant interviews, preliminary lab and Crime Scene Unit reports, and the so-called Sixty Sheets written up by the individual squad detectives. Once they were up to speed, they started in on the dead man's phone records, recently arrived via fax.

Nothing in DaCosta's regular Bell Atlantic billing records, or from his long-distance service provider, revealed much of interest. It wasn't until they got to the detailed billing sheets generated by the subject's cellular provider that things got more interesting. U.S. Cellular billed its customers for both incoming and outgoing airtime, so there was a record of every call DaCosta had placed or received over the past three months. Littel systematically went about noting any number the dead man had frequently called, along with the times of day and duration, while on another list, Terry did the same thing with calls DaCosta had received. That task completed, they looked up each of those numbers in the little personal phone book found stuffed into a phony wall outlet hidey-hole at the homicide scene. A frequently called 718 area code number had no corresponding notation in that book, so Littel took the next step and consulted a Coles Reverse Directory for Brooklyn, the Bronx, and Queens. He found the number in the Canarsie section of Brooklyn, listed to a cigar store in the 900 block of Remsen Avenue.

Of the numbers DaCosta had called most frequently, there seemed to be a pattern to the times those calls were placed. Each time the dead man received a call from the cigar store, he invariably made a call within five minutes to another 718 number. That number *was* found in DaCosta's little phone book, alongside the notation "Gina G." In the Coles directory, Littel found the same number listed to a Veronica Styles, residing at 209 John Street in Brooklyn, fifth floor. They tried the number, got no answer, and then tried other numbers listed in the reverse directory for residents of that same building. The first, third, and fourth floors were apparently occupied by businesses, while the phone on the second floor was listed to an N. Ebbcomb. Most first-initial listings were for women. They took a chance that N. Ebbcomb might know either Veronica Styles or Gina G., and tried her number first.

"Hello," a woman's voice answered.

"Yeah. This is Detective Littel from the Thirty-seventh Precinct in Manhattan, ma'am. We're conducting a homicide investigation and I'm calling about a neighbor, lives on the fifth floor of your building. You happen to know them?"

"Oh my God," she murmured. "Is she all right? She hasn't answered any of my calls since yesterday afternoon."

"Far as we know, ma'am. When is the last time you talked to her?"

"Gina? Yesterday morning. We sort of, um, had a fight."

Josh frowned at his partner, listening on another extension. "Actually, it's her roommate I'm calling about. Veronica."

"Who?" the woman sounded clearly confused. "If you're talking about my neighbor who lives on the fifth floor of my building, I think you've got the wrong person. My neighbor's name is Gina. Gina Galati."

"She doesn't have a roommate, maybe?" Littel asked.

"Nuh-uh. Just her little boy."

"That's strange," he said. "Your friend Gina. You mind describing her to me?"

Matt Stuart and Rhoda Bolivar were on the FDR Drive, moving parallel with the East River and headed north to attempt to locate Havana Hector Jaquez, when Josh Littel called them from his borrowed desk at the Sixth Precinct. Stuart snatched his cell phone from the seat between them when it rang.

"Stuart."

"Josh Littel, Lou. Got a couple more pieces seem to fit our puzzle." He described what they'd managed to cull from DaCosta's phone records that morning, and what they'd learned while pursuing those leads. "I ask the broad, lives downstairs from this Gina Galati, to describe her to me. Fits that sketch you got to a fucking T. We're headed to Brooklyn right now to show it to her."

Stuart searched his memory of Brooklyn geography, trying to pinpoint the stretch of Remsen Avenue where the cigar store from DaCosta's cell phone records stood. "I might be wrong, but seems to me the Brooklyn Terminal Market is just a block or so from that cigar store address," he said. "Which puts it in the heart of Albanese territory." Late last year, while working on the Angelo Albeneti file at Intelligence Division, he'd accumulated an encyclopedia's worth of knowledge about the Albanese organization. One interesting tidbit was how, in the face of a migration southward by Caribbean blacks who'd settled first in the East New York section of Brooklyn, the Albanese and their friends had managed to isolate whole blocks of central Canarsie and keep them Italian.

"This Galati broad turns out to be the same gal as in the sketch, and she ain't home, we'll need a warrant to search her place, Lou. How quick you think we could get it?"

"I'll reach out to Ogilvy soon as we hang up," Matt assured him. "Nice work, Josh."

"Piece of cake so far. But don't thank us yet. Not 'til we bring you something with a pulse."

Before dialing Ogilvy again at Intel, Stuart quickly brought Rhoda up to date. Once he'd finished, he glanced over and saw her wearing that expression of deep concentration she wore when crunching facts.

"Benny Cool saw DaCosta and our mystery woman together the night

Johnny Rodriguez went down," she said. "Then your guy—the one who supplied the description to the sketch artist—saw them together at Mom's Pie, too. Last night, you wondered if she was involved in the Santos hit. I'm wondering now, depending on what her actual relationship with DaCosta was, if maybe she didn't kill him, too. Eliminate a witness, you know?"

Before Matt could respond, his phone rang again. He supposed it was Littel, calling back to add some detail he'd forgotten to pass along. "Stuart," he answered.

"Al Goldstein, Matthew. Where you at right now?"

"Triborough Bridge interchange, headed to chase down Hector Jaquez. Why?"

"Something too strange to convey over an open phone line, old buddy. Logan and me are parked catty-corner from the southeast corner of the Holy Cross Cemetery. That's in Flatbush, on Cortelyou Road. You need to get your ass over here, quick as them wheels of yours can carry you."

For Suzanne Albrecht, it felt strange every time she returned to the Flatbush neighborhood where she'd grown up. Much had changed in her life since she'd left there twenty-four years ago, and all but the vestiges of her Brooklyn upbringing had long since been left behind. As the daughter of an Irish mother and an electrician father who'd moved to America from Austria as a small boy, Suzanne was nurtured in a melting pot of Old World European cultures and American middle-class values. Throughout her education in Brooklyn's public schools, she'd lived in constant contact with Italian, Jewish, Irish, and German kids from homes still strongly tied to Old Country ways. Since grammar school, she'd been driven by an ambition to succeed at something lofty and unique. She'd concluded early on that in order to accomplish it she needed to become as American as possible. If that meant turning her back on this place, on her Catholic faith, and on many of her parents' more simplistic ideals, then so be it. At Erasmus Hall High School, it became clear to her that power was what she craved, and that politics was where real power lay. Without money or connections to the city's political machine, the law seemed the most expedient path toward her goal. Later, as an overworked and underappreciated intern at a prestigious midtown law firm, she'd thrown over the legal profession as the means toward her end, and turned to the NYPD.

By the late 1970s, the Knapp Commission's findings had forced many of the old guard in the police department into early retirement. To compensate for a perceived injustice done to minorities and women, the Job was recruiting them aggressively. Suzanne had a law degree from Columbia University, which could only help improve her visibility, and she figured she'd be a shoo-in for quick advancement up the ranks. So, rather than take the bar exam, she'd taken the leap across the thin blue line.

Holy Cross Catholic Cemetery was full to capacity long before either of Suzanne's parents became eligible to be buried there. But today, as she entered it at five past nine, it was still a place of memories. Located two blocks across Clarendon Road and Ditmas Avenue from her childhood home on East Thirty-seventh Street, it was where she and childhood chum Rose Marie Sabatino had gone to smoke cigarettes the first time they'd ever cut class. In the late spring of her sophomore year in high school, she'd surrendered her virginity there to senior shortstop Frankie DiSalvo. Drafted by the San Diego Padres that same spring, Frankie was killed when he plowed his new El Dorado, purchased with signing money, into an elevated-train support column on Nostrand Avenue. Every time she entered the cemetery and smelled the fresh-cut grass, she was hit with a vivid memory of that initial sharp pain, then Frankie laboring at her like the greased piston of some infernal machine.

"You're late," Angelo Albeneti said, his voice coming to her from behind a weather-worn marble tomb. Nerves frayed, Suzanne started in surprise as Angelo stepped into view. He was dressed not in his usual stained undershirt and flour-dusted white chinos, but in a charcoal double-breasted suit.

"First instance I can recall you ever being on time," she replied. "How much of my life have I wasted standing around waiting for you to appear, Angelo?"

Without replying, he walked directly to her and reached with both hands to feign an embrace. Before he could get a hand between her breasts, searching for a wire, she pushed back abruptly.

"How stupid do you think I am, *paisan*? I record you, who can I run to with the tape?"

"Always had a nice bod on you, Suzanne. Too bad we never got together like that."

"In your dreams."

"So why the meet? I'm a busy guy."

As she stood a moment continuing to regard him, she recalled how he'd once reminded her of the screen actor Sal Mineo. If Mineo were still alive today, she wondered if he would have gone so far to seed, with tufts of black hair sprouting from his ears and the coif gone so perilously thin. Today, Angelo's body was thick with too much rich food and too little exercise. She doubted that an actor, no matter how old and dissipated, would harbor the same latent violence in his eyes. "You and your play pals have started a war you can't win," she replied. "In the process, you've probably scuttled any chance I had of becoming this city's next PC. If it's not already too late, I'm hoping I can talk some sense into you."

He shot an impatient glance at his oyster case Rolex. "Don't know what the fuck you're talking about," he said distractedly.

"Hogwash!" she snapped. "A woman who works for you killed one of my field associates and his Dominican girlfriend last Wednesday. A dirty Special Ops cop named DaCosta drove her to the hit. She's likely responsible for killing the chief of a drug-pushing crew in Washington Heights last Thursday. Hell, for all I know, she killed DaCosta too, last night."

"Sounds like one busy little broad."

Suzanne ignored him. "Yesterday, you, Tony Nails, and Gus Barone met with two Chinese tong members at a boat basin in Canarsie. We've identified them as high-level heroin traffickers, which means you're getting ready to go head-to-head with the Colombians who control the flow of narcotics into Washington Heights. And like I said earlier, it's a war you can't win."

"I'm a baker, babe."

"You're a capo in the Albanese crime family, about to start a full-scale drug war! Last night, the Colombian-Odessa Mafiya alliance sent a man to Washington Heights to kill Francisco Santos, only he never got his chance. Someone from your team got there first." She watched him closely as she spoke, and thought she saw him blink on absorbing that last bit of news.

"I shoulda offed you *and* my cunt of an ex when I had the chance," he complained. "Been done with both youse backstabbing bitches. But no, I gotta go all soft, and look where it gets me."

"You never had the chance and you know it," she shot back. "I had you cold, Angelo. And I'm the one who screwed up, not you. I should have thrown you in jail and given what Rose Marie had on you to the U.S. Attorney right then and there."

"You din't have no more chance than I did, you wanted your best friend to *survive* that fucking divorce," he sneered. "I went to jail, ain't no place far away enough she coulda hid. Bitch couldn't hurt me without hurting you, so both of youse had your hands tied, and I've had you by the cunt hairs ever since, babe. And me?" He spread his hands, shrugging and smiling. "I'm still makin' d' cheesecake."

"And starting major drug wars. I'm telling you, Angelo. Our guys are so close they can smell the stink of your lousy cologne. They decide to push the button, shoot a missile up your tailpipe, there's nothing in this world I can do to stop them."

"We're all big boys," he assured her. "This ain't our first rodeo, babe. But hey. I appreciate your touching concern."

Whenever she was around him, Suzanne found it extremely hard to control the rage he got boiling inside her. "The FA you had killed was on the take from Santos," she said, trying to keep her tone modulated. "I assume you knew that. DaCosta wasn't mine, at least not directly, but when this bomb you're so busy planting explodes, the fallout from it will affect the whole Job, of which I am the first deputy commissioner. Once the media gets finished raking the entire NYPD command structure over the coals, there's no way I'll get the top job come August."

He shrugged, the smile gone from his face but still smoldering in his eyes. "Woulda been nice to have the actual PC in our pockets, but hey. Ain't nobody ever said you had a lock on it, babe. Think of all the opportunities a broad like you will have in the private sector. Hell, we might wanna hire you ourselves."

"I thought you just baked cheesecakes."

"It's a growth bidness, babe. Name one person you know ain't got one kinda sweet tooth or another."

Stuart and Bolivar made good time retracing their route back down the FDR Drive. They took the Manhattan Bridge across the East River into Brooklyn and reached Grand Army Plaza, at the tip of Prospect Park and the Brooklyn Botanic Garden at nine-thirty, within twenty minutes of receiving Martini Al's call. Headed south on Flatbush Avenue, Stuart took advantage of light midmorning traffic and kept his foot in it. He was weaving in and out of gaps between cars when his phone rang again. He asked Rhoda to grab it.

"Lieutenant Stuart's line. Detective Bolivar," she answered. "Yeah, Sarge. Hang on." She handed the phone across. "Sergeant Goldstein."

Stuart wedged the instrument between cheek and shoulder as the light at the next intersection turned yellow. Halfway through, he had to swerve sharply to avoid a cabbie jumping the gun. "Yeah, Al?"

"Where you at?" Goldstein asked.

"On Flatbush. Less than a mile from you."

"Come across on Clarendon, and keep an eye peeled. You might get lucky enough to see an old friend. Not in her usual wheels, though. This ride's a navy blue Chevy Lumina."

"What's going on?" Stuart asked. He hated games and felt like he'd just been asked to play one.

"Like I said earlier, buddy. Not on an open line. You see what I hope you do, maybe I won't need to do quite so much explaining once you get here."

With the phone flipped shut and set alongside his thigh again, Stuart recapped the conversation for Rhoda.

"What old friend?" she asked. "I don't get it."

"Me neither, but it sounds like maybe I will. Al follows Albeneti out here, then feeds me this cryptic crap about an old friend. I'm assuming it's some sort of code." He shook his head. "I'm only firing on five of eight cylinders right now. Wouldn't be surprised if I'm missing something."

He saw sympathy in Bolivar's return smile. "So we keep an eye out for a dark blue Chevy Lumina."

Flatbush Avenue became more congested as they passed within a few blocks of the huge Kings County Hospital and Kingsboro Psychiatric Center complex. With the central commerce area of Flatbush just ahead, the sidewalks were more crowded with pedestrian traffic, too. This was the heart of Matt's last command before moving on to Intel Division, and he found himself on the lookout for the familiar faces of troublemakers. Old habits died hard, but most of those individuals had undoubtedly moved on, either into the state prison system or to their rewards. Four years was an eternity in the life of a mutt.

"When I ran the squad here, I thought the Seven-one was busy," he told Rhoda. "Guess I didn't have a clue, huh? Still, it's amazing how little things have changed in four years."

"Faces come and go, but the city stays the same," she waxed philosophic. Then, as Stuart eased them to a stop at a light too red to run, she sat up straighter to point diagonally across the intersection. "That's a Lumina, isn't it? Oh my God—" She stopped abruptly to gape.

Stuart looked that way, and for a heartbeat, his mind refused to believe what he saw. In the next instant, the implications of Suzanne Albrecht's presence in Flatbush, driving away from his destination, came down on him like an avalanche. Beyond her strictly professional interest in recent events in Washington Heights, she was also somehow involved in them in a way she couldn't control. She had to be. From Thursday last week when she'd summoned him to her office, he'd had an inkling that Suzanne was already two steps ahead in a race to avert a disaster that only she knew was impending. She'd gotten him "the money," and had already set the wheels in motion to make him Joe McMahon's replacement . . . *before* Officer Johnny Rodriguez was whacked. A good cop learned not to trust coincidence, and Matt realized he'd either forgotten that all-important axiom or been blinded by other feelings. He could see now that Suzanne must have known all along how dirty Macho Man Rodriguez was. Whether she'd also known he was due to have his ticket punched was a whole other question, and a frightening one at that.

"She's who met Albeneti," he murmured. A part of him had gone numb. He felt like time had suddenly slowed to a crawl.

"It's not possible," Rhoda protested. "I mean, I don't know the woman, but you listen to the stories, Suzanne Albrecht is the straightest arrow on the Job."

"I do know her," Matt replied. His gaze was still locked on the face across the intersection, waiting intently for the light to change. "And this could prove she's a lot more complex than I ever guessed."

When the light turned green, Stuart saw Suzanne's eyes automatically sweep the intersection for stragglers before she proceeded. It was then that she spotted him and Rhoda, and registered that most damning of all expressions: dismayed surprise.

Twenty-two

Like a submariner in a vessel crippled by depth charges, Suzanne Albrecht had scrambled for over a week to shore up leaks sprung the entire length of her hull. And like most mortals faced with the inevitable collapse of their worlds, she had embarked on that feverish attempt at damage control in denial. Even as late as last Wednesday, when Johnny Rodriguez was killed, she still held out hope that she could survive the current crisis, right her ship, and continue to sail on. She'd used Matt Stuart like a steel lolly-column to brace up the hull where it seemed most likely to cave in. Throughout the week since, she'd listened intently to news from other sectors, trying to anticipate where the next crack that could sink her might appear. News of Red Top crew chief Darryl Johnson's homicide was followed too quickly by Stuart's discovery of Macho Man's dirty-money stash, and yet she'd not really started to sweat until Clarence DaCosta was killed, just yesterday. That event, followed by her conversation with Stuart and Chief Ogilvy at the scene, had impacted with enough force to take her breath away. Before she could recover it, Francisco Santos was hit, and that morning, as she left Holy Cross Cemetery, Suzanne knew that everything she'd worked to achieve over the past twenty-two years was destined for the bottom of the sea.

The shock of seeing Matt Stuart waiting at the light across Tilden Avenue was nearly as profound as what she'd read in his expression.

That kind of surprise could only mean one thing. He'd been summoned to Flatbush in pursuit of Angelo Albeneti. Whoever was working the detail had already seen her there, in the Albanese capo's company. In light of that fact, Matt couldn't help believing that she had purposely inserted him at Intelligence two years ago in hopes of using him to keep tabs on their ongoing Mom's Pie/Angelo Albeneti investigation. He was probably recalling their pillow talk, and hearkening back to how she'd muscled him into taking the whip's assignment at the Three-seven last week. While Stuart was still in the dark, as she was, regarding the specifics of Angelo's current plan, he'd most certainly been led to one conclusion: she had used him, and his affections, with deceit beyond all dishonor.

Headed north on Flatbush Avenue, Suzanne suddenly realized she had no idea where she was going. On impulse, she turned left on Parkside Avenue to drive in the direction of the Gowanus Expressway. Through the dust and debris of dashed hopes and dreams, one thing *had* become frighteningly obvious. Angelo and his friends were rolling the dice and taking the biggest risk of their criminal careers. The parts of their scheme that didn't seem downright mad to her seemed wildly reckless. It was unclear to her how far Angelo was prepared to go with this campaign, but one thing *was* clear. Her own career was over, and she was no longer in a position to guarantee her friend Rose Marie Sabatino's safety.

When Angelo Albeneti left Holy Cross Cemetery to climb back into his Mom's Pie Company delivery van, he drove east on Cortelyou Road toward the Brooklyn Terminal Market in Canarsie. Al Goldstein sent Jack Hogan to follow him while he stood on the cemetery sidewalk, waiting for Stuart and Bolivar to arrive. When they pulled over to the curb opposite him five minutes later, he pitched a Roi-Tan smoked and chewed down to a two-inch butt into the gutter. The moment he climbed into the backseat of Matt's car, closed the door, and saw the expressions on their faces, he knew they'd seen what he'd hoped they would. His old buddy had a history there—no matter what kind of secret Stuart believed his affair with the first dep was—and Al hadn't wanted to be the guy to break that particular bad news. "Go figure, huh?" was what he said instead.

"I want to know exactly what went down, Al," Matt replied. "Who arrived first, how they met, how long they talked, and who left first. All of it."

"When she showed, he was already there, inside the cemetery," Goldstein reported. "She parked here on Cortelyou, same as him. Location of the meet was prearranged. Both walked to the same monument. He waited behind it 'til she came. They talked. Looked pretty animated and not that friendly, with her more pissed off than him. She really got into his shit about something."

"It went on how long?" Matt asked.

"Ten minutes, tops. She left first, but only by a couple steps. Don't suppose I need to say how bad this looks. I mean, the Job's first deputy fucking commissioner meeting with the likes of him?"

Stuart sat quietly a moment, then turned in his seat to face his second-in-command directly. "On the phone, you called her my old friend, Al. I wish I could dodge this particular bullet, but considering the circumstances, I don't think I can. Straight up, buddy. What is it you've heard?"

Goldstein had known Matt Stuart for a lot of years. In all that time, he'd never once doubted his former partner was a stand-up cop. Matt had been through hell, losing his little boy the way he had, then losing his marriage on top of that. Several years back, when he'd first heard the stories, he'd been unable to fathom what Suzanne Albrecht's appeal might be. He could only conclude she was taking advantage of him, exploiting an emotional need Stuart had. "There's been this rumor kinda dangling on the Detective Bureau grapevine, two, maybe three years now," he said slowly. "That you and the first dep were sneaking around onna side. I got no idea how widespread it is. People knew I was your ex-partner, y'know?"

Still eyeing him steadily, Stuart nodded. "Simon Ogilvy told me the same thing last night. Also told me he'd assumed Suzanne had inserted me inside his division as a spy. She didn't, and today he seems to believe me when I tell him that."

Goldstein didn't miss how Stuart had glanced in Bolivar's direction as he spoke, clearly trying to gauge her reaction to all this. In Al's judgment, she'd absorbed it with the same kind of cool detachment she brought to most new information. It was what made her an excellent detective: that ability to sit back and methodically process new data.

"I admitted one thing to him that he probably already suspected," Matt continued. "Suzanne was directly responsible for my being assigned to the Three-seven squad. Johnny Rodriguez was one of her field associates. Due to the circumstances of his death, it seemed obvious that he'd gone native on her. How much more she knew, I can only guess."

Goldstein took a deep breath and slowly blew it back out again. He knew how hard it had to be for Stuart to sit there and admit the things he just had. Hearing the pain in his friend's voice made Al want another cigar, and maybe an extended session with a birdbath in a dark, smoky bar. For the moment, he could have neither, so he tried, instead, to channel the anxiety he felt in a positive direction. "This thing between you two still going on?" he asked.

"Ended six months ago. She asked me to take the Three-seven assignment as a favor to her. Said she wanted to avoid a corruption scandal if she could help it, and I was the only guy she could trust to plug the leak. Quietly."

"Sounds to me like she had no idea what Albeneti and his pals were scheming," Al observed wryly. "You think?"

Though he shook his head, Stuart's expression was still troubled. "Frankly, I don't know what I think right now, Al. It could explain why her conversation with Cheesecake was so heated, as you say. But what her relationship with him might be, I still can't imagine. He's a made guy in the goddamn Mafia."

Rhoda spoke for the first time since they'd started down that particular path. "You do realize the mere fact of her consorting with the likes of Albeneti could implicate her in the murders of three civilians and two police officers," she said. "The instant she saw you staring back at her across that intersection, Lou, she knew you knew it, too."

Matt looked glum, plainly still trying to get his mind wrapped around the enormity of the first deputy commissioner's evident transgression. "It's probably less difficult for me to imagine than it is for you," he said. "I know how she's wired better than most. It's got something to do with the blind ambition that drives her, and the fact she took a wayward step somewhere, cut a deal with the devil. You do that, the payback's always a bitch."

"Be interesting to hear how she tries to explain it," Goldstein mused. "I can't imagine."

"I seriously doubt she'll go anywhere near the Big Building right now," Stuart countered. "If we're even close to correct in our suspicions, her whole life just plowed into the side of a mountain. She might even decide to run."

"Meanwhile," Rhoda interjected, speaking to Al directly, "we have a war we might want to prevent escalating to the point the governor has to call out the National Guard. We need to know where Albeneti is headed, and what shape the Albanese plan of attack is going to take. The lou and I had an interesting conversation with Candy Ignacio this morning, and another with Josh Littel. Candy tells us a woman named Gozon has been shacking with one of the Red Top crew's block captains. She might be who hit Uncle Frank last night, and if she's allied with the Albanese, then Roberto Santiago and his Odessa Mafiya friends could have a real fight trying to win that market back."

Goldstein turned this news over in his mind and nodded. The war was on and they were right in the middle of it. Any hope he'd held out for a quick and easy way to end it was fading fast. "What about Josh and Terry?" he asked.

"He and Gaskin think they're close to identifying the woman who killed Macho Man."

It wasn't until eleven o'clock that morning that Terry Gaskin and Josh Littel collected the search warrant ordered for them by Chief Ogilvy, and could proceed to Gina Galati's John Street address on the Brooklyn waterfront. The neighbor they'd contacted answered her intercom, then rode downstairs to examine their ID through the elevator gate before she would grant them access. Heavy-breasted, with short-cropped dark hair, Naiomi Ebbcomb was barefoot and dressed in paint-stained sweat pants and a T-shirt, and appeared to have been crying.

"We've got a warrant to search the fifth-floor premises," Gaskin said as he presented the document. "Is there a super who can get us in there?"

She sniffled and took a swipe at her nose with the back of one hand. "I'll call him. He lives up the block."

Littel produced a copy of the artist's sketch, unfolded it, and handed it across. "Is this your friend Gina?" he asked.

The partners watched her eyes widen, and then saw a look of caution develop. "It looks an awful lot like her," she admitted. "And a thousand other Italian women in Brooklyn."

"We're operating on the theory that she's the one in a thousand," Littel replied.

Stuart had contacted Chief Ogilvy with the name they'd fed him, and had it ring a bell. The OCCB had a record of one Santino "Sonny" Galati, a former brother-in-law of Angelo Albeneti. He'd twice been arrested on bookmaking and numbers-running charges, and according to their files was thought to be living in Florida now. There was no record of his having family, but OCCB was digging deeper there. "So. How long you known your neighbor, Miss Ebbcomb?"

The woman's distraught condition made Josh wonder about the nature of her relationship with Gina Galati. It wouldn't be politically correct to generalize and say the woman actually *looked* gay, but privately, he would concede the possibility.

"Two years," she told him. "She was three months pregnant when she moved in here. I baby-sit for her now and then."

"She got a job?" Gaskin asked.

The question earned a frown. "A freelance gig is what she claims, doing layout work for a family business in Manhattan. Whenever I've asked her anything about it, she kinda shines me on. All I know, she gets called to come to work at all kinds of crazy hours."

Layout work. Littel and Gaskin made eye contact, reading each other's minds.

"She ever have visitors?" Josh asked.

Her face clouded again. "Not too often. There's this greaseball Italian Stallion type, drives a shiny red Cadillac and comes around maybe once a week. Not her boyfriend or anything. In fact, I think she can hardly stand him. He's got something to do with the family business."

"Tall, short, full head of hair, thinning, how old?" Gaskin asked. He had his notebook out, pen poised.

"Big guy," she replied. "With a gut. Forty maybe? Lots of hair but not long or anything."

"You said greaseball," Terry prodded.

She nodded. "Like, why wear one or two gold chains when ten will do, you know? And no matter how hot it is, he's always wearing this black leather goombah jacket."

It sounded like a description of half the hoods in the city, but the red Cadillac might help narrow it down some. According to the file he'd read during that meeting at the whip's house Sunday, Angelo "Cheesecake" Albeneti's sometime visitor on Pleasant Avenue, Tony Fortunado, drove a red El Dorado. He pressed on as he finished jotting notes. "Anyone else?"

She paused, seeming hesitant about what she would say next, then practically sneered her reply. "Just some guy she spent the night with Saturday. A *real* cheeseball, you ask me. Light-skinned black guy with almost blond hair, in dreadlocks no less. He's wearing this Super Fly suit but drives a totally beat-to-shit Chevy or something."

DaCosta, Littel thought, which made for an interesting twist. They weren't only killing people together. He wondered if she'd pulled the classic black-widow act: killed him after screwing him. When he looked his partner's way, he could see Terry was thinking exactly the same thing.

"Let's go find this super," Gaskin suggested. "See if your friend Gina ever brings home any of this freelance work she does."

Suzanne Albrecht was in a full-blown panic by the time she reached Staten Island via the Verrazano Narrows Bridge. The implications of her being discovered in flagrante had become more damning the more time she had to think about them. Because she was driving a company car and had nowhere to run, even in different wheels, her options seemed severely limited. In a matter of hours, her credit cards would probably be worthless. She carried very little cash, her passport was locked in a wall safe in her apartment, as were her checkbook, a majority of the certificates in her stock portfolio, and any jewelry she owned. With the hopelessness of her predicament becoming ever more apparent, she scrambled all the more, seeking some avenue of escape.

Rather than proceed directly to Rose Marie Sabatino's house to warn her of the danger she was in, Suzanne had continued across Staten Island on I-278 and crossed into New Jersey over the Arthur Kill. Five miles north up the Jersey Turnpike at Newark International Airport, she'd used her ATM card and three major credit cards to withdraw the maximum cash advances obtainable from a variety of electronic teller machines. With that cash, she'd purchased a one-way ticket to Miami on a flight departing early that evening and rented a tiny Geo Metro automobile. It was her plan, still very much half-baked, to get a cut-and-dye job and purchase some flamboyant skirts, tops, and a bathing suit. Once she reached Florida, she would head for the islands.

It was noon before she'd retraced her route to Staten Island. Off I-278 she took the Todt Hill Road exit south toward Rose Marie's house on Otis Avenue, between the Grant Hill and New Dorp train stations. Her old friend often took her lunch hour at home, so she opted to try there first. As she slowed down in front of the modest gray clapboard dwelling, she saw she was both in and out of luck. Rose Marie's Oldsmobile coupe was parked in the drive behind a white Land Rover Discovery. Her friend appeared to have company. She supposed that Rose Marie's visitor might leave if she made it clear there was something urgent she needed to discuss, and with that hope in tow, she parked on the street to approach the front door up the walk.

When Rose Marie answered the door to Suzanne, she seemed more alarmed than delighted to see her there on her stoop. "Suzanne!" her old friend exclaimed. "What on earth are *you* doing here?"

It was a reasonable question. Suzanne was a notorious workaholic, generally difficult to pin down, yet there she was, standing at Rose Marie's door in the middle of a workday. "It looks like you've got company," Suzanne observed. "There's something we need to talk about, but if this isn't a good time . . ." She let it hang, giving Rose the choice of either inviting her inside or running her off.

Rose Marie saw the look of urgency in her friend's eyes and stepped back to clear the way. She waved toward the interior of the house with a gesture of unconcern. "The Land Rover? Belongs to my niece. She and her little boy are visiting for a couple days. You remember my brother Dom's little girl, Regina?"

Suzanne had a vivid recollection of a child no more than five or six years old, cute as a button, with dark hair and huge brown eyes. It had to be eighteen years ago, before Dominic Sabatino had that fatal run-in with the goons sent by his loan shark. "Sure do," she replied. "And you don't know how old it makes me feel, hearing you say she's got a little boy."

"Oh, I know. I feel the same way." Rose led the way toward her kitchen, gesturing excitedly with her hands the way she always did when she spoke. "You're lucky you caught me. I'm home from the office for a quick bite is all."

In the kitchen, a toddler sat in one of those portable high chairs that clamp to a table or countertop. He was being spoon-fed by a very pretty young woman with longish dark hair, dressed casually in shorts and a tank top. The instant the young woman's eyes met Suzanne's, there was a flash of that same kind of alarm seen earlier in Rose Marie. It made

Suzanne feel as though the very earth beneath her feet had shifted unexpectedly. What the hell was going on here?

"Gina," Rose introduced them. "I don't know if you remember my friend Suzanne Albrecht, from the old neighborhood. Suzanne, Gina Galati."

There was an unmistakable wariness in the young woman as she extended a hand to shake. "I remember, sure," Gina said. "Matter of fact, I seen you on the news just last night. Couldn't place the face for the life of me. Until right now, that is. Wow. So you're like a big muckety-muck cop now, huh?"

"She's the New York Police Department's first deputy commissioner," Rose Marie informed her. "The number two ranking cop in the entire city."

While listening to their exchange, Suzanne couldn't shake the feeling that they were communicating in some kind of code. She felt herself flush with anger. Her old friend would be dead right now, not a successful realtor living in the lap of security and comfort, if it weren't for her sticking her neck out.

"There's something come up that Suzanne and I need to talk about," Rose told her niece. "You'll have to excuse us a few minutes. You got everything you need?"

"Don't sweat it," Gina said with a shrug. "Nice seeing you again, Suzanne." She returned to spooning baby food.

Rose Marie led Suzanne down the hall to her study and closed the door. Once they were alone, their conversation sealed off from the world outside, Suzanne went on the offensive.

"What is it I saw just now, Rose? When you answered the door, and then again from Gina, the second I walked into the kitchen."

Rose Marie crossed to her desk, pulled out the chair, and dropped into it. Her head thrown back, she closed her eyes and took a deep, purposeful breath. "Gina's in some kind of trouble, Suze. She showed up at all hours last night, like she is on the run from something. First thing this morning, she asks about you. Says she saw you on the news last night. Then, out of the blue, you show up on my stoop. How do you expect me to react?"

It hadn't occurred to Suzanne that Gina might be in trouble. Nor did it occur to her now that the young woman's problem might in any way be connected to her own. She assumed, from the girl's coarse Brooklyn speech pattern and her tough-girl demeanor, that what she'd fled was something mundane like a drug deal gone sour or an abusive mate. The fact that Gina had recognized her from a news broadcast was nothing new, nor was the discomfort many people displayed on learning she was a cop.

"I had a talk with Angelo this morning, Rose," she said slowly, returning to her own dilemma. "At Holy Cross Cemetery."

Now there was only confusion in Rose Marie's expression. "You're kidding. In the old neighborhood? Why there?"

"He and Gus Barone have decided the Mafia needs to get back into the heroin business. In the past week they've killed two dirty cops and a couple of high-profile street dealers in upper Manhattan. Holy Cross is where we always meet to have our little chats. This morning, I went there to try and convince him that what he's doing is crazy."

"And he laughed at you, right?"

"That's not the worst of it. The stupid bastard was followed. By a surveillance detail from our Intelligence Division. They saw me there, too."

Rose Marie's hand went to her mouth. "Oh my God, honey."

Suzanne nodded. "You got it. I'm dead meat. And depending on Angelo's mood, you could be dead meat, too." She removed her ticket folder from her handbag to brandish it. "I've got a little under eighteen hundred in cash, a rental car, and a one-way flight to Miami. No matter how far I decide to run, they'll probably catch me. When they do, I'll be tried as an accessory to half a dozen murders. Just last week I was in line to become this city's next police commissioner. Saturday night, I went to a Yankees game as a guest of the mayor."

Rose Marie was suddenly on her feet and pacing. Her face had gone pale and her hands were clenched into fists. "You know I'll do anything I can for you, honey. Get you cash, contact anyone you need me to contact . . ." She stopped, fresh out of ideas and clutching at straws. "Hell, I owe you my pathetic life, Suzanne. I really don't know what to say. I'm sorry? Right now, it sounds a little lame."

"There's not much you can do," Suzanne replied. "Outside of watching your own back. With this craziness Angelo's started, all hell's going to break loose. When it does, he may decide to cut his losses, and you've always been a loose end. One he'll hate to leave dangling."

Rose slowly unclenched her fists and squared her shoulders. "I guess this was bound to happen someday, right? I mean, how nutty was I to think I could actually walk away from that asshole?" There were tears in her eyes as she reached to take Suzanne's hands in hers. She looked hard at her. "I'm so sorry, honey. Sorry I ever got you involved. It wasn't fair."

Suzanne pulled her hand from her old friend's grasp to wipe a tear from Rose's cheek. "Hey," she said, code-switching to the Flatbushese that she and Rose Marie had grown up with. "Whuddah friends foah, f'crissake?"

They threw their arms around each other, hugging with a ferocity that only thirty-five years of love and devotion could generate. Suzanne, too, began to weep.

The instant Suzanne Albrecht appeared in her aunt's kitchen, Gina Galati had jumped to an obvious but mistaken conclusion. The cops had somehow managed to identify her, and then her aunt's old friend had made the connection. She'd come there to arrest her quietly, out of deference to an old friend. But now, as Gina stood with an ear pressed to the door of her aunt's study, overhearing most of the exchange conducted within, she was able to piece together shards of what she couldn't hear, too. It was hard for her to believe that the prim, tightly wound woman she'd seen on the news last night was a product of the same neighborhood that had produced her Uncle Angelo, her father, and her hated stepfather, Sonny. Even with her polished businesswoman's demeanor, Aunt Rose Marie was unmistakably Brooklyn as well, but this policewoman could have been from almost anywhere.

From what Gina was able to gather, Suzanne Albrecht had used her office to help Rose Marie when her aunt had decided to divorce Angelo. Because her uncle was not only a made guy but a capo in one of the oldest and best-run organized crime entities in America, Gina couldn't imagine what kind of leverage would be necessary to accomplish such a feat. She knew how virtually impossible a divorce from a Sicilian mobster was. Malcontent ex-wives and troublesome girlfriends of Mafia goombahs were prone to despairing leaps from the Triborough Bridge and falling overboard from pleasure boats on Long Island Sound. It took one killer to really know another, and Gina knew firsthand the merciless side of her uncle's temperament, the fierceness of his pride. But that morning, when this policewoman and Gina's uncle were seen together by other cops, the uneasy truce between Angelo and Rose Marie had been shattered. The lady cop was on the run, and Rose Marie was left to face Angelo's wrath alone.

When sounds of weeping signaled the end of their exchange, Gina slipped quietly back into the kitchen. She lifted Claude from his playpen and pile of toys to clean his face with a damp washcloth. A good-natured baby, he returned her smile and made "buh, buh, buh" sounds, smacking his lips with each utterance. Gina cooed back at him as the study door opened. At that same moment, the pager she carried in the pocket of her shorts vibrated for the umpteenth time that day. The display would carry Tony Fortunado's contact number at the cigar store on Remsen Avenue. Before long, she needed to decide what her next move would be.

Twenty-three

The meeting that Matt Stuart was summoned to attend in the throne room on the fourteenth floor of One Police Plaza that Monday afternoon was attended by every bureau chief and division commander on the Job. It made for a crowd. Many individuals accustomed to having seats at these confabs were forced to stand. Together with Rhoda Bolivar and Chief Simon Ogilvy, Stuart stood facing the assembled company to one side of outgoing police commissioner Glen Massengale's desk. In deference to Ogilvy's status as boss of Intelligence, Matt let Simon do most of the talking. But when called upon to relate the circumstances that first landed him at Three-seven, and the gist of what he and his detectives had managed to put together in the week since, Stuart was more than happy to speak up. Listening to himself, he found it hard to believe so much had happened in so short a time.

"So let me get this straight," Chief of Department Bob Dunleavy addressed the Intel chief. "We still have *no* idea why the second-highest-ranking cop in the Job took a clandestine meeting with a man you've identified as a capo in the Albanese crime organization?"

"We can guess," Ogilvy replied. "But for the moment, I don't see any merit in it." He stopped and let his gaze roam from face to face around the room. "Here's what we *do* know. The opening salvo has been fired in what could be the biggest drug war this city's ever seen. The Albanese appear to have forged an alliance with Chinese heroin interests. They're both aiming to recapture control of a market they lost to the Colombians. It seems likely that First Deputy Commissioner Albrecht has compromised our ability to react to this threat by supplying the Albanese with intelligence on our investigations."

"How?" Commissioner Massengale asked.

"I've identified the field associate she assigned to my division, sir. Last night, this officer worked a wiretap surveillance where the Cali cartel's man in New York and a former KGB major were heard discussing a strategy for dealing with an Albanese threat. Later, that officer left his post to call First Deputy Commissioner Albrecht's apartment from a pay phone. This morning, Suzanne Albrecht met clandestinely with Angelo Albeneti."

This wasn't the first time Stuart had heard this information that day, but as he listened to it again, he was still having tremendous difficulty believing his former lover was really that corrupt. There had to be some explanation; one that went beyond the conclusion that Suzanne was some kind of twisted sociopath. Thwarted as her suitor, he'd seen her fickle nature more than once, and how consumed she was by her ambitions. He also knew that Simon Ogilvy and Al Goldstein both believed she'd played him for a fool, somehow managing to short-circuit a good cop's inherent sixth sense for spotting the con. But Matt wasn't buying it, or at least not *all* of it. There was more at stake than met the eye. Much more. Right now, he was less concerned about how corrupt Suzanne might be than he was about his former lover's safety.

"It's been two hours since she failed to answer my calls to her cellular phone and pager," Commissioner Massengale told them. "I've ordered a list compiled of every field associate under her control, throughout the department. When this meeting is over, I'm issuing an areawide APB for her apprehension. Twenty minutes from now, I travel to City Hall to update the mayor on these developments."

Short-timer or not, Stuart felt sympathy for the man. No one wanted to leave a career of dedicated service under a dark cloud, yet today's crisis threatened to create a scandal so black, memory of any positive Massengale accomplishment would be obliterated by it.

"So tell me, Chief," the PC continued to address Ogilvy. "How soon can you make cases strong enough to get racketeering indictments against all these people? The first deputy commissioner's disappearance is bound to create a media circus, but our first responsibility is to protect citizens from the impending bloodbath you've predicted."

"I've ordered blanket surveillance of every significant player now in the picture, sir," Ogilvy told his boss. "Lieutenant Stuart and his squad have done some excellent work identifying principals in a new drug-distribution hierarchy that is seeking to take control of Washington Heights. They've also identified the woman believed to have pulled the trigger in Officer Juan Rodriguez's homicide, and tied her at least circumstantially to the Albanese organization." He shrugged. "How soon we can nail them depends on how quickly they make their next moves."

Narcotics Division chief Danny Shoshany eased himself upright from the windowsill he sat propped against. "This recording your people made of Major Neyizhsalo and Roberto Santiago. It sounds about as damning as that kind of thing gets."

"We'll see," Ogilvy said. "My next stop is the Javits Building, for a sit-down with the U.S. Attorney. He'll tell us if we've got enough to take to a federal grand jury."

In all the years he'd been involved in dealing drugs, Kamil Imbongi had never seen anything like the crackdown currently being waged against Red Top crew activity by the NYPD. Early Monday afternoon, only hours after he thought it safe enough to finally sound the all-clear and send his troops back out into traffic, uniformed and plainclothes cops suddenly appeared in legions to start making wholesale arrests. None of the reports he'd received were of run-ins with the usual faces from the local station house. Instead, the antagonists were all interlopers. Squad cars involved in the arrests bore markings from precincts as far away as the One Twenty-third in Staten Island and the One-eleven in Douglaston, Queens. The cops in them had hit quickly. By best estimate, a full half of the street runners and pitchers engaged in Red Top commerce were now in custody.

At one o'clock, Imbongi ordered all remaining Red Top troops off the street, and every stash house shut down, its contents moved to the next location in the tightly protected secret rotation. He'd moved his own headquarters to a building six blocks from the last, on the corner of 157th Street and Amsterdam Avenue. As was his custom, he'd spent most of his time on the new rooftop watching the movement of traffic below and monitoring the neighborhood's pulse.

Shortly after his arrival there, Kamil called a council meeting of his twelve block captains. By three o'clock, all of them had assembled to loiter in the shade of the building's water tower. Most were nervous to be gathered in broad daylight, considering the state of siege that now existed in Washington Heights. For his purposes, Kamil wanted them to be nervous, and also wanted them angry. He called the meeting to order by slapping his flywhisk against one robe-clad leg, then pointed it accusingly at skinny, six-foot-seven-inch Richie Townsend.

"You and that trigger-happy Dominican bitch be what brung this shit down on us, Brother Richie. You, her, and that guinea gangster motherfucker you let her bring with her when we talk. Me? All I wanna know, Brother Richie, is why? Why Steady Eddy Tío Paco weren't good enough for us, you gotta let them stir up all this shit?"

While Townsend locked eyes with Imbongi, it was O. J. Dixon who piped up from where he sat cross-legged against a parapet wall. "Because that greaseball ain't the only motherfucker getting his dick sucked by no Dominican bitch around here, Brother Kamil."

Like lightning, Townsend spun on Dixon and brandished the 9 mm Beretta he carried concealed beneath his oversize basketball jersey. But before he could level the gun to aim it, he saw the muzzle of Dixon's Uzi already pointed at him.

"Bang, you dead, motherfucker," Dixon said quietly. "Why don't y'all answer the nigger's questions?"

Stuck between a rock and a hard place, Townsend still couldn't resist a bit of posturing before he backed down. He rolled his shoulders and head, never once breaking eye contact with his adversary, then mouthed the word "pow" and blew a kiss at Dixon before putting his weapon up.

"That true?" Imbongi asked Little Richie. "That Dominican bitch used pussy to get in your door? That trick be as old as the fucking Bible, nigger. All bitches know a man can't think straight, he got some hot mama sucking on his Johnson. That how this bitch get to you?"

Richie felt the heat of eleven pairs of eyes boring into him. A sheen of sweat broke out to coat his shaved head as his posturing turned into nervous foot shuffling. "Ain't none of you ignorant motherfuckers understand," he argued defensively. "Dominicans got their own politics, same as we got ours. Raquel, her sister, and a whole lotta other Dominican bitches in this neighborhood got plenty reason to hate Tío Paco. He send their dudes to the DR on his business and ain't half of them never come back. Then he evict the new widow bitches from their houses. That's how greedy the motherfucker was."

"And what that got to do with us?" Corky Cochran demanded.

"Jus' hear me out," Richie snapped. "Paco, he take most the money for hisself while every other motherfucker in this neighborhood bend his ass over backward, helping protect him and his turf. So lately, a buncha them pissed-off bitches decide they had enough. It ain't gonna be Tío Paco's game to call no more."

"And how long you know they be planning this little coup?" Imbongi asked. There was accusation in it.

His expression sullen, Townsend stared hard at him. "It's the guineas been planning this shit, not Raquel. They the ones got the hard-on here."

From his corner perch, Corky Cochran hopped down to stand within three feet of Townsend. He had to crane his neck to look up at him. "Darryl Johnson, Richie. That nigger like a brother to me. Some mother-fucker shot him down like a dog and it weren't nobody Tío Paco Santos sent."

"What you saying, bro?" Richie demanded. "That maybe I done him?"

Despite the difference in height, the diminutive Cochran wasn't back-ing off. The mean streak for which he was famous glowed bright in his eyes as he stood his ground. "Don't know. Maybe you, maybe the bitch you be fucking. But what I *do* know? T'other day, y'all had more reasons why Kamil shouldn't be the new crew chief than I got bastard kids. Why that be?"

"What?" Townsend snarled. "You pushing up on me, nigger? I gonna pretend I din't never hear that."

"Ee-nough!" Imbongi roared. "Both you niggers drop it! Now!" He'd drawn himself up to his full height, his mantua gathered in one hand to allow him freedom of movement. His flywhisk sliced at the air before him like Solomon's sword. "Fact we got bitches telling us how we gonna run our business be bad enough. But this brother-against-brother bullshit ain't none of us is gonna tolerate." He turned to stare directly at Townsend. "Y'all can't see how they using you, you a dumb mother-fucker, Richie. That divide-and-conquer bullshit be as old as Eve and the snake."

"This nigger dissed me," Townsend complained.

"No," Imbongi insisted. "He axed the same question been on all our minds. Ever since you and them Dominican bitches show up with the greaseball last night. It look to us like you helping them make their play."

Townsend decided he'd heard enough. He turned abruptly on his heels and stalked toward the stairwell access without another word. Nearly tearing the door off its hinges, yanking it open, he turned one last time to address the assembled company before he disappeared. "You niggers all gonna sorely regret how much y'all just pissed me off! This time next week, we see who come crawling to who." That said, he was gone.

The eerie silence that descended was broken as Imbongi slipped a handheld radio from a pocket of his robe, lifted it to his lips, and keyed the transmit button. "Richie don't leave the building," he said quietly.

It was three o'clock by the time Matt Stuart and Rhoda Bolivar arrived at the Three-seven to monitor the progress made by other members of the squad. Terry Gaskin had left a message reporting that he and Josh Littel could be reached at an Organized Crime Control Bureau number. They'd gone there in pursuit of information about Regina Galati, the woman now believed to be the Albanese organization's cop killer. Another message was from Simon Ogilvy at the U.S. Attorney's office downtown. His team monitoring the wire at the Dihsko Volya had overheard Mikhail Neyizhsalo's half of a phone conversation with Roberto Santiago. They'd apparently agreed to meet Gus Barone for a sit-down. Neyizhsalo was angry that Barone had refused to meet on neutral ground, insisting instead on nine o'clock at his Remsen Avenue social club in Canarsie. He had assured Santiago he would not attend without heavy backup, and Roberto had evidently concurred.

The most recent message, from Al Goldstein, was the one Stuart returned first. "You sounded antsy, Al," he told his second-in-command on connecting with him. "What's up?"

"Cheesecake ain't so much as walked his fucking dogs ever since he got back here from Canarsie. And we ain't heard a word from you about Suzanne Albrecht, or what else is cooking. We're going batshit here."

Stuart apologized, said he'd been on the run, and quickly brought him up to speed. "I'm guessing Albeneti will be in on this meeting tonight, but can't imagine what might go down. I'm calling Ogilvy next. I reach him, I'll ask him to get you and Hogan some relief. Come nine o'clock, we'll all want to be fresh."

"How *you* holding up, Matthew? You gotta be running on fumes."

"Wouldn't mind a few hours' shut-eye," Stuart admitted, "but I need to see how the next hour or so plays out. You get relief, don't forget to let me know your whereabouts."

When Stuart hung up, Rhoda was still on another line with Terry Gaskin. He punched the button to listen in. "I'm here, too, Terry," he announced.

"We think we may be onto something, Lou," Gaskin reported. "This Sonny Galati the OCCB identified for us earlier? A fourteen-year-old story has it he sent his goons around to dance on the head of this barber who got in too deep to him. They accidentally broke his neck. And get this. He married the dead guy's widow."

"Yea-a-ah?" Stuart wondered if he was missing something. Damn, he was tired. Since mention of the idea of a nap, he could swear his eyelids had taken on weight.

"Widow's name was Constancia Sabatino. Had a daughter by her first marriage name of Regina. Be twenty-four years old today. And better yet? Her dead first husband was the brother of Cheesecake Albeneti's ex-wife."

For a moment, Stuart's eyelids felt a bit lighter. From beneath them, he looked out into the squad room to where Rhoda Bolivar sat. She was looking straight back at him.

"Which makes DaCosta's 'Gina G.' Angelo Albeneti's niece," she murmured into her receiver.

"You got it," Terry replied. "And by the way. Guess where she's made a half dozen calls the past two weeks?"

"To a cigar store pay phone on Remsen Avenue," Stuart conjectured.

"Bingo, Lou."

Matt sighed, suddenly tired again. "We've either gotten incredibly lucky here, or these Gen X goombahs are way too sloppy." He checked the time and saw it was pushing three-thirty. "If we want to be fresh for this nine o'clock sit-down in Canarsie, we need a break. You and Josh crawl off, catch a couple hours' shut-eye," he suggested. "Leave a number with Operations where I can find you." He broke the connection a moment later and heaved himself to his feet to wander back into the squad.

"What are the beds like in the bunk room here?" he asked Rhoda.

"No matter how tired you are, I don't think you're that desperate," she replied. "They don't call this place the last frontier for nothing."

"I can call Chief Ogilvy from the car," he said. "We should go home for a few hours. Get some rest and something to eat. It could be a long night."

"One small problem."

"What's that?"

"Wheels. I caught a ride with Jack this morning."

Matt beckoned her to her feet. "Valley Stream, right? Come on. We get started now, we can hit the LIE before traffic starts piling up."

She grabbed her purse. "You sure? It's pretty far out of your way."

"But not that far from Canarsie. I'll get a bite somewhere. Sack out in my car if I have to. Right now, I'm so tired I could sleep on a bed of nails."

"Why not a guest room with a Sealy Posturepedic," she offered. "That, and half the *arroz con pollo* I was planning to reheat. You think you can handle my cooking, there's more than enough for two."

"Careful what you offer me, Officer," he warned. "I'm hungry enough right now I could skip the rice. Eat a *pollo* raw, feathers and all."

Ever since the meeting between Raquel Gozon and the new leader of the Red Top crew in the wee hours that morning, Tony "Nails" had hung around the smoke shop on Remsen Street waiting for his brother Marco to report in. When Marco finally did reach him at noon, he complained he'd been up most of the night and had only just crawled out of bed. Unwilling to discuss details over the phone, Nails set a three o'clock meet with his brother at a *caffè* and *dolce* joint near Marco's apartment on Arthur Avenue in the Bronx.

Arthur Avenue was one of several pockets of Old World Italian culture in New York that had refused to give way to the relentless influx of immigrants constantly changing the personalities of the city's five boroughs. A few square blocks were all that remained of a once sprawling Italian immigrant neighborhood, since flooded by waves of Hispanics from the Caribbean and African-American migrants from the South. Today, only those with the fiercest will to resist change continued to live there. The enclave they maintained had become almost quaint, with restaurants frequented by diners up from Manhattan for the adventure, or over the George Washington Bridge from New Jersey. In a city whose old traditions were fast being swallowed up by supermarket chains and name-brand retail outlets, Arthur Avenue was still lined with old-style shops, their plate glass windows loaded with Old World breads, pastries, salamis, and sundries still prized by local and visiting gourmands. It was said that one could leave a car double-parked at the curb, unlocked and with the keys still in the ignition. Nobody would touch it other than to set free another car trapped at the curb. Such was the strength of the Old World values that still prevailed there.

When Tony Fortunado arrived at the Il Positano coffee bar a few minutes past three o'clock, he found his brother already occupying a marble-topped corner table. A Vivaldi string quartet played low from speakers hung from the stamped-tin ceiling. A skinny, raven-haired girl with pert breasts and a tight little backside was placing a cannoli and a demitasse of espresso before the younger Fortunado. Otherwise, the dark-paneled interior was empty.

The big brother crossed the patterned ceramic tile floor to pull up a chair. "Nice breakfast," he greeted Marco. Toward the waitress, who couldn't have been more than fifteen or sixteen, he directed an empty, patronizing smile. "Gimme a cappuccino with a little Frangelico dumped in it if you got it. Glass of water, too." As she withdrew, he let his gaze linger on her fanny as he spoke again to his brother. "So. How'd it go with the niggers last night?"

Shorter than Tony but broader through the chest and shoulders, Marco was a weight-lifting fanatic who resented the underling role he was forced to play as a member of his brother's crew. He was impatient to move up the Albanese family command ladder, and thought with his dick too much, so far as Tony was concerned. Or maybe Tony was just jealous. Four months ago, he'd sent Marco off to establish contact and make inroads with a female Dominican faction disenchanted with Tío Paco Santos. In typical, dick-driven fashion, his baby brother had ended up mixing business with pleasure. He'd come back from his assignment, the best-looking Dominican bitch in the five boroughs on his arm. As valuable an asset for generating future revenue as she might prove to be, the fact that Marco was so taken with her was not lost on Angelo Albeneti and others. Hell, he'd even given the silly cow a diamond and asked her to marry him. A broad who wasn't even Sicilian.

"Didn't I tell you going in, you ain't got nothing to worry about there?" Marco complained. "This Imbongi fuck, or whatever we-wuz-kings-of-the-jungle bullshit name he calls himself, ain't got no choice but to play ball with us." As he spoke, Marco dumped an enormous amount of sugar into his coffee and stirred it with the tiny spoon. "And the tall, skinny nigger Isabelle's sister's been doing? Richie Townsend? He's got almost as much juice as Imbongi. The fat boy don't wanna play along, we whack him and put Townsend in charge." He lifted his cup to his lips and took a tentative sip. "Sonofabitch took seven slugs from a fucking machine gun couple years ago. Lived to tell aboudit. Them other niggers are all in awe of a dude with luck like that."

Tony nodded, wondering if he dare be satisfied. If his brother screwed this end of it up, it would reflect badly on him and his ability to run a tight ship. Gus Barone and his Albanese capos didn't miss things like that.

The waitress arrived with Tony's cappuccino and glass of water. He waited for her to clear off before pressing ahead. "You happen to see the news since you dragged your ass outta bed, Sleeping Beauty?"

Marco pointed to a copy of Monday's *Post*, folded on the chair beside him. "Looks to me like you didn't have no trouble getting to DaCosta, huh? Cops are saying it looks like a fucking overdose. Nice."

Tony brightened, reliving the memory. His presence on the threshold outside Clarence DaCosta's door Sunday afternoon was wholly unexpected. He'd never visited the renegade cop at home before, always making contact via telephone. He'd purposely tried to look agitated, which was understandable under those circumstances.

"Sonofabitch had no idea what was coming," he said. "Answers the door: Whassup, m'man? Please. Come on in. Me? I see this big fuckin' Colt Python he's got in his hand and about crap my pants."

Marco grinned. "No shit? He was braced?"

"No shit. So I go: What the fuck is this? DaCosta looks down, sees the piece in his hand, and stuffs it into his waistband all apologetic like. Tells me I don't ring the downstairs buzzer, how'z he supposed to know who the fuck I am? This is New York."

Tony looked back with satisfaction, remembering how he'd advanced further into the apartment and sniffed the air, disapproving of what he'd seen. He was a guy who washed his beautiful red El Dorado every day of the year, rain or shine, and had his wife scrub their kitchen floor on her hands and knees.

"He's got this high-dollar Mitsubishi big-screen TV in one corner and more CDs than Tower Records, but his apartment's a fucking pigsty," he'd continued. "Once I'm inside, I turn to him and say: What's this I hear, you had dinner with Gina Galati at Peter Luger last night? He's kinda confused by how I could know that and not sure how to react. It's then I happen to see this big blowup of some magazine cover on the wall. It's a picture of this nigger uniformed cop running outta some burning building with a baby in his arms. He's using it for a dartboard. The whole thing's shredded and tore up by a million hits with these darts he's been chucking at it."

"What the fuck was that about?" Marco asked.

"Just what I asked him. And y'know what the low-life crud says to me? He says he's got a problem with uppity nigger cops, kinda like the one he's got with people like me, sticking their noses into his personal business."

While contemplating his brother over the rim of his cup, Marco took another sip of his coffee. "Kinda asking for what he got, wasn't he?"

"Aint that right? I mean, no piece of nigger trash talks to Tony Nails like that without having to answer for it. So I grab him by the front of his fucking shirt with one hand, slam him up against the back of his front door, and take that iron outta his pants with the other. It's like he never knew what fucking hit him." He smiled inwardly, remembering the look of astonishment on DaCosta's face on having the barrel of the Python jammed up under his chin.

"Your *personal* business, I say. You work for the Albanese, you don't *got* no personal business, you fucking dirtbag. Then I tell him Gina Galati is Angelo Albeneti's niece, not some nigger cop's Italian whore. I said that was *his* mama."

For the first time since starting the confrontation with DaCosta, Tony remembered seeing real fear in the renegade cop's eyes. He hadn't taken issue with the fact that Clarence and Gina had eaten dinner together. It was what happened afterward. Of course he should be upset. The idea of her doing anything like that with a piece of shit like DaCosta made him almost physically ill.

"So what'd he say, for crissake?" Marco demanded. He was into Tony's narrative now, hanging on every nuance, really getting off.

"He tells me I'd better pull the trigger right then and there; any man calls his mama a whore is a fucking dead man. I tell him I'm really scared."

While Marco attacked one end of his cannoli with his spoon, Tony reached over with a stubby index finger to scoop some of the filling out and convey it to his mouth.

"Hey," Marco protested. "Get your own fucking pastry."

"Blow me." Tony savored the creamy sweetness that filled his mouth. "So, t'make a long story short, DaCosta decides he's a dead man anyway, he don't make some sorta move. He grabs for the gun and I surprise him by actually letting him get hold of it. That leaves his two hands tied up and one of my hands free. Me? I got this hot shot all ready to go in my pants pocket. Imagine the look in his eyes, I flash that needle, yank the cap with my teeth, and ram my knee into his nuts with everything I got."

"Bet he shit a brick."

"Went down like a load of them, I'll tell you that. The gun goes flying, and I'm down there on the floor, sitting on his chest like a heart attack. Slipped the spike into his arm before he knew what end was up."

Marco was hunched forward, trying to imagine the setting and the feeling, his pastry forgotten for the moment. "Jesus mother. He ODs on the shit with you sitting right there on *top* of his ass?" His estimation of his paunchy big brother was clearly on the rise.

"You ever see a man die like that?" Tony asked. "Goes all spastic, having these fucking convulsions. Makes for a pretty wild ride, until he starts shitting and pissing himself."

Marco paled and made a face of disgust.

"That's no shit," Tony pressed on, then paused to chuckle. "If you'll pardon the expression."

Rose Marie Sabatino took time off after lunch to visit her bank and get Suzanne Albrecht an additional five thousand dollars in cash. Suzanne changed into a print sundress and open sandals she'd purchased earlier and drove to a two o'clock appointment Rose Marie had made for her with a hairdresser at the Staten Island Mall. Along the way, she threw her business clothes into a Dumpster. At four, she emerged from the beauty salon onto the main concourse of the mall so totally transformed she hardly recognized herself. Without losing much length, her hair was now a tawny blond rather than auburn, cascading to her shoulders in a riot of loose curls. The stylist had suggested a burnt umber lipstick to set off her mouth, and a darker rouge than she would usually use to highlight her good bones. The eye shadow she'd applied accented the sparkling blue of her irises with just the sort of drama Suzanne had worked the past twenty years to avoid. She knew she had a decent body and better-than-average face, but the woman who peered back at her from every mirror she passed was actually quite beautiful. To see herself in that light was more unsettling than she could have imagined, and as she left the mall she was gripped by a powerful feeling of loss.

Rush-hour traffic was starting to clog city arteries as Suzanne drove aimlessly in her rented Geo, no longer fearful of being spotted by the forces most certainly combing the streets for her. As if pulled by some internal magnet, she slowly worked her way north and east toward the borough of her birth, the heaviest traffic moving in the opposite direction over the Verrazano Narrows Bridge as she crossed it. In her near-suspended state of distraction, she paid little attention to the occupants of other cars. At the Hamilton Parkway exit, she left the Gowanus Expressway, then went immediately west on the Bay Ridge Parkway toward Upper New York Bay. In a remote recess of her consciousness, she wondered how many times over two and a half years she'd driven down that very thoroughfare. The only thing missing today was the eagerness she'd once felt anticipating the turn south onto Narrows Road and then onto Harbor View Terrace.

Suzanne paused several blocks from her former lover's house to ask herself what she was doing, and could find no plausible answer. She had a flight departing Newark International Airport for Miami in less than three hours. Given what Matt had seen that morning, he couldn't believe anything but the worst about her anymore. And who could blame him? She was, by reputation, a master manipulator. Not only had she worn her ambition on her sleeve, she'd ultimately used it as an excuse to throw him over. Since that morning, it had to have eaten at him that Intelligence was where she'd placed him two years ago. That, and the knowledge that on more than one occasion, he'd discussed the Angelo Albeneti file with her.

Ultimately, Suzanne didn't hesitate on reaching Stuart's driveway. She turned in to pull up before the garage. As she stepped from the car to approach the house up the front walk, she was greeted by the familiar odor of sea air. She'd never removed the key to Stuart's front door from her handbag, and used it now to let herself in. Standing in the entry hall, other familiar odors and sounds were there to greet her. There was the ever-present tangy lemon of furniture polish. It combined with the lingering odors of meals cooked and fires lit in the hearth to create a scent distinctive to the three generations of Stuarts who had lived there. To one side of the archway to the living room stood the huge grandfather clock, its steady, resonant ticking the very tempo of tranquility.

She wandered into the kitchen, wondering what she would say in the note she meant to leave, knowing that nothing could possibly make things right again. It was a sun-drenched, friendly room, and as she moved through it, fingers lightly trailing across the surface of the breakfast nook table, memories of the lazy Sunday morning breakfasts she and Stuart used to share there flooded back. The easy intimacy of those mornings was something she'd treasured. To the odors of bacon frying and the sharp bite of fresh chopped onions bringing tears to her eyes, she would share snippets of news from the Sunday *Times*, sip orange juice with champagne splashed into it, and wrap herself in the comfort of simple contentment.

Without consciously deciding to, she opened the refrigerator and started to scan the interior. Suddenly, she was ravenous, realizing she hadn't eaten a thing all day.

Twenty-four

By the time he reached Rhoda Bolivar's Valley Stream, Long Island, home late Monday afternoon, Matt Stuart was exhausted. Still, in a situation like this, where a female subordinate was involved, the boss cop part of him was ever on the alert. The simple warmth he encountered upon walking into her house caught him off guard. Located in a typical postwar subdivision, the raised ranch-style structure had those tiny touches of character a place accumulates over four decades which set it apart from its neighbors. Inside, there was a dining L off the living room that opened into a big eat-in kitchen. One of the three bedrooms had been converted into a den or study of sorts, and looked like the place Rhoda spent most of her time. In it, a computer sat atop an antique oak desk, one wall was lined with books and CDs, and a big, comfortable leather chair faced a stereo and TV. Downstairs, half the basement was fitted out as a home gym with a NordicTrack ski machine, stair-stepper, inclined bench, and a rack of dumbbells. It explained why she was in such good shape.

"Still hungry?" she asked at the conclusion of her nickel tour. She flipped off the lights and led the way upstairs to the kitchen.

Her backside was at eye level, three feet ahead of him as he climbed the stairs. Matt forced his mind toward food. "Voraciously. Nice digs, Detective. How often you hit that equipment back there?"

"It's Rhoda, and not often enough, I'm afraid. Our schedule hasn't left me time to breathe, let alone pump iron."

In the kitchen he took a chair at a smallish table. Set before a sliding door that opened onto a deck, it had a view of the backyard beyond. From where he sat, Matt could see the fresh-tilled soil of a garden in preparation. "How long have you been here?" he asked.

Standing at the stove, she poured a small amount of oil into a large commercial skillet and started to heat it. "Four years. Bought it with the spoils of a hard-fought divorce. My ex got the loft in Tribeca."

Stuart did some quick arithmetic. Four years ago she was twenty-eight. "Wall Streeter?" he asked. "Your ex?"

"Commodities broker. How'd you guess?"

"A loft in Tribeca isn't cheap. There's only one kind of young guy in this town with that sort of purchasing power anymore. That, and the downtown location."

While spooning leftover *arroz con pollo* into the hot oil, she smiled. "Pretty good. Only one assumption I'd question: that he's young."

Matt shrugged. "You don't strike me as the sugar-daddy type." The odor of garlic in hot oil made his mouth water. He took a sip of the iced tea she'd poured, hoping it might calm the growling in his gut. "Smells wonderful."

"Thanks. I was twenty-four and Tim was twenty-six when we married."

"Where'd you meet?" he asked.

"The South Street Seaport, of all places. I was on patrol, working the happy-hour crowd. He asked me for my phone number on a dare. I've always been a sucker for the tall, blond, all-American boy type."

"If you don't mind my asking, what happened? To cause the breakup."

"Me. I was a woman with a mind of her own, working all kinds of crazy hours. I think he got more than he bargained for. I had myself on a fast track, trying to make detective. When I volunteered for a plain-clothes Narcotics detail, he went ballistic."

"Ah." How many times had Stuart heard the same story, where a civilian husband or wife failed to comprehend the demands and stresses of the Job? In nine cases out of ten, it spelled disaster for a marriage.

"So tell me something?" she asked as she stirred. "Once this case is resolved, will you go back to Intelligence? You and Chief Ogilvy seem to work pretty well together."

"Comes from mutual respect, I think," he replied. "Simon's a political animal and I know that, just like he knows I'm not. We don't threaten each other's ambitions."

"Which doesn't answer my question."

He smiled. "No, I guess not. There'll be some serious fallout from this, from the throne room on down. If Al Goldstein and Simon Ogilvy know Suzanne and I were lovers, I suspect others in positions of power know it, too."

She lifted a forkful from the skillet to her mouth to test it for warmth, then continued to stir. "Are you afraid they won't trust you, in light of what she's done?"

It was something he'd wondered any number of times since last night, when Ogilvy had revealed his knowledge of the affair with Suzanne. "Good possibility they won't," he replied. "In a police force with thirty-eight thousand members and legions of guys who have never shit in the nest, why take a chance on me?"

Rhoda stopped stirring, opened a cupboard to grab two plates, and pointed. "Flatware. Second drawer from the end. Napkins in the drawer to the right of it." She spooned a large helping onto each plate. "These past six days, I've watched the way you work," she said. "Chief Ogilvy has, too, Lou. There's nothing you're trying to hide or dodge."

"Matt. And I appreciate the endorsement, but you know as well as I do how everyone on the Job wants to distance himself from a leper." He was on his feet, collecting knives and forks from one drawer, then flower-print cloth napkins from the other. The table set, she carried their plates to it, then found salt, pepper, and Tabasco.

"You sticking with the tea or want something stronger?" she asked.

"Just tea, thanks." He held her chair as she sat, which prompted a bemused smile.

"You don't like it, you don't have to eat it," she said. "We can always order pizza."

"It's wonderful," he said, and raised his iced tea in a toast.

"Thanks." She clicked her glass with his. "So. They ostracize you. What then? I can't imagine anyone with your talent and drive sitting still for very long. You have an alternative plan?"

With another mouthful on its way, Matt paused and shook his head. "Not at the moment. No."

They concentrated on eating and let conversation lag. For the moment, the investigation, Matt's future, and everything else pertaining to the Job took a backseat to ravenous hunger. Once both of them had cleaned their plates, Stuart rose to carry them to the sink.

"And housebroken, too," she murmured.

He glanced over one shoulder as he opened the dishwasher to load it. "You don't mind, do you?"

"Hardly. You do ironing?"

"Keep dreaming," he told her. "Back while we were on the subject of alternative plans a minute ago, I was wondering about your plans. Detective first grade by age thirty-two, and bilingual. How much longer can you work an assignment like the Three-seven before you go stir-crazy?"

"I'm getting there," she admitted. "But the way I see it, there isn't a whole lot of room further up the chain of command for a Venezuelan-born woman with no political pull. A while back, the DEA's top banana at their New York Division office made a pretty serious overture. Don't know if he's more interested in my talents or my ass, but I'm considering checking it out."

Stuart knew several New York cops who had made the transition to federal drug enforcement. One had since moved to Miami and claimed to love the work. The others felt they'd more or less traded one batch of bureaucratic headaches for another. "You want, I'll be happy to put in a good word to Ogilvy for you," he offered. "He's always on the lookout for cops with skills like yours."

Those little creases of bemusement he'd seen before appeared at the corners of her mouth again. "And what, exactly, would those skills be?"

He finished placing the dishes in the dishwasher and turned to lean against the counter. "An affinity for the work, and a kind of creativity all the experience in the world can't teach. That's what's impressed *me* most."

She scraped her chair back and stood to cross to the stove. There, she picked up the empty skillet and carried it to the sink. "Darn. I was hoping you'd be *most* impressed by something a little more basic."

While scrubbing out the skillet, she stood so close that Matt could smell the crisp scent of her perfume. When she turned to set the pan in the drainer, he saw challenge in her frank brown eyes. "Careful, Detective," he warned. "You're way too attractive. You let it hang this far out, a sexually deprived workaholic like me just might grab for it."

"Good news," she replied. "Stripping naked to get your attention might seem wanton and undignified."

Acutely aware of an erection suddenly throbbing within the confines of his briefs, Stuart felt his exhaustion vaporize. "You hitting on me, Detective?"

"Yes, I am." She slid closer to lean into him. "And it's Rhoda, remember? Please don't make me grab you and throw you down on the floor."

When their mouths met, a jolt of electricity surged through him, clear to the soles of his feet. It seemed like an eternity since he'd felt this kind of hot, straining eagerness in his arms.

"Bed," she gasped when at last they surfaced for air. "We'll try the kitchen table some other time."

Suzanne Albrecht had assembled the ingredients for a mushroom, Swiss cheese, and onion omelet from Matt Stuart's refrigerator when she turned to his kitchen phone to call her voice mail. Maybe Matt had tried to reach her and left a way she could contact him outside the usual channels. She was disheartened to discover Stuart hadn't tried to communicate with her at all, while everyone else, from the PC to the mayor to the chiefs of Department, Intelligence, and Personnel had all left messages saying it was imperative she get in touch with them as quickly as possible. She hung up wondering—as she had a thousand other times that day—what had to be going through her former lover's head. He was undoubtedly certain she'd used and betrayed him, and that she had very possibly destroyed his career in the process. The idea of him hating her made her heartsick.

As wistful as she'd felt on starting to prepare her omelet, she found herself no longer hungry once it hit her plate. Seated alone in Matt's breakfast nook, she stared out across the rooftops to watch how the low sun gleamed on the waters of New York Bay. It was after six o'clock. She would never make her flight to Miami, but now it didn't matter. She no longer had the will to run. She wished Stuart would suddenly appear. She would try to explain, and magically, everything would be all right again. But nothing would ever be right again. She knew that.

She pushed aside her plate, stood, and walked listlessly from the kitchen to the entry hall stairs. Like a zombie, she ascended to the second floor to stand before the large mirror on the landing and contemplate the blond stranger reflected back at her. All those years wasted, she

thought; time spent living someone else's agenda. The ambition that
drove her had eaten her soul and stolen her youth. The beauty she studied now was brittle at its edges. She felt no love and damned little like
for the person behind it.

At Stuart's bedroom doorway she paused a moment to absorb how little had changed since the last time she'd set foot there, half a year ago.
He'd pushed himself hard that past week, but his bed was still neatly
made. The towels visible through the open bathroom door beyond were
hung in an orderly way over the bar alongside the tub. She advanced
toward the highboy dresser, opened the second drawer from the bottom,
and there, just where she'd left them, were a peignoir, negligee, and other
lingerie items. With a vivid memory of the last time she'd worn an emerald green satin camisole, she lifted it from the drawer by its spaghetti
straps. Holding it up against her, she studied her reflection in Matt's full-
length dressing mirror and how the green contrasted with her new
makeup and hair.

As she started to ask herself the self-pitying question of why her life
had insisted on taking this perverse turn, she abruptly stopped herself. It
had taken this turn because she'd taken no strong, counteractive action to
prevent it. Only she was to blame for who she was now, standing in deep
despair before this mirror. This wasn't who she'd labored twenty years of
her adult life to become. And neither was the fugitive she'd set out to become earlier that day. Running wasn't her style. Of that much she was
suddenly and totally convinced.

With anger burning so that it threatened to overwhelm her, Suzanne
turned and threw the camisole onto Matt's bed. She opened her handbag
to check the load of her service revolver, and then, with newfound re-
solve, walked from the room.

Just minutes after Gina Galati's aunt called from the office at 6:07 that
evening to say she was on her way home, the young hit woman's pager
vibrated for the dozenth time that Monday. Prepared to once again ignore Tony Fortunado's attempt to contact her, Gina checked the display
window. Much to her surprise, it wasn't Tony's number she saw there,
but her Uncle Angelo's, from a rarely used secure line in the Mom's
Pie office. Not wanting to compromise her aunt, Gina scooped up her
son, strapped him into his car seat, and drove to a pay phone at the New
Dorp train station. There, as commuters poured from a recently arrived

train and raced for the parking lot, taxis, and buses, she deposited the requisite thirty-five cents and dialed a number long since committed to memory.

"Yeah," her uncle answered.

"It's me, Unc."

"Where the fuck you been?" he demanded.

"Around. Busy."

"Where you now?"

"Pay phone. Don't sweat it."

"Jesus, Gina. Tony been tryna reach you all fucking day. He says you ain't been home, but the cops been there. What the fuck's up?"

"You tell me," she suggested. "Something I heard on the news last night kinda freaked me out, Unc."

"You didn't answer my question."

"I've gone to ground is what's going on." If he could refuse to answer a question, so could she. Gina was an old hand at this game.

"You don't return his calls, he starts thinking they mighta nabbed you."

"If he's responsible for whacking Clarence DaCosta, it's no thanks to him they didn't. Fuck-up left something behind. Cops traced it to me. I'm taking a long vacation, Unc. Somewhere tropical, with weak extradition laws."

"I might have some thoughts on that subject. Could be some help. But I got a favor to ask first. Think you could meet me here? Say, an hour from now?"

"What's the rush?" She was still very much on her guard.

"There's serious shit going down. Tonight. And I got a little problem I need taken care of. You know the side loading dock door. I'll leave it unlocked."

Gina's aunt was probably home by now, and would baby-sit if she asked nicely. "Tell your pal Nails, he so much as looks at my tits, I shoot him in the balls," she told her uncle. *"Capisce?"*

Rhoda Bolivar had suspected Lieutenant Matt Stuart might be a fairly decent lover. She'd watched how he moved, and witnessed the confidence with which he carried himself. What she hadn't anticipated was the level of pure animal eagerness. During their lovemaking he'd shown sensitivity to her needs as well as his own, and kept his ardor in check just long enough for *both* of them to reach the edge of the precipice and tumble over it together. It was rare in her experience to find a man who enjoyed giving pleasure as much as he liked receiving it.

Stuart had arrived at her house dead on his feet, taken sustenance, and then risen to her challenge. Ten minutes after their lovemaking, he'd fallen into a deep sleep, while she was so energized that her toes literally twitched. She lay on her back, staring at her bedroom ceiling with vivid memories of what had just transpired flashing past her mind's eye: delicious little bits and pieces she wanted to lock onto and save as fuel for future fantasies.

When the phone at her bedside rang, Rhoda was so wrapped up in those memories she was tempted to ignore it. Then her sense of duty got the better of her. She rolled over to reluctantly snatch up the receiver.

"Hello?"

"Lieutenant Stuart left this phone as a reach number," a male voice replied. "He there?"

"Sacked out in the next room," she lied. "Who's calling?"

"Manhattan North Operations, ma'am. I've got Chief Ogilvy from Intel Division holding."

Evidently, Stuart hadn't mentioned *whose* number it was, and for that Rhoda was grateful. She told the man to hang on, covered the mouthpiece, and gave her lover a nudge. When he came awake with a start, clearly disoriented, she murmured an apology for the intrusion and offered him the phone. "Chief Ogilvy. I told the Op Desk guy you're asleep in the next room," she whispered.

Before accepting the receiver, Matt caught Rhoda's hand and kissed it, then tried to shake his head clear. "Yeah, Chief. What's up?" He dragged the fingertips of his free hand across the underside of Rhoda's left breast, listening to Ogilvy's reply. The pad of his thumb lightly brushed her nipple, producing a little tingle that gave her gooseflesh. Then his expression clouded. "Jesus. Made it when?" As he listened, he slowly withdrew his hand. "Okay. On my way. Be twenty, thirty minutes."

"What?" Rhoda asked as he handed her the receiver.

"Suzanne Albrecht called home to check her voice mail . . . from a phone in my house half an hour ago. Local uniformed patrol just did a drive-by. No cars in the driveway, no sign of life. Which doesn't mean she's not holed up in there."

"I don't get it," Rhoda said. "*Your* house?"

He threw back the bedclothes and shoved himself upright. "Guess we'll find out the why soon enough. Ogilvy's convinced the PC to hold off ordering a move until I get there. Meanwhile, they've got the block sealed off."

The nervous tension that gripped Gina Galati as she approached Mom's Pie Company up Pleasant Avenue from the south was the same kind she imagined a fox would feel sneaking past a farmer's house toward his chicken coop. With the time change now a month old, seven in the evening was still broad daylight. The cops were onto her identity now, and it stood to reason they also suspected who employed her. To improve her odds of walking clear of danger once this little drama was played out, she had taken extra care while dressing for this meeting. Her hair was tucked out of sight beneath a blue New York Giants cap. She'd wrapped her torso in ten feet of Ace bandage to flatten her breasts, and wore huge, calf-length denim shorts, a T-shirt hanging to mid-thigh, and men's Nike basketball shoes to further disguise her sex. Through hours of practice, she'd perfected a classic Brooklyn male street swagger. Unless an observer was directly on top of her, she could easily pass for a slender teenage boy.

Opting to approach up Pleasant Avenue on foot, Gina left her Land Rover three blocks from Mom's Pie at a meter. The retail end of the business closed at 7 P.M. on Monday, and her uncle had told her he would leave the loading dock door unlocked. As an added precaution, he'd also left a truck parked there in loading mode, its cargo doors open. Nearing the bakery, Gina spotted the first surveillance team in a late-model Ford Crown Victoria diagonally across the avenue. She imagined there would be a second pair of detectives positioned within view of the dock around the corner and decided to make her approach through the Laundromat next door. From there, she climbed out a bathroom window, up the fire escape, and across the roof. Angelo's soundproof and electronically sterile office was located in the basement of his building, one level below the bakery proper. Gina knocked at the external door her uncle used to access his sanctuary from his apartment two flights upstairs. Seconds later, she saw the security peep darken.

"What's this?" Angelo complained as he opened up. "Why didn't you come the way I said?"

"You been outside lately?" she asked. "Street's lousy with cops."

He led the way toward his office past pallets piled with bulk baking ingredients. Even down here, the atmosphere was heavy with tantalizing odors. Adjacent to the office door, Gina paused at the silver tray Angelo kept stocked with that day's baked delicacies, and grabbed a cookie. As she bit into it, satisfying sweetness filled her mouth.

Her uncle entered his office to take the chair behind his desk, propping his flour-caked shoes atop one corner of it. In a grimy tub chair in front of him, Tony Fortunado lounged with his black leather jacket hanging open to reveal his paunch. Before she joined them, Gina started to ease the door closed.

"Don't do that," Nails complained. "Air-conditioning's on the fucking fritz."

"So sweat," she said, tossing her black tote into the chair opposite him and jerking a thumb in Tony's direction while looking to her uncle. "You get into this dimwit's shit yet about how he did DaCosta?"

"Hey!" Fortunado protested. "You watch your fuckin' mou—"

"Why?!" she snarled, turning on him. "You didn't leave something behind you shoulda found and taken care of, there's no way the cops are onto who I am. And whose bright idea was it, giving him a fucking overdose? Lotsa people gotta know how much that man hated drugs."

"Hated drugs but loved white pussy, yeah?" Fortunado sneered. "Me? I can't believe you spread your fucking legs for that piece of nigger trash."

Gina felt her blood start to boil and told herself to cool it. She had to keep a clear head. Ignoring his gouge, she turned instead to her uncle to address the business at hand. "What's this job you're so eager for me t'do? And where you got in mind I'm gonna take this so-called vacation?"

Albeneti grabbed a manila envelope off his desk to sail it in her direction. Gina caught it, midair, and opened it. The first items she extracted from within were two Alitalia ticket folders.

"First class to Palermo," her uncle said. "You and Claude can stay with my cousin Sophia, until you get settled. I was you, I'd get a little villa on the sea. She lives in Termini, halfway between Palermo and Cefalù."

Gina had never heard of any cousin Sophia, but knew that her uncle, like so many other Sicilians in America, maintained strong ties to family in the Old Country. In his business, a place to hide, protected by family grateful for all the money he'd funneled to them over the years, was imperative. She ignored the tickets and reached again into the envelope to remove an eight-by-ten color photograph paper-clipped to a typewritten dossier. On recognizing the individual in the picture, she felt her heart skip a beat. It was Suzanne Albrecht, the woman who had visited her aunt at lunchtime that afternoon, the first deputy commissioner of the New York Police Department.

"You're shitting me," she murmured.

"You know who she is?" Her uncle sounded surprised.

Gina turned to the dossier to scan it. "Saw her doing a press conference outside DaCosta's building last night. On the news."

Suzanne Albrecht was fairly certain the surveillance team working 118th Street across from the Mom's Pie Company loading dock had seen her approach and enter the building via the side door there. Considering the extreme nature of her makeover and the kind of clothing she wore, she was pretty sure they didn't recognize her. It seemed a stroke of pure luck that one of the bakery vans was in the process of being loaded at the time of her arrival and both it and the loading dock door were left wide open. Angelo's precious Shih Tzus were undoubtedly restricted someplace where they couldn't wander outside and into traffic. If her luck held, the heavily soundproofed basement walls would prevent them from spoiling the surprise she had in store for their master.

No deliverymen or other bakery personnel appeared as she picked her way past trolleys loaded with cooling racks, then pallets stacked with flour, sugar, and salt. At the top of the basement stairs, the compressor on a large walk-in cooler just below her kicked on. It created a din that helped mask the sounds of her approach from alert Shih Tzu ears.

Moments later, Suzanne stood just outside the bakery office, weapon in hand and trying to decide how she should make her next move. The door, left ever-so-slightly ajar, allowed a young woman's muffled voice to leak out from the other side. She leaned closer to listen.

"Crissake, Unc. She's the second-highest-ranking cop in the city. Job like this is gonna cost you."

Angelo's voice as he growled his reply was unmistakable. "How's two hunnerd grand sound?"

Unless Suzanne was wrong, the young woman attached to that first voice was the niece she'd met that noon at Rose Marie Sabatino's Staten

Island house. The timbre was distinctive, and "Crissake, Unc," tended to confirm it. Even more unsettling was the subject of their discussion. Unless she was very much mistaken, they were talking about her. *Killing* her.

"Half up front," Regina Galati replied. "And this scumwad so much as mentions my tits again at the payoff, I shoot him inna fucking nuts."

"Hey!" a second, muffled male voice protested.

So there were at least three of them in there. Suzanne eased back the hammer on her service weapon and reached for the doorknob. What the hell? She'd come this far. Try as she might, she could find nowhere else to turn.

Twenty-five

B y the time Matt Stuart and Rhoda Bolivar reached his house on Harbor View Terrace in Bay Ridge, it was after eight o'clock. In the rush to leave her place, Matt had forgotten his beeper on Rhoda's nightstand. He wondered what else he'd left behind. The measly hour of shut-eye he'd managed to catch had left him with a headache.

At the intercept line set up by the Sixty-eighth Precinct to seal off the south end of his block, they were greeted by Simon Ogilvy, Chief of Department Robert Dunleavy, and the Brooklyn South Detective Operations commander. An arrest of the Job's first deputy commissioner was no small matter. Stuart was surprised not to see the PC also on hand.

Almost before they'd stopped moving, Chief Dunleavy was in Matt's face. "Any idea what she would be doing in there, or why in God's name she'd come here?" he demanded.

Stuart sneaked a peek in Ogilvy's direction, hoping to learn what Simon had already said. The Intel chief returned an almost imperceptible shake of his head to say Matt was in the clear. "None," he replied to Dunleavy. "Last time I spoke with her was last night. At the DaCosta homicide." He surveyed the street in front of his house and wondered why, if Suzanne really was inside, she hadn't recognized the hopelessness of her situation. There were RMPs parked to create barricades at both ends of the block, light bars flashing. Inside the frozen zone, a half

dozen unmarked cars sat unoccupied. At least twenty detectives and uniforms loitered in clusters, awaiting word on what would happen next.
"Don't know how she got here, given there's no car. But if she took a cab
or something and isn't sound asleep, I'd say she definitely knows we're
out here."

Ogilvy stepped over to tell Dunleavy he'd like a word with Stuart
alone. The Department chief saw something in Simon's look that told
him back off, let him handle this.

Led to one side, Matt glanced back at Bob Dunleavy as he spoke.
"How much does he know, or at least suspect?" he asked his former boss.

"Might've heard the rumors on the grapevine," Simon replied. "But
after talking to him the past fifteen minutes, I'm inclined to doubt it."

"Powermonger like him?"

"Careful. He's a peer."

"Political animal. Excuse me."

"All the more reason this must look pretty strange to him, right? How
do you feel about talking to her?"

Stuart shrugged. "It's my house. And no, I'm not afraid she might
shoot me. We parted on amicable terms."

The Intel chief's public persona cracked long enough to allow a quick
smile. "Umm. I don't suppose she would have dragged you into all this
other craziness if you hadn't."

"Or that I'd have gone along," Matt agreed. "Give me ten minutes.
You don't hear anything by then, call the hostage negotiators."

Ogilvy wished him luck and Stuart started across the street past
dozens of watchful, curious eyes. On the front walk, headed for his veranda, he felt very much alone and exposed. He studied his front windows for signs of movement and saw none. At his door he paused a
moment, pretending to sort through his keys, and asked himself how he
intended to deal with Suzanne. In less than twelve hours, everything
about the world they'd once occupied as lovers had changed. She no
longer held his fate in her hands, and he no longer ached for the intimacy
they'd once shared.

Unable to come up with anything workable, he shoved his key into the
lockset, turned the knob, and took the plunge. The instant he took a first
breath of the air inside, he knew someone had been there recently. The
lingering odors of cooking emanated from the kitchen, smelling like

someone had recently made breakfast. A dirty frying pan and uneaten omlet in the kitchen confirmed it.

"Suzanne!" he called out as he started back through the dining room for the entry hall and the stairs. Not a peep. On the second floor, at the open doorway to his bedroom, he stopped abruptly, first spotting one drawer of his highboy left open, and then an emerald green camisole abandoned on his bed.

"Hell is this?" he murmured. "A stroll down memory lane?" He had no idea where she'd meant to head, taking that course of action. Of one thing he *was* fairly certain. Suzanne was no longer there, and this visit was meant as a message to him. Ice Maiden or not, she cared about the time they'd spent together in this house. She'd wanted to reach back and touch it again.

The orders given Taras Pidvalna by Major Mikhail Neyizhsalo were specific. On arrival outside the Palermitan Social Club in Canarsie, six hours before the meet with Gus Barone, the former KGB assassin was to secure a defensive position Neyizhsalo had already picked out for him. From it he would observe comings and goings at the club, and any suspicious activity up and down Remsen Avenue. Major Mike expected the Albanese to have beefed-up security, and figured Roberto Santiago would bring muscle, too. He'd therefore ordered Pidvalna to maintain an extremely low profile. Taras was to surface only should a crisis demand his intervention.

At 2:48 that afternoon, Taras had arrived in the neighborhood driving a painting contractor's van complete with ladders, drop cloths, buckets, a spray rig, and other tools essential to that trade. That morning, a minion in Major Mike's organization and his very pregnant wife had gone apartment hunting in the block of Remsen Avenue across from Albanese headquarters. By ringing bells, contacting building superintendents, and speaking with shopkeepers, they had located an empty apartment suitable for Pidvalna's purposes. Later, a well-spoken attorney in Neyizhsalo's employ had contacted the landlord of the building claiming to be the prospective tenant's father-in-law. He'd offered payment of first and last month rents in cash and proposed he incur the expense of getting the place painted. His daughter was eight months pregnant with her first baby. She wanted a bigger apartment in a safe neighborhood and needed to ready the apartment for occupancy as quickly as possible.

For Taras, it came as no surprise when, within half an hour of his arrival, a man claiming to be a neighbor in the building had knocked on the door to introduce himself. By then he'd spread drop cloths, scattered tools, gotten Spackle on his hands, and smeared a dab of it on one cheek. His visitor's manner was too suspiciously observant for him to be anything but a cog in the opposing team's security apparatus, but Pidvalna's act appeared to convince him. For the past five hours, as tape recordings of "Taras Bulba" and "Kupalo" played to mask the silence of his watchfulness, Pidvalna had occupied a darkened bedroom overlooking the avenue, a spotting scope to his eye and his sniper rifle within easy reach.

When the appointed hour of his meeting with Roberto Santiago and Major Mikhail Neyizhsalo arrived and all of the principals but two were assembled in a back room off the kitchen of the Palermitan Social Club, Gus Barone wondered what could be delaying Angelo Albeneti and Tony Fortunado. It was Cheesecake who had masterminded the business plan that had convinced him it was time for the Albanese to get back into the drug trade. Without him, Gus felt exposed. Angelo was integral to a meeting such as this. Even with his oldest friend and trusted consigliere, Alfonse Palma, and the physically intimidating Louie "the Crab" Di-Caprio on his side of the table, Gus couldn't imagine fighting the war he'd declared without Albeneti.

Taking a sip of grappa to cut the phlegm coating his throat, Barone nodded to the two men and their muscle seated across the table from him. "Gentlemen. My associate, Mr. Albeneti, has clearly been, uh, delayed. But we don't wanna keep youse any longer than necessary." He paused to nod toward Chinese drug lords Lyman Fat and Fu Chiang, seated past DiCaprio on his left, and fixed Santiago with a steady, solemn gaze. "I'm assuming, once you saw our friends arrive, you got a better idea just what kinda hand we're gonna play. Yours ain't a monopoly anymore, Mr. Santiago. We got the goods and we got the know-how to compete with you straight up."

Santiago's anger smoldered behind a mask of barely maintained civility. "Do you believe you can kill off key elements of our distribution network without retribution, Señor Barone? Surely, you are not that big a fool." He nodded to indicate the former KGB major at his side. "We also have a strong hand to play. Or do you not read the newspapers?"

Barone eased back in his chair and patted the air between them with open palms. "Whoa there, amigo. Them broads that whacked Tío Paco Santos last night? If that's what you're talking about, my information says they was Dominican, same as him. They wanna buy dope from us, it ain't because we twisted their arms. We either got better product or better prices."

"You have sold drugs stolen from Santos," Santiago said flatly. "To the Jamaicans in East New York." He nodded to Fat and Chiang. "Not their drugs. Ours."

Gus smiled and slowly shook his head. "Afraid you got your facts outta whack there, amigo. A renegade nigger cop named DaCosta did that. Same guy who killed them crew leaders in Washington Heights last week. You read the news or watch TV, you know he won't be making no more trouble like that here on in."

Staring back at Barone, Santiago made no effort to hide his contempt. "You wish me to believe this policeman was working for himself, and not for you? I find that *muy dificil*."

"How difficult you find it's your problem, amigo. We're bidnessmen, same as you. We don't need no trash like him doing our dirty work for us." Barone looked meaningfully down his side of the table toward Louie "the Crab." "We got our own resources in that area."

Seated to Santiago's immediate right, Mikhail Neyizhsalo had remained impassive throughout this exchange. Now he sat forward and looked directly into the Albanese godfather's eyes, his expression as hard and cold as marble. "We do not come here to listen to you threaten us," he said, speaking so quietly that Gus had to strain to hear him. His gaze moved to also encompass Lyman Fat and Fu Chiang. "You do not want to fight a war with us," he assured them. "Why? Because I do not think you are willing to pay the price we are to win it."

Before Barone could respond, Lyman Fat beat him to the punch and met the former KGB officer cool for cool. "Who makes threats now?" he asked. "And seeks to flatter himself at the same time. We will not make the same mistakes our elders made. They underestimated the Colombians' strength." He paused, looking toward Roberto Santiago. "But we are not our elders. If you choose bloodshed, many of your own will also fall. You cannot attack our right to do business on the same streets as you and expect us not to fight back."

As Barone opened his mouth to add something, he was interrupted by the loud clatter of an object falling down the range-hood vent pipe in the adjacent kitchen. No sooner did it hit with a bang inside the hood than the rattle of a second falling object followed, and then a third.

"Hell is that?" Barone demanded of Louie DiCaprio.

With the third tear gas cannister let loose to tumble with a satisfying echo down the thirty feet of vent duct from the social club roof to the kitchen, Gina Galati knelt in the gathering gloom and contemplated how long she had waited for the satisfaction of this moment. Much of what made her feel as good as she did right now was directly related to the events of two hours ago, after she and her uncle had reached agreement on the terms of the Suzanne Albrecht contract. Now, as she knelt listening for shouts of surprise and confusion, she fondled the trigger guard of her SPAS 12-gauge automatic shotgun, savoring the memory of those last moments in Angelo's office.

Her uncle had dropped his feet to swing around in his chair and face a squat, century-old safe parked against the wall behind his desk. He'd spoken with that customary smug confidence as he spun the dial. "Half up front? No problem. Problem is gonna be finding her. I'm told she's dropped outta sight."

Almost on cue, the outer door to the bakery was thrown open and there stood the contract herself, .38 Smith & Wesson Model 37 Airweight in hand. Angelo had his back to her as he worked the safe combination, but Tony Fortunado was facing her straight on. When the two dogs sleeping in one corner leapt up suddenly and commenced barking, Nails reacted as any man confronted with a loaded gun might. He saw a weapon in Suzanne Albrecht's hand, aimed at his boss, and went for his own, tucked into the waistband of his slacks. It was a move that probably saved Gina's life. Suzanne saw it and turned to fire before he could get his weapon cleared. Her shot caught him where his jaw met his left ear, spattering the pinup calendars hung on the wall behind him.

That one instant of distraction was all Gina had needed to pull the weapon she'd already had her hand on inside her tote. As Suzanne Albrecht turned back toward a startled and confused Angelo Albeneti, the fire of maniacal hatred burning in her eyes, Gina capped her with one shot from her noise-suppressed 9 mm Beretta. As the slug buried itself in the target's thorax, the force of impact was enough to propel her backward out the door through which she'd come.

"Jesus mother!" Angelo gasped, struggling to rise from his knees and collapsing into his chair. He stared about him with a look of astonishment frozen on his face, first at the corpse of Tony Fortunado, half his head missing, and then at the still-twitching corpse of Suzanne Albrecht in his office doorway. In an attempt to regain his cool, he tossed banded stacks of cash in Gina's direction and forced a shrug. "Didn't know she'd make it quite that easy for you, kid. I mean, how hard was that?"

Considering the effects of that sudden adrenaline rush on her own heart, Gina could only imagine how hard and fast her uncle's must have pounded. "That don't look like no two hundred grand, Unc," had been her reply. "A deal's a deal."

With reluctance, Angelo had returned to the safe and removed more cash to pile alongside the money already scattered on his desktop.

Gina crossed to scoop it up, ignoring the mess Fortunado had made of the adjacent wall's bright white paint job. "I s'pose I don't need to count it?"

"Gimme a break here, huh?" he complained. "I'm fucking family."

Gina had returned to where she'd left her tote, stooped to stuff the cash into it, and straightened with the noise-suppressed 9 mm automatic still gripped in her right hand. "My father was family, too," she'd replied. "And look how you let Sonny Galati treat him. I'm a bright little bitch, Unc. The kind that learns from the example of her elders."

"Fuck is dis?" Angelo complained. "What? I ain't treated you like my own daughter?"

"At least you never tried to fuck me," Gina replied. "I gotta give you that."

The dogs had watched that exchange with cocked heads, then started in barking all over again when she shot her uncle mid-chest. Ready to shoot either one of them if they tried to bite her, Gina had heaved her uncle's corpse aside to see what other treasures might await her in his safe.

Two hours later, Gina Galati now knelt alongside the rooftop vent while thirty feet below, Louie "the Crab" DiCaprio was on his feet and moving toward the noise in the Palermitan Social Club kitchen.

"No idea," DiCaprio replied to Gus Barone's query. "Sounded like something fell off the fan or something, maybe."

From where he sat, Gus could see the restaurant range through the open doorway. When a sudden hissing noise was followed by a dense, vaporous cloud pouring from beneath the stainless steel hood, he leapt to his feet in panic. "Gas!" he yelled.

While Barone tried to fathom who could be behind the attack, and why, everyone started to scramble at once. All of the principals involved in the current dispute were there, inside the social club with him. Several had gone for weapons, but none had produced a gas mask, or otherwise seemed to have anticipated this particular eventuality. The look he got from Roberto Santiago was every bit as accusatory as the one he threw back.

The Crab, with his trademark Ingram Mac 10 mm machine pistol clutched in one hand, blazed a trail through the liquor storeroom past the walk-in refrigerator and freezer to the delivery door at the back of the building. Moving at speed, he hit the door-release bar hard, ready to lay down fire as he hurtled into the back alley beyond. The door started to open, then stopped abruptly, staggering him. "Chained," he grunted. "Fuckizdis?" In the next instant, he'd reversed field to race back through the building toward the street.

For Taras Pidvalna, the first indicator that something had gone awry inside the Palermitan Social Club came when the front door flew open and a big, powerfully built Sicilian staggered onto the sidewalk enveloped in a cloud of smoke or gas. Doubled over and coughing, the others, including the major, followed quickly on his heels. Instantly, men brandishing weapons emerged from adjacent cars and doorways to converge on the scene, some Albanese, some Chinese, and some Cali cartel.

Taras heard a first booming shotgun blast, followed quickly by a second and a third, but saw no muzzle flashes. One of the Chinese from inside the social club, Roberto Santiago, and the big Sicilian who'd led the charge from the building crumpled to the pavement. The acoustics between buildings on either side of the avenue made it difficult to determine where the shooter was, but when gunmen from each faction saw their leaders hit, a spontaneous firefight erupted.

Convinced that he could be of no help to his employer now, and wary of being struck by a stray bullet, Taras started to duck below the windowsill. Across the avenue, he caught sight of movement on the social club rooftop and stopped to train his scope in that direction. Directly above the front door, a slender young man crouched with an automatic

12-gauge shotgun, methodically picking off individuals on the sidewalk below.

Taras took aim with his sniper's rifle, having no idea whether Mikhail Neyizhsalo was any longer among the living. Nor could he guess what this youngster with grim hatred frozen on his face hoped to accomplish with such wholesale and apparently indiscriminate slaughter. What he did know, with certainty, was that he had a good, clean shot at a target, and should take it.

As Gina stood at the parapet wall overlooking the street with feet planted wide, the Franchi SPAS 12-gauge alive in her hands and the bodies of her sworn enemies littering the sidewalk below, she felt nothing but a curious kind of emptiness. She had no idea how many of those men she'd actually killed or who they were, but felt no remorse as they fell. All of them played the same game, and were therefore the same detestable scum. In another light, the fact that they and their henchmen were also shooting at each other might have struck her as poetically just. But the memory of her dead father's addiction, and the brutal, calculating coldness of Sonny Galati, had long since obliterated all sense of irony in her. She'd wanted to look into her Uncle Angelo's eyes as he died, and had. The rest of them, she just wanted to hurt in a way they'd always remember. Who they were and the code by which they lived had led to the murder of her father. It had allowed men like Sonny Galati to prosper.

Gina watched in fascination as Gus Barone crawled frantically toward the curb, trying to reach the cover of a parked car five feet away. One crimson blotch stained his white shirt high on his right shoulder, and another, the back of his left thigh. She thought of her son Claude, fathered by a beautiful French soccer player she'd met at a Manhattan nightspot and dragged home for a one-night stand. She wanted Claude to grow up as far removed from Gus Barone's world as his imagination—and the small fortune soon to be delivered into her aunt's care—could take him. That place wouldn't be Sicily, and the home of some cousin named Sophia, or anywhere else his heritage of violence might one day come to haunt him. She wanted her son to grow up happy and not so full of hatred that his humanity lay forever buried beneath it.

She aimed at the middle of the scrambling Albanese godfather's back and felt the satisfying jolt as the 12-gauge jumped in her hands. In the instant before Barone collapsed, she would swear she'd seen the sidewalk through the hole the magnum buckshot load had created in his torso. With him dead, her job there was finished and her thoughts turned to the escape route she'd planned. She took a step backward out of view from the street, and as she straightened, a bullet fired from a window across the avenue tore into her throat, severing her spinal cord at the nape of her neck. In the long moment of surprise before her heart quit, Gina caught a glimpse of that irony that was life. At last.

Twenty-six

Word of the gunfight out in front of the Palermitan Social Club in Canarsie reached Harbor View Terrace in Park Ridge at 9:22 P.M. Members of the Intelligence Division surveillance teams who had witnessed it were still trying to sort out the who, what, and why when Simon Ogilvy got a call from his ranking officer at the scene. Moments later, Chief of Department Bob Dunleavy received a similar call from the Brooklyn South watch commander.

Confronted as he'd been with a barrage of probing questions posed by Job brass—what exactly *was* his relationship with Deputy Commissioner Albrecht? how had she gained access to his house without forcing entry? why would she have wanted to? was she in the habit of making herself at home in his kitchen, and where else was she in the habit of doing such? etc.—Matt Stuart was clearly relieved to be delivered from their interrogation by developments elsewhere. Considering the circumstances, Rhoda Bolivar thought he had comported himself with admirable dignity. No, he had not been in communication with First Deputy Commissioner Albrecht at any time since observing her in her car on Flatbush Avenue that morning. Yes, he had given her a key to his house three years ago. No, it hadn't occurred to him that she'd never returned it. Yes, he and Suzanne Albrecht had been romantically involved for a period of time. And no, he had no idea what her relationship with

Albanese capo Angelo Albeneti might be, and wouldn't want to guess. As Rhoda listened to his answers, butterflies fluttered in the pit of her stomach. Was she jealous of the intimacy Suzanne Albrecht had shared with Matt and the fact that she'd chosen *his* house as a temporary safe haven?

Simon Ogilvy had no trouble justifying why Matt and Rhoda should tag along with him to Canarsie. His current investigation of Albanese family drug-dealing activities was a direct outgrowth of the Three-seven squad's investigation into the murder of Officer Juan Rodriguez in Washington Heights. As they approached Stuart's car, Rhoda asked for his keys and told him she would drive.

"I look that bad?" he asked.

"Awful would be kind."

He dug them from his pocket and handed them across.

As Rhoda joined the procession of cars moving past the barricades set up at the south end of Harbor View Terrace, she felt Stuart's eyes on her and glanced his way. "What?" she asked.

"I'm sorry you had to listen to all that. My private life laid bare."

A sympathetic smile crept from the corners of her mouth and eyes as she slowly shook her head. "I'm a big girl. It's not like you never mentioned it. I've got plenty of my own dirty laundry."

"It's been over for months," he reiterated. "Current evidence to the contrary."

Rhoda believed him and was a little surprised that she did. She'd never met Suzanne Albrecht, but from what she'd seen of the woman from afar, she couldn't put her and Matt Stuart in the same bed together.

By the time they reached Remsen Avenue, a better picture of what had transpired there was starting to come clear. Albanese godfather Gus Barone had met with Mikhail Neyizhsalo and Roberto Santiago at the Palermitan Social Club as scheduled. Also on hand were Albanese consigliere Alfonse Palma, an enforcer named DiCaprio, and the two Chinese caught on film at the Paerdegat Basin marina that past weekend. All of them were flushed from the club when tear gas was dropped down a kitchen vent pipe from the roof of the building. Santiago, Louie DiCaprio, Lyman Fat, Fu Chiang, and others had been rushed to Kingsbrook Jewish Medical Center, all in critical condition. Barone, Neyizhaslo, and two others were already dead.

Stuart, Rhoda, and Chief Ogilvy were briefed by Intel Division detective Joey Lozano. When Mikhail Neyizhsalo left Brighton Beach for the meeting, Lozano and his partner, Pete Ogborn, had followed him to Canarsie. They were in their car, a block south on Remsen, when all hell broke loose.

"Just like that, we got goons from every faction here crawling outta the woodwork," Lozano continued to describe the action. "Four Chinese guys jump outta the back of this van here." He pointed to a blue Ford Windstar. "Same time as a half dozen Colombians climb outta that Transport over there. Everybody's armed to the fucking teeth. The goombahs got at least a dozen guys hanging in doorways and inside businesses up and down the block, and they all come running."

"Who fired first?" Ogilvy asked.

Lozano gestured to where several uniformed and plainclothes cops could be seen moving around on the roof of the social club building. "That's where it starts to get geechy, boss. You know the sketch we been circulating? Of the tomboy broad in the ball cap, works for Angelo Albeneti? We think it's her who dumped the gas down the vent pipe. She definitely fired the first shot."

"You sure?" Stuart asked, suddenly excited.

"I seen her with my own eyes, Lou," Lozano replied. "Leaning over the facade up there, this twelve-gauge assault gun in his hands, picking them off like carnival targets."

"How do you know it's her?" Rhoda pressed him.

The Intel detective shrugged. "She's laid out on the tar up there, deader'n a mackerel. Took one in the throat."

Stuart was thinking fast. "We all expected Angelo Albeneti to be at this meeting," he told Ogilvy. "He wasn't, and neither was Tony Fortunado. What have you heard from our teams watching Mom's Pie?"

"Just that a woman with lots of curly blond hair let herself in the loading dock door around seven-twenty. Jack Hogan described her as a pretty hot number . . ." The Intel chief stopped to look toward Rhoda. "His words, not mine. Nobody's been seen coming or going since."

"The dead woman on the roof turns out to be Gina Galati, it's time we get a warrant," Stuart urged his ex-boss. "First Albeneti doesn't show here, then every major player in the New York drug game is either killed or knocked out of the box by a shooter in his employ."

"Take some pair of balls, wouldn't it?" Ogilvy murmured. "A major power play both inside and outside his own organization, all in one night."

"But exactly what it looks like he's done."

"I'll call Central Warrants," Simon agreed. "What's your next move?"

From up the block, Stuart saw Terry Gaskin threading his way through the commotion inside the frozen zone, headed in his direction. He and Josh Littel were part of the police presence on Remsen Avenue at the time of the shootings. He would be able to add detail to Joe Lozano's briefing. "I want to call my guy, Raymond, get a positive ID as soon as the dead woman up there reaches the morgue." He tried and failed to stifle a yawn. "Him, and maybe that neighbor of hers who my guys interviewed." He paused to watch Albanese godfather Gus Barone, zipped into a body bag, unceremoniously loaded onto a gurney. "Meanwhile, the connection between Suzanne and Albeneti still bugs hell out of me. I want to take a look at her apartment."

"Search warrant shouldn't be too hard to get there," Ogilvy said. "We've got reasonable cause galore."

Matt wondered what it would feel like to invade Suzanne's private space now, just as he wondered how she had felt invading his that afternoon. He looked Rhoda Bolivar's way. "I know how tired you are. You up for it?"

"There a doorman, or someone else who can get us access?" she asked.

"Pretty sure the super has a key. Let's just hope Albeneti hasn't gotten there first."

While watching Matt Stuart start away from him toward that crew-cut detective from his squad, Simon Ogilvy saw weariness in the set of his shoulders.

"When I heard he got the Three-seven, I wondered whose hat he'd crapped in," Joey Lozano growled at Ogilvy's side. "Looks like every cloud's got its silver lining, though, huh? Just like they say."

Roused from his rumination, Simon turned to him. "Say what?" he asked.

"Detective Bolivar. That's one great-looking piece of ass."

"I'm sure she'd be pleased to know you think so, Detective," Ogilvy growled. "Where's your partner?"

"Petey?" Lozano scanned up and down the street. "Beats me. Been acting strange ever since we got word the first dep went on the lam this morning. Wandered off to find a shitter twenty, thirty minutes ago. Come to think, that's the last I seen of him."

"Tell him I want a word," Ogilvy said. He turned away, looking for the chief of detectives. He scanned the blood-spattered landscape, the survivors since removed to area hospitals and corpses to the morgue. If Stuart's theory proved true, that Angelo Albeneti had made a play to consolidate a power base both inside and outside the Albanese organization, the mobster had to be deranged.

Stuart gave Rhoda the address of Suzanne Albrecht's apartment building on East Eighty-first Street and York Avenue, then occupied himself during their journey around the bottom of Brooklyn by calling Al Goldstein. When he reached him, the Three-seven squad's second-in-command was eager for news of what had transpired in Canarsie.

"All we're getting is bits and pieces," Martini Al complained. "Littel calls, says all hell's broke loose, and where the fuck's Cheesecake? Then he calls back, says they got the Galati broad dead onna rooftop; that she's the one flushed Barone outta the joint with tear gas. What the fuck happened there, Matthew?"

"You have the gist of it," Stuart replied. "Sidewalk out front looks like Omaha Beach on D day. Four dead, ten wounded. Barone, Neyizhsalo, and one of the Chinese are history. An Intel guy who saw it all go down thinks the bullet that killed Gina Galati—if she *is* Gina Galati—came from a building across the street. Ballistics is checking it out. Littel and Gaskin are picking up the neighbor they interviewed this morning; taking her to the morgue to do an ID."

Al's tone softened when he spoke next. "We heard about the first dep making them phone calls from your place, Matthew. Any guesses where she's gotten to by now?"

Stuart shifted his gaze to Rhoda's profile, her eyes intent on the traffic ahead. "Halfway to Rio be my best guess. She'd have to have some sort of contingency plan, lest the shit hit the fan. That's just her nature." Matt watched Rhoda at the wheel beside him, her jaw set in that determined expression she wore when in deep concentration. "Meanwhile, we still need to figure out what her connection to Cheesecake Albeneti is. If she was feeding him intelligence, there's no saying what kind of advantage he might have right now."

"Better find something concrete, Matthew. Fact that this Galati broad was his niece, and was seen picking up a cake at his place, ain't exactly incriminating. *Or* the fact somebody at a cigar store in Canarsie called her number. With that kinda evidence, we pick his sorry ass up for questioning, some shyster in a Brioni suit and Tanino Crisci loafers has him back on the street before you can say depraved indifference."

When Detective Pete Ogborn finally surfaced again at the Remsen Avenue crime scene, Simon Ogilvy thought he looked like a man with a noose around his neck. Joey Lozano had delivered the message that the boss wanted to see him. He now trailed ten yards in Ogborn's wake, trying to look disinterested. Without inviting Lozano to join them, Simon asked Pete to sit with him in the backseat of his car.

"You look kinda rough, Detective," he commented when they were settled. "Why's that? Conscience finally caught up with you?"

Ogborn had to know something like this was coming, yet he blinked and stared at his boss, clearly surprised. "My conscience? I-I'm not sure what you mean by that, sir."

"At two-thirteen this morning, you placed a call to First Deputy Commissioner Albrecht's apartment from a pay phone two blocks from your listening post outside the Dihsko Volya," Simon said flatly. God, was it only that morning? It seemed like an eternity ago. "I've known about your FA status from Jump Street, Pete. It's my job to know, and my job to protect our more sensitive investigations. I did it by either feeding you crap or keeping you totally in the dark."

"Jesus," Ogborn whispered. If it was possible for a man already pale with shock to turn any whiter, he may have. "I didn't ask for the assignment, Chief. She recruited me."

"And once you agreed to it, you were only following orders, right? So why does your conscience bother you so much right now, Pete?" Simon shifted to stare out at the street, where camera strobes from Crime Scene Unit photographers streaked the night. His gaze wandered toward the roofline above the Palermitan Social Club as he still tried to puzzle out why, if this was a major Albeneti offensive, Cheesecake had sent just one slender kid to perform so herculean a task. If Gina Galati—the man's niece, no less—was such a formidable threat, wouldn't he consider her an almost invaluable asset and want to protect her better than he had?

When Simon returned his attention to Ogborn, he shook his head and grunted in disgust. "Whatever you told your boss this morning, it threw her into a panic, Detective. First thing she does is run off to Flatbush and take a meeting with Angelo Albeneti. You probably weren't aware we've been watching him like a hawk the past couple days."

Ogborn's eyes bulged.

"Didn't think so. Our surveillance caught them together this morning. Worse for her . . . she spotted our surveillance, which is most likely why she ended up going on the run."

"You're saying it's *my* fault?" Ogborn's question was barely audible.

"Not hardly," Simon scoffed. "She hung herself. But before she did, she provided Angelo Albeneti with information that may well have dictated what happened here tonight. Information you gave her." He nodded out the window as the last two EMS techs heaved the doors of their ambulance closed and started to roll. "Those three dead guys and one dead gal might have been dope-dealing scum, but wouldn't you agree they've been denied due process?"

Twenty-seven

Suzanne Albrecht's address at East Eighty-first Street and York Avenue on Manhattan's Upper East Side was a ten-story prewar building with a blue awning stretching to the curb out front. The lone uniformed doorman who worked the lobby at eleven o'clock that Monday night was relaxing inside the door with the Yankees-Orioles game on a tiny television. He moved with reluctance when two detectives appeared brandishing gold shields and demanded access to the first deputy commissioner's sixth-floor apartment. The superintendent seemed only a trifle more eager to cooperate when roused from his basement digs, but forced himself to appear interested while Stuart explained that a search warrant would soon be forthcoming. A politician at heart, he knew how displeased the affluent owners of the building's co-op apartments would be should he alienate the police. Eventually, he produced a key.

For Stuart, it felt strange to walk back into Suzanne's apartment under current circumstances, just two days after his last visit. Everything looked exactly the same as it had Saturday evening: the newly acquired Persian carpet and the familiar art rearranged on the walls since their breakup last November.

"Nice," Rhoda commented. She advanced through the living room to peer out the south-facing window. The bustle of traffic on York Avenue and apartments in the building directly across East Eighty-first were most of the view, but parts of the Fifty-ninth Street Bridge and the tram to Roosevelt Island were also visible twenty blocks to the southeast. "Two bedrooms?" she asked.

"With formal dining room, eat-in kitchen, and two baths. She used the second bedroom as a combination TV room and study. A lot like yours."

Rhoda drifted to a bookcase alongside the fireplace and examined a cluster of photographs grouped there on one shelf. Matt knew some were of Suzanne's parents and grandparents, and one was of her as a child. Featured prominently, in an eight-by-ten silver frame, was her official graduation picture from the Police Academy. In it, Suzanne was twenty-four years old and six months out of Columbia Law School. She had her hair tucked away beneath her uniform hat, and unlike the Palace Guard persona she'd cultivated over time, she'd worn contacts then, and makeup.

"Wow," Rhoda murmured. She'd lifted the picture from the shelf and turned in Stuart's direction. "Pre-Ice Maiden."

"Hadn't changed all that much, really," he said. "Just learned how to camouflage it."

Something she heard in his voice gave Rhoda pause. She let the photo dangle at her side and looked harder at him. "You okay with this? Being here?"

Stuart remembered in a flash his hiding that green camisole in his dresser before signaling the all-clear to the cops assembled outside his house. He felt a lump form in his throat. "Hell no, I'm not all right with it. I'm standing in my fugitive ex-girlfriend's apartment preparing to go through her dirty underwear with you."

She returned the picture to its perch and started in his direction. Her tone was sympathizing when she spoke. "We can call Jack and the sarge, Matt. Trade details. They're only forty blocks north of here. A straight shot up First Avenue."

Stuart swallowed hard and forced a grateful smile. "You spend almost three years with someone, you think you get to know them. Turns out I really didn't know Suzanne at all, and that fact bugs the shit out of me." He shook his head. "Do I want to run away from this? Nuh-uh. If there's something here that explains what we saw this morning, *I* need to find it, not Jack Hogan or Martini Al Goldstein."

"Where do you want to start?" she asked.

"I'll take the study," he said. "Why don't you start with her bedroom."

*   *   *

Almost an hour had passed since Martini Al Goldstein was last brought up to date on developments at two opposite ends of the city, and a half hour since he, Hogan, and the Intel Division detectives at Mom's Pie had finally given up waiting for Angelo Albeneti to make a move. When he reached Suzanne Albrecht's voice mail at her apartment, it was the second time he'd dialed the number inside a minute, hoping Matt Stuart would pick up. "Yeah, Matthew. If you can hear me, pick up the goddamn phone."

There was a click, then the noise of someone fumbling with the receiver at the other end of the line. "What's wrong with my cell phone?" Stuart asked, sounding preoccupied.

"How long you been on that particular battery?" Al asked.

Stuart must have heard the urgency in his voice, even over the din of frantically barking dogs. "Why? Albeneti not there?"

From a telephone at the top of the stairs leading to the basement offices of Mom's Pie, Goldstein could see past a walk-in refrigerator and pallets stacked with flour sacks to where the two Shih Tzus were tied to a support column. Just beyond, detectives from Manhattan North homicide loitered, watching a medical examiner's pathologist methodically examine the corpse discovered in the office doorway. "Oh, he's here all right. Suzanne Albrecht and Tony Fortunado, too. Problem is, they ain't saying nothing, or going anywhere but to the morgue."

There was a pause on the line, then Stuart muttered, "Jesus."

"Tony Nails took one in the jaw. Gun in his hand unfired. One spent round in the cylinder of the first dep's thirty-eight. From the angle of where she was standing, the lab guys think she's the one probably killed him."

Stuart's head was spinning. "*One* spent round? Who killed Angelo?"

"He got it in the heart, sitting at his desk, no weapon in sight. Means there was a fourth party involved, Matthew. We don't know who. There's a floor safe with the door left hanging open. All we found inside was a few papers and a gold Rolex oyster case watch."

"Which retails at close to eighteen thousand."

"Kinda rules out a robbery motive. Not that I ever considered it."

"Damn," Stuart complained. "None of this makes sense. If Albeneti wasn't making a grab for the brass ring, who's left, Al? Every major player in the city is either wounded or dead."

"Dunno, Matthew. We had it figured out: who DaCosta and the Galati broad were working for; how the Albanese were moving on Washington Heights. I still don't think we was wrong, but there's something missing."

"A *major* something," Stuart murmured. He sounded weary, and Al could well imagine why. His old partner had been on the move nonstop for the better part of three days. "Any idea what time those hits went down?" Matt asked.

"Pathologist is still working on it. The counter crew locked up and left the building around seven-fifteen. Basement has better soundproofing than the fucking Oval Office. We never even heard the dogs bark."

"Give me another buzz soon as he pins it down."

"Check your phone, Matthew. I might not be the only one been trying to get in touch with you."

As soon as he disconnected with Al Goldstein, Stuart dug his tiny portable out of the breast pocket of his jacket and found it switched off. He'd kicked himself earlier for forgetting his beeper in the rush to leave Rhoda's house, and guessed he'd used the phone half a dozen times between eight o'clock and nine-fifteen, turning it on and off between calls to conserve power. No sooner did he switch it on than the damned thing rang.

"Stuart," he answered.

"Uncle Lou? Your nephew, Raymond. Where you been? I been trying to get hold of you all night."

"Call me at this number," Matt instructed his cover. He recited Suzanne's and flipped the cell phone shut. Tempted as he was to pull Sapienze that weekend, he'd resisted. Chances were, Sal was one of the counter help Martini Al had referred to: those employees who'd closed up the bakery at seven-fifteen. The telephone in Suzanne's study rang on cue.

"Go ahead," he answered.

"You know that tomboy-looking broad I described to the sketch artist?" Sapienze asked. "I saw her again tonight, Lou. Not at the bakery, but three blocks down Pleasant Ave. Makes me think she might live in the neighborhood."

The massacre in Canarsie had hit the ten o'clock news, but Sal couldn't know that Gina Galati had played a major part in perpetrating it. "You're sure it was her? The same woman?" he asked.

"I'd bet the farm if I had a farm, Lou. Same sorta clothes, same Brooklyn street swagger, ball cap, everything. Only this time, insteada getting into a beat-to-shit gypsy cab, she climbs outta this spanking new Land Rover Discovery. White, loaded."

"You get a plate?" After the day he'd had, Matt was surprised he had any adrenaline left, but felt more of it kick into his bloodstream to lift him all over again.

"I said I was weary of this life, not *totally* burned out," Sapienze chided. His professional competence had been called into question. He recited the tag number back to his control, then asked the expected next question. "What's this I heard on the news, Lou? About a fucking massacre outside Gus Barone's social club on Remsen Avenue? Albeneti in on it or what?"

"Looking more doubtful by the hour," Matt replied. "But your role in this is over, Sal. We're pulling you. Tonight."

"No shit?" There was no mistaking the relief heard in the undercover cop's voice. "Why? What gives?"

"Where are you now?"

"Home."

Home was Brooklyn. "How soon can you meet me at the morgue?"

"Dunno. Forty-five minutes?"

"The tomboy's name is Gina Galati, Sal," Stuart told him. "Or was. We found her on the roof of the Palermitan Social Club two hours ago with a bullet hole in her neck. If you make a positive ID, it looks like she was a very busy girl tonight."

Once Matt hung up with Sapienze, he dialed Chief Simon Ogilvy's mobile number. Rhoda wandered into the study as Matt waited for his call to connect. She carried what looked like a yearbook, an index finger marking her place in it. "Eureka," she said softly.

Matt held up a finger to stop her as the Intel chief picked up.

"Ogilvy."

"Stuart, Chief. I just got a call from Raymond. He's meeting me at the morgue."

"Where the hell you been?" Ogilvy complained. "I've been trying your cell phone *and* your goddamn pager ever since I heard what happened at Mom's Pie."

"You need to have your guys search the neighborhood there. Look for a white Land Rover Discovery," Matt replied, not attempting to explain. He recited the plate number to his former boss.

"What's this about?" Ogilvy sounded tired, too, and like his fuse had grown dangerously short.

"Raymond thinks he saw Gina Galati on Pleasant Avenue tonight. Around seven-fifteen. Looks like she drove out to Canarsie afterward to start the ruckus there." The notion that Suzanne was actually dead still hadn't penetrated to the level of emotional response yet. All Stuart felt was a vague numbness. "If that's the scenario, boss, it puts a new spin on things."

"What spin is that?" the Intel chief complained. "She worked for Albeneti, didn't she?"

"That was one of our assumptions. I'm still working on the why not, but it could be it's not entirely true."

"How's that?"

"Don't know yet. It's why they call these things investigations."

"Lack of sleep turns you into a real asshole, Lieutenant. You make any progress where you are?"

Stuart glanced over at Rhoda, who now had the yearbook open on the desk between them and wore a look of impatience. "I'll keep you posted," he replied. "Let me know about the Land Rover." This time he made sure he left the power switched on when he folded the phone closed. "Suzanne Albrecht is dead," he said. "Killed in a shoot-out in Angelo Albeneti's office at Mom's Pie. He's dead, too." He went on to relate what Al Goldstein had reported from the scene.

"Jesus," she murmured.

"Before the phone rang you said 'Eureka.' "

She turned the book his way. "Check this out. Yearbook from Erasmus Hall High, nineteen seventy-four. I found it in her lingerie drawer, this tucked inside." With a flourish, she produced a yellowed article cut from a newspaper, complete with faded black and white photograph. "Angelo Albeneti's wedding announcement, dated June 15, 1977."

Matt accepted the announcement from her outstretched hand.

"You notice who served as the bride's maid of honor?" she asked.

Matt knew from his work on the Mom's Pie investigation at Intelligence that a woman named Sabatino had divorced Angelo Albeneti in 1986. What he didn't know was that Rose Marie Sabatino and Suzanne

Albrecht were old friends. "Damn," he marveled. "This was over twenty years ago."

"Probably knew each other a lot longer than that," she said. "Look at this." She pushed the yearbook at him. "Senior class pictures. Albeneti and Albrecht come one right after the other."

As an eighteen-year-old high school senior, Suzanne had worn her hair long and straight like Michelle Phillips or Cher. She had more baby fat in her face than six years later at her academy graduation. In his picture, Angelo Albeneti sported a modified Italian Afro. Both of them looked impossibly young and innocuous, like life had hardly yet dented them. "And Rose Marie Sabatino?" he asked.

"Here." Rhoda flipped pages and planted a finger. "Reminds me of that actress Linda Fiorentino."

Matt could also see the resemblance. "Definitely be someone might catch Albeneti's eye," he said.

"Then there's this." Rhoda produced a videocassette. "It was hidden along with this other stuff."

Stuart took the tape and turned it over in his hand. It bore no markings to indicate what it contained, or how long it might play. "I've got to meet this guy at the morgue in half an hour. Someone we've been running deep under at Mom's Pie," he told her. "You want to tag along or stay here, see what's on this?"

"I think I'll tag along. Tired as you look, I don't trust you behind the wheel of a car."

Twenty-eight

Stuart was pleased when Rhoda invited him to spend the night at her place. He didn't want to be home alone with his memories. Meanwhile, everyone associated with their investigation was now either dead or hospitalized. Viewing the tape they'd discovered in Suzanne Albrecht's apartment could wait until morning. Together, they'd traveled to the morgue on First Avenue and East Thirtieth Street to meet Sal Sapienze. They'd stayed only long enough for him to confirm that the dead woman found on the social club roof was the same woman he'd seen on Pleasant Avenue earlier than night. From there, Rhoda drove through the Midtown Tunnel into Queens, then straight out the LIE and down the Cross Island Parkway to Valley Stream. It was two o'clock before they tumbled into bed. Both were too tired to do anything but agree not to set an alarm.

Stuart had never felt this exhausted. For the first half hour after his head hit the pillow, he was too wired by the rush of all that had happened to do anything but stare into the darkness and replay it in memory. Stretched out beside him, Rhoda had fallen asleep almost instantly. The light from a nearly full moon leaked into the room through gaps in the vertical blinds to illuminate her form beneath the bedclothes. Matt watched the easy rise and fall of her rib cage and thought about what was happening between them. Nothing, lately, had gone in a direction he could have anticipated. He was wise enough to recognize the futility of speculating on where things would go from there.

His thoughts turned to Gina Galati, and the doubts he'd harbored until Sal Sapienze confirmed that she was the woman he'd seen on Pleasant Avenue that evening. Gina Galati had gone on a rampage, and Matt still had no idea why. Her motives were as unfathomable to him as transubstantiation or the Virgin birth.

The relief on Sal Sapienze's face as he was being delivered from the private purgatory he'd inhabited for the past eighteen months was as uplifting as watching Rhoda's slumbering beauty, outlined in moonlight. Matt took a deep breath, closed his eyes, and tried to lock in these comforting memories.

Tuesday morning, the crying of her infant nephew, Claude, was the first indication Rose Marie Sabatino had that her niece had not returned from wherever she'd gone last night. A second clue was the absence of Gina's Land Rover from her driveway. Rose had hurried to the guest room to gather the baby from his crib and carry him to the kitchen to make coffee when the phone rang. The caller was her cousin Anna, from Flatbush. She asked if Rose had seen the news yet and told her to turn on CNN.

It was nine now, three hours after she'd learned Suzanne Albrecht had been killed last night along with her ex-husband and a slew of others, including Albanese godfather Gus Barone. According to a broadcast she'd watched several times over a span of two hours, police had yet to disclose the identity of a female casualty found at the Remsen Avenue scene. Rose could guess it anyway. The woman had to be Gina. The reports were saying she killed Angelo sometime after Mom's Pie Company closed for business last night, then drove to where Barone was having a meeting. Fourteen people were either dead or wounded outside the Palermitan Social Club in Canarsie. It seemed likely that Claude was now an orphan.

Still in shock, Rose Marie barely heard a car door slam outside. She started in surprise when the doorbell rang, and moved to the front of the house to peer into her driveway past the dining room curtains. She expected to see police cars, but instead saw a delivery van from a Manhattan-based messenger service idling outside her door.

The bill of shipping the driver asked her to sign was preprinted, the delivery charged to a Mom's Pie Company account. Rose Marie carried the big, overstuffed envelope into her kitchen, where Claude sat contentedly in his high chair, making a mess of a banana. Filled with apprehension, she tore the flap. The last thing she expected to see tumble forth onto her countertop was money.

The envelope contained a quarter of a million dollars in cash, all in fifty- and hundred-dollar bills, and a hastily scrawled note from her niece:

Rose,

    The fact that I'm not there to get this delivery probably means I'm dead. Sorry about Suzanne. She walked in on my surprise party. Started shooting before I knew what was happening. The money is yours, which don't hardly make up for me dumping my baby on you. Still, I hope it'll help. I've hated Angelo ever since he let Sonny kill my father. I'd planned to kill both those rotten fucks, but what plan is ever perfect? Maybe, I get lucky, I'll meet Sonny in hell.

           Ciao, Gina

Located in the New Dorp section of Station Island, the home of Angelo Albeneti's ex-wife, Rose Marie Sabatino, was a gray clapboard ranch-style that reminded Rhoda Bolivar quite a lot of her own. It was modest, well kept, and in a neighborhood built during the same postwar era. Stuart had the wheel today, and Rhoda was left free to catalogue her impressions as they made the turn from Richmond Road onto Otis Avenue. There was a late-model Oldsmobile sedan parked in the drive, bracketed by mature pink azaleas in full bloom. Everything about the setting proclaimed that Rose Marie Sabatino was a solid middle-class citizen. So did a background check done by the OCCB earlier that day. It revealed nothing out of the ordinary about the woman, other than her having an ex-husband who was a made guy in the New York Mafia. She was a licensed commercial real estate broker with an income of approximately $120,000 per annum. She had purchased this house after the 1987 downturn for $152,000, and paid off the fifteen-year mortgage three years early. The Buick was financed, her 401K plan was funded at an equitable level for a working woman forty-two years of age, and her

Chemical bank checking account currently contained a little over $12,000. Rose Marie Sabatino was comfortable, nothing more, nothing less.

Neither Rhoda nor Stuart was able to sleep past eight o'clock that morning. Rhoda was surprised by how refreshed six hours of uninterrupted shut-eye made her feel. And Stuart had been all energy the moment his feet hit the floor. He'd taken the first shower while Rhoda made coffee, then contacted OCCB to ask for the lowdown on Suzanne Albrecht's high school friend. By the time Rhoda had dried her hair and applied a little makeup, Matt was halfway through the videotape they'd found last night. He'd brought her up to speed, reading from hastily jotted notes, and then pressed ahead. The entire forty-eight minutes of footage was of Rose Marie Sabatino. In her late twenties or early thirties when the tape was shot, she sat at a table relating stories and showing exhibits in an effort to reveal everything she knew about her husband's criminal activities. To collect this information she'd recorded telephone conversations, photocopied sensitive documents, and taken photographs of gatherings. Thirteen years ago, had it been placed in the hands of a federal grand jury, this tape contained enough dates, places, names, and other specifics to have put Angelo Albeneti, Gus Barone, Alfonse Palma, and a half dozen of their Albanese cronies in prison cells for the rest of their lives.

Rhoda wasn't surprised that the woman who answered the front door seemed to be expecting them.

"Morning, Officers," she greeted them. Neither Rhoda nor Matt had yet produced ID. "No, I don't know who killed him, and yes, I'm glad the sonofabitch is dead."

"Mind if we come in?" Matt asked.

She frowned at the gold lieutenant's shield and identification card he held up, then shook her head. "Don't see why you'd need to, Lieutenant. I just told you everything I know."

"You didn't mention that Gina Galati is your niece," Matt replied. "Or was."

Rhoda watched the woman's face closely. As the ex-wife of a made Mafia guy, she had had practice hiding her feelings, and did a pretty good job of it now. But not good enough. The flicker of pain Rhoda saw in her eyes, though gone in an instant, gave her away.

"I don't know what that has to do with anything," she replied coolly.

And then a child let out a wail somewhere deeper in her house. "Oh fuck," she muttered, the defensive shell crumbling.

"Gina had an eighteen-month-old son," Rhoda said softly. "Your brother, her mother, and now her uncle are all dead. I imagine you might be the boy's only close living relative."

A single tear leaked from the corner of Rose Marie Sabatino's right eye and started its slow journey down her handsome face. Without bothering to wipe it away, she stood back and held the door. "Make you a deal," she said. "You tell me what you already know, I'll do what I can to fill in the blanks."

None of the expectations Rhoda carried into that house were met. Where she'd anticipated seeing slick lacquer and chrome furnishings à la *Goodfellas*, she found tasteful reproductions of Mission designs. The living room walls were hung with framed Art Nouveau posters by Mucha. The lighting fixtures, oriental carpet, and a display of ceramics were from that period, too.

From somewhere beyond the dining room—probably the kitchen—the baby let out another wail.

"You might as well sit down," Ms. Sabatino invited them. "I'll only be a second."

Left alone in the room with her, Matt turned to Rhoda. "She may be more inclined to talk to another woman. Why don't you carry the ball awhile?" He removed the videotape from a side pocket of his jacket and handed it across.

When Rose Marie returned, she carried a towheaded toddler in her arms, a blue plastic pacifier stuffed into his mouth. When he saw them, the baby scowled and shook his head from side to side.

"Cops," she said. "Considering his bloodlines, he's probably predisposed to take the negative view."

Rhoda advanced slowly. "A blond." She held out a hand to him, smiling as she wiggled one finger. "Who's his daddy?"

"A French soccer player. Gina said he was gorgeous. Beyond that, I don't think he was anything more than the donor."

Rhoda appreciated the woman's frankness and tried to say so with her expression. Rose Marie Sabatino had ten years on her but didn't look it. She had the kind of dramatic bone structure a camera loves, a wide, expressive mouth, and penetrating dark eyes, all framed by ash blond hair cut in a businesslike bob. To judge from how the suit she wore fit her, she stayed in good shape. "We found your tape," she said, and held it up to her. "Hidden in your friend Suzanne's lingerie drawer, along with your high school yearbook and wedding announcement."

"Ah. Could be fewer blanks to fill in than I thought."

The baby grabbed Rhoda's finger as she met his bright blue eyes. He pulled at it and then let go to slap playfully at her hand. "It explains how your ex-husband managed to turn the tables on Suzanne Albrecht, and why she wanted to kill him, but it doesn't tell us anything about why your niece went on that rampage last night."

Rose Marie sighed and leaned forward to set the toddler gingerly on his feet. At eighteen months he was fully capable of walking, and headed straight for a playpen full of toys. "My brother, Gina's father, was a sweet man. Unfortunately, he had an addiction. Spent six, eight hours at a whack in the OTB at Aqueduct. Got in so deep with a bookie named Sonny Galati, he couldn't pay the vig anymore. Sonny sent a couple goons around one day to rough him up. They accidentally killed him. Six months later, Sonny married Gina's mother."

"Christ," Rhoda said.

"Gina was ten. Sometime in that first year after he married her mother, Sonny caught her alone in the garage fixing her bicycle and raped her. I didn't know any of this until just the other night. If I had, I would have cut the bastard's cock off."

To judge from the bitterness in her, Rhoda believed she was capable of doing just that. "It's a horrible story," she said softly, "but it doesn't ex—"

"Why the rampage? Rage. Sonny continued molesting her for almost four years. She hated her mother for failing to protect her, hated Angelo for not protecting her father, and hated Sonny Galati for being the brutal pig he was."

Stuart entered the exchange for the first time, elbows planted on both knees as he leaned forward in his chair. "Did she mention she'd done work for your ex-husband?"

Rose Marie frowned at him. "What kind of work?"

"Killing people."

The shock Rhoda saw register looked genuine.

"Jesus." The woman slowly shook her head. "There was this side of her I could never figure out. If she *did* work for Angelo, I imagine she had some plan in mind."

"Like what she did last night?" Rhoda asked.

Too much reality had caught up with her at once. Rose Marie's shoulders sagged as she shrugged. "Who knows? Maybe."

Matt pointed to the videotape in Rhoda's hand. "We're assuming it was Suzanne Albrecht who helped you get the leverage it took to make the break with your husband. Correct?"

She nodded, her eyes misting again. "When my little boy was killed, I realized how much I hated the life I'd married. There was no way Angelo would let me go. Not with all I knew. Suzanne bought my life with hers. In exchange for my freedom, she promised not to hand the tape over to the U.S. Attorney. A year or so later, Angelo turned that against her."

Ever since his divorce from Rose Marie Sabatino in 1986, Angelo Albeneti had been blackmailing Suzanne Albrecht. The night he'd ordered Officer Johnny "Macho Man" Rodriguez killed, everything Suzanne had worked for since her Police Academy days started to come unraveled. Yesterday's meeting in that Flatbush cemetery was just the last thread, pulled from the fabric of her dreams and ambitions.

Midmorning, after joining the PC and chiefs of Department and Detectives in the mayor's City Hall office to recap what had transpired yesterday, Chief Simon Ogilvy crossed the Brooklyn Bridge, headed for his Intel Division office on Poplar Street. Halfway across the East River, he told his driver he wanted to stretch his legs and get some air. He asked to be dropped at the intersection of Furman Street and Cadman Plaza at the foot of the bridge. It was another gorgeous late May day, the sun warm on his face and a breeze gently fingering his hair as he strolled out along the East River bulkhead. The sight of wheeling gulls, gamboling on updrafts off the water, made him yearn for more innocent times, when the reality he'd known was less bloody, the fights he'd fought less hopeless. He considered again how impossible so much of what he'd sought to accomplish in his adult life had proved to be, and how, if he'd had it to do all over again, he would undoubtedly choose to beat his head against those exact same walls.

At the water's edge, Ogilvy stood a moment staring out across it to the towering spires of Manhattan's Financial District. To his right, the elegant weblike support structure of the Brooklyn Bridge loomed over him, starkly outlined in brilliant sunshine. As he stood considering the contrast between that gorgeous day and the dark ironies of life within the Job, he removed his cell phone from his pocket and called his exec, Phil

Cassidy. When Cassidy came on the line, Simon was brief and to the point.

"Where's Pete Ogborn this morning, Phil?"

"Banged in around eight," Cassidy replied, using the Job vernacular for calling in sick. "Said he'd come down with a flu bug or something."

"After our meeting with Hizzoner, I cornered the PC, said I want Matt Stuart back on my team again, ASAP," Simon told him. "Chief Rose wants to move Stuart's old partner, Al Goldstein, into the whip's slot up there, and promote another detective named Hogan to fill the second's slot. That leaves the Three-seven squad a man short, and I told him I've got just the detective for his vacancy."

There was a pause from down the line. "Ogborn? Jesus. He ain't never worked streets even half as mean as those. He don't *qualify* for duty that rough. The natives will eat him alive, boss."

"Umm," Ogilvy agreed. He was thankful his exec wasn't there to see the twinkle in his eye. "Actually, I'm kinda hoping they deep-fry him first."

Epilogue

It was mid-July in south Florida and unmercifully hot. The cooling fan on the heat-exchange unit of retired Albanese bookmaker Sonny Galati's air conditioner had picked that morning to start making a terrible racket. When the doorbell rang at noon, exotic dancer Wendy Hashimoto thought it was the repairman Sonny had called. Instead, she was confronted by a man in a ski mask, brandishing an automatic pistol and a roll of duct tape. The gun had one of those silencer things attached to its muzzle, just like Wendy had seen in movies. The way the stranger prodded her with it, pushing her back into the house, told her he meant business.

"Where is he?" the intruder demanded in a low, throaty whisper.

One of Wendy's abiding fears was that some whacko from the titty bar where she worked might follow her home some night. But she hadn't danced in almost a week, and this was broad daylight. The idea of Sonny being a target had never occurred to her, though to judge from the house on the Intracoastal Waterway where he lived, and how he threw money around, he was probably rich. But he was sixty years old, fat, and hardly someone Wendy would call a threat.

"I-I don't th-think you have the right h-house," she stammered.

The way the man looked her up and down, like he was appraising an outfit on a mannequin at the mall, was unnerving. It was impossible to read his expression behind that mask, but Wendy got the impression that even in her thong bikini and three-inch stiletto heels, she hadn't scored high in the stranger's estimation.

"I've got the right house," the stranger snarled. "And you're gonna tell me where that fat fuck is, or I'm gonna blow your tits off." He eased the barrel of the gun beneath Wendy's right breast to prod her backward across the terra-cotta tile of the entryway.

Despite the heat, Wendy felt a cold sweat coat her body. "By the p-pool," she whispered, hardly able to speak. The stranger had called Sonny "that fat fuck." It was a fairly apt description. As unlikely as it seemed, he was his target all right.

"Alone?"

The hard, cold metal of the noise suppressor induced pain each time it prodded. Wendy's mouth had gone so suddenly dry, all she could do was swallow hard and nod.

The intruder looked past her to scan the glassed-in sunroom beyond the entry. It fronted a pool terrace, where Sonny Galati was stretched on a chaise in the sun. "Sit there," he ordered, and pointed at a white wicker armchair.

Wendy hadn't understood what the duct tape was about until a first strip was ripped from the roll and slapped over her mouth. Horrified, she watched as the stranger wrapped more of the tape around the bared flesh of her abdomen and upper arms, binding her to the back of the chair.

"You breathe?" her captor asked.

Wide-eyed with apprehension, Wendy nodded.

"Good." The man knelt to start on her legs, taping each ankle to the chair.

"Wendy!" It was Sonny, calling from the pool terrace. He'd turned his head their way, and for a moment, Wendy's captor froze. Then, realizing that the light out there was so bright, it wasn't likely he could see inside the house, he relaxed.

"Get your ass out here, rub lotion on my back. I'm fuckin' burning up heah."

With Wendy immobilized, the stranger's demeanor seemed to soften. Peering out from behind the mask, his eyes actually appeared to smile as he patted one of his captive's bare thighs.

"Not to worry, sweetmeat. I'll take care of him."

Wendy watched the stranger ease open a sliding glass door and slip onto the pool terrace. With his muscular, weight lifter's physique, it was difficult to guess how old he might be. Early thirties, maybe? She had noticed how big and well shaped his hands were. He had a nice tight ass, too. An exotic dancer noticed those things about men.

Stretched out on his stomach, his face turned away from the house, Sonny was oblivious to the stranger's approach. He remained unaware of that presence until the muzzle of the noise suppressor was placed against the back of one knee and the intruder pulled the trigger. Then, Galati's entire body jerked like he'd been zapped with a cattle prod.

Wide-eyed with horror, Wendy watched Sonny's blood drench the cushion of his chaise as his attacker calmly took aim again and shot him in the other knee. Even through a barrier of triple-glazed glass she could hear his screeching wail of pain and terror as he twisted, trying to heave his bulk over to confront his nemesis. Almost nonchalant, the shooter removed a silver hip flask from a back pocket of his shorts and unscrewed the cap. Wendy saw his lips move and wished she could hear what was said. To judge from how he suddenly froze, Sonny seemed to recognize either his assailant or something the man said. When doused from head to toe with the contents of the flask, he started to scream all over again. Indifferent to his terror, the stranger produced a book of matches, struck one like Bogart lighting a cigarette, and set the wailing fat man aflame.

As unlikely as it might have seemed six weeks ago, Matt Stuart's life had returned almost to normal. At an inquiry into the death of Suzanne Albrecht, her motivations for visiting his house were again called into question by Job brass. Simon Ogilvy had gone to bat for him, and within the month he was back working for his old boss at Intelligence. There was no escaping where Suzanne had chosen to make her last stand, or what that implied. The media had dug hard looking for information it could use to turn her death into a full-blown police scandal, but the mayor had decided to stonewall them. He'd buried what Stuart's investigation had brought to light.

A month ago, Matt had placed the house built by his grandfather on the market. Nearly overnight, a young bond trader from Wall Street snapped it up for the princely sum he was asking. With part of the proceeds, he'd purchased a smaller house a block from the Atlantic on Rockaway Point. From several large windows and his back deck, he could see the open ocean. He could walk to the beach in less than three minutes. When he closed his eyes at night, the smell of salt air was still with him. But it did mean he lived in Queens now, not Brooklyn, and how normal could that ever be?

While much had changed in those six weeks, years would pass before some memories faded enough to be called distant. It was one of the facts of a street cop's life that he learned to live with, or else found other work. Stuart was no longer Rhoda Bolivar's boss, which was undoubtedly a good thing. The beautiful Venezuelan detective had become an enduring fixture in his romantic life. It was easier for him to feel open and easy with her in this new house than it ever would have been in the old, and she loved the sea as much as he did. Last night, a Saturday, she'd stayed over. They'd grilled fresh-caught bluefish and taken a long walk out to the Rockaway Point jetty and back.

It was a month before he finally caught up on his sleep and was able to relax into the regular hours of an Intelligence Division routine that included most weekends off. That Sunday morning, as Matt opened the *New York Times* on the back deck, savored a first sip of fresh-brewed coffee, and thought about breakfast, he recalled the Sunday in late May when a similar scene was interrupted by Simon Ogilvy's phone call. That evening, he'd spoken to Suzanne Albrecht for the last time. The next morning on Flatbush Avenue was the last time he'd seen her alive.

Today, the first article to catch his notice was a Metro section piece written by Luis Esquivel, recently honored by the mayor with a citation and hired by the *Times* to cover an inner-city drug-crime beat. It detailed how, since the shootings of Mikhail Neyizhsalo and Roberto Santiago in Brooklyn and the murder of Dominican *patrón* Francisco Santos in upper Manhattan, new alliances had been forged, possibly stronger than ever. Esquivel contended that traffic in heroin and cocaine now ran even more smoothly than before the late May shake-up. In his article, he targeted four people for portrayal. The first was a relatively unknown Odessa Mafiya front man named Pidvalna. The second was the Cali cartel's new strongman in the Northeast, Oscar Bienvenudo. The third was Raquel Gozon, the queenpin of a new Washington Heights drug-dealing matriarchy. And last was an apparently bright and ambitious new breed of African-American street dealer who called himself Kamil Imbongi. According to Esquivel, these disparate individuals were working in an atmosphere of heretofore unheard-of cooperation. The result was a new, well-oiled drug-dealing machine.

Stuart read the particulars of Esquivel's exposé and was visited by more of those vivid memories he hoped might fade one day: dead and wounded scattered across the Remsen Avenue sidewalk in Canarsie. Tío Paco Santos lying dead outside his bodega. A tall, skinny block captain named Townsend, found dumped in an alley later that same day Matt and Rhoda had visited Rose Marie Sabatino. It never ceased to amaze him how quickly the criminal element could put the wheels back on and get their wagon rolling again.

The second item to grab his notice was a smaller article buried deep in the paper's front section. A retired Brooklyn loan shark and bookmaker who'd moved to Boca Raton, Florida, five years ago was murdered Saturday in his home. Local authorities were calling it an apparent reprisal killing. Santino "Sonny" Galati was long suspected by the NYPD's Organized Crime Control Bureau of having ties to the Albanese crime family. He and a Lauderdale-area exotic dancer had been accosted at noon, Saturday, by a masked intruder. Galati's companion, bound and gagged, had witnessed the intruder shoot him in both knees, then douse him in gasoline and set him aflame.

Considering Sonny Galati's relationship with his stepdaughter, Gina, immolation seemed appropriate to Stuart. In the investigation he'd conducted subsequent to the Angelo Albeneti and Gus Barone homicides, they uncovered a messenger delivery made to Albeneti's ex-wife on Staten Island the morning after his death and billed to Mom's Pie Company. Though Albeneti's office safe was looted, no money was found on either Gina Galati's person or in her car. It seemed reasonable to assume she might have sent it somewhere. After a brief discussion with Simon Ogilvy, Stuart had decided to forgo a follow-up on those leads. Rose Marie Sabatino was raising her dead niece's child. If a chunk of unreported income had fallen her way, then so be it. Matt also considered it unlikely her ex-husband was the only mobster to whom she had ties. If the aunt wanted to avenge her niece, she undoubtedly had the connections it would take to get the job done.

Stuart finished the article, refolded the paper, and thought again about the decision he and Ogilvy had made. He guessed that Simon would sooner or later see the same news item and ask himself the same questions. There wouldn't be much doubt in his mind, either, as to who had sent the masked man to set Sonny Galati aflame. Neither he nor Stuart would ever mention having seen that article in the *Times*.

Matt heard the patio door and turned his head. Rhoda stood barefoot in the opening, clad in an oversize DEA T-shirt, her raven hair tousled with sleep. Her new job had taken her to Washington that week for training. The hours had been long. Last night she'd looked tired, but this morning she looked radiant.

"Sleep well?" he asked.

"Like the dead. What's for breakfast?"

"I was thinking French toast."

"Umm. I take it you've got decent bread?"

"Challah?"

"Decent enough. You brush your teeth?"

"I've been up for two hours."

"Didn't answer my question."

He rolled his eyes. "What do you think?"

"Then kiss me, you fool . . . and take me back to bed. Breakfast can wait."

• A NOTE ON THE TYPE •

The typeface used in this book is a version of Times Roman, originally designed by Stanley Morison (1889–1967), the scholar who supervised Monotype's revivals of classic typefaces (Bembo) and commissioned new ones from Eric Gill (Perpetua), among others. Having censured *The Times* of London in an article, Morison was challenged to better it. Taking Plantin as a basis, he sought to produce a typeface that would be classical but not dull, compact without looking cramped, and would keep high readability on a range of papers. "*The Times* New Roman" debuted on October 3, 1932, and was almost instantly in great demand; it has become perhaps the most widely used of all typefaces (though the paper changed typeface again in 1972). Given its success, it is noteworthy that it was Morison's only original design. Ironically, he had pangs of conscience, writing later, "[William] Morris would have denounced [it]."